PRAISE FOR CAROLYN BROWN

The Daydream Cabin

"I absolutely loved this novel. With moments of laughter and tears, I could not stop reading and imagining the beautiful changes that were taking place within each character's heart! Author Carolyn Brown's novels always give me a feeling of hope!"

—Goodreads reader review

Miss Janie's Girls

"[A] heartfelt tale of familial love and self-acceptance."

—*Publishers Weekly*

"Heartfelt moments and family drama collide in this saga about sisters."

—*Woman's World*

The Banty House

"Brown throws together a colorful cast of characters to excellent effect and maximum charm in this small-town contemporary romance . . . This first-rate romance will delight readers young and old."

—*Publishers Weekly*

The Family Journal

HOLT MEDALLION FINALIST

"Reading a Carolyn Brown book is like coming home again."

—*Harlequin Junkie* (top pick)

The Empty Nesters

"A delightful journey of hope and healing."

—*Woman's World*

"The story is full of emotion . . . and the joy of friendship and family. Carolyn Brown is known for her strong, loving characters, and this book is full of them."

—*Harlequin Junkie*

"Carolyn Brown takes us back to small-town Texas with a story about women, friendships, love, loss, and hope for the future."

—*Storeybook Reviews*

"Ms. Brown has fast become one of my favorite authors!"

—*Romance Junkies*

The Perfect Dress

"Fans of Brown will swoon for this sweet contemporary, which skillfully pairs a shy small-town bridal shop owner and a softhearted car dealership owner . . . The expected but welcomed happily ever after for all involved will make readers of all ages sigh with satisfaction."

—*Publishers Weekly*

"Carolyn Brown writes the best comfort-for-the-soul, heartwarming stories, and she never disappoints . . . You won't go wrong with *The Perfect Dress*!"

—*Harlequin Junkie*

The Magnolia Inn

"The author does a first-rate job of depicting the devastating stages of grief, provides a simple but appealing plot with a sympathetic hero and heroine and a cast of lovable supporting characters, and wraps it all up with a happily ever after to cheer for."

—*Publishers Weekly*

"*The Magnolia Inn* by Carolyn Brown is a feel-good story about friendship, fighting your demons, and finding love, and maybe, just a little bit of magic."

—*Harlequin Junkie*

"Chock-full of Carolyn Brown's signature country charm, *The Magnolia Inn* is a sweet and heartwarming story of two people trying to make the most of their lives, even when they have no idea what exactly is at stake."

—Fresh Fiction

Small Town Rumors

"Carolyn Brown is a master at writing warm, complex characters who find their way into your heart."

—*Harlequin Junkie*

The Sometimes Sisters

"Carolyn Brown continues her streak of winning, heartfelt novels with *The Sometimes Sisters*, a story of estranged sisters and frustrated romance."

—All About Romance

"This is an amazing feel-good story that will make you wish you were a part of this amazing family."

—*Harlequin Junkie* (top pick)

The Strawberry Hearts Diner

"Sweet and satisfying romance from the queen of Texas romance."

—Fresh Fiction

"A heartwarming cast of characters brings laughter and tears to the mix, and readers will find themselves rooting for more than one romance on the menu. From the first page to the last, Brown perfectly captures the mood as well as the atmosphere and creates a charming story that appeals to a wide range of readers."

—RT Book Reviews

The Barefoot Summer

"Prolific romance author Brown shows she can also write women's fiction in this charming story, which uses humor and vivid characters to show the value of building an unconventional chosen family."

—*Publishers Weekly*

"This story takes you and carries you along for a wonderful ride full of laughter, tears, and three amazing HEAs. I feel like these characters are not just people in a book, but they are truly family and I feel so invested in their journey. Another amazing HIT for Carolyn Brown."

—*Harlequin Junkie* (top pick)

The Lullaby Sky

"I really loved and enjoyed this story. Definitely a good comfort read, when you're in a reading funk or just don't know what to read. The secondary characters bring much love and laughter into this book; your cheeks will definitely hurt from smiling so hard while reading. Carolyn is one of my most favorite authors. I know that without a doubt that no matter what book of hers I read, I can just get lost in it and know it will be a good story. Better than the last. Can't wait to read more from her."

—*The Bookworm's Obsession*

The Lilac Bouquet

"Brown pulls readers along for an enjoyable ride. It's impossible not to be touched by Brown's protagonists, particularly Seth, and a cast of strong supporting characters underpins the charming tale."

—*Publishers Weekly*

"If a reader is looking for a book more geared toward family and long-held secrets, this would be a good fit."

—RT Book Reviews

"Carolyn Brown absolutely blew me away with this epically beautiful story. I cried, I giggled, I sobbed, and I guffawed; this book had it all. I've come to expect great things from this author and she more than lived up to anything I could have hoped for. Emmy Jo Massey and her great-granny Tandy are absolute masterpieces not because they are perfect but because they are perfectly painted. They are so alive, so full of flaws and spunk and determination. I cannot recommend this book highly enough."

—Night Owl Romance (5 stars and top pick)

The Wedding Pearls

"*The Wedding Pearls* by Carolyn Brown is an amazing story about family, life, love, and finding out who you are and where you came from. This book is a lot like *The Golden Girls* meets *Thelma and Louise*."

—*Harlequin Junkie*

The Yellow Rose Beauty Shop

"*The Yellow Rose Beauty Shop* was hilarious, and so much fun to read. But sweet romances, strong female friendships, and family bonds make this more than just a humorous read."

—*The Reader's Den*

Long, Hot Texas Summer

"This is one of those lighthearted, feel-good, make-me-happy kind of stories. But, at the same time, the essence of this story is family and love with a big ole dose of laughter and country living thrown in the mix. This is the first installment in what promises to be another fascinating series from Brown. Find a comfortable chair, sit back, and relax because once you start reading *Long, Hot Texas Summer* you won't be able to put it down. This is a super fun and sassy romance."

—*Thoughts in Progress*

Daisies in the Canyon

"I just loved the symbolism in *Daisies in the Canyon*. As I mentioned before, Carolyn Brown has a way with character development with few if any contemporaries. I am sure there are more stories to tell in this series. Brown just touched the surface first with *Long, Hot Texas Summer* and now continuing on with *Daisies in the Canyon*."

—Fresh Fiction

The
Hope Chest

ALSO BY CAROLYN BROWN

CONTEMPORARY ROMANCES

Hummingbird Lane
The Daydream Cabin
Miss Janie's Girls
The Banty House
The Family Journal
The Empty Nesters
The Perfect Dress
The Magnolia Inn
Small Town Rumors
The Sometimes Sisters
The Strawberry Hearts Diner
The Lilac Bouquet
The Barefoot Summer
The Lullaby Sky
The Wedding Pearls
The Yellow Rose Beauty Shop
The Ladies' Room
Hidden Secrets
Long, Hot Texas Summer
Daisies in the Canyon
Trouble in Paradise

CONTEMPORARY SERIES

THE BROKEN ROADS SERIES

To Trust
To Commit

To Believe
To Dream
To Hope

THREE MAGIC WORDS TRILOGY

A Forever Thing
In Shining Whatever
Life After Wife

HISTORICAL ROMANCE

THE BLACK SWAN TRILOGY

Pushin' Up Daisies
From Thin Air
Come High Water

THE DRIFTERS & DREAMERS TRILOGY

Morning Glory
Sweet Tilly
Evening Star

THE LOVE'S VALLEY SERIES

Choices
Absolution
Chances
Redemption
Promises

The Hope Chest

CAROLYN BROWN

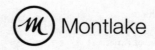

Published by Montlake, Seattle

www.apub.com

Amazon, the Amazon logo, and Montlake are trademarks of Amazon.com, Inc., or its affiliates.

ISBN-13: 9781542029506
ISBN-10: 1542029503

Cover design by Amanda Kain

Printed in the United States of America

Dedicated to
Margie Hager and Janet Rodman,
with thanks for all the support and
love you shower upon me.

Chapter One

"I t's a good place to be *from*," Flynn O'Riley muttered as he looked at the bright-red T-shirt printed with "Where the heck is Blossom, Texas?" that was hanging on the wall. He scanned Weezy's Restaurant for his two cousins, but evidently he was the first one to the meeting that afternoon.

The mixed aromas of burgers, grilled onions, and coffee filled the place, bringing back memories of his childhood when his mother would pick him up at the local diner in Blossom. He always spent two weeks with Nanny Lucy, and even as a toddler he would cry when it was time to leave his grandmother's house. Stopping for a hot dog had started out as a ploy to keep him from crying when he left, but as he grew older, it became a tradition. One that he'd wished had never started after he was fifteen. That was the year his mother was killed in a terrible car wreck on her way to pick him up in Blossom.

He crossed the room, found an empty booth, slid into it, and tried to shake off the memory of the last time he'd sat in that same booth. Weezy's had only been open for a little while, and he and Nanny Lucy were meeting his mother there for the first time. Before, they'd always met at a different café in town. He still remembered the smell of the steaming coffee that Nanny Lucy had ordered. He looked at the table in front of him and got a visual of the half-eaten hot dog sitting before him that day when the policeman came in and whispered something to his grandmother.

Nanny Lucy told him bluntly that his mother had died in a car wreck that morning on the way from Austin to Blossom. "I loved that woman as much as if she'd been my own daughter, but your dad didn't appreciate a good thing when he had it." Matthew, Flynn's father, was her estranged son.

Nanny Lucy was a tough old girl, and Flynn had never seen her cry, not even that day to sympathize with him. He wept until he had no more tears, and then Nanny Lucy told him that his life would never be the same, but that he was strong and would endure whatever got thrown at him.

"You can stay with me until the funeral is over, but then you have to go live with Matthew," she had said. Flynn knew better than to argue with Nanny Lucy, but anything—living in a cardboard box under a bridge—would be better than living with his dad, who Flynn was sure didn't want him. He could count on the fingers of one hand the times he'd seen his father from the time his folks divorced until his mother died.

"But Nanny Lucy," he argued with tears streaming down his face, "Daddy doesn't even want me for weekends or a couple of weeks in the summers."

"You'll have to learn to get along with him," Nanny Lucy said.

The next three days were a blur. The graveside service was held at the cemetery in Blossom. Only a handful of people were there. His mother had been the only child of parents who had been only children, and they were gone. The only family he had were his two cousins, April and Nessa, and then Nanny Lucy and his father, neither of which had wanted him. His father came to pick him up the very next morning. That was the year that Matthew had filed for divorce from stepmother number three, so for the next couple of years, it was just Flynn and Matthew in a fifth-floor apartment down near Bay City, Texas.

"I'm not changing my lifestyle one bit, boy," Matthew had said when he'd shown Flynn the bedroom he would be using. "You can earn your keep around here by taking care of this apartment and learning to cook, and you are responsible for your own laundry. As soon as you're sixteen, I'll get you a job in the oil field business doing odd jobs after school and on weekends. Good hard work will keep you out of trouble."

"Yes, sir," Flynn had said, and he had borne his grief alone. He blinked away the past, coming back to the present. According to the sign on the wall, they still had coconut pie like Nanny Lucy had ordered that day. He imagined that hot dogs were on the menu, but he still gagged at the thought of biting into one. The taste always took him back to that terrible moment.

"Flynn O'Riley?" a masculine voice asked from the end of the booth.

"That's me," Flynn said, glad for the interruption that put an end to the sad memories.

"Paul Jones, Lucy O'Riley's lawyer." He stuck out one hand, pushing his wire-rimmed glasses up his nose with the other.

Flynn shook with him. "Pleased to meet you. Nessa and April should be here soon."

"I'm a little early," Paul said, "and I've got a lot of papers for you grandchildren to sign. Would you mind if we moved to that table"—he nodded toward the other side of the café—"to give us more room?"

Flynn slid out of the booth and followed the short gray-haired man across the room. Paul took a seat at the head of the table, pulled one of the extra chairs around to sit beside him, and put his briefcase on it. He flipped it open and began spreading out papers in three stacks.

A waitress came from a booth full of ladies, laid two menus on the table, and asked, "What can I get you guys?"

"Coffee and a cherry fried pie," Paul answered, but he didn't look up.

"Just coffee for now," Flynn answered. "Maybe something to eat after we take care of this business, and we'll need another menu or two by then."

"Sure thing." The young girl left smiling and returned in a couple of minutes with their order and extra menus.

"I'll wait until your cousins get here to go over all this"—Paul motioned at the stacks with a flick of his wrist—"but I can tell you that Lucy's son Isaac didn't have a leg to stand on when he protested this will. All he did was prolong this day for six months. It had to be tough on Vanessa to take the stand against her own father. I wondered why you and April didn't show up then. But most of all, I'm wondering why you're here today, since I'm sure Vanessa told you the details of the will and the court proceedings."

"I don't know about my cousins, but I need a month away from my lifestyle to get some perspective. But if you'd have asked me to testify back then, I would have been there. Nessa and I couldn't find April at that point, so she probably didn't even know there was a will or that Uncle Isaac had contested it. He probably thought being a preacher put God on his side." Flynn chuckled.

He's not on my *side, that's for sure. I need this month away from women. Away from my father. Away from myself,* he thought.

"Blossom is a good place to get away from everything, for sure, and you're right about Nessa. The Reverend Isaac was pretty full of himself in court, but Vanessa proved him wrong. He was pretty angry when things didn't go his way. I've wondered if it caused a split between him and his daughter." Paul nodded and changed the subject. "I love the cherry pies in this place. And their hot dogs are amazing."

"I'm a burger man myself," Flynn said.

"They're pretty good, too," Paul agreed.

"I really thought Uncle Isaac would convince the judge that Nanny Lucy was out of her mind when she made her last will. He's very persuasive and usually gets what he wants. But Nessa is tough. I imagine that she did fine without me and April to back her up." Flynn looked up as the door opened and was glad to see that April had arrived with Nessa.

"She sure did." Paul nodded.

Flynn was only five feet, eight inches tall, but Nessa was even shorter. Her curly red hair was pulled up on top of her head, adding about three inches, with springy curls going every which way. She marched across the floor with the same no-nonsense expression he remembered her having when they were kids. The sunlight coming through the window lit up every one of the hundred freckles on her square face, a face the same shape as Nanny Lucy's. He hadn't seen Nessa since Nanny Lucy's funeral six months ago, but his cousin hadn't changed a bit. She gave the impression that she could spit in a charging bull's eye without hesitation.

April was a different matter. She was only four months younger than Nessa, but she looked ten years older. She'd always been tall and thin, but today her clothes hung on her like a burlap bag on a broomstick. Her blonde hair was pulled up in a ponytail, but a few strands had escaped to stick to the sweat on her narrow face, and her green eyes looked haunted as they darted around the restaurant. She finally managed a weak smile when she locked eyes with Flynn. He hadn't seen her in at least ten years, and she'd definitely changed—a lot.

"Sorry I'm late. I got stuck in construction traffic around Wichita Falls." Nessa pulled out a chair and sat down at the table.

"And I'm running on a prayer and four bald tires, so I didn't dare go very fast." April sighed as she slid into a chair beside Nessa.

"So this is it, Mr. Jones," Nessa said. "Is Daddy still cussin' you through his lawyer? He's tried every way in the world to find a loophole to appeal this will."

"Please, call me Paul. There are no loopholes. Miz Lucy O'Riley made sure of that when she had me draw it up," he said, "and you ladies aren't late. We've only been here a few minutes." He adjusted his bifocals and focused on April. "You're the youngest one of the grandchildren, right?"

"Yes," she answered. "I'm April, born in that month. Nessa was born in January, and Flynn on the last day of February, so I'm just barely the youngest, and I'm pleased to meet you." April's eyes seemed to be glued to the last bite of pie on Paul's plate.

"Do y'all want a cup of coffee or a fried pie?" Flynn asked. "I'm going to wait until we get done here before I order."

"I'll wait, but I am hungry. I skipped lunch so I wouldn't be too late," Nessa said.

"I'd like a sweet tea," April said.

Flynn caught the waitress's attention and ordered tea for April and refills for Paul and himself.

"Are we ready, then?" Paul handed each of them a folder. "This is a copy of her will. In simple language, it says that you three grandchildren inherit her entire estate to be held jointly, which is the two-bedroom house, her quilting shed, the four and a half acres that it sits on, and everything in the house. The property cannot be sold. She wanted it to always be there in case one of you needed a place to live or just wanted to use it for a vacation home. There is a quilt in the frame out in her work shed, and before any of you can leave, you have to hand-quilt it. She was adamant about that part of the will. It cannot be quilted on the sewing machine. If any of you fail to work together, then you forfeit your third to the other two." He flipped through a few more papers. "There is a hope chest, also known as a cedar chest, that you will put the quilt in when it is completed. That hope chest is now in the care of Jackson Devereaux, her friend and nearest neighbor, and it will remain in his care until one of you gets married. The person who marries first inherits the chest. Jackson also has the key to the hope chest and will open it for you when the quilt is finished. You can see whatever is inside when you open it, and at that time, the contents will belong to you three grandchildren. She didn't even tell *me* what's in the chest, so it will be your surprise."

"It's probably some of her extra pillowcases," Nessa said.

"Or maybe she kept all her money in there rather than burying it in quart jars out in the backyard." Flynn chuckled. She had to have money hidden somewhere. She'd lived frugally and sold her quilts and quilt kits for a high price, so what had she done with the profits?

"What if we don't give a damn about the hope chest or what's in it?" April asked.

"That's your choice, but I would advise you strongly to at least finish that quilt and find out what Lucy has left you. Now, the last thing we need to consider is her car. It is part of the estate and cannot be sold. The keys are on this ring with the house key." He handed the ring to Nessa and then laid out a stack of papers with yellow, red, and blue tabs. "Each of you need to sign on every sheet. This is acknowledging that I have explained the terms of the will and that you are accepting them. April, you are yellow. Flynn, you are blue. And Vanessa, red."

Nessa picked up the pen first and began flipping pages and signing on the appropriate lines. "What if none of us want to leave at the end of the quilting stuff?" She tucked an errant strand of curly red hair behind her ear as if focused on the document, but her steely blue eyes floated in tears.

Leave it to Nessa to ask that question. She'd always been Nanny Lucy's favorite of the three, even when she rebelled against her father's strict religion and did not marry the guy he had picked out for her. Nessa looked like Lucy and was the daughter of her favorite child.

"Then I suggest you learn to live together in harmony," Paul answered as he pulled envelopes from his briefcase.

"Did she leave any money at all?" April asked as she took her turn with the pen.

That's April, Flynn thought. When Nanny Lucy's only daughter, Rachel, died just four days after April was born, Granny had taken her in and raised her, given her a home until she graduated from high school and moved to San Antonio to live with a group of her friends. She had been a pretty little girl with a round face and blonde hair, but from the looks of her now, life had not been too good to her.

"There's a thousand-dollar check for each of you up front," Paul informed them. "Beginning today, you will be responsible for the electric bill. I've taken care of having the bill put in Nessa's name. Y'all can figure out how you want to split the payment. The propane tank is full, and the water comes straight from a well. I'm not sure what there is in the house in the way of food. She died quite suddenly, as you all know." Paul passed the three envelopes around, one to each of them.

"On Christmas Day." April wiped a tear from her cheek with the sleeve of her chambray shirt. "I didn't even get to come to the funeral."

"That's on you." Nessa glared at her. "I tried to get in touch with you."

"Don't look at me like that," April said. "You're not God. I lost my job, got kicked out of my apartment, and was living in my car with no phone. Not all of us—"

Nessa's finger shot up so fast it was a blur. "Don't start with that poor, poor, pitiful me crap. It's not like I was royalty. I worked hard to get my teaching degree. I've taken care of myself since I was eighteen and Daddy cut me off. Granny raised *you* herself, so you had it better than me or Flynn, either one."

"Yeah, right." April folded her arms across her chest and turned to stare out the window.

"We don't need to air our dirty laundry in public." Flynn shot stern looks across the table.

"I think that concludes our business," Paul interjected, "but maybe I will remind you, again, that on the second page of the will, it states that Jackson Devereaux, your next-door neighbor, not only has possession of the hope chest, but he also has the key that opens it. The Blossom Quilting Club will inspect your quilt when it is finished, and if they give you a passing grade on it, he will open the chest to add the quilt to whatever it holds. Then the chest itself will remain in his custody until one of you gets married." Paul closed his briefcase. "My business card is attached to each of your copies of the will. If you have questions, feel free to call."

"Thank you," Flynn said. "We appreciate you meeting us here."

"You are welcome." He smiled and adjusted his wire-rimmed glasses. "Blossom isn't that far from Paris, and I'll take any excuse to come to Weezy's. I love their pies." He picked up his briefcase and disappeared out the door.

"Well, you've each got a thousand dollars," Flynn said. "Are y'all really serious about leaving or staying? I think I'll stick around. My curiosity wants to know what's in the hope chest."

Besides, I need a place to see if I can become a better man, he thought as stared at the menu. *I don't like the person I am right now. I need some direction, and I hope coming back to Blossom will turn me around.*

"I'm not going anywhere. I finished up the school year yesterday, and I don't go back to Turkey, Texas, until the middle of August"— Nessa picked up a menu—"if I go back at all. I'm serious about that much anyway. I may look for a job in this area. It all depends on how things go around here." She picked up the menu.

April shrugged. "I don't have anyplace to go. I've been living out of my car again for the past week, and I'm broke. Flynn, are you looking forward to quilting?"

"No, I'm not." Flynn said. "But I learned to do all kinds of things when I had to move in with Dad, so I can manage to thread a needle and sew on a button. Don't worry about me. I'll do my share, and I'm here for the summer, too. Let's have something to eat before we go out to the house—I'm starving. It's my treat today, but don't expect it to happen very often." He couldn't bear to see anyone go hungry, not even his pesky cousins, who had driven him crazy when they had been teenagers.

❖   ❖   ❖

"I'll have a chicken-fried steak." Nessa focused on Flynn. "Are you still buying?"

"Yes, I am." Flynn flashed one of the smiles that had always drawn women to him like flies to a jar of honey. He had gotten his brown eyes and dark hair from his Latina mother, but he'd gotten his charm from his father, the girls' uncle Matthew. His short height he could blame on Nanny Lucy, since she had been barely five feet tall.

All that oozing charm wasn't necessarily a good thing because, when it came to women, the grass was always greener on the other side of the fence for both Uncle Matthew and Flynn O'Riley. Uncle Matthew was working on his fifth wife these days—Nessa's brow wrinkled when she frowned—or was it his sixth? The way he changed wives, he would never live long enough to see a golden anniversary. Flynn had followed in his father's footsteps and had flitted from one woman to another since he was fifteen. The only difference between the two O'Riley men was that Flynn had never married—or stayed with one woman long enough to form a relationship.

They were a far cry from Nessa's father, Isaac, who had married his college sweetheart thirty-five years earlier and had pastored a huge all-faith church near Canyon, Texas, for the past twenty years. Nessa figured he never even glanced at the grass on the other side of the fence, and if he had, her mother, Cora, would have taken him straight to the cleaners. If religion could be measured on a scale of one to ten, Uncle Matthew would come in at a minus four, and her father and mother would each rack up a score of at least fifteen. Looking back, Nessa figured Uncle Matthew was proud of his only child, since he'd followed right in his footsteps, whereas her father probably had calluses on his knees from praying for *his* only child, who had rejected his faith and joined a more liberal church.

At that thought she glanced down at her knees. She'd spent plenty of hours herself kneeling beside her bed over not doing exactly what her parents thought she should. They'd tried to shove their religious views down her throat, and she'd rebelled by refusing to date any boy who went to their church. That meant sneaking around with bad boys— sometimes even meeting them at the church and going inside to make out in a Sunday-school room.

Nothing seemed to satisfy her. She couldn't commit to a relationship— not in college or since she'd become a teacher. She had realized that something was missing in her life right after Nanny Lucy's funeral, but nothing she tried seemed to satisfy the longing for change. When the court ruling finally came down and she and her two cousins owned their grandmother's property, a peace had settled over her heart and soul. She was going back, at least for the summer, to the only place where she'd ever felt free and happy—to her perfect grandmother's house.

"Y'all ready to order?" a waitress asked.

Her voice startled Nessa and jerked her right back from her woolgathering.

"I'd like the double meat cheeseburger, fries, a root beer, and a couple of those apricot fried pies," Flynn said.

The waitress looked over at Nessa. "And for you?"

"Chicken-fried steak with mashed potatoes and white gravy, corn, and green beans, sweet tea, and a cherry pie, please," Nessa said.

"I want the fish dinner and a slice of coconut pie," April said before the waitress got finished writing. "And could we have an order of onion rings for an appetizer?"

"Next time, I won't be so quick to offer to pay." Flynn grinned.

"I haven't eaten a real meal in two days," April said. "I've been living on potted meat sandwiches and water, so thank you for the meal, Flynn, and thank you for calling me when you did to tell me about the will, Nessa. My phone service was cut off pretty much right after you made that call."

"What happened to you?" Nessa asked.

"Bad choices, bad men, bad everything." April shrugged. "I'm hoping that this move will give me a new start."

"Me too," Flynn said.

April cut her eyes across the table at Flynn. "You've had women falling all over themselves to get at you since you were a teenager. You've had a good job, and I figure one of those big dual-cab trucks out there belongs to you." She pointed out the window. "So why do you need a new start?"

"That's a conversation for another day, but yes, the black truck is mine," Flynn answered. "I see the waitress coming this way with our onion rings."

Like April, Nessa wondered what the mystery with her male cousin could be. Had he gotten hurt by some woman, or was he truly tired of being like his father?

"You're Flynn O'Riley, right?" The woman set the plate of onion rings in the middle of the table, passed the drinks around, and then pointed to the name tag on her shirt. "Remember me? I'm Tilly Waters. I thought I recognized you, but I didn't want to interrupt when you were talking to the lawyer. He comes in here pretty often for a slice of pie. Haven't seen you since we were in junior high school, and you used to come to church with your grandmother. Where have you been keeping yourself?"

Nessa bit back a giggle. The women couldn't keep their eyes and, probably, most of the time, their hands off her cousin, even when he had onions on his breath. She'd always heard that women liked tall, dark, and handsome men, but evidently they didn't mind if he was on the short side if he had the dark-and-handsome bit down pat.

"I've moved around a lot," Flynn answered. "Houston, Galveston, El Paso."

"Well, I'm divorced and have two kids, but I'm always up for a good time," Tilly said with a broad wink. "You can call me here from noon until closing, six days a week, or . . ."—she lowered her voice—"I'll put my cell phone number on the back of your ticket."

"I'll keep that in mind." Flynn picked up an onion ring.

"Your orders will be out in about five minutes." Tilly rushed off to wait on another customer.

"You going to call her?" April whispered.

"Hell, no!" Flynn snapped.

"Have you gotten religion like Uncle Isaac?" April picked up an onion ring and bit into it.

"Hell, no, again," Flynn said.

"Then what's the matter with you? Did you fall into bed with one too many women, and now you've got something wrong?" April whispered. "Are you sick? Good Lord, Flynn, do you have a sex-related disease? You do still chase every skirt that passes by you, don't you, or have you reformed?"

"I'm not sick, but I need to get away from women for a while," Flynn growled. "And I'm not talking about why. I'm here for a few weeks, and then I'll probably be on my way. I'm not interested in dating while I'm here."

"Are you dying?" Nessa asked.

"I told you, I'm not sick," Flynn said.

April leaned forward and eyed him closely. "But are you telling us the truth? You and Uncle Matthew have never been able to resist a pretty woman, so something is definitely wrong."

"I also told you that I'm not talking about it," Flynn said. "We have to do this job of quilting together. It's a joint effort, like the one we have with the house. If I'm not there to buffer, y'all will argue more than you'll work. And Nanny Lucy has raised my curiosity about that hope chest. Is that the thing that sat at the end of her bed?"

"Yes," Nessa answered. "Grandpa had their neighbor make it for her for their first-anniversary present. I've always thought that was the sweetest thing."

"D. J. Devereaux made it? I never knew that." April grabbed the last onion ring.

"I remember him," Flynn said. "He used to come to Thanksgiving dinner at Nanny Lucy's. I only got to be there a couple of times after my mother died and I went to live with Dad, but before that, Mama and I went to Nanny Lucy's almost every year for that holiday. According to Mama, Nanny Lucy had high hopes that my dad would settle down when he got married and had a son, and she was so disappointed when he didn't that she washed her hands of him. But she was always nice to Mama even if she was an ex-daughter-in-law."

"I liked Aunt Gabby," Nessa said. "She was always sweet to me."

"Me too." April nodded. "Is this the Jackson that's keeping the hope chest hostage? I wonder what the *D* stands for."

"D. J. died a while back," Flynn said. "Nanny was all broken up about it when I called her to wish her a happy birthday. She said his nephew Jackson had taken over the custom furniture business. I suppose that's the person with the hope chest and the key to open it."

Nessa remembered her grandmother talking about Jackson coming to live with D. J. about five years before. Since she was never there except for a couple of days in the summer, she'd never met the nephew—or was he a great-nephew?

"His name was Dow Jackson Devereaux," Nessa explained. "I asked Nanny Lucy about it when D. J. passed away. D. J. and his brother both started out in law and had a firm together in the beginning. But the business about drove D. J. crazy, so he left it and began to do woodwork. Jackson's father is James Edward, and he named his son after his brother. So now we have the second Dow Jackson Devereaux. He got tired of lawyer stuff, too, and just like his uncle he turned to woodworking."

"I remember D. J. being very quiet but having kind eyes," April said. "So he was D. J., and the nephew is Jackson. I wonder if the brother, James, ever regrets naming his son after D. J. Kind of marked him, didn't it?"

"Maybe so," Nessa answered.

Things like that did happen. Her parents' strictness had sure enough marked her, and now she was having trouble figuring out what was rebellion and what was just plain old Irish stubbornness.

"I remember D. J. being kind of odd," Flynn added. "Nanny Lucy said he was a recluse. When I was a little boy, she told me not to go to his house and bother him. I didn't know what a recluse was in those days, but the word kind of scared me. His family must have loved him a lot since his brother named one of his kids after the old guy. Either of y'all ever meet this Jackson guy?"

Nessa and April both shook their heads.

"Maybe he's a recluse as well," Nessa said.

"Lord knows that place out there is a good place for hermits," April said. "Only two houses, and both of them are at dead-end roads."

Tilly brought out their food and refilled their glasses. She laid the ticket on the table and said, "I'll be looking for your call. We need to catch up, Flynn."

"He's going to be very busy for the next few weeks," Nessa said. "We've got lots to do out at Nanny Lucy's place."

Tilly laid a hand on her heart. "I loved that woman. She was in the quilting club with my granny and in the garden club with my aunt. May her sweet soul be resting in peace. I know she'd be so happy that you kids have come back to Blossom to live." The door opened and she dropped her hand. "I've got more customers. I'll be looking forward to seeing y'all real often here at Weezy's."

"Can either of you cook?" Flynn asked when Tilly was out of hearing distance. "I hope you can because I don't intend to spend much time here."

"I can open soup and make a pretty mean sandwich." April picked up a piece of fish with her fingers and took a bite.

"I'm a fair cook, nothing gourmet," Nessa answered. "Nanny Lucy lived by the goose and gander law, if I remember right, so you should be able to make grilled cheese sandwiches and heat up canned soup, just like us."

"I can do a little better than that." He squirted ketchup on his fries. "We'll work out the duty schedule when we get to the house, and I'm sure we'll have to make a run up to Paris to the grocery store this evening."

So many decisions, Nessa thought. The idea that her two cousins would even consider staying around for a little while surprised her. She had thought she was coming halfway across the state to clean out the house and maybe hunt down a teaching job near here. She'd had no idea that April or Flynn, either one, would even stick around long enough to help her clean up the place. And since, under the terms of the will, the place could never be sold, she planned to at least spend every summer in Blossom.

One thing was for sure: if Nessa had to get married to inherit the hope chest that she had coveted since she was a little girl, there was no chance. She hadn't had much luck with the dating game—seemed like she picked losers who cheated on her. So Flynn or April could have the hope chest, even if, after the way they'd treated Nanny Lucy, neither of them deserved it or a share of the property. They'd gotten to be around Nanny Lucy more than Nessa, and neither of them appreciated what they'd had.

What makes you think you're so high above your cousins? the annoying voice in her head asked. *Sure, you might have come around a little more through the years than they did, but maybe they had their reasons not to, just like you have yours for not wanting to spend much time with your folks.*

Nessa had only gotten to see their grandmother for a couple of weeks in the summers and on the occasional holiday. After they were grown, neither Flynn nor April had spent as much time with Nanny Lucy as Nessa had, and Lord only knew she hadn't done right by her grandmother, either.

They can have the hope chest, though, if it means getting married, she vowed as she dug into her chicken-fried steak. *I've got to figure out who I am before I can even think about a relationship.*

Chapter Two

April sucked in a lungful of air and let it out slowly as she parked her twenty-year-old Chevy in the front yard of the small house where she'd been raised. Miranda Lambert's song "The House That Built Me" was playing on the radio. One line said that if she could just touch the place, the brokenness inside her might start healing. April liked the idea, but she couldn't count all the fears and guilt trips that had been born in that house. Like an untreated sore, they had festered and become infected years and years ago, until now they were more like a cancer. She had known down deep in her heart that the only way she would ever be cured was by coming back to the house and facing the past. Maybe then she could begin to heal the way Miranda sang about in the song.

"How can it heal me when this is the place that broke me to begin with? I guess the only way to answer that question is to give it a try." April sighed. "Am I coming back to mend the break or to make peace with the fact that it will never heal?"

More than a dozen years ago, when she was eighteen, she'd driven away in the same car that she'd come back to Blossom in that day. The vehicle had not had as many dings in it back then, and the upholstery had been in good shape. But the car, like the owner, had been through some rough times over the years. She'd driven away with high hopes of making it big and returning to Blossom to rub Nanny Lucy's nose in her success. All she'd done was prove her grandmother right. God only knew she wasn't in any better shape these days than the ripped seats in her vehicle.

She could get another job and start over like she'd done so many times, but that would just start the vicious cycle all over again. She would work awhile, get involved with a sorry excuse of a man, let him take advantage of her, and lose everything. It was like alcoholism or an addiction to gambling. Each time she would tell herself she was going to get it right this time, and yet she never did. Then, after the last time around, when she was down and out, she'd seen a quote on a plaque in a convenience store: "What you call rock bottom, I call rebirth."

If it hadn't cost almost ten dollars, she would have bought it and laid it on her dashboard. After that, every time she thought of the plaque, she wished she had purchased it.

She opened the car door, but since the air conditioner had quit years ago, there was no difference between the inside and outside air. "You told me when I left the day after high school graduation that you hoped I would have regrets about my decision. Well, you were right, and I do, Nanny Lucy. I just hope that this is the beginning of my rebirth process. This time around I *will* learn to love myself and get off this roller coaster of destruction."

The last guy she'd let into her life had yelled, "You are the problem, not me!" as he stormed out of her apartment. That probably hadn't been true in his case, but the words had stuck in her head, and she'd realized that until she learned to love and accept herself, she was never going to be at peace.

Flynn pulled his big, shiny black truck in on one side of her car, and Nessa parked her dark-blue SUV on the other.

"First step is always the hardest." April put her feet on the ground, and an empty potato-chip bag flew out of the car. The wind carried it across the yard to hang up in the red rosebush right beside the porch steps. She carefully picked it out of the thorns, wadded it up, and shoved it into the pocket of her faded jeans.

This is me, she thought as she waited for Nessa to unlock the door. *Empty, worthless, and trashy.*

Stop it! the voice in her head scolded. *It's never too late to start all over. As long as you have breath in your lungs and a brain in your head, you can take the bull by the horns, spit in his eye, and make a new and better life for yourself.*

"I hope so," she muttered.

I was right about you, but you've still got time to prove me wrong before you die. It was the first time she'd heard Nanny Lucy's voice in her head, and it startled her.

A musty, closed-up smell hit April in the face when she walked into the familiar living room. Very little had changed over the past decade. The same brown-and-orange floral sofa sat against the north wall, with a log-cabin quilt hanging behind it on an oak rod. The end tables were new, but the old entertainment unit with the television in the center was still straight ahead, and two wooden rockers flanked the sofa. Nanny Lucy had told her that she had rocked all three of her children and all three of her grandchildren in the burgundy one. She seemed proud of that fact, but April would just as soon that she had never rocked April or been responsible for her raising, either one. The green rocking chair had belonged to their grandfather, who had died six months before April's mother was born. Nanny Lucy had said that he had died without even knowing that she was expecting a third child.

Nanny Lucy was only a little older than I am right now when her husband died, leaving her pregnant with my mother, and with two teenage boys to finish raising alone. No wonder she was so short-tempered, April thought. *But I've seen other women who survived similar situations.*

Nanny Lucy had either been happy, quilting until dawn and singing hymns, or else having one of her bad days, when it seemed like she begrudged April the very air she breathed. Flynn and Nessa seldom saw her on those horrible days, but when they left, April knew that one or maybe a whole week of them was bound to come around.

Flynn stopped in the middle of the floor and then began opening windows. "I'd forgotten that there's not an air conditioner in this place. Would it be against the rules if I bought a couple of those small ones and hung them in the windows?"

"Can't happen," April said. "She tried to put one in the living room before I left, and the wiring in this place wouldn't handle it. She took it back to the store and got her money back."

"Well, I can fix that issue in a few days," Flynn said.

"I thought you were a hotshot supervisor in the oil business these days," Nessa said.

"I was until Nanny Lucy's lawyer called with the news that Uncle Isaac's case against the will had fallen through," he said. "Now I'm just an unemployed guy who is a third owner of this hot house with no air-conditioning."

"You quit your job over this?" Nessa waved her hand to take in the whole place.

"I needed a change anyway," Flynn said, "and this gave me a good reason."

Nessa grabbed a tissue from a box on the end table and wiped the sweat from her brow. "Daddy had his heart set on using this property for a religious retreat for his church deacons and the heads of his committees. He thought he might have to buy out Uncle Matthew to get it, so he'd already started a church donation fund to do that. The church owns a nice bus they could have used to transport the people from there to here, and Mama said he was thinking about setting up a fund for a little airplane."

"Have you talked to him since . . . ?" April asked.

Nessa raised a shoulder in a shrug. "I've listened to him rant and rave about things, but lately I've been ignoring his calls. I got tired of hearing him yell about the unfairness of the court system," she answered. Then she changed the subject. "Flynn, how do you know anything about rewiring a house?"

He shrugged. "I took classes for that kind of thing in vo-tech when I was in high school. Then I started at the bottom in the oil field business before I ever graduated. They had me doing everything from wiring to digging ditches." Flynn opened more windows in the living room and dining area. "I learned how to do all kinds of electrical things as well as the regular oil business." He returned with two oscillating fans and plugged them in.

"Are you going to use the money she left you to rewire the house?" Nessa asked.

"Yep, and then some of my own money to put an air conditioner in that window." He pointed. "I came here to get my life in order. I don't have to sweat to death while I'm doing it. Thank God it's June first and not the middle of July or August when it feels like it's seven degrees hotter than hell in this part of the world. I don't mind the heat in the day. I got used to that back when I was working outside all the time, but I hate to sleep without cool air."

"Want to elaborate on that business about getting your life in order?" April felt like her feet and legs were filled with concrete and she couldn't move past the middle of the living room floor. Memories of the pain, both physical and mental, that she'd felt in the bedroom she'd used when she was growing up flashed through her mind. The switch across her legs, the guilt trips when Nanny Lucy told her how much she had sacrificed to give April a decent, God-fearing home, and the way the walls seemed to close in on her when she was put in her room for hours on end all flashed through her mind. She couldn't make herself take a step toward that room. She'd forgotten that she'd even asked a question until she realized Flynn was talking.

"I do *not* want to talk about anything right now," Flynn said. "We all three share DNA, but I don't really know either of you. I hadn't seen you"—he nodded toward Nessa—"in six or seven years before Nanny

Lucy's funeral." He turned to focus on April. "And it must be ten years since I've seen you. So I don't feel like baring my soul to either of you."

"Fair enough," April said. "I guess we'll get to know each other pretty quick when we work on the quilt out in the shed, though, won't we?"

"I'd like to go out there and take a look at it." Nessa headed for the door. "And then I'm going to unpack. I suppose April and I will be sharing a room."

"You can have the room." April didn't want to sleep in the room where she'd cried herself to sleep too many nights to count. "The sofa folds out into a bed, and it's a lot more comfortable than sleeping in the back seat of my car or on the trundle bed in that room." She didn't even look down the short hallway toward the door leading into the room.

"Poor little April." Nessa's condescending tone was just short of pure whining.

April whipped around and pointed a finger only inches from Nessa's nose. "Don't judge me. You haven't walked even a foot in my shoes, so you don't get to talk down to me. Sometimes one person's heaven is another person's pure old hell."

Nessa threw up her palms defensively. "All right. I won't fight you for the sofa. I'd rather have it, since your old room just has a twin bed, but if you want to sleep in the living room, who am I to deny you that?"

"Before I'll go in that room, I'll go out to the quilting shed and use a sleeping bag. I've slept under the quilt frame plenty of times." April marched through the living room, the dining area, and the kitchen and out the back door.

Nessa followed her. "We're going to have to try to get along. This house isn't big enough for us to hide from each other."

"No, it's not." Flynn came out right behind them.

"You lived in a nice place with a lovely bedroom and two parents who loved you the whole time you were growing up, didn't you, Nessa?" April hadn't come to Blossom with intentions of being hateful or pouting. Like Flynn, she had come for a fresh start, and hopefully, to find closure, but dammit, Nessa had always known just which buttons to push to make her mad.

"Yep, and the church was close by if I really wanted to hide, or if I wanted to meet my boyfriend and make out in one of the Sunday-school classrooms," Nessa said. "Let's don't get into the joys of being a preacher's daughter." She reached out and turned the knob on the door of the quilting shed, and the door opened. "I wonder why this door isn't locked."

"Probably because everyone in these parts was too afraid of Lucy O'Riley to ever even think about stealing one of her quilts," Flynn said. "With her red-haired temper, she would have shot first and asked questions later. I guess she's still got that shotgun in the house somewhere. Would you know where, April?"

"The shotgun is always loaded and under her bed, and her .38 revolver, loaded also, will be under her pillow. If you need to use them, just remember to cock the hammer," April answered.

She had asked her grandmother once why she slept with a gun under her pillow and another one under her bed. Lucy had told her that one or both could take care of snakes, both the kind that slithered and the two-legged kind. Maybe that was where April had gone wrong. She never had a gun to take care of those two-legged varmints that seemed to be always taking advantage of her.

No! she fussed at herself. *I'm here for that rebirth stuff, not to think about all the times I've failed in the past.*

Chapter Three

essa walked around the edges of the patchwork quilt that was stretched on a wooden frame. She'd never tackled anything this big, and it was a little scary, especially when she thought about the Blossom Quilting Club passing judgment on the thing when they were finished. She remembered that two other women had made up the club with her grandmother, but it had been years since she'd seen them. Nanny Lucy had talked about them—Stella and Vivien—when Nessa called her.

She closed her eyes and took a deep breath. Even after being closed up for six months, the shed still smelled like roses. Nanny Lucy had always kept a rose-scented candle burning on top of the filing cabinet in the corner. She glanced over that way, and sure enough, a large jar candle with three wicks was waiting to be lit. Nessa wondered if rose-scented sachets were still tucked away in Nanny Lucy's dresser drawers, too.

"Wonder what's so important that we need to finish this thing?" she muttered. "And why do we have to work on it together? I wish I had faces to go with their names—Stella and Vivien, two sisters."

"Guess we'll have to get it finished to find out why," April answered. "It's sure not something I'm looking forward to doing. I hate anything that has to do with needles. Stella and Vivien had been friends to Nanny Lucy since they were all just kids."

"Didn't you ever get to help quilt?" Nessa asked.

"*Get* to help?" April's chuckle was brittle. "More like *had* to help. Don't worry about me messing things up so we don't pass the test. I can do the job, but I won't enjoy it."

Nessa couldn't imagine not enjoying sitting beside Nanny Lucy and quilting. She was amazed by the quilt in the frame, though. Nanny Lucy's quilts were intricate and fancy, like the one hanging behind the sofa. For that matter, Nessa loved every step of making a quilt. Cutting the pieces out was like the beginning of a friendship when two people are getting to know a little about each other. Sewing those pieces together was like building all those little shapes into a quilt top. Then the final step was putting the backing, batting, and top all into a frame, where it was stretched tight. That was the tedious part of a hand-quilted piece of work. One stitch at a time to hold everything together. That process reminded Nessa of life.

The colors in the squares of the quilt top before them looked like they had been thrown together haphazardly by a drunk—and Nanny Lucy had sworn that not a drop of liquor had ever entered her mouth. "That has to be the ugliest quilt I've ever seen. Did she make y'all sew this up when I wasn't around? It looks like something a beginner might do, not an accomplished quilter like Nanny Lucy."

"Not me," Flynn said. "You were here when I was."

April shook her head. "Me either. I never put a top together in my life. Like I said, I hated anything to do with sewing."

Nessa took a deep breath. "Do y'all remember this place always smelling like roses? And did you ever wonder why she used a quilt as decoration behind the sofa and not family pictures?"

"Of course I remember the smell of roses. They're planted everywhere, so it stands to reason that in the summer it would smell like roses around here." Flynn frowned and pointed toward the quilt. "I'm glad she didn't hang that thing above the sofa."

"She loved the scent of roses. Maybe they made her think of good times in her life. She seemed to be happiest when she was quilting or else working with all the roses in the front yard," April said. "And I agree with Nessa. This does not look like one of Nanny Lucy's projects. Maybe Uncle Isaac was right when he said she was losing her mind. As far as the pictures go, I don't think she liked any of her kids or grandkids well enough to put our pictures on the wall. She tolerated us, but that's about as far as it went. I learned when I was pretty small that she had good days and bad days, and to steer clear of her on the latter ones."

"Shhh . . ." Nessa put a finger to her lips. "If the wind or the angels in heaven carry that statement about her not being in her right mind, Daddy is liable to take us back to court again and put you on the stand. Can't you just hear it? 'Judge, I think my mother was insane because she made an ugly quilt.'" Nessa laughed, but she wondered if Nanny Lucy had suffered from depression from a young age, and if so, if it was something genetic that Nessa would inherit someday.

She shook her head to get such thoughts out and poked Flynn in the arm. "I always gave her rose-scented sachets for holidays. You might want to take them out of her dresser drawers before you unpack your things. The women might not flock around you like flies on a fresh cow patty if you smell like roses."

"Then I will leave them right where they are," Flynn told her.

"What's this?" A chill chased up Nessa's spine. Was Flynn having the same kind of emotional turmoil as their grandmother? "The playboy isn't on the prowl anymore? Do give us details."

"Like I said, it's a conversation for another day, maybe never if we don't become friends." Flynn's tone left no doubt that there was a story hidden deep in his heart—or maybe his soul.

"Did you find a picture of Jesus in your morning toast and decide to turn your life around?" Nessa asked.

Flynn turned toward her and gave her a dirty look. "Uncle Isaac would disown you for a comment like that."

Nessa ran her hand over the first few squares in the quilt. "I doubt that. He would love to find a picture of his Lord and Savior in a pancake or in his morning oatmeal. That would make him famous." A heavy, tense feeling hovered in the shed as they all stared at the quilt again. "I loved coming out here with Nanny Lucy and watching her quilt. She had the neatest little stitches, so even and uniform." Not even the good memory eased the tension.

"I was practically raised in this shed." April sighed. "I spent hours under the frame when I'd done something bad, like remind her of my mother. I learned to stay down by the waterfall as much as possible just to stay out of her way. When Nanny Lucy put me under the quilt, I got tired of listening to them singing hymns and talking about the healing properties of the Spirit of God and patterns for making future quilts. I often wondered if God had quilting frames in heaven, and if He didn't, would Nanny Lucy be happy there? I always felt like her quilting business, the ladies from the church, and her garden club women came before me. I was just the burden from my mother's death."

"I wanted to live here when"—Flynn hesitated for a second—"my mother passed away. Nanny Lucy told me that she couldn't raise another kid, and maybe if my father had to take care of me, it would straighten him out, but she was wrong. Nothing could ever straighten Matthew O'Riley out."

"You might have been luckier than you realize." April whipped around and glared at Flynn, bringing even more tension into the shed. "Nanny Lucy was over fifty when I was born and thought she was done with raising kids. She told me that on a daily basis. When my mother died, she said that God told her she had to raise me." She pushed a hand through her hair. "But enough of that depressing old story. Let's get out of this place."

"You're not the only one who didn't have a perfect life, girl. It's a wonder that I ever got to come spend time here with you and Nanny Lucy," Nessa said as she started outside. "Daddy used my time here as a disciplining tool, and believe me, I was not a perfect child."

"Did you have to eat your carrots to get to come to Blossom?" April did a head wiggle when she smarted off.

"I wish that's all it was." Nessa didn't even try to smile. "But it was more like 'Vanessa, if you don't say your prayers for at least thirty minutes, you don't get to go to Blossom this summer.' Or from Mama it was, 'Nessa, if I catch you wearing makeup again, you won't be visiting your Nanny Lucy this summer. Jesus says I have to love Mother Lucy, but she's a bad influence on you, and I don't love that.' Carrots had nothing to do with the way things were done in the Reverend Isaac O'Riley's house."

"I had no idea." April followed her out of the shed. "I figured that since you had parents, both of you were so much better off than I was."

"I thought that since you got to live with Nanny Lucy, you were so much better off than me or Flynn." Nessa closed the door behind her. She had brought her own baggage to Blossom with her, but somehow her problems seemed minor compared to what she could see in her two cousins. "What about you, Flynn?"

"I'm not ready to talk about the past, but I would rather have lived here, no matter how tough it was, than live with my dad," Flynn said.

Strange that they all had different views of their grandmother. To April she had been a reluctant parent. To Flynn she'd been a wonderful grandmother whom he would have chosen to live with over his father. To Nessa she'd been an escape from an ultra-religious household for a couple of weeks every summer.

Flynn finally broke the silence when they reached the porch. "Let's all load up and go to Paris to stock the place with food. I'll drive. We can start on the quilt tomorrow."

"First we make a list." Nessa was good at making lists and organizing everything from her desk drawer to her time. "It won't take but a few minutes. Flynn, you can make one, too, of everything you need for rewiring. April and I can go to the grocery store, and you can go to the hardware store."

Flynn glanced over at April. "Guess you can take the teacher out of the classroom, but you can't take the bossy out of the teacher."

"If I'm going to get the name, be damned if I won't have the game." Nessa tilted her chin up a notch. She didn't want to ever be a submissive woman like her mother. "We will take my SUV since it looks like it could rain, and we'd have to put the groceries in the back of your truck. You can both put up with my bossy, or else don't bother unpacking."

"The preacher's daughter cusses," April teased.

"The preacher's daughter has also had men that stayed the night with her and has been drunk off her butt a few times and is still bossy," Nessa said. "With an overbearing father, I had to learn to stand up for myself or else I would have been married for more than a decade and had a houseful of kids by now." She stopped at the door and turned around. "April, you can help me make our grocery list. Since you don't like to cook and wouldn't know cinnamon from paprika, I'll do the checking and tell you what to write down."

"Yes, ma'am." April snapped to attention and sharply saluted her cousin. "Thank you, ma'am, for allowing me to follow your orders."

"And now the smart-ass that I remember comes out." Flynn chuckled. "Where have you been hiding it?"

April dropped her hand, and the expression on her face changed from sassy to blank in a fraction of a second. "Under lots of stuff that should be forgotten. For now we've got things to take care of this afternoon so that we can get out here in the morning and start quilting. The shed gets pretty hot in the afternoons, so we should work when it's at least semi-cool, in the mornings."

Nessa could relate to what April said. So many painful memories should be forgotten, but according to some of the things she had overheard the school counselor saying, talking about them was the best way to overcome your problems.

"What if we put a window unit out there?" Flynn stopped by his truck and took a couple of suitcases from the back seat.

April did the same thing, only her things were in two white garbage bags.

Nessa went back out to her SUV, hit the button to raise the hatch, and picked up two suitcases from a stack of boxes.

"Good God!" Flynn stared at the packed SUV. "Did you bring everything you own?"

"I don't know about Nessa, but I sure did," April said. "This is it, lock, stock, and barrel. A car that runs off fumes and bald tires, what clothing I own, and I think there's a bottle of water left somewhere in the back seat."

"I came with intentions of staying at least until the end of summer," Nessa said, "so I cleaned out my fridge and my pantry. If I stay past the end of August, I'll have to make a trip back out to the Panhandle and get the rest of my stuff."

She rolled the suitcases across the gravel driveway and hoisted them up the steps to the porch. Then she took them, one by one, to the bedroom that she and April had shared when she came to visit. The room looked the same—trundle bed on one wall, dresser on the other, small closet, window with lace curtains overlooking the backyard.

Nanny Lucy had told her that when her boys, Isaac and Matthew, were growing up, there had been bunk beds in the bedroom. Her daughter, Rachel, hadn't come along until the boys were fourteen and fifteen, and her husband had already passed, so she had kept the new baby in her room until she was two years old and then moved her crib into the living room. It wasn't until the boys had left home, at eighteen and nineteen, that Rachel had gotten her own bedroom.

Nessa pulled back the curtains, slid the window up, and propped it open with a wooden stick, probably the same one that had been used back when her father was a small boy. The fresh air blowing through the screen brought in the scent of roses with just a touch of mint mingled with it. She inhaled deeply and made a mental note to water the flower beds, and then she went back out to bring in the boxes of stuff that would go in the kitchen and pantry.

"How long will it take you to make your list?" Flynn kept arranging his tools in an old leather belt when she came through the living room.

"Maybe fifteen minutes." Nessa looked up at the ceiling. "You do realize that it's going to be a hot job rewiring this place."

"I'll sweat in a hot attic any old day rather than having to crawl under the house," Flynn answered. "I've worked in extreme heat, and I don't mind it, but I'm just a little claustrophobic."

"Did your daddy ever put you in a closet when you disobeyed him?" Nessa remembered spending some time in the pantry with the door closed when she was a child. She was supposed to be asking God for forgiveness for whatever sin she had committed, but instead she'd usually spent the time eating cookies, or even just brown sugar.

"Of course not," Flynn answered. "My dad was too busy to care what I might or might not do wrong. As long as I did my chores, he pretty much left me alone."

"Did you have to crawl under houses?" Nessa pushed the issue.

"Few times, but mostly they were trailer houses, and that's enough interrogation for today. Arrest me or I'm leaving." He grinned.

"When you two get done arguing, I've got a question," April said.

Nessa and Flynn both turned around to look at her.

"Is it all right if I put Nanny Lucy's things in the coat closet in bags or boxes and store them in the garage?" April nodded toward a closet door to the left of the television. "I need a place for my things."

"Sure," Nessa told her. "Do what you need to do, and you can use half the dresser drawers in your old room if you want to or need them."

"Thanks, but no thanks. I can make do with the shelf in the closet. I'll take care of that job when we get back from Paris." April held up a pen and a piece of paper. "Are you ready to make that list?"

"Almost," Nessa answered. "I've got a few more things to bring in."

What is it about that bedroom that spooks April? What kind of memory would do that to a grown woman?

The same kind as being put in a dark pantry or sent to my room to pray for what seemed like eternity, she thought. *How is it that I never realized April was so unhappy living here?*

"Then I'll get a few of Nanny Lucy's old coats out of the closet while you do that," April said. "I'll put them in trash bags, and we can store them in the garage until we figure out what we want to do with them."

Nessa nodded as she left the musty-smelling house, exiting into the scent of roses permeating the air outside. Grumbling under her breath about how her two cousins hadn't offered to help her bring in the boxes, she hauled them in by herself and set them on the table and counters. "Thank you both for all the help." Sarcasm dripped from her words.

"All you had to do was ask." April carried two large bags out into the garage.

Nessa shot a dirty look her way. "I shouldn't have to ask."

"Did you help bring in our things?" Flynn asked as he passed through the kitchen and into the garage. He pulled on a rope and brought a ladder down from the opening in the ceiling to the attic. "I'm going up to see what I need up here, and if I *do* need anything, I *will* ask."

"Oh, hush!" Nessa began to unload her boxes onto the table.

"Everything I own is dirty," April said, "so I'm starting a load of laundry at least to get stuff rinsed. I already checked, and we're about out of detergent, so I put it on the list. We'll need to go by the bank and cash the check the lawyer gave me so I can pay my third of whatever we buy today." She left the door to the garage open and was back in a couple of minutes.

"I'll cover the grocery bill this week. You can get it next time we go." Nessa opened the refrigerator to find it totally empty. "I wonder who did this," she said as she moved on to the pantry, "and this."

"What?" April sat down at the table and picked up the pen to make notes.

"Cleaned out everything. The pantry has a few cans of food, but the flour and sugar canisters are empty. There's nothing in the fridge," Nessa answered.

"Kind of like us," April muttered. "We're empty, and hoping that we—"

"All of us are bringing baggage to Blossom," Nessa butted in before her cousin could finish. Sometimes the way to help was called tough love. April didn't need mollycoddling, as Nanny Lucy used to call it when one of them thought they needed babying. She needed to realize she wasn't the only one who had lived through hard knocks. "You aren't the only one with dirty laundry. I brought a load with me, too—both real and otherwise."

"Moving on, then." April set her mouth in a firm line. "I've written down milk and bread."

Flynn came through the still-open garage door with a frown on his face. "I saw a mouse up there and got to wondering about Waylon. There's no way a mouse would dare show his beady little eyes in this house if that old tomcat was still alive. Did Nanny Lucy tell either of you that he'd died?"

"Last time I talked to her, she said her third Waylon cat was celebrating his fifth birthday. That would have been a week before Christmas," Nessa answered.

"She called him Waylon the Third," April said. "Remember the summer that Waylon Sr. died?"

"Oh, yes—we were eight years old," Flynn said. "We had the funeral for him out under the pecan tree in the backyard, right?"

"Nanny Lucy wanted to put him in a plastic trash bag and throw him in the dumpster," April said, "but Nessa started to cry, and she caved in and let us bury him. I'm telling you, girl, she always did like you the best."

"Yeah, right!" Nessa had forgotten about that day, but a lump formed in her throat at the memory. "Mama and Daddy never let me have pets, so that was my first time to deal with death. I cried until I got the hiccups. Later, Mama and Daddy dragged me to every funeral that was held in our church, but I never cried as much over those folks as I did over poor old Waylon. I wonder what happened to the newest Waylon when Nanny Lucy passed away so suddenly."

"Hopefully, someone took him in and gave him a good home." Flynn brushed the cobwebs from his arms. "I don't think anyone's been up in the attic in years, and April, you're right, that wiring is so old that there's no way it would support even one air conditioner. We should just have central heat and air installed."

"That would cost a fortune," April gasped.

"Let's don't do something that radical until we see how things go around here." Nessa didn't want to put up a third of the money for such an expensive unit, and April sure didn't have those kinds of dollars stashed away. Nessa would be surprised if her cousin had twenty bucks in her purse.

"I guess as small as this place is, we can make do with three window units. One for each of the two bedrooms and one for the living room. We can get those for about a hundred dollars each," Flynn said. "Y'all about ready to go?"

"Almost," Nessa answered. "I'll buy the unit for my bedroom to help out."

"Me too," April agreed.

Nessa was about to offer to pay for April's window unit. The only money her cousin had was the small endowment their grandmother had left her, and that would have to last until April found a job.

"No worries. I'll gladly buy all three if you won't make me quilt." Flynn grinned.

Nessa appreciated the gesture and the fact that Flynn had a soft heart—even if he wasn't looking forward to stitching up a quilt.

April shook her finger at him. "You are going to put as many stitches in that quilt as me and Nessa. I'll give you the money for the air conditioner in the living room since that's where I'll be sleeping, but I was totally honest when I said I was broke. If you want the money for it today, you'll have to stop at a bank and let me cash the check that the lawyer gave me."

"And my answer to that dumb idea of you not quilting is hell, no!" Nessa added.

The noise of a car coming up the gravel driveway made all three of them stop and look out through the old wooden screen door.

"Who would be coming out here?" Flynn asked.

"Could be the folks from the electric company," Nessa offered. "The lawyer said that we'd have to get things arranged with them to keep the power hooked up."

"Anybody home?" a loud voice called out, and then there was the sound of footsteps on the porch.

"Come on in, Stella!" April yelled.

"Who's Stella?" Flynn asked.

"That's one of the ladies from Nanny Lucy's quilting club. You'll remember her when you see her. She hasn't changed much since we were teenagers," April explained in a low voice. "I'd know her raspy smoker's voice anywhere. I used to steal cigarettes from her purse when she came to club meetings."

"Good God," Nessa gasped. "Do you still smoke? If you do, you'll have to take your nasty habit outside. Nanny Lucy didn't allow anyone to smoke or drink or use bad language on her property."

"Nope, I do not smoke, and believe me, I know all the rules, upside down and backwards," April said. "I never even lit up a cigarette. I gave them away to kids at school. I thought it would make them like me, but it didn't, so I stopped stealing them."

Flynn opened the door for the short, thin woman who made April look downright overweight. Her face was just skin stretched over a skeleton. Her hair had been dyed a shade somewhere between orange and red, but gray roots were showing.

"I heard you kids were here. I brought a chocolate cake for you. Lord, I miss Lucy. She was a rock in both of our clubs." Stella talked as she carried the cake to the dining room table and set it down.

"Thank you so much," April said.

Stella turned around and stopped in her tracks. "I swear to God, Nessa, you look just like Lucy did when she was thirty years old and we started our garden and quilting clubs. April, darlin', you look tired. Flynn, you've got Matthew's good looks. That's not necessarily a good thing." She fussed with the cake on the table. "Maybe things would have been different if Gabby had lived to finish raising you. I still get weepy when I think of the good Lord taking your mama home to be with the angels at such a young age." She wiped a tear from her eye, straightened, and then headed toward the door. "I'd love to stay and catch up with you kids, but my sister, Vivien, and I are going to the animal shelter. We volunteer there for a few hours once a week. If y'all need anything, you feel free to call me." She was gone with a wave before any of them could say a word.

"Did that really happen, or did I dream it?" Nessa shook her head.

"Stella makes the best chocolate cake in the whole world, and there's one on the table, so I think it was real," April answered. "Y'all should remember Stella, if not by her face, by her voice. She was here on Wednesday afternoons every single week with Vivien for the quilt-club meetings. There were about six or seven of them, and they would exchange tips and all kinds of patterns in addition to talking about God and repeating church gossip. There's a file cabinet full of the patterns out there in the shed."

"When those women came around, I went down to the waterfall," Flynn admitted. "I didn't like being around them, and there were always leftover refreshments, so I didn't figure I was missing anything."

"I loved listening to their stories," Nessa said, "and Nanny Lucy would give me scraps from the quilt pieces to play with."

"Then maybe you should join the quilting club," April said. "Since the shed is here, they'll come around asking us if we want to join."

"Are you going to join?" Nessa asked. "What if they want to use the shed for their projects? I'd hate to join and then be in the middle of a quilt when they needed the frame and space."

"Nope!" April's tone left no room for argument. "After we get that job finished in the shed, I don't care if I never go out there again. I'm going to look for work somewhere around Blossom, though, because I'm tired of running from my problems."

"And your problems are?" Flynn asked.

"Like you said earlier, I don't want to talk about it with a couple of strangers, even if we do share DNA," April told him.

"I can't wait to get into the filing cabinets, but I don't think I'd join the club even if they asked me," Nessa said, responding to April's earlier suggestion. "I've never been much of a joiner in anything. Any club or organization I was allowed to join when I was growing up had to be affiliated with the church, and"—she shrugged—"Daddy didn't like it, but if I couldn't be in 4-H at school, then I refused to join the young ladies' auxiliary at church."

"And I thought you were an angel." April smiled.

Nessa shot half a smile toward her and changed the subject. "I'm hoping the mice haven't been into the fabric cabinet in the garage. We could probably make more than one quilt while we're here."

"Whoa!" Flynn put up a palm. "Speak for yourself. If you want to sew every day this summer, then I won't stand in your way, but darlin' cousin, when we get the quilt finished that's in the frame, I'm done."

"Guess our DNA *is* a little bit alike." April almost grinned. "But what do you intend to do to stay busy all summer, or until we get the quilt done? Whichever comes first." April hung her purse on her shoulder and headed out through the front door this time.

"Rewire this house, put in new electrical outlets, and hang some air conditioners to start with," Flynn answered as he headed toward Nessa's SUV. "After that, I'll either find something to do, or I'll sit on the porch and listen to the birds sing."

April opened the door and slid into the back seat. "Or go down to the waterfall and listen to the water rushing over the stones, like I intend to do if I can't find a job."

"I love that waterfall, and the time we spent there—except for the last day." Flynn fastened his seat belt.

"That was the highlight of my visit when we were all here. How could you not like the last day?" Nessa frowned. "That was when Nanny Lucy fixed a picnic and spent the day with us. I always thought it was a perfect ending to the time we got to spend here in Blossom. At the end of that day, Mama either picked me up here or at the café when I got a little older."

"I liked swimming, but I didn't like that picnic," Flynn admitted. "It meant our time here was over, and I had to go back to Dallas to live in a fifth-floor walk-up apartment. I missed the open space and the waterfall, having y'all to talk to even on the days when we bickered and argued. Every time I climbed the steps, I wished I was back here in the country."

❖   ❖   ❖

April hadn't liked the day that her cousins left the place, either. Once a year, in the summer, then maybe again on Thanksgiving Day or Christmas, were the only times she got to be with them, and those were special days for her. She and the cousins might argue and fuss the whole time they were there, but when they were gone, she was all alone for the rest of the summer with only one of the Waylons for company. Just thinking of the loneliness of living out in the country on a dead-end road made her stomach hurt like it had when she was a kid and her cousins left.

In those days, if Nanny Lucy wasn't packing up patterns and quilt kits to mail off to her customers, she was either sewing up a quilt top in the house or doing the hand-quilting out in the shed. April quickly learned to stay out of her way and to entertain herself.

A vision of Nanny Lucy standing in the middle of the living room came to mind. April had just graduated and had a decision to make about going to college or getting out on her own. It was one of her grandmother's bad days, when she was mean and hateful.

"You can either live here and commute to college," Nanny Lucy had told her, "or I'll give you the amount of money that the first semester would cost me, and you can have what you've saved through the years to go with it. But if you take the money, don't ever ask me for another dime."

She'd taken the money and blown every bit of it by Christmas. No matter how down and out April had been, Nanny Lucy had stayed true to her word and never offered to help her out again.

That's no excuse for the decisions I've made, April thought as she watched the scrub oak trees and the mesquite thickets go by at seventy-five miles an hour. *I didn't have to mess up my life, but I did.*

"You sure are quiet back there," Flynn said.

"Just enjoying the cool air and the scenery," April said.

"Maybe we should sleep in the SUV tonight," Nessa suggested.

"I'll take the sofa and a fan before I ever spend another night in a vehicle," April said, "even if one is hot and the other is cool. And I call first dibs on the bathroom for a shower when we get home."

She felt like the prodigal son in the Bible stories that she had learned in Sunday school as a child. Nanny Lucy had dragged her to church four times a week: Sunday morning, Sunday evening, Wednesday-night Bible study, and Friday-night choir practice. By the time she was a teenager, not even the social aspect of going to church was something she liked, but by damn, Nanny Lucy said she would go, and she did.

"Maybe we should all go to the waterfall and have a swim before we take our showers. If I'm remembering right, that part of the creek is spring fed, and the water is cool all year round," Flynn said.

"Sounds good to me," Nessa agreed.

April let her mind go back to the hours and hours she had spent at the falls when she was a teenager. A few times she'd even gone skinny-dipping and let the cold water wash over her naked body. Nanny Lucy would have picked a switch and given her ten licks with it if she'd caught her, but she'd gotten away with it every single time. Not once had she felt like she should drop down on her knees and repent for swimming in the nude.

The time that she had taken a deep breath, gone under, and let it out slowly came back to her mind. When her lungs had begun to burn, she had surfaced and wished that she'd had any mother in the world other than Rachel. Why did she have to die? Even though she was just a teenager, she might have loved April. April would have even taken super-religious Aunt Cora, but her favorite would have been her aunt Gabby. She had thought that Flynn was the luckiest boy in the whole world.

You have the chance to start over, the voice inside her head said. *Now it's up to you to make the most of it. Don't ruin it like you've done in the past.*

Nessa snagged a parking spot close to the door at Walmart and turned off the engine. "Flynn, do you want to go to Home Depot for what you need? We should be done in half an hour at the most." She tossed him the keys.

"Yeah, right!" Flynn chuckled. "A woman in Walmart for only thirty minutes. That would be a miracle."

"Maybe one of *your* women would take two hours, but Nessa and I have a list, and I don't have money to blow on junk. What cash I've got has to last for a whole month while we finish a quilt." April unfastened her seat belt and opened the back door of the SUV. "And then I have to look for a job."

A job with no skills needed except waitressing, tending bar, or selling plants in a greenhouse, she thought as she stepped out of the cool vehicle and into the sweltering summer heat that seemed to suck the life out of a person.

Kind of like being stuck under a quilt frame in the middle of the hot summer, she thought.

"You can use Nanny Lucy's car anytime you want," Nessa said. "It belongs to all of us, so you've got as much right to it as we do."

Flynn rounded the front of the SUV, slid in behind the wheel, and restarted the engine. "I'll be right here waiting for you in thirty minutes. If you aren't out in an hour, I'm going to steal your vehicle and go home."

"I will track you down, and you'll be sorry that you took something that belonged to me," Nessa told him without cracking a smile.

Flynn chuckled as he put the vehicle in gear and left the two women standing beside the place where folks returned their carts.

"I guess we'd better hustle," April said, "or he'll never let us live it down."

"He wouldn't dare leave us." Nessa started toward the entrance. "Hey, look, it says that Walmart is hiring. You want to work here?"

"Nope," April answered. "My car barely made it to Blossom. I need a job that's close enough to home that I can walk if I have to."

"Girl, I told you that you can use Nanny Lucy's car anytime you want. I wouldn't trust the tires on your car to take you from the house to the highway. First time you hit a pothole, one of those tires is going to blow," Nessa told her. "It's not brand new by any means, but she kept it in good repair."

"I don't need or want handouts or charity," April said. "I'm going to make my own way from now on, but I might use Nanny Lucy's car since it's part of the estate and not a pity gift from you or Flynn."

"All right, then," Nessa said.

"For a redhead with a temper, you sure don't have a hard heart." April grabbed a cart and handed Nessa the list. "Since you're buying, you can decide on the good products or the generic. I'll push the cart for you."

"I'm a shrewd shopper," Nessa said as she headed toward the dairy aisle.

"I'm a professional cart pusher," April said. "Next week, you can shop for me since that's my week to pay for the food. I'll give you the money if you're all that good at this job, and I'll push the cart for you. When it's Flynn's turn, we'll just hope that we get food for a week and not just ice cream and chocolate cupcakes."

"You remembered." Nessa grinned.

"If he didn't outgrow it, he's got a sweet tooth worse than anyone I've ever known." April pushed the cart down the dairy aisle. "This week, please get two gallons of milk. I could drink half a gallon all by myself."

"Then we'd better get three, because if he still drinks as much as he did when we were kids, Flynn will go through a gallon by himself," Nessa said. "I remember Nanny Lucy saying that she needed a cow during the week or weeks we were in Blossom."

"What do you think his problem is?" April asked.

Nessa put three gallons of milk, two pounds of butter, and four dozen eggs into the cart. "I think he might be sick, as in really sick and dying. After all the women he's been with, he might have caught something from one of them."

"God, I hope not," April gasped. "He's too damn pretty to die, and too young to die at thirty-one years old."

"I don't expect there would be many women who would disagree with you," Nessa giggled, "but something is wrong with him for sure. Losing his mother and then having to live with Uncle Matthew, who's always been a womanizer, kind of ruined him. There's something going on with him, and I'm just as nosy as I am bossy, so I intend to figure it out."

"Good luck with that. Underneath all the good looks and charm is a pretty stubborn guy," April said. "Some people are blessed, some of us aren't."

"It's not a blessing if he's dying of some weird disease that he got from a one-night stand," Nessa argued as they moved on to the produce aisle.

"What would we do if . . ." April couldn't make herself say the words.

"If he gets really sick, we'll take care of him. He's our cousin, and we'll bury him beside Nanny Lucy. That reminds me"—Nessa put a bag of potatoes in the cart—"we should go to the cemetery and clean up her grave sometime this week, maybe even put some flowers out there."

"I don't want Flynn to die," April said.

"Me either, and he's probably not really going to die, but he's got something wrong with him that he doesn't want to talk about," Nessa said. "Maybe he's got something that Viagra won't cure, and his days of chasing women are over."

"Good God!" April gasped. "He's not old enough to need the little blue pills."

"Honey, he's that age by the calendar, but he's used up sixty years' worth of his stuff with probably dozens upon dozens of women. Nanny Lucy always said that he was just like his father, and my dad used to pray out loud that I wouldn't turn out to be a fornicator—his words, not mine—like my cousin," Nessa whispered.

"How many sex years do you figure you have used up?" April asked.

"Not nearly enough," Nessa answered. "I was so protected and sheltered as a teenager that I'm probably only twenty-one right now in sex years. It's like dog years. How about you?"

"I'm pretty close to my real age." April shrugged. "I'm not an angel, and I made bad choices, but FYI, I never turned tricks or worked the streets. We need to go down the next aisle. That's where the detergent and cleansers are."

"Are we going to make Flynn clean house?" Nessa asked.

"Hell, yes, we are." April nodded. "Unless he's working in the flower beds, or maybe painting the house. He can pull his share of all the work. Did you notice that the paint is peeling and the porch is down to bare wood?"

"No, but as small as the place is, we could probably take care of the whole job in a couple of days if all three of us worked together," Nessa said as she put a huge jug of detergent in the cart and then checked the list. "Cinnamon and ginger. We need to go down the spice aisle, and we need flour and sugar, too. I brought partial bags from home, but they won't last a whole week."

Thirty minutes later, they rolled their cart, now loaded with full bags, out to the parking lot to find Flynn sitting in the same parking spot as before. April pushed the cart over to the SUV, and Flynn got out to help unload.

"Right on time." He looked up at the sky. "A miracle may float down from heaven."

"The only thing that's coming out of those clouds is rain, and lightning to strike you if you don't watch your mouth," Nessa told him.

"I always knew you were a witch, but I didn't know you could control the lightning," he said.

"Never underestimate the powers of a redhead," Nessa shot back at him.

"Did you get everything you needed?" April asked.

"Except for the air conditioners," Flynn answered. "But they've ordered three small window units that I can pick up on Thursday. We'll have a cool house by this weekend."

Together they situated the bags in the back of the vehicle, and then April got into the back seat again. She wasn't sure how they'd all three live together as adults, but there was a bed and a shower, and judging from all the groceries Nessa had paid for, she wasn't going to go hungry. For all those comforts, she could put up with Nessa's smart-ass attitude and Flynn's secretive smugness. If they were still around at the end of the summer, she would use what money she had made at whatever job she could find to locate her own place. She didn't intend to live with them forever.

Chapter Four

*J*ackson Devereaux had always loved the sunsets in North Texas. Maybe it was because he took the time to enjoy them more than he had when he lived in Austin, but in those days, he'd seldom seen the sunrise or the sunset. He'd worked eighteen-hour days at the law firm back then. Most of the time he had been in his office before daylight and hadn't left until after dark. Nowadays he knocked off work by five thirty. His muscles might be tired, but his mind had not been tied up in stress knots since he left the city.

He sat down on the porch steps, and his big yellow dog flopped down beside him. "How did your day go, Tex?" He scratched the dog's ears. "Did you chase any rabbits or tree a squirrel or two?"

The dog gave a short yip.

"Miz Lucy's grandkids have come back." He stretched his long legs out from the top step to the bottom one and leaned back on his elbows. "Rayford Jones came by this evening to pick up the hope chest he'd ordered for his granddaughter's sixteenth-birthday present. He said all three of them had met with the lawyer in Weezy's this afternoon, so we have neighbors again."

The dog lay down and rolled over on his back.

"You don't care if anyone lives in Miz Lucy's house or not. You're just interested in getting your tummy scratched, aren't you?" Jackson used both hands to give the dog a good working over. "We'll pay them a visit tomorrow and take Waylon home. You should be happy about that much, at least."

The dog jumped up, made a lap around the yard, and then came back to flop down at the bottom of the steps.

"That idea makes you happy, does it? I guess getting rid of Waylon will clear the way for you to get to come back inside the house." Jackson swatted a mosquito away from his arm. "It would have been nice if you and Waylon could have been friends, but maybe it was for the best. If you'd been friends, you would have missed him, like I do Uncle D. J. and Miz Lucy. But you'll be glad to see your archenemy leave." He stood up, crossed the wide porch, and went into the house.

The Devereaux place was only a quarter mile from Miz Lucy's place as the crow flew or on the old, rutted pathway where Jackson and Lucy had often walked back and forth from one place to the other. If he had to go by vehicle, it was a mile trip. The drive down to the fork in the road was half a mile, and then a sharp turn to the left and another half mile before Hope Creek Road ended at Lucy's place.

Waylon, the big black-and-white cat, was a blur as he ran down the hallway and went straight for his food dish. He reared up with his paws on the cabinet and meowed loudly while Jackson opened a can of food.

"Starving, are you?" Jackson asked.

Waylon changed positions, and with all four feet on the floor, he began to purr and weave around Jackson's legs.

Jackson set the cat food on the floor and then went about opening a can of gumbo for himself. "Tomorrow morning bright and early, you are going home. I'll miss you, but Miz Lucy would want you catching mice at her place and getting to know your new owners. This was just a temporary home until they could get here. You'll have three people to spoil you, and no dogs to pester through the screen door. If you don't like it over there, you can always run away and come back, but sneak up to the back door so you don't have to fight with Tex."

While his soup heated, Jackson cut a couple of thick slices of Italian bread from a loaf and laid them on a plate. Uncle D. J. had liked gumbo, both from a can and homemade, and they'd had it at least once a week. They would work all day in the shop, sometimes only exchanging a few words about whatever project they were working on, but supper had been their time to visit. That was when he'd learned that Uncle D. J. had fallen in love when he was a young man, and that only a few months before the wedding was to take place, his fiancée had been diagnosed with cancer and had died six weeks later.

He poured his soup into a bowl and carried his supper to the table. He sat down in the same chair he'd used since that first day all those many years ago when he had come to visit his uncle, and he bowed his head. After a moment of silence, he opened his eyes and raised his head.

"I always liked it that neither of us said anything out loud when we said grace," he told the cat, who was now sitting in one of the other three chairs. "Seemed more personal that way."

After he'd eaten supper, he took a long, cool shower. He dressed in a pair of loose-fitting shorts and a tank top, got a beer out of the refrigerator, and sat down to watch a couple of episodes of *Longmire*. Waylon jumped up on the sofa beside him, turned around several times, then curled up next to his thigh.

Jackson fell asleep sometime in the middle of the second episode and woke with a start when the theme music began playing at the end. He turned off the television and headed to his bedroom, with Waylon right behind him. "You better enjoy sleeping on the foot of my bed tonight, old boy. Those people over there might put you in the garage at night, and you'll have to spend the nights alone."

❖ ❖ ❖

Nessa awoke before daylight with so many things spinning around in her head that she couldn't grab hold of one before it slipped away and another thought took its place. She couldn't go back to sleep, so she got out of the narrow bed, tiptoed down the hallway so she wouldn't wake April, and stopped dead in her tracks. Even in the dark, she could see that the sofa had been put to rights and the bedding was folded neatly on the coffee table.

April had left, and from the lack of the aroma of coffee floating through the house, it was clear she hadn't even bothered to make a pot before she sneaked away in the night. Now that Nessa didn't have to be quiet, she went to the kitchen and made coffee in the old percolator with blue cornflowers on the front.

"Next week, when we go back to Paris, I'm going to buy a drip machine," she declared.

"Why?" April came inside through the front door. "That old thing makes the best coffee in the whole world. It's strong enough to melt the enamel off your teeth and has enough flavor to make you want a second cup."

"Where have you been?" Nessa eyed her carefully. "I thought you'd left when you weren't on the sofa."

"I told you that I'm not going anywhere." April's tone was icy cold. "Not necessarily because I'm all sentimental about being here, but the truth is, I don't have anywhere else to go. My life has brought me full circle right back here to face my past. I guess it's a good thing. We'll see in a few weeks or months. So I hope you weren't giving thanks that I was gone and hoping you might wind up having this place all to yourself."

"Where were you?" Nessa asked.

"I couldn't sleep, which isn't unusual. I can't remember ever sleeping without nightmares, and once I'm awake, I can't get back to sleep. I went down to the waterfall. We got too busy last night to go, and it's always been where I go to think," April answered. "I'm just really glad that creek can't talk."

"I'm jealous that you got to spend so much time down at the falls when you were a kid. I used to draw the falls and write poems about it.

My writing and the art were horrible, but I missed it so much." Nessa poured two cups of coffee and headed toward the front door. "Let's watch the sunrise. They're always so much brighter in the country than in the city."

April followed her, and they sat side by side on the top step of the porch. "Turkey, Texas, can hardly be called a city. It's not even as big as Blossom. And that waterfall and creek are the only things I missed when I left here. When I went there this morning, I was glad that it hadn't changed. We need some things in our life that stay the same."

"Turkey might not be a huge city like you're used to living in, but it's bigger than two houses, both at a dead end, on Hope Creek Road," Nessa argued. "Look, you can see an orange thread out there on the horizon."

April cocked her head to one side. "Shhhh . . . I hear something."

Nessa listened intently for a moment. "Probably deer coming up to feed on the mesquite leaves."

"Sounds like a cat," April said.

"Do you think Waylon is . . . ," Nessa started, but was interrupted when a guy pushing a wheelbarrow rounded the end of the house.

"Guess you folks are early risers, too," he said in a deep Texas drawl mixed with just a hint of southern Louisiana. "I'm Jackson Devereaux, and I'm returning Miz Lucy's cat. I've taken care of him over at my place since she passed away, but I'm bringing him home to you all."

"Pleased to meet you. I'm Nessa O'Riley, and this is my cousin April. Flynn is still sleeping," Nessa said.

Mercy sakes, but Jackson was a good-looking guy, and that voice of his would make a woman melt in a puddle at his feet. He set the cat carrier on the porch and then unloaded a bag of litter, the plastic pan that it went into, and several cans of cat food. Then he hefted a ten-pound bag of dry food off his shoulder and put it beside the carrier. "I usually keep his dry food bowl full and give him wet food in the evening. That's the way Miz Lucy took care of him. I took him to the vet for his shots last month when I took my dog, Tex, so you don't have to worry about that for another year."

"Thank you," Nessa said. "Want a cup of coffee?"

"Thanks, but no thanks. I've got a full day ahead of me, so I'd better get on back home and get busy. You ladies have a nice day, now." He tipped the bill of his cap toward them and pushed his wheelbarrow back around the house.

"What's going on out here?" Flynn pushed his way out onto the porch and almost tripped over the cat carrier.

"That's Waylon," April said.

"The neighbor, Jackson, has been taking care of him," Nessa explained. "He could be a recluse like his uncle."

"Why would you say that?" Flynn yawned.

"Because I get the impression that he planned to put Waylon and all of that stuff on the porch and then leave," Nessa answered. "He told us what to do with the cat and then hurried back out into the dark like he didn't want to talk to us."

"He seemed surprised to see anyone up and around this early," April added. "He's younger than I thought he would be."

"Oh, yeah?" Flynn yawned again.

"Yep," Nessa said. "I figured he'd be middle-aged at the very least. D. J. was at least eighty, so a nephew would be forty or fifty."

"Maybe D. J.'s brother didn't have Jackson until later in life." Flynn picked up the carrier. "We're all waking up early because Nanny Lucy used to kick us out of bed before daylight." The cat began to howl and wiggle around in the carrier. Flynn set it back down. "When we come here, we think that's what we have to do. The house or the place has its own rules, and we've been trained to follow them," he said above the noise of the cat, and then picked the carrier up again and set it inside the door. "I'm going to turn this noisy critter loose and get a cup of coffee. Is it strong enough to curl my toenails? What did Jackson look like?"

"Of course, it's good coffee." April stood up and gathered as much of the canned food into her arms as she could carry. "It was still dark enough that we couldn't see the man very well, but I'd guess he's about our age. He was taller than you, and I could see dark hair under his baseball cap. That's about it."

"You don't have to rub it in that I'm not tall," Flynn said.

"I didn't say that you were short. I said that Jackson was taller than you," April said.

"Same difference," Flynn argued. His dad, who had been touchy about his height, too, was only an inch taller than Flynn.

Nessa could hear them still going at it after they were in the house. She sipped her coffee and watched the morning light slowly turn the dark blobs out there in the distance into individual trees. She could stay right here in Blossom for the rest of her life if she wanted, and peace filled her soul when she thought about doing just that. Before, every time she'd come to Blossom, there had been a dreaded deadline—a week, two weeks at the most, maybe to come back later for just an overnight visit—but today she didn't have to worry about leaving.

"Your phone has been ringing, stopping, and then ringing again." Flynn opened the door and crossed the porch. "Can't imagine who'd be calling any of us this early." He handed the phone to her and went back inside.

"Hello, Daddy," she answered on what was probably the eighth or ninth ring, wishing that she'd left her phone turned off.

"Are you in Blossom?" he asked.

"Yes, sir." She was glad that she didn't have to talk to him face-to-face.

"That court decision isn't right, and you know it. Mother should have left that property to me since I'm the oldest child. Matthew is too busy chasing women to ever settle down, and Rachel's been dead since she was sixteen. I would have done something good and right with the place," Isaac said.

"What makes you think the three of us can't do something good with it, too, like maybe turn our lives around and get on the right track?" she asked.

"Flynn is just like his daddy. He'll never settle down to anything. April has always been a problem child like her mother was, and if I thought for one minute that property would make you come back to the arms of this church, I'd be happy." Isaac had taken on his big, booming preacher tone.

"You know the terms of the will, Daddy," Nessa said. "We can't ever sell this place. It says so in the will. Is Mama up and around this morning?" She tried to change the subject.

"She's at the house, having the church ladies over for prayer group," Isaac answered. "I'm at the church, practicing my sermon for tonight's midweek service. You aren't planning on staying in Blossom and living in that house, are you?"

Nessa shut her eyes and remembered the too many times that she had been made to sit in the front pew of the church and listen to her daddy practice his sermon. If she fell asleep, she'd had to go pray in her room.

"Well?" Isaac said in a stern voice.

"Right now I'm taking it one day at a time. And this day we're going to start quilting as soon as we all have breakfast." She avoided his question.

"That was the craziest notion my mother ever came up with," Isaac growled. "I know beyond a shadow of a doubt that she was losing her mind when she made that will. Too bad the court didn't agree with me. Making you quilt in order to get a hope chest is downright stupid. What on earth could be in that old piece of junk that would be important enough for any one of you three to follow her orders?"

"Maybe nothing." Nessa clenched her free hand into a fist and gritted her teeth. "Or maybe she just wanted us to sit still and get to know each other as adults."

"It's still a crazy notion," Isaac said. "Are you planning to spend the whole summer there? Your mother and I are taking a church group to Israel right after Independence Day. We've got one place left in the package deal, and we would like it if you would go with us."

Who dropped out, and do you have to fill the quota to get the deal? she wondered as she shook her head. "Sorry, Daddy, but I am going to spend the summer here. I may even fire up Nanny Lucy's quilting business. If it does well, I may quit my job in Turkey," she said, and she waited for his reaction.

She could almost hear him trying to get words to come out of his mouth. "I love to quilt," she added. "It makes a song in my heart and peace in my soul."

"That's got to be the most insane notion I've ever heard!" He yelled so loud that she held the phone out from her ear. "But then I'm not surprised. Every time you went to Blossom, you came home bewitched. It's that house. It's got a hold on you."

Nessa wasn't a bit surprised. Isaac always raised his voice when he was angry or trying to make someone agree with his viewpoint. "Maybe you should bring your Bible and perform an exorcism over the house."

"You should have been born to Matthew instead of me." Isaac's voice dropped to a whisper, like it did when he was about to explode.

"You were the one that said the house was possessed and had a hold on me." Nessa knew she should hold her tongue, but she didn't have the power to shut her mouth. "If it's all that bad, then why did you want it for a church retreat? Who knows what might have happened to the VIP folks if you'd brought them here? The house might have bewitched them all, and they could have left your church, moved to Blossom, and started growing turnips down by the waterfall."

"I'm not listening to your sass," Isaac said, and he ended the call.

Nessa rolled her eyes toward the sky. "Thank you, Nanny Lucy, for giving me a healthy dose of sass. I must learn to use it more often than I already do." She stood up, picked up the litter in one hand and the pan in the other, and went into the house, but her hands were shaking. Her father would have considered her smart-ass remarks blasphemous. She'd put her foot down before and told him that she wouldn't marry right out of high school, but she had not talked to him in that tone of voice in a very long time—maybe not since then.

"Y'all ready for breakfast?" she called out. "I'm thinking french toast and bacon. And where does this pan go, April?"

"In the garage," April answered. "Waylon sleeps out there at night. And count me in for breakfast."

"I'll second that. French toast sounds great," Flynn said. "Do we have to start quilting today? I thought I'd get busy on the rewiring."

"Only after we quilt for two hours," April said. "I want to get it finished so I can get out there and find a job. You two might have money in the bank, but I don't." She needed structure in her life. Get up. Go to work. Come home. Figure out that she was needed.

"I agree with April about working on the quilt a couple or three hours every morning while it's a little bit cooler." Nessa got a loaf of french bread from the pantry and sliced it into thick slabs.

"When we get done with quilting today, I'm going to weed the flower beds. Nanny Lucy would turn over in her grave if she saw how pitiful they look. The roses need to be deadheaded and the lantana pruned back." April took plates down from the cabinet and set the table.

"So you know something about flowers?" Flynn asked.

"Don't look so surprised." April gave him the old stink eye. "I do know how to do a few things."

"Did you ever work in a flower shop?" Nessa asked as she whipped eggs and milk together, then added sugar and cinnamon.

"No, but I worked in several greenhouses," April answered. "Of all the jobs I've had since I left here, those were my favorite ones."

"Good, because I don't like to work outside, and I hate to get dirt under my fingernails. I'll gladly do the cooking if you'll take care of the flower beds and the lawn," Nessa said.

"It's a deal." April nodded.

"What about me? Do I get to sit on the porch and watch you two work?" Flynn refilled all their coffee cups.

"No, honey." Nessa reached over and playfully pinched his cheek, then browned four pieces of toast. "You get to sit on the porch and wait until a pretty woman comes by. Then you get to chase her down and seduce her."

"You haven't changed a bit." Flynn slapped her hand away. "I think they mixed all of us up as babies. I should have been a preacher's son, and you should have been the daughter of the greatest smart-ass in Texas."

"That's pretty much what Daddy told me this very morning. You wouldn't have lasted overnight in the house I grew up in." Nessa went back to the stove and browned more toast in a big cast-iron skillet.

"As bossy as you are, Nessa, and as smug as you are, Flynn, y'all would have wilted and died if you'd grown up here," April said. "Nanny Lucy was a wonderful lady, but she could put a guilt trip on a person that went all the way to the bottom of the soul, and believe me when I tell you that she knew very well how to wield a switch. Ten licks was the minimum."

"Are you serious?" Nessa was stunned.

"Y'all knew her as a sweet nanny for two weeks. Somehow you being here was when she had good days," April answered. "But I was the bastard offspring of the daughter who had disappointed her and then died four days after I was born. At least once a day, more in the days after y'all left and went back home, she reminded me that I had my mother's genes, and I knew that was a bad thing from her tone. It didn't seem to matter if she was having a good or a bad day. I was always a thorn in her side."

Nessa could well understand what April was saying. Looking back, she'd always felt like one of those thorns for her father. "I guess that's where my daddy got his ability to make me feel guilty about even the air I breathe." Nessa talked as she cooked breakfast. "He could put a guilt trip on Jesus, and he practiced on me almost daily."

Both women glanced over at Flynn.

"Hey, my dad was too busy either chasing women, getting married and then chasing women, or getting divorced because his wife caught him chasing women to ever even talk to me." Flynn shrugged. "I was just a bratty kid that he didn't want to raise but had to when my mama died. I pretty much did what I wanted from the time I went to live with him—no questions asked except on payday, when he held out his hand for half of what I made to pay for my room and board in his house."

"We should call that childhood the O'Riley curse." Nessa set a platter of toast and bacon on the table.

"Amen," April and Flynn both said at the same time.

Chapter Five

When they went out into the shed that morning, Nessa walked all the way around the quilt. "I can show you how Mama and I did the smaller throws when we were making quilts for the elderly folks, but this is at least four times bigger than what I'm used to working on. On one like this, with only five-inch squares, my advice would be that we start on one side and work our way across, quilting around each square. This doesn't look a thing like what Nanny Lucy usually made."

"Why not start in three of the corners so we're not all crammed up so close to each other?" Flynn asked. "With your temper, I sure wouldn't want to accidentally stick you with a needle."

"If you do that, then when you get to the middle, you'll have wrinkles and bumps. You start on one side, then if there's excess, it works itself out on the other side," April explained. "Don't look at me like that, Nessa. I know how to do the job. I just don't like it, and neither did my mother."

"How do you know what Rachel liked?" Flynn asked. "You were only four days old when she died. You can't possibly remember anything about her."

"No, I don't. What I do know is that Mama was too wild to ever learn to do something profitable like quilting. But I never heard anything about what she did right, so I guess you're right. I don't know a lot about her, other than that I'm tall and blonde like she was, and I'm a total disappointment just like she was, too," April answered.

Nessa wondered if the fact that Rachel had slept in the bedroom back before April had was the reason April didn't want to go in there. Did she truly believe that the house had powers and a mind of its own to cause her pain and misery? And if she did, then why would she ever come back to Blossom?

"Must be that O'Riley curse we were talking about earlier," Nessa said. "I didn't get praise when I did something right, but I sure got yelled at when I did something wrong."

"The curse presents in different ways. I wonder if Nanny Lucy's ups and downs were part of the thing. Maybe that's what got it all started to begin with." Flynn sat down, picked up a spool of white thread from the edge of the quilt, and threaded a needle. "It's nine thirty. I'm not putting a single stitch in after the clock hits twelve."

"Me either." April had already gotten her needle ready and had begun to stitch her area.

"After we eat lunch, I'm diving into the quilting cabinets in the garage." Nessa hummed an old country tune as she stitched.

"Is that a hymn?" Flynn asked.

"Nope," April answered for her cousin. "That's Miranda Lambert's song 'The House That Built Me.' In its own way, maybe this isn't the house that built us. Maybe it's what broke us all in some way because we are the kids that were produced from the kids that grew up here."

Nessa nodded along to the lyrics in her head that said she'd gotten lost in the world and couldn't remember who she was. She looked to her left at Flynn, and then to her right at her other cousin. April had been right. All three of them were broken—maybe in different ways, but broken all the same—and they were products of what had gone on in this house years ago.

❖　❖　❖

Jackson used a piece of sandpaper wrapped around a block of wood instead of an electric sander to put the finishing touch on what he built. It gave him better control, and his pieces never had the swirls that a sander could cause. He'd been working on a hope chest to take to the next craft fair and thinking about the law firm he'd left behind five years ago. He'd never had a single regret, but here, lately, he'd found himself wishing for someone other than Tex to talk to during the long stretches between craft fairs, or when someone drove out to his place to pick up a piece of furniture.

He cocked his head to one side. Footsteps were approaching his shop, yet Tex hadn't barked. Thinking it might be a customer, Jackson waved over his shoulder. When he reached the other end of the hope chest, he laid the block of wood down and turned around.

"Hello, I'm Flynn O'Riley," the guy standing in the doorway said.

Jackson removed his work glove and stuck out a hand. "Jackson Devereaux. You're Miz Lucy's grandson, right?"

"That's right." Flynn had a good strong handshake. "My two cousins and I are living in Nanny Lucy's house."

"Welcome to Blossom." Jackson dropped Flynn's hand. "There's only two places out here by Hope Creek, so it's a small neighborhood. What brings you out this way?"

"Well, I figure Nanny Lucy talked about us enough that you know the basics of why we're in Blossom. But for today, I've been up in the attic all afternoon," Flynn said, "and needed to take a walk and stretch my legs, so I came over to thank you for taking care of Waylon for us."

"You're welcome," Jackson responded. "Mind if I work while we talk?"

"Not at all," Flynn answered. "I should be going anyway."

"Don't rush off," Jackson said. "What were you doing in the attic?"

"I'm rewiring the place so we can have air conditioners," Flynn said.

Jackson picked up the block with sandpaper wrapped around it. "Y'all will appreciate that. This is just the beginning of summer, and we've already had temperatures up in the midnineties. It's going to be a hot one for sure."

"Amen!" Flynn focused on what Jackson was doing. "What are you working on?"

"Another hope chest. I can't make them fast enough. Folks used to order coffee tables, end tables, even rocking chairs, but in the last five years, I've had more calls for these hope chests than anything else." Jackson went back to sanding. "Pull up a chair and have a seat. There's cold water and tea in the cooler if you want something to drink."

"Thanks." Flynn opened the lid to the red cooler and took out a bottle of water. He sat down in one of the old metal folding chairs over by the wall. "So you knew Nanny Lucy pretty good."

"She and Uncle D. J. were good friends, so she kind of took me in because of him, and because she missed her family." Jackson had often felt sorry for Miz Lucy, living over there all alone. She'd had her quilting buddies, gardening friends, and church family, but those were not family.

Flynn shrugged. "Life gets in the way."

"Don't I know it. I hadn't been around to see Uncle D. J. in ten years until five years ago. I remembered some good times when I came to see him as a kid, so when I got burned out with the law business, I came out here—he'd gotten tired of it back when he was probably about my age," Jackson said.

"Did you intend to stay when you came here?" Flynn asked.

"No, but he talked me into staying all weekend. The morning after I arrived, he took me to the shop and handed me a block of wood like this"—Jackson held up what he was working with—"and I sanded a chest of drawers he had built. That night I slept better than I had in years, and the next day we worked side by side from about eight o'clock until after five. I was hooked after that, and I never left. What about you? You going to stick around here? Miz Lucy said you had a good job with some oil company." Jackson went back to work.

"I'll be here for a few weeks, maybe longer," Flynn answered.

"Ever done any sanding?" Jackson asked.

"Not on wood." Flynn turned up the bottle and drank a third of what was in it.

"Want to give it a try?" Jackson wrapped a piece of sandpaper around a block and offered it to him. "See that box over there? It's the beginning of a hope chest. Sand with the grain, but without too much pressure. You want a smooth finish, so it's better to go over it several times rather than dig into the grain."

Flynn stood up, crossed the messy shop floor, and started sanding. "Like this?"

"Yep, that's good." Jackson smiled. Miz Lucy had said that all three of her grandchildren were as misguided as her kids had been, and that she hoped making them spend some time together would help them. Sanding that chest of drawers had sure put Jackson on the right track. Maybe sanding a hope chest would do the same for Flynn.

❖   ❖   ❖

Nessa had a glass of cold sweet tea in her hands when she heard Flynn and April talking in the backyard. Leaving her drink, she got up from the porch steps and went around to where April was pruning rosebushes and Flynn looked like he had rolled in cornmeal.

Nessa's finger shot up and pointed right at Flynn. Somehow her arm felt separate from her body. She wondered if it had moved on its own. "Where have you been, and what's that all over you?"

"I don't think anyone has asked me that question in fifteen years." Flynn grinned. "Does that mean you care about me?"

"Not in the least. It means that I'd like to know where you've been. I thought maybe you'd seen a pretty woman and headed for the nearest motel," Nessa threw back at him.

Flynn dusted the sawdust off his shirt with the palm of his hand. "I went over to Jackson's place to thank him for bringing Waylon home, and I spent a couple of hours sanding on a hope chest. It wasn't finished, but I really enjoyed doing that. Is supper ready?"

Nessa wondered if Flynn had found a way to work through his problems. If so, she hoped that he'd go visit Jackson every day. "Leftovers are on the stove," she said. "April and I have already eaten, and we are going to the waterfall for a swim."

"I'll see you after I eat." Flynn whistled as he headed into the house.

April kept nipping the dead buds off the bushes and catching them in a paper bag. "Go on without me. I've got one more rosebush to prune, and then I'll be down there."

"Don't take too long. The sunsets are always beautiful over the falls." Nessa picked up her towel and took the first steps down the pathway to the creek.

She dropped her towel on the grass beside the water, slipped off her oversize chambray shirt, and kicked her flip-flops to the side. The grass was cool and soft beneath her bare feet, just like she remembered it from when she was young. She wished that she were an artist or a poet so she could do justice to the only place where she'd ever truly felt content. She had always associated being here with her grandmother, but after some of the vibes she got off April, maybe she had been content here simply because she needed a happy place to go to when things were rough at home. Evidently, things were different when April was alone with Nanny Lucy.

She stuck her toes in the water and gasped.

"It's not all that cold," a deep voice said from the top of the rocks that formed the actual falls. "Miz Lucy said the red-haired granddaughter was Nessa. I guess that's you, right? We met when I brought Waylon home."

"Yes, we did." She nodded. "What are you doing here?"

"My property line cuts right across the middle of the falls. You're sticking your feet in my part of the creek. I don't mind, but we've got 'No Trespassing' signs put up all over the property."

"Well, then you're probably sitting on my rocks," she said. When he had brought Waylon home, it had been too dark to really see what he looked like, but oh, my goodness, he set her heart to fluttering like she was a schoolgirl at a Blake Shelton concert.

"How about we be good neighbors and share?" He flashed her another grin and dived down into the water. When he surfaced, he looked like a Greek god as water sluiced over his broad bare chest and wide shoulders.

Nessa was struck speechless. D. J. had been a short fellow with thinning gray hair and a pudgy, round face. Jackson looked like he should be on the cover of a romance novel, or even in the movies. Nessa would have stood in line for six hours to buy a poster of him if it looked just like him right at that moment.

"Well?" Jackson asked as he waded over toward her.

"Yes, I guess we should share since we're neighbors." Her voice sounded hollow in her own ears. "I understand you're holding our hope chest and the key to unlock it hostage until we get the quilt finished."

He came out of the water and plopped down on the grass a few feet away from her. "That's what Miz Lucy wanted, so I'll obey her wishes. Are you going to stay long enough to get to take it home with you? You can open it to put the quilt in when you finish it, but no one takes it out of my house until one of you gets married. Miz Lucy figures I'll have it until I die."

"I'm not planning on going anywhere until the end of summer, if even then, and I expect that either April or Flynn will inherit it," Nessa answered.

"Well, hello!" April said from behind them. "I thought I recognized your voice from this morning, when you brought Waylon home."

"Is he doing all right?" Jackson glanced up at April.

"He went straight to Nanny Lucy's room and hopped up on her bed. He slept there all day, then about half an hour ago, he decided that it was suppertime," April said as she dropped her shirt, revealing a faded one-piece bathing suit underneath. "I'm getting in the water. See y'all later."

She took a deep breath and dived right into the cold water, splashing both Nessa and Jackson.

"She's braver than I thought she'd be. When I first get into the water, I usually ease in slowly," Jackson said.

"What makes you say that about April? Did Nanny Lucy talk about us?" Nessa asked.

"A little," Jackson answered, and there was a long pause before he said anything more. "You are sassy and bossy. April is a lost soul. Flynn needs closure. She went into detail, but that pretty much sums it up."

Nessa thought about what he'd said for a few seconds before she said a word. Nanny Lucy had been right about all of them, but the way they had been raised had sure made a difference in the three. She couldn't help but wonder what else Nanny Lucy had told Jackson about them—especially her. She wished that Nanny Lucy had told her more about Jackson, like maybe how old he was or how handsome. "So, what would she say about you in five words or less?"

"A hermit who . . ." He held up a hand and shook his head. "No, that would be more than five words. A neighbor and a hermit. Five words."

"That tells me what you are, not who you are," Nessa said.

"Miz Lucy was right about you. I guess we'll have to get to know each other this summer to know *who* we are, won't we?" He grinned as he gathered up his shirt and towel. "I live about a quarter of a mile down that path. My door is always open for visitors, especially neighbors."

"Ours is, too." She watched him disappear down the path.

April surfaced and then walked out of the water. She draped a towel around her shoulders and sat down on the grass. "You can have him."

Nessa could feel a slow burn on her cheeks. "What and who are you talking about?"

"The sexier-than-hell Jackson," April answered. "You can have him. I won't fight you for him. I've sworn off men. Somewhere down deep, they're all worthless."

"What if I've sworn off them, too?" Nessa asked, remembering the last relationship she'd been in. The guy had wanted to run her life for her, tell her what to wear, where to go, how long to stay. If she'd wanted that, she could have married the guy her dad had picked out for her. She'd told him to hit the road, and she hadn't trusted herself to date since.

"Sworn off what?" Flynn sat down on the other side of her. "I saw Jackson on the way down here. He explained our property lines to me. I had no idea that the falls was on both our properties."

"Me either. Not until he told me, but we've agreed to share the falls. Should I have asked you two about that first, or should we put up a barbed wire fence and divide the creek?" Nessa tried to change the subject before the blush on her face set fire to every freckle.

April raised an eyebrow. "Like I told Nessa, I've sworn off men, including the sexy Jackson, so you can have him if you've given up women, Flynn."

"Not me." Flynn turned toward Nessa. "That leaves you, Nessa."

"Hey, I'm sitting right here between you two smart-asses." Nessa stood up. "Or at least I was. Number one, I don't need permission from either of you to like a man, and number two, what makes you think I even want to date anyone? Did you ever think that you two aren't the only ones in the world who are having trouble with the opposite sex?" She made her way to the top of the waterfall and dived into the cold water. April was right—jump right in and the chill wasn't so bad.

Chapter Six

Flynn sighed with resentment as he took his place between his cousins at the quilting project the next morning. Big, black clouds covered the sun, and the smell of rain was in the air. The old thermometer on the front porch said that it was only seventy degrees, and a slight breeze ruffled the leaves on the big pecan tree that shaded the house and shed.

The weather reminded him of another morning, more than a decade ago. It was his seventeenth birthday and the first time that his girlfriend had stayed for the whole night. She had tried to sneak out, but his dad had caught them kissing at the front door. Matthew had just smiled and said, "Good taste, Son. Is her mama married or divorced?"

"What was that sigh all about?" Nessa asked.

"It's fairly cool. There's a little wind blowing. I could be up in the house finishing up the wiring job so that we could set the air conditioners tonight, but oh, no! I've got to be out here quilting," he answered without mentioning that particular memory.

"Poor baby," April teased. "How about Nessa and I go get the air conditioners this afternoon while you finish up the wiring?"

"Ouch!" Flynn flinched and almost turned over his chair when he stuck himself with his needle. He'd forgotten how much the prick of a needle could smart.

"Don't be a wuss," Nessa laughed. "A drop of blood isn't going to get you out of doing your job. Nanny Lucy keeps Band-Aids in the cabinet above the file cabinet. Put one on your boo-boo and keep working."

Flynn dropped his needle on the quilt and carefully pushed back his chair. Nanny Lucy would claw her way through six feet of dirt and haunt his dreams if he ruined this special quilt, even if they all agreed that it was as ugly as a wild hog. He used a tissue to wipe the blood away, applied a bandage, and went back to his chair.

"I've figured out our system," April said. "This is a king-size quilt, so there's thirty rows going up and down"—she waved her left arm back and forth—"and twenty-four going across."

"And that means?" Flynn picked up the needle and was a lot more careful this time.

"It means that we each stitch around each of ten squares every morning," April explained. "One long five-inch section will be done, then we move on to the next one."

"And we'll be done in twenty-four days." Nessa hummed as she worked.

"Do we work seven days a week?" Flynn asked.

"We should talk about that and also agree on whether we get to leave when we finish our ten squares for the day," April said.

"We can't very well work ahead because of wrinkling." Nessa frowned.

"I vote that we get to leave when our portion is done," Flynn said.

"But only if your stitching is as good as ours," Nessa told him. "The quilting club will never let it pass inspection if your stitches are an inch long."

Flynn checked the work on both sides of him, and his work was every bit as nice as theirs. "The club won't find a bit of a problem with what I'm doing, and when I get my ten squares done, I'm gone."

"Guess that decides that, then." April didn't even look up from her work. "But don't pout when we get done before you do."

"Oh, honey." Flynn cut his chocolate-brown eyes toward her. "It will be you two who are still working when I leave this shed."

"The race is on." Nessa giggled. "Only it's between you two, not me. I love this work, so I intend to take my time and enjoy it."

"Well, would you look at this?" Flynn was amazed at the fabric square he had started to sew around.

"What? Did the poor baby poke his finger again?" April asked.

"Nope, but I did figure out part of the reason why this crazy-looking quilt is so important, and why there seems to be no rhyme or reason to the pattern. Like Nessa noticed earlier, Nanny Lucy's quilts were all so intricate, but this one is not. So do you wanna know?" Flynn grinned.

"Of course we do!" Nessa said, and then she sucked in air. "I know what you're talking about. I see it now."

"Well, clue me in," April said.

"Pay real close attention to your ten squares," Nessa told her. "What does that piece you are sewing around right now remind you of?"

April frowned and studied the square for a moment, then smiled. "Well, how about that? This is a piece from the dress Nanny Lucy made for me to wear on the first day of kindergarten. I wouldn't even remember it, but she showed me a picture of me wearing it once when I was a little girl."

"And this"—Flynn pointed to the portion he was working on—"is scraps from the shirt she made for me when I was about that same age. She used to sew a few shirts for me every summer while I was here, and Mama would make me save my new ones for the first days of school."

Nessa touched the piece she was sewing. "Yep, and I'm looking at the scrap from a dress she made for me about that same time, and if you look across the whole quilt, I betcha every square is cut from a remnant of something she made for us. This isn't just a haphazard thing she threw together, it's a memory quilt. I'm amazed that she has kept scraps all these years. Do you think she made out her will and then this quilt because she knew she was going to die?"

"Who knows about Nanny Lucy," April said. "She only talked to me when she was mad, and that seemed to be most of the time."

"Do any of us really want it bad enough to get married?" Flynn's memories of the time he'd had with his mother and the weeks he'd spent with Nanny Lucy in the summers were good. But over there on the other side, after he had gone to live with his father, were some painful times that he'd just as soon keep locked away in the back of his mind until he figured out how to deal with them.

"Remember the summer"—April kept stitching as she talked—"that I pulled my first baby tooth? Y'all were here, and Flynn was so mad because I was the youngest one of us and lost the first tooth."

"I was jealous, too," Nessa admitted. "The tooth fairy left you two quarters that night."

"Nanny Lucy made me put one of them in my piggy bank for my college fund," April said. "But I got to keep the other one. I bought a snow cone with it after y'all left."

"You had a college fund at six years old?" Flynn hadn't had a college fund when he graduated from high school. He'd had to work forty hours a week and take night courses to get his degree. "What happened to you, April?"

She shrugged. "Nanny Lucy said she would match my savings, dime for dime, until I graduated. The deal was if I had enough to pay for most of my first semester and I passed all my courses, then she would pay for the rest of the years until I got my degree. If I took the money and didn't go to school, she wouldn't pay a single penny on my education or help me out of any binds I might get into. But I couldn't stay here anymore. The rest is history. You already know most of it."

"Not the details." Flynn glanced down the row to see that she was at least two squares behind him on the morning job.

"Those aren't important." April's voice was as haunted as the look Flynn had seen in her eyes when she first arrived.

Flynn wondered if his tone was like that or if his eyes took on that same look when he talked about the past. Did the pain come through as plainly as it did with April? He had no doubt that she'd returned to Blossom to find closure for all the things that had made her the way she was. He'd come back to find peace, but was there really peace in this place, or was he chasing an illusion?

Nessa nudged his shoulder. "You sure got quiet."

"Just thinking," he said as he put in the last stitch on his section, "and now I'm going into the house to finish up that wiring. I'll have to turn off the power for a little while." He wished he could turn off his thoughts as easily as opening a breaker box and throwing a few levers. He stood up and stretched the kinks out of his neck and back and, with a wave, left his two cousins behind to do their sections.

❖ ❖ ❖

Nessa was still working on her daily portion of the quilt when April finished hers a few minutes later. "I'm going to water the flowers while you finish up," she said, and she was gone before Nessa could say anything.

She kept sewing, but the shed felt empty now, and more than a little gloomy. The dark clouds kept rolling in from the southwest, and that edgy feeling she always felt when a storm—either natural or mental—was approaching washed over her. She hated the heavy feeling in her chest, but not even the breathing exercises the school counselor had given her for anxiety when she was a kid were working today.

She'd just finished the last stitch and was threading her needle for the next day when her phone rang. The noise startled her so badly that she jabbed herself in the thumb, and a bubble of blood appeared immediately.

She hurried to the back of the shed, wrapped a tissue around it, and fished her phone from her hip pocket. "Hello, Mama," she said.

"I was about to hang up," Cora said. "What took you so long?"

"I was quilting," Nessa explained, "and stuck my thumb with the needle. Had to get a tissue to keep from getting blood on the phone. How are you and Daddy?"

"I'm fine," Cora said. "He's in a funk because of the way things went about that property out there. To tell the truth, I'm glad he lost. I don't want to move out to that godforsaken place. I like where we live—and our friends are here—but losing in court has shattered all of his retirement dreams. I told him that getting that property wasn't God's will for us, and he agreed, but he's still bummed out over it."

"Retirement dreams?" Nessa frowned. "Daddy is only sixty-two years old. I figured he'd preach a sermon on Wednesday night and drop dead right after the last amen was said when he was about a hundred and ten."

"That's sacrilegious," Cora scolded.

"Well, it's the truth." Nessa put the phone on speaker mode and put a Band-Aid on her thumb. "What were all these big dreams, anyway?"

"He was going to get the retreat going in that area, show his deacons here what a lovely place Blossom is, and then, in about four years, we would move there. He's always dreamed of coming back to his hometown and building his own church. If some of our good friends here in the church family saw the place, he believed that they would fall in love with it and follow him—kind of like the people did with Jesus." Cora sighed. "But your grandmother ruined it all. I will never understand why she did that, since Isaac is the only child that she could have put a bit of pride in. Rachel was a troubled child from the time she took her first steps, and Matthew was a complete disappointment. How Isaac could share DNA with those two is a mystery."

"Daddy used to tell me that disappointments were good for the soul. They taught us to depend on God and to realize that He was in charge. I knew that wasn't right because Daddy was the one in charge at our house, not God," Nessa said.

"That's downright mean." Cora's voice went all high and squeaky. "Your father's disappointment is aggravating me. He's moping around here like a six-year-old kid whose mama forgot all about his birthday. I'm glad we're going to the Holy Land next month. That's the only thing that's keeping him going. I wish you'd go with us. Samuel has agreed to take that last ticket we had to use to get the group rate. I'm sure he'd be delighted to have you along."

Nessa shivered at the very idea of spending two weeks with Samuel right beside her. He was the guy her dad had insisted that she marry when she was just eighteen years old. Six years older than she was, he had already finished college and was a successful pharmaceutical rep. He was as vanilla as a guy could be. Nessa craved someone with at least a little bit of wildness in him. He didn't have to ride motorcycles or have tattoos, but he did have to make her *want* a kiss from him instead of want to run away from one.

"Are you still there, Vanessa?" Cora asked.

"I'm here, and thanks for the offer, but no thanks. Samuel wasn't the man for me more than ten years ago, and he's still not," Nessa answered.

"Poor thing," Cora sighed. "He loved you so much, but he realized that you weren't the one for him at that young age when you . . . Well, you did get wild after you made that decision to go to college"—another sigh—"and then Samuel married Ruth Ann that very next year and lost her four years later. I've always thought that he was just waiting for you to grow up and come back into his life."

"He'll be waiting for a long time if that's what he's doing," Nessa said. "I don't love Samuel."

"You could give him a chance." Cora's voice turned slightly icy.

"No, thanks," Nessa said.

"Well, then, can't you let your dad use that house for a retreat in the winter months when you're back in Turkey at your job?" Cora asked.

Now we're getting to the real reason for this call, Nessa thought.

Cora O'Riley was a master manipulator, and she'd played her hand well. Nessa should feel so guilty for not going to Israel with the group that to make up for it, she would agree to let the Reverend Isaac use the house.

"Only if April and Flynn both agree to the idea," Nessa said, "and I doubt they will. They both say they're sticking around for a long time. There just wouldn't be room for any more adults in the house."

She was amazed at how good it felt to be able to say that to her mother, but somewhere in the back of her mind, she expected to be sent to her room to pray for forgiveness for talking to her mother like that.

"Sometimes I wonder how two godly people like your father and me ever produced a child like you," Cora said.

Nessa could easily visualize her mother setting her jaw and her mouth in a firm line with her dark, perfectly arched brows drawn down in a frown.

"You should have studied his mother a little more before you married Daddy," Nessa said. "They say I'm just like Nanny Lucy."

"God forbid!" Cora said, and she hung up on her.

April stuck her head in the door. "You about finished? Flynn says he'll be ready to set the air conditioners in a couple of hours, and it's looking like it could blow up a pretty fierce storm out here."

"I'm ready," Nessa answered. "Just let me run to the house, make a trip through the bathroom, and grab my purse. You can wait for me in the SUV if you want to. Just get the AC going."

April nodded and jogged in that direction as Nessa closed the shed and took off in a slow run to the house. *Storms aren't always on the outside of a body,* she thought as she cleared the porch and ran to the bathroom.

She could hear her father quoting that verse about loving thy mother and father. "I do love you," she muttered, "but the Bible doesn't say I have to like you."

❖ ❖ ❖

April hated thunder and lightning, but at least she had a roof over her head, and if things got too bad, she could always take shelter in the cellar. She wasn't too fond of that closed-in space, either, but she and Nanny Lucy had spent lots of nights down there waiting out a storm.

Her skin itched at the thought of going down into the cellar. She always felt like spiders or bugs were crawling on her body, or that a mouse was chasing across her feet.

She covered her ears at the first distant rumble of thunder, like she had when she was a little girl. Not wanting Nessa to think she was a big baby, she removed her hands when her cousin slid in behind the steering wheel. She needed a diversion, something to talk about while the lightning zipped through the sky and left another clap of thunder in its wake. "Did Nanny Lucy ever tell you the tornado story?"

Nessa started the engine and shook her head. "No, come to think of it, she didn't say an awful lot to either me or Flynn while we were here. Do you know that story?"

"Yes, I do," April answered. "She was deathly afraid of storms, and we relived the story every year during tornado season. I made up my mind that I would never go down in one of those shelter things again when I left home. I hated the smell even more than the spiders and scorpions that lived down there."

"Tell me what it was that y'all relived," Nessa said as she backed the vehicle out and started down the dirt road toward the highway.

"She and Grandpa Everett were engaged," April started. "Grandpa was working on the railroad, and Nanny Lucy had just finished high school. He had come to see her that evening in the house south of Blossom where she and her folks lived. A storm came up, but it wasn't just a thunderstorm like this, but a full-fledged tornado. The four of them, Nanny Lucy, her parents, and Grandpa, were crammed in a cellar along with several neighbors for over an hour, waiting for the tornado to pass over. She said . . ." April's hands went to her ears when a streak of lightning hit a nearby tree, and the thunder that followed it sounded like it was sitting on top of Nessa's SUV.

"That was pretty close." Nessa's voice quivered. "We're more than halfway there, so what do you want to do? Go home or go on?"

"Might as well go on." April dropped her hands and felt compelled to go on with the story, too. Maybe there was something in it that would make more sense to Nessa than it did to her. "It tore up a lot of property around town. Nanny Lucy said that the whole time she and Grandpa were in the cellar, she prayed that God wouldn't let the tornado ruin their little house that Grandpa had bought for them up by Hope Creek, the very house that we're living in now. She promised that she would raise her kids up in the church if God would spare hers and Grandpa's life and their house. He did, and she was faithful in taking her kids to church after that, even though Grandpa wouldn't go with her. And she was terrified of storms from then on, so every time the wind blew, we had to go to the cellar."

"Daddy never mentioned that, but he sure gets antsy when it storms. He says that it's God's way of showing us He's still in control." Nessa turned right and headed toward Paris.

"I always figured tornadoes were spawned by the devil, and that God was turning Lucifer loose with them to punish us for all our sins with tornadoes. That's the short form of what Nanny Lucy said when she was having one of her days." April closed her eyes tightly and shivered all the way to her toes when another streak of lightning zigzagged across the sky. "I hate storms to this day."

Nessa nodded. "Flynn had it easier than we did. He didn't have to go to church and be scared to death of the devil, or even of God."

April shivered again when a clap of thunder followed the lightning. "Nanny Lucy used to say that her kids were like little seeds. She planted them all, but at harvest time God got one, and the devil got the other two."

"I'm not real sure about all that." Nessa turned the windshield wipers on low when the first drops of rain fell. "If you'd had to live with my father, you might think the devil got all three of the seeds. He preaches a good sermon, but he's got a hard heart."

"What about us three?" April asked. "What would she say about us?"

"That I'm bossy. You are a lost soul. And Flynn needs closure," Nessa answered. "That's what Jackson told me she said about us."

"She got it right about us, but what would Flynn need closure about?" April wondered out loud.

"Who knows? Maybe when he trusts us, he'll tell us what he's hiding in his heart. What are *you* hiding?" They passed the exit to Sun Valley, Texas.

April pointed to the sign. "See that? I lost my virginity when I was fifteen up there in that little town. I was supposed to be at my girlfriend's house from noon until night church, but I went with my boyfriend up to an old barn, and we had sex."

"What's that got to do with anything?" Nessa asked.

"You asked what I'm hiding," April said.

"I'm sure you've had sex with other guys since then, right?" Nessa asked.

"Nanny Lucy found out that I wasn't at my girlfriend's house and grounded me until the end of the school year. Then it was summer, and she extended the punishment for three more months." April kept her eyes on the wipers going back and forth across the windshield.

Nanny Lucy had met her at the door, Grandpa's old leather belt already in hand, and the punishment had been twenty licks for sneaking around. She could almost feel every single lick she'd felt then as the doubled belt slapped against her bare legs and back.

"You're not hiding it if she found out," Nessa told her.

"She didn't find out about the sex, because I wouldn't tell her. But she ranted at me the whole time she whipped me with a belt, saying that if I wasn't at my girlfriend's house, then I had to be out with some worthless boy. She accused me of being just like my wild mother and told me if I'd gotten myself pregnant, I could go live in a box under a bridge," April said. "When I asked her why she hadn't kicked my mother out, she said a mother didn't throw her kid out in the street. Then she reminded me that I *wasn't* her child, and she *would* throw me out."

"'What would God think if I did that?' Or 'What would the people in Blossom think?' she said each time she swung that belt. She said she'd hoped that I would be a godly child to make up for my mother, but that it looked like the devil was going to get another one."

"You didn't get pregnant, did you?" Nessa asked.

"No, but I sure sweated it. I skipped two periods and was making plans to run away so that Nanny Lucy wouldn't have to even know about it when I finally started just before I'd missed the third one, and from that day until I left home, I didn't have sex again," April said.

"That first time isn't what it's cracked up to be at all, is it?" Nessa pulled into the Home Depot parking lot. "I was pretty disappointed. It was far more of a thrill knowing that I was doing something that I shouldn't on the sofa in my dad's study at the church than the actual sex."

"Holy smoke!" April gasped. "Did you really?"

"Yep, I did, and this is the first time I'm admitting that, too." Nessa slung the door open and picked up an umbrella from the back seat. "Sit tight. This thing is oversized, so we can both use it."

"So?" April asked when she was under the umbrella with Nessa. "Were you afraid that you might be pregnant?"

"Nope, I made sure the boy used a condom," Nessa said. "If I'd gotten pregnant in high school, Daddy would have guilted me to death, and Mama would have probably sent me away to an unwed mothers' home."

April felt closer to her cousin in that rainy moment than she ever had before. "Do you think that tornado that ripped through Blossom back then is still affecting us?"

"Kind of like the butterfly effect?" Nessa asked as they entered the store.

"Something like that," April answered. "If the tornado hadn't scared Nanny Lucy so badly, she wouldn't have been so adamant about going to church. If she hadn't pressured the boys, then your dad wouldn't be so strict on you, and Flynn's daddy and my mother wouldn't have rebelled. Are we ever going to be free of it?"

"I don't know. The question now is, What are we going to do about it?" Nessa headed toward the customer service counter.

April followed right behind her. "Never have kids would be the sensible thing, wouldn't it?"

"Do you want to have a family?" Nessa asked.

April nodded. "I love babies and little children, but I wouldn't want . . ."

"May I help you?" the woman behind the counter asked.

Nessa handed her a sales slip. "We're here to pick up these three air conditioners."

"Bring your vehicle around to the loading area, and I'll have someone bring them out to you," the woman said, and then she turned to the next customer.

"Well, that was easy enough," April said as they headed to the exit door.

"We were talking about children and having a family." Nessa popped the umbrella back up and sighed. "I'd like to have kids, but before I can even think about that, I've got to get my life straightened out. Like you, I've trusted the wrong men. You had guys that took advantage of you. I seemed to get involved with cheaters." Just saying that much brought back a measure of the pain she'd felt the last time she was in a relationship.

"What's that mean?" April asked. "You're a teacher. You have a job and a steady income."

"That's who I am on the outside." Nessa waited until April was in the passenger seat and then rounded the back of the SUV and got into the driver's side. She closed the umbrella, shook as much water from it as she could, and then put it on the back floorboard. "I'm as big of a mess on the inside as you are. I just hide it better."

"Want to talk about it?" April asked.

"Not today. We've had enough cousin therapy for one day. Let's go by the pizza place and get a couple to take home for supper, and maybe find a convenience store with a drive-by window to get a six-pack of beer to go with it," Nessa said.

"Nanny Lucy will for sure claw her way up out of the grave if we take beer into her house." April's tone was dead serious. "But that sure sounds good."

"Shhh . . ." Nessa put a finger over her lips. "I won't tell if you don't, and if Flynn does, we'll make him sleep in the cellar tonight."

April's frown turned into a smile, and a tiny weight lifted from her heart.

Chapter Seven

Flynn woke up on Friday morning with the covers pulled all the way up to his chin, and it felt so good to be breathing cold air after nights of sweltering heat. Waylon was lying on the pillow next to him, evidently trying to stare him awake with those big, green, unblinking eyes.

"Good mornin'." Flynn yawned. "Kind of nice to wake up in a cold room, isn't it? Is that where you slept when Nanny Lucy had this room?"

Waylon's meow sounded like he was saying yes.

"Don't you lie to me," Flynn chuckled. "I remember Waylon number two very well, and Nanny Lucy made him go to the garage when it was bedtime. You are a con artist."

Waylon meowed pitifully, got to his feet, and then jumped down off the bed and stood by the closed door.

"Guess that means you're hungry or that you need to get to the litter pan, right?" Flynn tossed back the covers and shivered as he made his way over to the air conditioner and turned it down to a low setting. He opened the door, and the smell of coffee and bacon wafted down the hallway.

The cat took off in a black-and-white blur.

"Guess he's in a hurry for his breakfast." Flynn chuckled as he got dressed in faded denim shorts and a stained T-shirt. Today he had plans to start painting the house when they finished their time in the quilting shed. He looked at the calendar on his phone and smiled. "I'm one week sober today."

You've never been an alcoholic. His father's voice was so clear that he glanced over his shoulder to be sure the man hadn't sneaked into the house during the night.

"A woman addiction is worse than alcohol," Flynn whispered. "But I've made it a week without a one-night stand, so I'm on my way."

You won't get a one-year token for that. The voice continued to argue.

"No, but hopefully, I won't be on wife number six, or is it seven, when I'm sixty-one." Flynn slipped his feet into a pair of old shoes, tied them, and left his father's antagonizing voice in the bedroom.

"Good mornin'," he called out as he headed toward the smell of bacon mixed with the aroma of coffee.

"Yes, it is," Matthew said from the end of the kitchen table.

"Dad?" Flynn blinked several times. What in the hell was his dad doing in Blossom, and why would he bring a woman with him?

Good grief! Flynn thought. *He's about to get married again, and he wants me to be his best man for the fourth, or is it fifth, time?*

"Hello, Son. I'd like you to meet Delores, my fiancée." Matthew reached over and held up the woman's hand to show off an engagement ring. "We're on our way to Kansas so I can meet her children. I figured I'd stop on the way. As soon as I charm her kin, we will announce our plans that we will be getting married at the end of the month. Want to be my best man?"

Poor Delores had no idea that he could turn on the charm like a faucet and turn it off when he got bored.

"Pleased to meet you, Delores." Flynn hoped his smile didn't look too fake.

The woman had platinum-blonde hair straight out of a bottle. She would probably be dying it some shade of red within six weeks of the wedding. Wife number three had been a brunette at first, but she'd soon dyed it to please Matthew. Wife number four, or was it five—Flynn had trouble keeping them all straight—had started out with light-brown hair, and when they divorced, she was a redhead. He wondered if his father's addiction to red-haired women was because Nanny Lucy had had red hair, and he had a hang-up about wanting her to love him as much as she had Isaac.

Delores's bright-red V-neck shirt showed three inches of cleavage and clung to her curvy body, just like her skinny jeans with the lines of her bikini underwear showing through.

"Likewise." Delores's husky tone and the slightly yellow marks on her fingertips left no doubt that she was a heavy smoker. "Matty, darlin', you didn't tell me that your son looked like that movie star that plays on *NCIS*. Nick is my favorite character—next to Gibbs, of course. How did a tall blond like you ever produce such a dark-haired, sexy son like this?"

"His mother was Latina," Matthew explained.

"I *have* to introduce him to my daughter Lisette." She scanned Flynn from his black hair to his toes. "Her father was Italian. They would make us some gorgeous grandbabies."

"Maybe they'll meet at the wedding," Matthew said.

"Sorry, Dad," Flynn said. "You're on your own with this one. I won't be done with the quilt by then, so I'll have to stick around here. Wish y'all all the best, though. Nessa, do you need some help?"

"We've got it covered," April said from the galley kitchen area. "You just get a cup of coffee and go on out on the porch so you can visit with Uncle Matthew in private."

Flynn shot a dirty look her way when he poured himself coffee and topped off his father's mug. Delores held her hand over her cup and said, "I can't have any more. Matty is the big coffee drinker in our house, not me. One cup in the morning is my limit. Course, Lisette goes with a cup in her hand all the time, especially after this last divorce. I've got a picture of her and her sister, Julie, that you should see since y'all are going to be shirttail kin." She pulled her phone out of her purse and flipped through several screens before she landed on the right one. "Right here. Lisette is twenty-one, and Julie is twenty-five."

"Good-looking ladies." Flynn managed a smile. His last stepmother had been about Julie's age, and the marriage hadn't lasted a year. At least this one was a little closer to his father's age if she had daughters in their twenties.

"Julie was born when I was sixteen," Delores said.

Flynn did the math in his head and bit back a grin. He'd been right after all. The woman was twenty years younger than Matthew and only ten years older than Flynn. That was a little more like his father. Delores fidgeted with a case that held her cigarettes, then noticed a plaque hanging on the kitchen wall that said, "Anyone Caught Smoking in My House Will Be Shot." She put the case back in her purse and said, "Lisette came along when I was twenty. Julie's daddy was twenty-eight, and he died when she was a year old. Lisette's daddy was forty, and he died when she was five years old." Delores sighed dramatically.

Yep, Flynn thought, *he's got a type, and she's it to a T. Talks too much. Lots younger than him. Dad, what are you doing here? You hardly ever visited Nanny Lucy, and when you did, it was only for an hour or two.* Flynn looked up from the picture and caught both Nessa and April staring at him. Nessa slid a sly wink his way. April raised both eyebrows. No doubt they were wondering if his dad had gotten tangled up with a black widow, because he was thinking the very same thing.

He handed the phone back to Delores. "Maybe someday I can meet them."

"Christmas would be great. They always come to see me wherever I'm living for Christmas. We'll have a huge family dinner, and . . ."

And you may not even be around by then, Flynn thought as he tuned out both her and his father and sipped his coffee. *I don't think Dad's ever married a ready-made family, and he might figure out really quick that this isn't what he wants.*

"Why don't you and Flynn take a short walk around the place while the girls finish breakfast?" Delores suggested. "I'll just step out on the porch and have a cigarette while y'all are gone."

Matthew leaned over and kissed her on the lips.

"Breakfast will be ready in ten minutes," Nessa said.

The front door swung open, and Isaac came into the house. A big man with blond hair and blue eyes, like his brother, he had a presence that filled the small living room. He glared first at Matthew and then at the woman at the table.

"What are *you* doing here?" Isaac asked.

"Daddy?" Nessa asked, her face going ashen. "What are you doing here?"

Matthew stood up, and tension engulfed the room like a wildfire. "I might ask you the same thing, Isaac."

Flynn started across the living room floor. Nessa came from the other side.

Cora stepped out from behind Isaac and got between the two men. "Y'all act like brothers. You're going to grieve the heart of God acting like two tomcats squaring off with each other."

Matthew dropped his chin a notch and glared at Isaac, who returned the icy-cold stare.

"I came to have a face-to-face with my daughter, to talk her out of this crazy notion of staying in this godforsaken place." Isaac knotted his fists. "Evidently you brought your new woman for your wild son's approval."

"I did, but that's not a damn bit of your business," Matthew answered.

Flynn hadn't even had so much as a phone call from his father in weeks. Was he there to ask for any money that Flynn might inherit, to claim what he thought was his inheritance by right?

Every muscle in Flynn's body tensed. His dad had never asked his approval on anything, especially not his multitude of women. Not once had Matthew said, "What do you think of this lady or that one?" No, sir! He had simply come home and said he was getting married again, and he'd expected Flynn to be his best man.

Nessa seemed to be frozen in place, but finally she crossed the room and hugged her mother. "Have y'all had breakfast?"

"We ate at Weezy's this morning before we came on out here," Cora said as she held out her arms toward April. "I'd forgotten how little this house is. How are you, April? Are you doing all right?"

"I'm fine, Aunt Cora." April walked into her arms and hugged her. "Better than I've been in a long time. Being here with Flynn and Nessa has been a blessing."

"About that walk you and Flynn were going to take? Why don't you step outside? And after that we should really be leaving," Delores finally said.

"I reckon him and me could go see the waterfall." Matthew took Delores's hand in his and headed for the front door.

Flynn followed behind them, glad for the chance to get away from the double ambush. Hadn't any of Nanny Lucy's sons learned how to use a phone? Cora was right. The house was way too small for the two O'Riley brothers to be inside it at the same time.

Delores sat down on the porch, stretched out her long legs, and put her bright-red spike heels on the bottom step. "Y'all boys don't leave me alone too long, now." She giggled as she lit up a cigarette. "I thought I was going to have a withdrawal fit in there, darlin', with all that tension. I'm sure glad I never had a brother, or boys, for that matter, if that's the way they act. I'll be right here when y'all get back."

"Where'd you find this one?" Flynn asked when they were halfway to the waterfall.

"That's harsh," Matthew answered. "Don't you want me to be happy?"

"Of course," Flynn replied. "We all deserve to be happy, but some of us have to work at it."

"I found her at the office." Matthew laughed out loud. "And, Son, I do work at it, probably harder than any other man. Sometimes I find it for a season, but when I'm not happy, I'm smart enough to move on."

"You have got to be kiddin' me." Flynn couldn't believe what he was hearing. His dad never went for the women who worked in the oil field offices.

"Truth!" Matthew crossed his heart. "There's this old two-story house in Bay City that's been converted into a bar called the Office. That's where I met her a month ago, right after my divorce was final."

"You do know there's other places to meet women, don't you?" Flynn said. "And you might even marry a keeper someday."

"At my age, it's the best place." Matthew chuckled. "I like the chase. I like making a woman feel special when I ask her to marry me."

"And breaking her heart when you divorce her or cheat on her?" Flynn asked.

"Collateral damage." Matthew shrugged. "I leave them with beautiful memories, though. I swore when I left this place that I'd never live in a marriage like my folks had. When I got tired of being married, I wouldn't stick around for a kid or because I might hurt her feelings."

"Why not just love 'em and leave 'em? And what do you mean like your folks' marriage?" Flynn really wanted to understand the thinking behind the way his father was and the way Flynn himself had been.

"I like being married. I like coming home to a woman and not having to go chase one down every weekend like you do, but then"— another shrug—"I start craving that chase and the thrill again."

"Have you ever wondered why you do this?" Flynn frowned.

"Nope, because I don't care why. I just know what makes me happy, and I don't try to heal happiness." Matthew pointed toward the waterfall. "I spent a lot of time out here at these falls when I was a kid, and then when I was a teenager. We never knew what kind of mood Mama would be in. She'd be high as a druggie after a fix one day, praising God and going to church every time the doors were open. A week later she would bottom out and forsake the church and cry all the time. Either way, I tried to steer clear of her, because she was quick to grab that belt and lay into me for anything at all. Isaac prayed a lot under that old scrub oak tree over there." He pointed downstream a little way. "I had a lot of sex both in the creek and on this bank, starting when I was fifteen. Weren't you about that age when you lost your virginity?"

"You know very well when that happened, and I was seventeen." Flynn flinched at the memory.

"Yep, I do." Matthew nodded. "The only difference in me and you, Son, is that I do marry one of my women every so often. You just love 'em and leave 'em, as you say. What happened to Amelia? I thought for sure she'd be the one that taught you how much fun a wedding and a honeymoon could be."

"We broke up," Flynn said.

Matthew laid a hand on Flynn's shoulder. "Too bad, but look on the bright side. There's always more fish in the sea."

"Dad, why are you and Uncle Isaac so different?" Flynn shook off his father's hand and raked his fingers through his dark hair. "And why do you hate each other? You're brothers, for God's sake, and you acted like you could kill each other up there at the house."

Matthew turned to look at Flynn. "If you think living in that house was a picnic for any of us, you're badly mistaken. The stress in the place was always so thick you couldn't cut it with a knife. Isaac and I just took the religion and . . ."—he paused a minute before he went on— "and everything else in different ways. My brother couldn't wait to go get close to Jesus four times a week. I couldn't wait to go get in some girl's underpants. We both got what we wanted in the same place—at the church. He was constantly on my case about religion. That's why I decided to never have but one child. I was afraid I'd produce a throwback like him and Mama. You should be thanking me, not acting like I'm the devil and Isaac is Jesus."

"Maybe, but I'm trying to figure things out about myself," Flynn replied. "I have to understand *why* in order to change."

"Why in the hell would you want to change?" Matthew was visibly taken aback by Flynn's words.

"Because I don't want to be your age and still be thrill seeking. I want to settle down and have a family. I want to be more like Mama and less like you. I went to a therapist, and he told me that what we both have is a form of addiction. We'll always be afflicted with it, but we can overcome it with time. We just have to want to change, and I do," Flynn answered.

"If that's your reasoning, it might be best if you aren't my best man at this one. Your attitude would spoil the whole party." Matthew's tone went downright icy. "I don't think Delores and I will stay for breakfast after all. We'll get something at Weezy's and get on up the road."

"Probably for the best." Flynn wasn't one bit disappointed. "I won't be coming to the coast for Christmas."

"You going to get religion like Isaac?" Matthew threw over his shoulder as he turned to walk away.

"No, just hoping to get my life on some kind of sane track." Flynn sat down on the grass and let the bubbling sound of the water falling over the rocks calm him. "I wish you luck this time."

"Don't need it." Matthew stopped and turned around. "I know who I am, what I like, and what I'll do next time when I'm tired of this one. Like the old saying goes, you can't change a leopard's spots, and, Son, you might look like your mother, but you've got a big dose of my DNA."

"Do you ever think about those sacred vows you make when you get married?" Flynn asked.

"Not since I broke the first ones with your mother. They're just words, but they sure help a fella seal the deal." Matthew chuckled, and then he disappeared down the path leading back to the house.

Flynn wondered what had happened in his youth that would cause Matthew to be the way he was. Had he inherited some of Nanny Lucy's ways, so that he liked the euphoric days better than plain-old-living times? Did he even realize that was why he was the way he was? Maybe that preference was why he could never seem to be a real father to Flynn. He had never seen Flynn as a "good time" but as more of a huge, unwanted responsibility.

Flynn stretched out on his back and watched the dark clouds cover the sky for the second day in a row. "I don't want to be like him," he whispered, "and I can change. I know I can."

❖ ❖ ❖

Nessa had come to Blossom to find peace, and there was the absolute opposite of that standing before her in the form of her father.

"I'll go outside," April whispered.

Nessa shook her head and mouthed, "No!"

"Y'all come on in and sit down at the table. I've got biscuits in the oven and was just about to scramble some eggs. Even if you have had breakfast, you can have a cup of coffee with us." Nessa whipped around and headed back into the kitchen.

"I'll be glad to pour y'all a cup," April said.

"Yes, please." Cora pulled out a chair and sat down. "How in the world are all three of you living in this tiny place?"

By the look in her hazel eyes, Cora was tired, embarrassed, and more than a little on edge, but even when she was angry with her husband, she would be submissive, even if it went against every nerve in her body. Nessa knew the signs from her earliest memories.

Just like she remembered, her mother's narrow shoulders slumped, and she clasped her hands together. No doubt that was to keep them from shaking with anger. True enough, she was a religious woman, but after living with Isaac O'Riley for more than thirty years, she could probably rewrite the book of Job.

Nessa crossed the small place and laid a hand on her mother's shoulder. "We manage pretty well."

"I take my coffee with two sugars." Isaac's back was ramrod straight when he sat down. His blond hair, as ever, was in place. Nessa had always wondered if he used gel or spray to keep it that way.

"This is an intervention." Isaac tucked his chin down a notch and glared at Nessa.

"For which one of us?" Nessa could feel the heat of his eyes, but she refused to turn around and look at him. "If it was for Uncle Matthew, I guess it failed."

Matthew pushed his way into the house. "I heard what Nessa just said. You and Mama tried that intervention crap too many times for me to remember. Give it up, Isaac. I'm not changing my ways."

"I gave up on you years ago," Isaac growled. "The demons in you have made a home, but I do pray for you every day."

"Don't waste your breath, Brother." Matthew grinned. "I own my demons. You just cover yours up with self-righteous robes. I came in to tell my nieces goodbye. It wouldn't seem right to run off without saying thanks for the coffee and the warm welcome. I probably won't come back to this place again. The hate seems to come right out of the walls. Come see me if you're ever in Houston." He turned and headed out, then stopped at the door and turned around with a frown on his face. "Take my advice and burn this place to the ground, then run as far away as you can."

"That's not my advice," Isaac growled as the door shut behind his brother, "but I do think you are wasting your lives even thinking about staying here."

"Maybe we're finding out who we are by living here," April said as she set their coffee on the table.

April had looked a little like a deer in the headlights when both of the O'Riley brothers were in the living room, but she'd done some kind of a turnaround to be able to say that to Isaac. Nessa gave her a brief sideways hug.

"Thank you," she whispered.

April's head bobbed once in a quick nod.

"That's crazy talk, but then I wouldn't expect much more from Rachel's kid," Isaac said.

"That's uncalled for, Daddy," Nessa said. "April can't help who her parents are, any more than I can help who mine are. You can say the same about Nanny Lucy and Grandpa. What happened in this place anyway to make you and Uncle Matthew hate each other?"

Isaac glared at her. "This was not a happy home. Mama had bad days, and Matthew seemed to be the one that brought them on. She'd be doing fine, and then he'd make her mad. She'd either start crying and telling us we didn't appreciate a thing she did for us, or else she'd grab a belt or a length of garden hose, or whatever was at hand, and whale away on both of us."

"We should have our coffee and leave," Cora said.

Isaac put up a palm and shifted his glassy stare toward his wife. "No! She wants to know why Matthew and I can't get along, so I'll tell her. It's like Jesus and the devil trying to be friends. They are enemies and never will be friends. That's the reason."

"That's judging," Nessa reminded him.

"That's telling the God's honest truth," Isaac growled. "If he'd been a better child, Mama would have had more good days than bad ones. It's his fault that she lost her mind and gave this place to you three kids. I should have inherited it. I gave up everything to live a Christian life like she wanted."

"That's ugly," Cora whispered.

"Yes, it is," Nessa said, "but it's past time for us to air out what we've got to say like adults. Why did your mother have those kinds of days?"

Nessa removed the biscuits from the oven and broke several eggs into a bowl, then whipped them up and put them in a skillet to scramble.

"That's all I'm saying about that." Isaac folded his arms over his chest and snapped his mouth shut.

"That's your choice, but it sounds to me like you and Uncle Matthew both need some counseling. For now, though, April and I are going to have breakfast. We've got quilting to do this morning while it's cool, and then we've all got other jobs to do around here. So we've got maybe half an hour to visit."

She and April both piled bacon and eggs onto their plates, added a couple of biscuits, and carried the plates to the table. "I'm not leaving until the end of summer, if at all. You need to understand that, Daddy. Your intervention failed. I haven't made up my mind about my teaching job for absolute positive yet. That said, now y'all talk while we eat," she said as she sat down.

"Your mother and I have prayed about this, and we feel that's a bad decision. This place has done nothing but make you rebellious, and God does not like that in a person," Isaac said.

"I've prayed about it, and God told me that it's the best decision I could ever make—that somehow I will find myself here." Nessa stared her father right in the eye and did not blink.

"Me too." April nodded. "Don't know if Flynn has, but I do know he's battling demons of his own. We're all here for a while, so suck it up, Uncle Isaac, and let us do what we have to do."

"That's disrespectful," Isaac said through clenched teeth. "You were always a rebellious girl, and being an adult hasn't done anything but make it worse."

"You always made me feel like I was something you stepped in out in the yard," April said. "Aunt Cora was sweet to me, but answer me this question since you think I'm disrespectful: Why did you treat me like that?"

"Because I never liked your mother. Mama was worse after she was born, and no matter how hard I prayed for my mother, she didn't get any better. Then you came along, and things went from bad to worse," Isaac said.

"Now that's disrespectful—taking your anger with your mother out on April?" Nessa said.

"Enough!" Isaac banged his fist on the table, and coffee sloshed out everywhere.

Cora hopped up, grabbed a paper towel, and wiped up the mess. "Sorry about that," she apologized.

"You shouldn't have to say you're sorry for the truth," Isaac said. "We'll be going now. I'm disappointed in both of you."

"Not Flynn?" Nessa asked.

"I never did have hope for him, and very little for April, but I did for you. Come on, Cora. Let's get on back to Paris to the church conference." Isaac stood up so fast that he knocked over his chair.

Cora picked it up and pushed it back under the table, then bent down and hugged Nessa. "He means well."

"Maybe so, but my mind is made up," Nessa said.

Isaac stormed out of the house with Cora right behind him.

"What do we do now?" April asked.

"We have breakfast and then go see about Flynn," Nessa answered.

"For the first time in my life, I was glad that my mother wasn't around to be a part of that fiasco," April said, and then she bit off the end of a piece of bacon.

"And you thought you were the unlucky one," Nessa said.

❖ ❖ ❖

Flynn had sat up, but his eyes were glued to the waterfall when Nessa sat down on one side of him and April on the other. The charcoal-colored clouds moved off to the east as if they knew he didn't need any more darkness around him that morning. He wanted his father to come back to the waterfall and answer a dozen questions, like, What had made him and Isaac take two completely separate paths?

"We brought you a couple of biscuits stuffed with bacon and eggs," Nessa said.

"And hot coffee." April held up Nanny Lucy's old silver thermos. "How did things go with you and Uncle Matthew?"

Flynn sat up and took the offered paper plate from Nessa. "He says I can't change. That I'll always be like him where women are concerned. It's been years since I've been around him and Uncle Isaac at the same time. I knew they didn't get along, but that was like . . ."—he paused— "pure black hatred filling the house."

"The difference between you both is that *you* want to change, and he doesn't." Nessa drew her knees up to her chin and looped her arms around them. "My dad blames Uncle Matthew for all the bad moods that Nanny Lucy must've had most of her life. Your dad must blame mine for being Nanny Lucy's favorite because he was so religious. What a mess."

"I can't even imagine how life was for my mother," April said. "That was one helluva morning. I'm glad those uncles don't live close enough to drop in very often."

"Talk about baggage," Flynn said.

"Compared to them, we've got very little," Nessa said.

"Way I figure it is that we have to come back to the root of our problems, and that's the only way to get rid of them," April whispered. "Your fathers don't want to get rid of theirs, so they're letting them fester and ruin any hope of a relationship between them."

"Amen to that." Flynn bit into the first biscuit and remembered his mother making him biscuits just like these to bring along on their trip to Blossom. Tears welled up in his eyes, but he was a grown man, and according to his father, men did not cry.

"To hell with it." He let the tears loose and didn't even flinch when they dripped from his jaw onto his shirt, leaving wet spots.

He held his free hand to his cheek, remembering the first time he'd busted a knuckle in the oil field, when he had shed tears. His father had rocked his jaw when he slapped him with an open palm and said, "Men don't bawl like babies, and women hate weakness."

April laid a hand on his shoulder. "Are you all right? Talk to us."

"No, I'm not," Flynn answered. "Mama made this same kind of biscuits for me on the last morning that we came to Blossom. She hugged me and said she'd see me in two weeks. The next time I saw her, she was in her casket, and Nanny Lucy turned me over to my dad. Nothing was ever the same in my life again."

"That's a tough memory," Nessa volunteered.

"It may sound horrible"—April picked up a rock and skipped it over the surface of the creek water—"but I'm glad that if I had to lose my mama, that I was too young to remember it. Nanny Lucy used to say that hard work would help me get through anything. Let's go do our quilting, and then, if it doesn't rain, I'll help you paint the house today."

"I have to go get the paint first," Flynn said, "but I'll take all the help I can get."

"Count me in, too," Nessa said.

"Thanks"—Flynn wiped his wet cheeks on his shirtsleeve—"for coming out here to see about me."

"Hey, we're family. We might all three be screwed up, but we're still family, and we're going to work through all this rotten baggage together," Nessa told him.

April nudged his shoulder from the other side. "Remember that part of the Miranda Lambert song about the house that built her? It says that she thought that maybe she could find herself."

Flynn and Nessa both nodded.

"That's our story," April said. "Now we've just got to figure out a way to get away from the past and look at the future. It won't be easy, but like Nessa said, we're family."

"Thank goodness for that." Flynn finally grinned. "If we weren't, there's no way I'd put up with you two."

"If we weren't, we would have sent you off with your new step-mom," Nessa teased.

"And we're not ever going to act like Uncle Matthew and Uncle Isaac," April said. "Give me your promise right now."

"You got it," Flynn said.

"I promise," Nessa agreed.

"Good. Y'all are my rock and anchor. Let's keep it that way. And speaking of stepmoms," she said, changing the subject, "the black widow looked like she could have you for breakfast when you came wandering into the kitchen this morning."

Flynn shook his head slowly. "I've sworn off women, especially ones that would be attracted to my dad. Either they're crazy when they meet him or they will be by the time he's done with them."

"Don't know which is worse, your dad or mine," Nessa said.

"It would be a toss-up." Flynn finished off his breakfast and poured a mug of coffee from the thermos. "Thanks again for this and for the support."

Chapter Eight

April woke with a start, sweat pouring off her body. She threw off the covers and immediately shivered when the cold air from the window air-conditioning unit cooled the sweat on her body. Lightning flashed through the window. For a split second she could see everything in the living room; then suddenly it was absolutely dark again.

"One, two, three." She covered her ears and counted like she had when she was a child. When she got to ten, thunder rolled off in the distance. That meant the storm was ten miles away and could possibly make a turn and not even come near Blossom.

Wake up, April! her grandmother's voice screamed inside her head. *We've got to go to the cellar. God is punishing me for my sins.*

April tried to shake the *storm voice*, as she had called it when she was a child, from her head. She never knew why God was punishing her grandmother, or how she could have possibly sinned when she was in church every time the doors opened, but in the recurring nightmares, Nanny Lucy kept repeating the same thing over and over.

"You were so religious that there's no way you sinned," April whispered just as another flash lit up the room. In that instant she didn't know if she was really awake or if she was still dreaming, because she could swear that Nanny Lucy was sitting in her rocking chair at the end of the sofa.

"One, two, three." She counted again and could tell that the thunder was getting closer.

"Screw this," she said as she pushed back the sheet and got out of the sofa bed. She tiptoed across the room and discovered that no one was sitting in the old rocking chair and what she had seen was a quilt that had been haphazardly thrown over the back. She grabbed it, wrapped it around her body like an oversize shawl, and then went into the garage. She pulled back an old rug, raised the trapdoor into the cellar, and went down the steps.

The old familiar smell of mustiness met her when she reached the bottom. She groped around in the dark for the string that would turn on the light. In the process, the wooden thread spool attached to the bottom of the string slapped her right between the eyes. She felt her way over to the cot in the corner, sat down, and waited for her eyes to adjust to the dark.

The rain sounded like golf balls hitting the metal roof. When a tiny flash of light came through the window in the garage and down into the open cellar door, thunder followed behind it immediately. The storm must be moving fast to have gone from ten miles out there to right on top of them in only a few minutes.

She stood up and waited for the next bolt of lightning to tell her where that abominable spool was and finally located it. She gave it a tug, and a low-watt bulb lit up the cellar enough so that she could see the oil lamp over in the corner. Nanny Lucy's rule was that they were only to use the electricity to find what they needed; then they had to turn it off.

April lit the lamp's wick and adjusted it to the right level. Nanny Lucy fussed if there was black soot on the chimney when it was time to leave the cellar. She crossed the narrow room to where the shelves were built in to hold jars and jars of canned fruits, jams, and vegetables. These days they were sparse, which meant that Nanny Lucy hadn't done much preserving in her final years, but there were still more than a dozen jars of peaches crammed up in one corner. And back behind them, lying on its side, was an almost full bottle of Jack Daniel's bourbon.

"I'm surprised you didn't find this, Nanny Lucy," April whispered as she opened the bottle and took the first long drink. "I left it here years ago, but the storm stirred up too many memories tonight. You telling me that you had sinned reminded me of my own sin in hiding it on your property. I'm not an alcoholic, but tonight I need a drink, or two or three. I can't imagine you ever sinning." She sat down on the end of the cot and threw the quilt off her shoulders. "I actually thought that you had angel wings under those cardigan sweaters you always wore. There was no way I could ever measure up to . . ."—she turned the bottle up again and then wiped her mouth with the back of her hand—"someone as perfect as you, so somewhere along the line I stopped trying. I just wanted you to love me, Nanny Lucy, but evidently you thought I was unlovable. How could you put Aunt Gabby on a pedestal and your own daughter in a deep hole?"

The storm raged, both outside and inside April's heart, as she kept taking drinks right out of the bottle. She could visualize her grandmother sitting in the old ladder-back chair at the end of the cot and giving her dirty looks.

"Well, at least I didn't disappoint you." April held the bottle up toward the empty chair. "I'm just as worthless as my mother. There will never be angel wings on my back or a halo above my head."

When the bottle was half-empty, she screwed the cap back on it, set it on the concrete floor, and curled up on the cot in a fetal position. "I think I'm drunk, Nanny Lucy. That's one more thing you can send me to my room for doing. 'Go on in there and be just like your mother.' That's what you used to tell me. I hated that room because I thought it was what made me . . ." She passed out and dreamed of her grandmother slamming the door to her old bedroom.

❖ ❖ ❖

Nessa awoke when the second wave of the storm seemed to take up residence over Blossom, Texas. Something wasn't right. She could feel it down deep in her soul when she sat up in bed and pushed back the covers.

Had she left the windows down a little in her SUV? No, she remembered seeing the clouds coming and going all day as they painted three sides of the house. She'd checked the vehicle twice before she went to bed. She looked at her phone and found that it was three o'clock, and then she fell back onto her pillow.

"Something still isn't right," she whispered as she got up, padded out into the kitchen, and turned on the light above the stove so she wouldn't wake April. She poured herself a glass of milk and took a fistful of peanut butter cookies from the jar in the middle of the table. She sat down with her back to the living room and had eaten the first cookie when Waylon came up the hallway, meowing at the top of his lungs.

"Shhh . . . you're going to wake April," Nessa scolded.

"She might as well get up. We're both awake. Damn cat must be afraid of storms." Flynn yawned and stopped beside the sofa on his way to the kitchen. "Where is April?"

"She's right there." Nessa turned around and pointed, pausing. "No, she's not."

Her blood ran cold in her veins, chilling her to the bone. She remembered that April had been terrified of storms in their youth, but she absolutely hated the cellar. She might have gone to the waterfall, which was a horrible place to be when lightning was flashing every few seconds.

Flynn turned around and looked down the short hallway. "Bathroom door is open, so I don't think she's in there. Did she leave us in the middle of a stormy night?"

Nessa stood up so fast that her chair wobbled before she stretched out her hand to right it. She hurried around the sofa bed and peeked out the window just as another streak of lightning lit up the sky. "Her car is sitting out there, so she must be here somewhere. I hope she didn't go to the waterfall in all this mess."

Waylon became a blur as he ran through the open garage door, still caterwauling loud enough to give the thunder competition.

"I understand why he wants to go out there. That's where his litter pan is." Flynn started that way. "But why would April be in the garage in the middle of the night?"

"Cellar? It's storming, and Nanny Lucy was terrified of storms. Remember how she'd stand out on the porch and tell us if we heard thunder, we were all going to the cellar?" Nessa brushed right past Flynn and pointed at the open cellar door. "You ever been down in that thing?"

"Nope, but I do remember her being afraid of storms," Flynn answered. "Have you ever gone down in the cellar? Is it concrete or just dirt?"

"Nanny Lucy sent me down there for a jar of peaches one time," Nessa answered. "It's dark, damp, and kind of spooky, but it's all concrete, even the floor. There was a whole bunch of granddaddy long-legged spiders there. I hate spiders, but I got the peaches and hurried back up the steps as fast as my legs would go."

"Why would April go down there?" Flynn looked down the wooden steps.

Nessa led the way, and when she reached the bottom, she picked up the whiskey bottle. "I found the reason. I wonder when April hid it. Nanny Lucy thought the devil would come up out of the ground, grab you by the ankles, and pull you straight to hell if you took a single drink of alcohol."

"She told me that very thing when I was a little boy," Flynn said as he started down the stairs. "Scared the bejesus out of me. I went home and cried when Mama poured herself a glass of wine that evening." Flynn seemed to fill the small space when he reached the bottom of the steps and saw April passed out on the floor. "What do you think happened here, Nessa?"

One of Nessa's shoulders rose in half a shrug. "I don't know. Maybe it's the storm. One thing's for sure: if April is ever going to get fixed, we need to help her figure things out. How are we going to get her up to bed?"

"Like this," Flynn said as he scooped April up in his arms like a baby and carried her up the steps.

Nessa followed behind him and closed the cellar door to keep Waylon out. "Put her on the bed in her old bedroom. I'll pull out the trundle and sleep on it. She may need me before morning."

"What she's going to need if she drank that much whiskey is a bucket or a trash can." Flynn carried her across the living room and down the short hallway. He gently laid her on the bed.

"So sorry, Nanny Lucy," April muttered. "How did you sin?"

Nessa lined the small trash can next to the dresser with a plastic bag and set it within arm's reach. If April started gagging, she could at least hold the can with one hand and hold her blonde hair back with the other one.

Flynn dragged the trundle bed out for her. "Call me if you need me. I'm going to leave my door cracked so Waylon can get in if he wants to."

"Thanks," Nessa said. "I wonder what she's talking about. Nanny Lucy was a saint. She never sinned. She had mood swings, but she was too close to God to sin."

"Just the ramblings of a good old-fashioned drunken stupor, I'd guess." Flynn started out of the room. "But, honey, I don't think there's a saint on the face of this earth. We've all sinned."

"And come short of the glory of God," Nessa quoted from scripture. "I wonder how April knew that Nanny Lucy sinned, and what it was."

"She probably said *damn* or *hell*, or maybe took the Lord's name in vain when she stuck herself with a needle." Flynn chuckled. "Sounds like the worst of the storm has passed. See you later."

Nessa stretched out on the bed and laced her hands behind her head. April muttered in her sleep, but the only two words Nessa could make out were *mother* and *sin*. How could the grandmother that Nessa had thought hung the moon make such a horrible mess of raising her own three kids and then her granddaughter?

The next morning, warm sunshine flowed through the window, the heat warming Nessa's face and bringing her semi-awake, but what made her sit up was April moaning in her sleep. Nessa grabbed the trash can and held it up to the side of the bed.

April's eyes popped wide open, and she shivered from her head all the way to her bare toes. "What am I doing in here? I told you I hate this room." She grabbed her head and closed her eyes. "Dear God, my head is pounding."

"I think maybe it should be 'dear Jack Daniel's,' not 'God.'" Nessa set the can back down. "Two questions. How long had that bottle been hidden down there, and what did you mean about Nanny Lucy sinning?"

"I can't remember anything." April put her pillow over her head. "Go away and let me die in peace."

"There's not an ounce of peace in your heart, so you might as well wake up and get past the hangover." Nessa set about making up the trundle and pushing it back under the daybed.

Flynn threw open the door and brought in a banana. "One banana coming right up." He sat down on the edge of the bed and took the pillow away from April's head. "Sit up slowly and eat this. After that, you'll go take a shower, and then come to the kitchen for a piece of bacon and a poached egg on toast. Then you can have a cup of coffee and two aspirin."

"I'll need that trash can if I eat a banana." April turned over and faced the wall.

"You might if you *don't* eat it." Flynn took her by the arm and gently pulled her up to a sitting position. "When I was fifteen, I had to figure out a cure for hangovers for my dad and his women. Dad is a happy drunk and the life of the party when he's drinking, but he's downright mean and hateful when he has a hangover. It didn't take me long to figure out how to bypass the temper and oftentimes the abuse. So eat your banana, go take a shower, and I promise by the time you get finished with the coffee, you'll be feeling a lot better." He peeled the banana and handed it to her.

She took the first bite. "I was dreaming, and then Nanny Lucy was still in my head when I woke up. She said that she was being punished for sinning.

"I remembered coming here several years ago, and I knew better than to even try to hide my bottle of whiskey in my suitcase, so I made an excuse and went to the cellar when I needed some liquid strength to get through the visit. Since it was open, I couldn't travel with it in my car, so I hid it." She took several more bites. "It had been down there for years. I'm surprised she hadn't found it and poured it all out on the ground."

"What do you think she was talking about when she said she was sinning?" Nessa asked.

"I don't have any idea." April finished the last bit of the banana.

"It was just a crazy dream brought on by the storm," Flynn said. "Now, off to the shower while Nessa and I make breakfast. We've got a quilt to work on, and you sure can't do it with a hangover."

"I'm not an alcoholic," April said as she got to her feet. "I could have been. I like the taste, but I don't like the aftereffects, so after I had a few mothers of all hangovers, I seldom ever drank anymore. I just want y'all to know that."

"Why does it matter what we think?" Nessa asked.

"We're living in this house together, all of us searching for something that's missing in our lives. We should be honest with each other." April shuffled out into the hallway, a hand to her forehead and groaning the whole way. "I still hate this room, even more than I hate that cellar. If I ever pull a stunt like that again, just leave me down there until I sober up."

"Why?" Nessa asked.

"I was born while a storm was raging, and they couldn't get my mother to the hospital. Nanny Lucy delivered me right here in this room, and she said that she knew that night I'd be just like my mother. She tried to beat it out of me, shame it out of me, and even guilt it out of me, but none of that worked," April answered. "She scared me half to death when she said that my mother's spirit was still lingering in this room and that she would never rest in peace because she hadn't been a good girl."

The tone of her voice sent chills down Nessa's spine that had nothing to do with the cold air blowing from the air conditioner in the window. "I thought you were born in the hospital over in Paris. Isn't that where your mother died?"

"When the storm passed, Nanny Lucy took my mother and me to the hospital. Mama had got an infection and died four days later. I wonder if that's what she meant when she said she had sinned. Did she feel guilty because she hadn't battled the storm to get my mother the proper care? Maybe the storm wasn't that bad, but she thought if Mama had me at home, I would die." April frowned.

"That's horrible. Do you really think she had that in mind?" Flynn asked.

"We'll never know, but I've always wondered," April answered.

"I'm so, so sorry," Nessa said. "I wish we'd gotten together before she died—while she could tell us how she felt about things, like what April said and us coming every summer."

"We'll never know for sure about all that, but we will know what's in that hope chest," April said. "We'll finish the quilt and open the hope chest. Who knows, maybe she left us a note explaining everything."

"We wouldn't be that lucky." Nessa started toward the kitchen.

"She probably took whatever had upset her to the grave with her," Flynn added.

"You're both probably right." April went into the bathroom and closed the door.

"Ready to go make bacon and eggs?" Flynn asked Nessa.

"Where were you with this magic cure when I had my first hangover?" Nessa asked.

"What did Uncle Isaac do when he found out his angel had been out drinking?" Flynn chuckled.

"By then I wasn't his angel anymore, and I let him think I had the flu," Nessa replied. "If he'd found out otherwise, I wouldn't be standing here today. I'd either be six feet under or in a convent."

"Uncle Isaac isn't Catholic," Flynn reminded her when they had reached the kitchen and he had gotten out a cast-iron skillet.

"Wouldn't have mattered," Nessa said. "He would have put me in one anyway."

Chapter Nine

*I*t wasn't that Jackson hated Sundays. It was more like they bored him. He wasn't a churchgoing guy, never had been. He'd usually stayed home even on the occasional times when Uncle D. J. felt the need to go to Sunday services. His uncle had always said that if the almighty God rested one day a week, then humankind should do so, also, whether he went to a church-house building or not. So any kind of work in the shop was taboo on Sundays.

After putting in sixteen- and eighteen-hour days as a lawyer, Jackson had decided that Uncle D. J. was right in his thinking and had always put aside his work and rested on Sundays. That week he had his usual breakfast of a bagel with cream cheese and strawberry jam smeared on top and two cups of coffee, and he was headed outside when he noticed the hope chest sitting against the wall in the living room.

The key had been taped to the back and wasn't visible, and there was no way he would betray Miz Lucy's trust and open the old thing. But he couldn't help wondering about what could be inside. Those three grandchildren of hers seemed like decent sorts, so why hadn't she just given them their inheritance—whether it was just a bunch of keepsakes or a bundle of cash—instead of making them quilt?

"She was a haunted soul," Jackson said out loud as he carried his phone out to the porch and sat down in Uncle D. J.'s old wooden rocker with the wide arms. *I could feel a kinship with her. I don't know what she had faced in the past, but I felt like I didn't belong anywhere until I came here. I'd only gone into the law business to please my brother and sister and my folks. I wish I had told Miz Lucy how much our visits had meant to me before she passed.*

He was about to bring up the contact list on his phone and give his folks a call, like he always did early on Sunday morning, when the phone rang. He smiled when he saw his mother's name pop up on the screen. "Good morning," he answered cheerfully. "How are things in Bay City?"

"Great!" his mother said. "You are on speaker. Your dad is right here beside me. We're ready for church, but it's a little early to go that way. How are things in Blossom?"

"You ready to come back to work yet?" James's deep southern voice asked.

"I work every day, Dad." Jackson smiled.

"You know what I mean. You were a crackerjack lawyer."

"And now I'm a crackerjack hope chest and furniture builder. I don't have an ulcer, and I don't have to take depression pills." Jackson bit back a sigh.

"You never did have those things wrong with you." His father's tone was curt.

"No, but I was well on the way to having both." Jackson had had this same conversation too many times to remember. "I've got neighbors now. Miz Lucy's grandkids have moved into her house. Two women and a guy. It's kind of nice knowing someone about my age is over there."

"I guess it would be," his mother, Linda, said. "You haven't been around anyone but old people in five years. When are you coming home for a visit?"

"Maybe Christmas." Jackson said the same thing he always did. That was when he would go back to South Texas, even though just a few days away from Blossom felt like years. Until then he was busy with his business. "But my door is open anytime y'all want to get away for a weekend and come to Blossom."

"We just might do that," Linda said.

Jackson wasn't about to hold his breath. His face wouldn't look good in that shade of blue. He smiled at the old adage he'd heard both Uncle D. J. and Miz Lucy say many times when they knew some event wouldn't happen or someone wouldn't come through with a promise.

"Let me know a day ahead of time, and I'll thaw some T-bones and grill them for you," he said.

"Will do," James answered, "and you know you've got a place in the firm anytime you get tired of messing around in that little Podunk town. Right now, it's time for your mother and me to go to church."

"Y'all have a good day," Jackson said.

"You too." This from his mother.

"And that ends the Sunday phone call," he said as he shoved the phone back into his shirt pocket.

Tex came around the side of the house and plopped down beside him. Tongue hanging out and panting, the dog laid his head on Jackson's knee.

"Been out for an early-morning run?" Jackson heaved a sigh of relief that the weekly phone call was over. "Your feet are wet. I bet you made a side trip by the creek, didn't you? We belong right here in our little part of Blossom, Texas, don't we?" He rubbed the dog's ears. "Maybe if my brother and sister hadn't been teenagers when I was born, things would be different, or if I hadn't overheard my folks talking about me being an 'oops baby' to their friends, I would have felt like I belonged in their world. But that's all water under the bridge. I tried to make them happy, but I was miserable."

The dog jumped up, almost in a hunting-dog point at the side of the house. The hair on his back stood straight up, and he growled deep down in his throat.

"What is it, old boy?" Jackson asked.

❖ ❖ ❖

Nessa peeked around the corner of the house. "Does he bite?"

"No, he's all bluff," Jackson answered. "Come on around and meet him. Once he gets to know you, and that takes about two minutes, you'll have a friend forever. I might warn you, though, he doesn't like Waylon, so if he comes visiting over at your place, don't let him in the house. I tried that when I first brought the cat over here, and it did not end well. When the fur stopped flying, Tex had a scratched nose, and Waylon had a bloody ear."

Jackson laid a hand on the dog's neck. "Tex, this is Nessa. She's kin to Miz Lucy. Remember her? She saved soup bones for you. Nessa might do the same if you're nice to her."

Tex began to wag his tail and slowly made his way off the porch. He raised a paw when Nessa was a foot away. She stooped slightly and shook with him. "Pleased to meet you, Tex. And yes, I will save you a bone the next time I make a ham."

Nessa could have sworn that the big yellow dog actually smiled at her.

"Want a cup of coffee?" Jackson asked. "I made a whole pot."

"I'd love one." Nessa nodded. "When I was a little girl, it seemed like a lot farther between our house and this one, but in those days, I didn't notice how rough the roads were to either of our places."

Jackson stood up and motioned toward the swing on the other end of the porch. "County don't pay a lot of attention to roads that only go back to two houses, but every now and then they bring out a load of gravel and smooth it out a little. Come on up and have a seat. I'll bring out the coffee. Unless you want to come inside?"

"This is fine." Nessa crossed the porch and sat down on the end of the swing. "It's going to get hot this afternoon, so we might as well enjoy the cool morning while we can."

"My thinking exactly." Jackson whistled as he went inside.

In a couple of minutes, he poked his head out the door. "Sugar or cream or both?"

"Just black," she answered.

Another minute passed, and he pushed through the old wooden screen door and carried two big mugs of coffee outside. He handed one off to her and then sat down on the other end of the swing.

"Thank you. So you've been living here five years? Ever wish you were back in the city?" Nessa asked.

"Not one time," Jackson answered. "The peace and quiet out here kind of grows on you. After you've been here a few weeks, go on back to the city for a visit and see how discontented you'll be."

"I don't have to do that," Nessa said. "When I was a kid, I came here every summer for a couple of weeks and usually cried myself to sleep every night for weeks when I went back to the Texas Panhandle."

"Miz Lucy said you're a teacher," Jackson said. "Are you planning to look for a job around here?"

"Maybe, but what I'd like to do is make quilts and pick up Nanny Lucy's business where she left it off," Nessa said.

"She made a great living that way. We used to go to craft shows together, and we always had a really good time. She would sell whatever she had made up, and she always took along boxes of patterns and quilt pieces already cut out so folks could make their own," Jackson said.

"When are the fairs?" Nessa asked. "I'm totally new to this thing, but I love to quilt. There's something both soothing and satisfying about the job."

"Starting in September, there will be several each weekend. Miz Lucy, Uncle D. J., and I went to the ones closest to home, for the most part, but we always had good sales at one down near Waxahachie, so we tended to go there, even though it meant staying in a hotel overnight," he said. "Get a couple of quilts made up and some boxes ready, and you can go with me. I'll show you the ropes."

"You'd do that for me?" Nessa was amazed.

"Sure, we're neighbors." Jackson's smile lit up the whole porch. "Besides, I've never been to a fair by myself, and I'd appreciate the company. I've got an enclosed trailer that we use to transport our wares."

"How many quilts should I have ready to go by the first fair?" Nessa was already doing the math in her head. She had three weeks left in June and the whole months of July and August to work. If she used the time to make a simple pattern and had a few of the more complicated quilts cut out and ready to sell as do-it-yourself projects, she might have a few things to show. She and her mother had made quilted throws for shut-ins and for the members of her dad's congregation who had moved to nursing homes, and she'd always loved the work.

"That's up to you," Jackson said. "Miz Lucy seldom brought anything home from a fair. She sold her quilts for anywhere from six hundred to two thousand, depending on how much detail was in them, and the kits started at two hundred."

If she sold just two quilts a week and the kits, Nessa thought, she'd be making far more than she ever had teaching.

"Kind of makes you wonder why you didn't start quilting when you were younger, doesn't it?" Jackson asked, but went on before she could answer. "My dad and mom are both lawyers. My older brother and his wife are both lawyers in the Devereaux firm, and my older sister is a lawyer. Her husband is a surgeon. I make almost as much as they do with my woodworking projects. I sure wish I'd come to Blossom right out of high school and gone to work with Uncle D. J."

"What did they think when you decided to build furniture?" Nessa asked as she sipped her coffee. She could already hear her father preaching at her, and without closing her eyes, she could see the aggravated expression on her mother's face.

"Being a lawyer was what was expected of me, so that's what I did. Dad says I was good at my job, but I wasn't happy," Jackson said. "So I took a two-week vacation and came to Blossom to think. They were fine with that since all my cases were settled and I had the time to take.

But they weren't happy when I told them I was staying here and not coming back."

"I don't imagine my folks are going to be happy if I tell them I'm resigning my teaching job, either." Nessa's voice sounded tense to her own ears.

"It's been five years. I talk to them on Sunday mornings, and they're still trying to convince me that I need to come back to the firm." He chuckled. "Don't expect your folks to support you in what they'll think is a crazy decision. Your father is the preacher, right?"

"Yes." Nessa nodded. "The apple of Nanny Lucy's eye. He's the only one that grew up to be what she wanted. We were all surprised when she didn't leave her place to him."

"From what little she said about her family, I think she was disappointed in all of her kids in some part," Jackson said. "She didn't go into detail, but she did say that she regretted the way she'd raised all of them."

"It's strange how I thought I knew her so well, and I didn't really know her at all," Nessa said.

"Does anyone ever really know another human being? I thought I knew Uncle D. J., but I find out new things about him every day—even since he passed away. Little things, like once I found an old newspaper tucked away in the patterns that had an article in it about him making a hope chest for the daughter of the Texas governor." Jackson finished off his coffee. "Want a refill?"

"No, I should be getting on back to the house, but thanks for the coffee and the visit. Want to join us for Sunday dinner about noon today?" she asked. "I've got a big pot roast in the oven." And then she wondered if maybe she should have asked April and Flynn about inviting someone to dinner.

Why would I think that? It's my home as much as theirs, she scolded herself.

"I'd love to. I'll bring dessert," he said. "Did you say noon?"

"That's the plan, but I've already got an apple pie ready to go in the oven, so just bring a healthy appetite." She handed him her empty coffee cup and stood up. "See you then."

"I'll be there, and thanks," he said.

She could feel his eyes watching her as she rounded the end of the porch. April would tease her terribly if she knew that Nessa threw an extra swing into her walk.

Chapter Ten

*J*ackson had been to lots of Sunday dinners at Miz Lucy's place, both when his uncle D. J. was still alive and even after he had passed on. That first Sunday he'd gone over there after Uncle D. J. died was tough. He and Miz Lucy had played checkers rather than dominoes that afternoon, because they couldn't bear the memories of D. J.'s love of the game.

"Never been in that house when four people were gathered around the table," he told Tex as the two of them started down the path. The clouds from the past couple of days had moved on, and there was nothing but clear blue sky above him. A slight breeze ruffled the leaves in the gnarly oak trees on either side of the well-rutted pathway. Over to his left, he could hear the waterfall bubbling over the rocks. All in all, a beautiful day with, most likely, a good Sunday dinner waiting, so why did he feel so antsy about going?

They turned off the trail into the backyard, and Tex ran on ahead. When Jackson got closer, he could see the dog on the front porch with April, his head in her lap. "Traitor," he mumbled. "You were supposed to stay with me."

"Hello!" April waved with her free hand. "Is this your dog? If not, I'm going to adopt him."

Jackson stopped at the bottom of the stairs. "I reckon I'll claim the mutt. I inherited him when Uncle D. J. passed away. He usually doesn't take to people so quickly."

"I like animals," April said. "D. J. must have gotten him after I left Blossom. I don't remember him having pets."

"Tex is eight years old." Jackson smiled. "He's been around since I got here."

"I've been gone more than ten years, so that explains it. He's beautiful." She stroked the dog's blond fur. "He's part Lab. What's the rest?"

"Great Pyrenees," Jackson answered. "Makes for a good watchdog, but the mix also makes for a big old teddy bear. The only time he gives me much trouble is when I take him to the vet. He whines the whole way and looks up at me so pitiful that I hate to make him go in for his shots."

"My dream job would be to work for a vet," April said. "I loved working in greenhouses, but to be around animals all day would be even better. We had Waylon back when I was growing up, but Nanny Lucy wouldn't let me have any other pets. Waylon was here to catch mice, not to be a pet. Dinner should be about ready, so come on in the house." She bent forward and whispered to Tex, "I'll bring out scraps for you if you'll hang around on the porch."

"You've made a friend for life," Jackson chuckled, and he followed April into the house. His stomach growled when the aroma of fresh-baked bread and cinnamon rushed out to meet him. "Something sure smells good in here."

"Come on in," Nessa called out from the kitchen. "I'm putting it on the table right now."

"Anything I can do to help, and is it all right if I wash my hands in the kitchen sink?" Jackson asked.

"We've got it covered." Flynn carried a basket of hot rolls to the table.

"And yes, feel free to wash up at the sink," April said. "I'll get the dog smell off my hands in the bathroom."

Jackson had washed his hands in the kitchen sink dozens of times over the past years, but today he seemed to be clumsy, bumping into Nessa three times. Once when she passed by him on the way to the table with a bowl of corn in her hands, again when he reached for a towel, and then again when she took a platter of meat, potatoes, and carrots across the tiny galley kitchen to the dining area.

Jackson had had a few dates since he'd moved to Blossom, but nothing had caused the sparks and electricity to fly like they did when he brushed against Nessa O'Riley.

That's downright crazy, he thought. *She's not my type.*

And that is? Miz Lucy asked.

Tall, blonde, and brown eyed. He crossed the room and took a seat at the table. Nessa pulled out a chair on one side and sat down. When her knee touched his under the table, he got another jolt. He could not get involved with Nessa. She was his neighbor, and quite possibly in the next few weeks would be his cohort at craft fairs. If he started something with her and it went south, things would be terribly awkward.

"It's your turn, April," Flynn said as he bowed his head.

April's chin dropped to her chest and she closed her eyes. "Dear God, thank you for this food. Amen."

"That was short and sweet," Flynn said.

"It covered what I wanted to thank God for, and we still say grace in this house because Nanny Lucy would throw a hissy fit if we didn't. I just don't see any need to thank God for everything from dirt to the bull that gave his life for us to eat today." April slid the meat platter close to her plate and took a generous helping. "Nanny Lucy thinks we should thank God for it, and I'll do it, even though it seems kind of crazy to me since Nessa bought and prepared the food. I'll help with cleanup, but nobody ever thinks to thank God for the dish soap or the hands that wash the dishes. They only thank Him for the food and the good things that happen to them."

"You've got a pretty good point there," Jackson said. "I don't think I've ever thanked God for Tex, and he's been a loving, faithful companion that's kept me sane the past couple of years. There's been weeks when he was the only living thing around this place."

"We had at least a five-minute prayer before every meal, including all of us reciting the Lord's Prayer at the end of Daddy's grace," Nessa said. "I appreciate a short-and-to-the-point prayer." She put roast, potatoes, and extra carrots on her plate, then passed the platter on over to Jackson. Their hands touched in the process, and there was that surge of heat again.

"Thank you." His voice sounded slightly hoarse in his own ears. "This all smells delicious."

❖   ❖   ❖

"Nanny Lucy could make biscuits that melted in your mouth, but she never did master yeast rolls." Nessa wondered how words went from her brain to her mouth with all the chemistry between her and Jackson dancing around the room. She hoped that April and Flynn were so focused on dinner that they couldn't see it, or they would tease her later.

Jackson was going to be kind of like a partner in her craft business, and she could not mess that up. She would not fantasize about seeing him without that shirt on at the falls. She couldn't start something up with him. That was as far as she got with her vows, because she did visualize him without a shirt on—his broad chest muscles under her hands, the soft black hair that had to be on his chest tickling her fingertips.

"Nessa!" April's tone brought her back to the present.

"What?" She came near to jumping out of her skin. The adrenaline from the shock of April's voice sent her heart to pumping double time.

"You were staring off into space like you were high," April said. "Flynn asked you to pass the butter."

"I'm not high." Nessa's face suddenly felt hot. "I was trying to remember exactly what time the apple pie comes out of the oven." Yes, it was a lie, but she *had* forgotten to set the timer.

"In ten minutes," Flynn replied. "Apple pie is one of my favorites, so I won't let you burn it."

"Thanks." Nessa sent the butter dish around the table to Flynn. "So, Jackson, what have you been working on this week?"

"Three more hope chests," he answered between bites. "I could use some part-time help, but . . ." He shrugged and went back to eating.

"What's the problem?" Nessa asked.

"I bet getting people to come out here to the sticks for just part-time work would be tough, right?" Flynn asked.

"Yep." Jackson nodded.

"I'll take the job," Flynn said. "I don't know a lot about building anything, but I can fetch, and I can learn. I've been wondering what I'm going to do now that the house is painted and rewired. I can be over there right after dinner tomorrow and work until five or six, whatever time you quit."

"Are you serious?" Jackson asked.

Nessa crossed her fingers under the table. That would get Flynn out of the house half the day. It didn't take a psychoanalyst to see that he was going to get bored if he didn't have something to do. And if he was bored, he might slip back into his old ways. She remembered that he'd always been a little hyper, even as a kid. While she was content to read a book or sit and watch Nanny Lucy cut out fabric for quilts, he was always running here, there, and yonder. She'd never given a thought to the fact that he had to live in a walk-up apartment when he went home, or that he spent a lot of days alone while his mother worked. Then when his mama died, he had to live with his father, and that couldn't have been pleasant. No wonder he'd felt free as a bird let loose from a cage when he came to Blossom.

"I'm very serious," Flynn answered. "I'll work the first week for free. If we get along and you think I'm learning the job, then you can start paying me the second week. That sound fair?"

"More than fair," Jackson answered. "You sure you want to start tomorrow afternoon?"

"Sounds good to me." Flynn nodded.

"That's not fair," April said. "I'm the one who needs a job, and I bet I could learn just as fast as Flynn can."

Nessa slathered a hot roll with butter and wished that she could throw in her name for the job. But that would never work. She got hot flashes just sitting close to the guy. Working right beside him in a small workshop was out of the question.

"You said you like animals, right?" Jackson smiled across the table.

"Love them. Animals and flowers never break your heart," April said.

"Our vet is an older lady, and she also has an animal shelter right beside her small-animal clinic. When I was in there last week, she mentioned that she'd like to hire part-time help. It's getting harder and harder to get enough volunteer help for the shelter, and she can't keep up with the small-animal practice and run the shelter, too," Jackson said. "She said what she needs is someone who's willing to go back and forth from clinic to shelter as she needs them. I can call her in the morning and put in a word for you if you really need to work, but again, this is only part-time."

"I only have time for part-time since we have to finish the quilt." April's tone was full of excitement.

"I'll give Maudie a call first thing in the morning," Jackson said. "The animal clinic is right off the highway on the east side of Paris."

April groaned.

"I told you that you can use my car, or I don't see any reason why you couldn't drive Nanny Lucy's car. Like the house, it belongs to all of us," Nessa reminded her, hoping that she would get the job. That would leave her with a quiet house in the afternoons to work on her quilt tops. Nanny Lucy said it was all right to make the tops on the sewing machine, but she wouldn't have one of those big quilting machines in her shed. Oh, no! In her opinion, a *real quilt* had to be hand-stitched.

"Are you sure?" April asked.

"If she isn't, I am," Flynn said. "I can walk over to Jackson's place. I won't need the truck during the afternoons."

"Thank you, Flynn, for the offer, but I can drive Nanny Lucy's car. I had forgotten all about it. I sure hope she hasn't filled the spot," April said. "And I can't believe that even the possibility of something like this just fell into my lap. Thank you, Jackson."

He shrugged. "No problem. Maudie can use the help, and so can I."

Nessa had no reason to be jealous about a woman she'd never met and a neighbor she'd only been around a handful of times, but she was.

"What's her last name?" Nessa asked.

"West," Jackson answered, "but everyone just calls her Maudie or Doc."

"I don't remember Nanny Lucy ever mentioning her," April said.

"She moved here from out in West Texas when she retired about ten years ago. Her sister and mother were living in Paris back then, and when they passed, she got bored and opened up a small-animal clinic, but the place was previously set up for horses and cows as well, so she turned that part into a shelter," Jackson explained. "She said that people kept dropping strays at her door, and she had to do something with them. When I took Tex and Waylon in for their shots, there were balloons and flowers in her office. She had turned eighty that day. I don't know how she's doing everything with only volunteer help from Stella and Vivien one day a week."

"That's amazing," Flynn said.

"Yep," Jackson answered. "As active as she is, she'll probably live to be a hundred."

Nessa felt a little guilty about being jealous, and mildly embarrassed about the relief that had washed over her when she found out that Maudie was eighty. "I want to grow up and be like her and Nanny Lucy. I want to work right up until I drop dead."

April shivered. "Don't talk like that."

"It's the truth, and it's also time to take the pie out of the oven." Nessa pushed back her chair, got a couple of hot pads from the cabinet drawer, and carefully removed the pie.

"That smells so good." Jackson smiled at her.

"We'll have it warm with your choice of cheese melted on top or a scoop of ice cream." Nessa's heart threw in an extra beat, and her skin got all warm.

It's just a smile, she scolded herself, *and you are not in high school, so act your age.*

Chapter Eleven

April drove five miles under the speed limit and was still ten minutes early to her interview that morning at the Honey Hill Vet Clinic. When she had parked in front of the low redbrick building, her sweaty palms clamped the steering wheel of Nanny Lucy's little compact car in a death grip. Even after it had been sitting out beside the house with a cover over it for six months, the smell of roses lingered in the vehicle. She could almost visualize Nanny Lucy sitting beside her with a disapproving look on her face.

You're all excited about a job taking care of dogs and cats? Flynn has worked his way up to an office in some fancy oil business. Nessa is a schoolteacher. Her grandmother's voice rang loud and clear.

"You told me that if I like a job and do it well, then I'm a success," April muttered. "You liked quilting and cutting out pieces, and you were very successful."

I didn't have the chance to make something better of myself like you did, the voice in her head argued.

April shook it off, and with a racing heart, she turned off the engine and slowly opened the car door. She didn't just want this job. She needed it. Sure, she still had money left from what the lawyer had given her, but it wouldn't last forever.

She put her boots on the ground, and doubts flooded over her.

Should I have dressed up more? she worried as she smoothed the front of her shirt and sent up a silent prayer. She wouldn't vow to be in church every time the doors opened like Nanny Lucy had done during the tornado, but she did tell God that she would be forever grateful if He could help her turn her life around.

She crossed the parking lot and reached for the doorknob, but before she could touch it, the door swung open and a short gray-haired lady motioned her inside. "You must be April. I'm Maude West, but my friends and neighbors all call me Maudie." She stuck out her hand.

For a woman who just came up to April's shoulder, she had a firm handshake. Her bright smile reached her crystal-clear blue eyes.

"I'm pleased to meet you. I didn't bring a résumé. Jackson didn't think I would need one. I've worked at many jobs, but never in a place like this." April dropped Maudie's hand. Was that the right thing to say?

Should she have just let Maudie ask the questions and not volunteered any information until she was asked? Did saying that she had worked at many jobs make it sound like she'd been fired?

Questions raced through her mind so fast that they made her dizzy.

"Jackson is right. Anyone can fake a résumé. What I'm interested in is someone who loves animals and will work hard." Maudie led April into her office.

"I can do that for sure." April glanced around the small room. A laptop computer sat on an old, scarred oak desk right in front of her. The office chair behind it looked like it had come out of a 1920s movie, and the only other seat in the room was a padded wingback chair that was covered in a floral tapestry and had a cat curled up on it.

"Jackson described you perfectly. Have a seat." Maudie pointed to the chair where the biggest cat April had ever seen was sleeping. The critter opened one eye and looked at her like he was daring her to touch him.

Was this a test to see if she could get along with a big, lazy cat? If so, she sure hoped that cat liked to be awakened.

"I love cats." April scooped him up in her arms and sat down. She buried her face in his thick fur and then put him in her lap and kept petting him. Not only was the cat a huge boy, but his big, loud purr matched his size.

"You're hired," Maudie said. "Can you go to work right now?"

April jerked her head up and stared at Maudie, who looked even smaller in the chair behind the desk. Surely she hadn't heard the woman right. "You don't need to ask me any questions about my past employment or anything?"

"Nope, Willie there is my test, and you passed it. I don't care about the past. My only concern is whether you like animals. The last person who applied for the job refused to touch Willie and sneezed three times. Can't have someone with allergies working with animals all day. She came in here wearing a fancy little suit and high-heeled shoes. I don't know what she thought she would be doing here," Maudie chuckled. "You're wearing the right clothes for a place like this."

"I *can* start right now." April thought about pinching herself to see if she was dreaming.

"Good. The shelter is through that door." Maudie pointed. "Just put Willie back on his chair and go to work. Be here at twelve thirty every day and stay until five thirty, when we close up shop. I'll pay you minimum wage until Friday. If you still want to stay after this week, I'll increase it by a dollar an hour after that. Do we have a deal?"

"Yes, ma'am." April nodded. "What do you want me to do first?"

"I haven't been in the shelter since Saturday night. You'll see what you need to do." Maudie smiled. "I imagine that you're thinkin' I'm out of my mind, hiring a person on the way they treat my cat, but I'm a good judge of character. I've been wrong a few times, and when I am, I admit it, fire the person I hired, and get on with life. I speak my mind. I don't pussyfoot around things, and if you don't like me at the end of the day, you know where the door is. But for now I'm glad to have you,

April. I've got a feeling you and I are going to get along just fine. Leave the door open. Willie likes to go visit his buddies."

April gave the cat a kiss on the top of his head, got to her feet, and put him back in his chair. "Thank you, Miz Maudie. I appreciate this job more than you'll ever know."

"You are very welcome. Now I've got to go check on a couple of cats that got their little testicles removed this morning. I'll holler at you about three, and we'll have a fifteen-minute break. Do you like coffee, tea, or maybe a soda pop?"

"Sweet tea is my drink of choice." April headed toward the closed door.

"Mine, too. See you in a bit." Maudie disappeared through a door on the other side of the office.

The stench of dirty cages met April when she walked into the large room. If it hadn't been air-conditioned, it could have been much worse—that's what she told herself. Two dozen cages on one side of the room held cats that were meowing at the top of their lungs. Half that many cages on the other side held puppies and small dogs. April crossed the floor, opened the cabinet doors on the far end, and took stock of what all was available. Pads to put in the cages, food and water, but nothing was organized. She could fill water bowls from the stainless-steel sink at the end of the cabinets, but the dish soap was on a shelf beside the extra bowls. When she got finished with the cleaning, she fully intended to get the place put to rights.

"All right. Let's get to work." She opened the first cage and decided to move the little orange kitten in it over to the only empty cage in the place. "You can stay in here, darlin' baby, while I clean up your apartment. Has it been a long weekend?" she crooned to the kitten as she carried it over to its temporary cage.

She talked to each animal as she carefully took it from its cage, and by midafternoon she had finished cleaning the cages. She grabbed a broom in the corner and was busy sweeping the floor when Maudie arrived with two bottles of sweet tea in her hands. She handed one to April and motioned her back into the office.

"Have a seat." Maudie pointed to the chair again. "Willie is sleeping under the desk right now. You've really done good. The shelter looks clean, and the animals seem happier than I've seen them in a while. Are you a cat and dog whisperer?" She twisted the cap off her tea and took a long drink.

"I've teased folks about that," April said. "I just love animals. I think they know when you're afraid of them or don't like them. I'm so glad that Jackson told me about this job."

Maudie raised an eyebrow. "You got a little crush on Jackson?"

"Not me," April answered. "My life is in too big of a mess for guys right now."

"Smart girl." Maudie nodded. "And a hard worker. I remember Lucy talking about you grandchildren when she brought Waylon in for his shots. You're the oldest, right?"

"No, that would be Nessa. Then Flynn was born the very next month. I came last, but we were all born within four months of each other," April explained.

"Then your mother was the sixteen-year-old that died when you were just a few days old. The baby of the O'Riley family, right?" Maudie asked.

"Yes, ma'am," April answered. "My mother was the youngest child. Uncle Isaac was the oldest, and he's the preacher. Uncle Matthew is in the middle, and he's Flynn's father."

"She talked about Isaac more than Matthew," Maudie said.

"Do you have children?" April asked.

"No, I don't. My sweet husband, who was also a vet, and I were married for thirty years. He's been gone for thirty years now. We wanted a big family, but the good Lord never saw fit to give us children. Maybe that's why we loved working with animals so much. If you love them, they know it, and"—a grin covered her face—"they never talk back."

"You got that right," April chuckled.

"It's hard to believe that now he's been gone for thirty years." The grin faded as Maudie sighed, no doubt remembering the good times she'd had with her husband. "I never remarried. I figured that once you've had steak, it's kind of hard to go back to bologna."

"Amen to that." April smiled and pointed to the clock. "Break time is over. I'm going to scrub the floor in the shelter and then get the cabinets all put to rights, unless you've got something else for me to do?"

"Nope." Maudie grinned. "If you have time after you get that done, you can take the animals out one at a time again and give them some TLC. Poor little things get tired of being caged, and I hardly ever have time to love on them."

"I can sure do that." April threw her empty bottle in the trash can and headed back into the shelter. She hummed a lullaby as she cleaned the floor and organized the cabinets. She kept humming as she took the first kitten out and held it like a baby in her arms. When it got tired of being petted and began to squirm, she put it back and got another one out, alternating working and loving on all the sweet animals. By five thirty she had the cabinets in decent order. She had given each of the cats and dogs a little individual time. She made sure they all had food and fresh water and then waved goodbye to them as she closed the door.

❖ ❖ ❖

Flynn didn't have a dry spot on his T-shirt when it was time to close up shop that afternoon. The hours had flown by as he listened to the radio—thank goodness he and Jackson shared a love for the same kind of music—and sanded two hope chests. But in spite of the sweltering work, he felt so much more alive than he had when he'd finished a day in his air-conditioned office down in South Texas.

"Ever think of air-conditioning this place?" he asked as Jackson locked the door to the shop.

"Oh, yeah, lots of times," Jackson answered, "but the building isn't insulated. The electric bill would eat up all my profits. Uncle D. J. used to say that sweat was good for us. I do use a couple of space heaters in the wintertime, and on the rare occasion that it snows, I take a few days off. Want to cool off in the house and have a beer before you go home?"

"Love to." Flynn followed Jackson across the backyard and up onto the porch.

Tex was already waiting for them at the door, his tail slinging drops of water every which way when he wagged it.

"Looks like he's been splashing around in the creek to cool off. I might do the same before I make a sandwich for supper." Jackson opened the door and stood to the side. "Welcome to the Devereaux home. Have a seat anywhere. Got a preference for your beer? I've got Coors in bottles and Budweiser in cans."

"Coors, and thanks." Flynn could see that a woman hadn't lived in this house in a long time, if ever. No fancy throw pillows on the sofa or knickknacks sitting around. A single painting of the waterfall hung above the sofa. The coffee table had scrapes and scars made by boots being propped on it, and the end tables were dotted with circles that came from sweating beer bottles and cans.

Flynn was way too dusty and sweaty to sit on the sofa, so he took a seat in an old wooden rocker like the ones in Nanny Lucy's living room. This one had been stained and varnished at one time, but the finish had worn off the wide arms. He set it in motion with his foot and just enjoyed the cool air while Jackson was in the kitchen. This was the life—no headaches or paperwork to take home at the end of the day.

"There you go." Jackson handed him a longneck bottle of Coors and then twisted the cap off his own. "So are you coming back tomorrow, or have you had enough? You really are good with wood." He sat down in the other rocking chair and propped his feet up on the coffee table.

Flynn removed the cap from his beer and took a long drink. "I'll be back. I'd forgotten how good a cold beer tastes after a hot day of work, and it's been a long time since I could say I was finished at the end of the day."

"Miz Lucy said that you worked in the oil fields. Wasn't that hot work?" Jackson asked.

"Back when I worked outside it was even hotter work than what we've been doing, but for the past three years, I've been behind a desk," Flynn answered. "Working with my hands sure eases the stress, even if it does make me sweat."

"Yep," Jackson agreed. "I got to where I hated to go to work every day when I was a lawyer. I got up with a heavy feeling in my chest. I came home after sixteen hours in the office or the courtroom, fell into bed, and even though I was mentally exhausted, I fought sleep, because I knew the next morning would just start things all over again."

"You're preaching to the choir, but my days were probably only ten hours, not sixteen. At the end of the day, I took a full briefcase home with me." Flynn noticed the hope chest sitting beside the sofa. "Is that what you're guarding until we get the quilt finished?"

Jackson nodded. "Miz Lucy brought it over here last year in the back of her truck. I tried to talk her out of leaving it with me, but she'd made up her mind. She said that she didn't have long to live, and that she'd been to see the lawyer earlier that day about her will. She made me promise that I would take care of it, so I just shoved it over there in the corner, and it's been there ever since. When are y'all going to get the quilt done?"

"By the end of the month if we keep on schedule," Flynn answered. "You ever been nosy enough to peek inside?"

"Nope." Jackson grinned. "Knowing Miz Lucy, it might be booby-trapped. I liked her, and she was a good neighbor, but she did have her moments. Uncle D. J. said that she had mellowed a lot in the last five years, but things were different when she was younger."

"We're slowly finding that out," Flynn said.

"Which one of you do you think will be married first and take this away from my house?" Jackson asked. "Not that it's in the way or a problem for me to keep it. I owe Miz Lucy that much."

"Why do you think you owe her anything?" Flynn asked.

"Lots of Sunday dinners, dominoes and games of checkers, and long talks about what I wanted to do with my life," Jackson answered. "She was always willing to listen to me. She didn't give a lot of advice, but she was a good listener. Of course, I could always tell within a few minutes if she didn't want company, and I'd make an excuse to leave."

"I never talked to her much about what to do with my life, but I did spend time with her every summer, so I guess I owe her, too." Flynn turned up his bottle and took another drink before he went on. "And I expect that it will be Nessa who gets that hope chest. I'm not even looking for a relationship, and I get the impression that April isn't, either."

"Nessa is looking for a relationship?" Jackson asked.

"All three of us are kind of messed up right now," Flynn said. "No, that's not right. We've been messed up for a while, and we need to get our lives straightened out. Nessa may be the lightest of the list, but she's got baggage. She'll probably get her ducks in a row before me and April. That's why I said she might wind up with the hope chest."

He glanced over at the rectangular box that used to sit at the foot of Nanny Lucy's bed. Of all the things in her house, what made it so important? It just looked like an aged cedar chest with a tarnished brass keyhole in the front. Flynn wasn't even sure that he wanted the thing at all, but he couldn't shake the need to know what was in it.

"I came here with baggage," Jackson said. "It took me quite a while to feel like I was making progress getting rid of it. Uncle D. J. was a little old guy who didn't talk much, but, looking back, he knew exactly what I needed. Time and hard work, and he gave me both."

"Well, I've got time, and you've given me a job that involves hard work, so maybe I'll see some light by the end of summer." Flynn finished off his beer and stood up. "Thanks again for the beer. I should be getting on back. Nessa usually has supper ready about six. Want to come eat with us?"

"Thanks, but no thanks," Jackson said. "I've got my heart set on having a nice cool dip and then diving back into a mystery book I've been reading."

"Maybe next time." Flynn held up his empty bottle. "Where's the trash?"

"Just leave it on the coffee table. I've got a couple of recycling bins out back," Jackson told him.

With a slight nod and a wave, Flynn went outside, took a minute to pet Tex, and then headed home. He was only a few yards down the rutted pathway when he realized he was whistling. He hadn't done that in years, especially not at the end of a workday.

❖   ❖   ❖

Nessa put away the sewing machine, cleaned all her quilting business off the dining room table, and was stirring a pot of marinara sauce to go on spaghetti when April came into the house. The hours had flown by, and most of the afternoon she had hummed as she worked. That alone told her that she should give this quilting business a chance. She loved teaching, but toward the end of the school day, the minutes turned into hours and she could hardly wait to get out of the classroom.

"I guess you got the job, or else you started to run away with Nanny Lucy's car and figured that she would haunt you if you did that," Nessa said as she slid a loaf of Italian bread into the oven.

"Got the job. Love it, and it never entered my mind to run away." April went straight to the kitchen sink, lathered up her hands, and then rinsed them. "I told you I came back here to face my demons and get my life into some kind of order. I'm not going anywhere but to work and home until that happens." She dried her hands, took down three plates from the cabinet, and set the table. "Why aren't you looking for a job?"

"I've got paychecks coming in all summer, so I don't need to work until fall, plus I've saved enough that if I'm very careful, I won't have to work until January," Nessa answered.

"Must be nice to have a savings account." April sighed. "I'm going to get me one of those as soon as I start getting a paycheck."

The blank look in April's eyes had faded somewhat, and her smile didn't look pasted on. Strangely enough, Nessa was happy for her. The way she'd acted those first few days, Nessa had kind of hoped that she would leave in the middle of the night. That haunted look in April's eyes had made Nessa wonder if maybe she'd been dabbling in drugs. If so, Nessa wouldn't have cared even if April *had* taken Nanny Lucy's car with her.

"Tell me about your work." Nessa brought out a head of lettuce and a tomato from the refrigerator and made a bowl of salad while the pasta cooked.

"I take care of the shelter, for the most part. That's what Maudie had me doing today. I cleaned all the cages, then played with the cats and dogs until it was time to come home," April answered.

"You get paid to play with kittens and puppies?" Nessa asked.

"Hey, you got paid to be a glorified babysitter to kindergarteners," April told her.

"I had to teach them a lot of things," Nessa argued. "And I had to deal with parents. You just get to have fun, with no lesson plans or three or four sets of parents involved. Do your pets learn to read?"

April cocked her head to one side and frowned. "How does a kid get that many parents? I didn't even get one. That's not fair."

"They have a daddy and stepmother, a mama and stepfather, and at least one set of grandparents that usually sees them more often, because the parents have to work," Nessa explained.

Before April could say anything else, Waylon came down the hallway, stopped at the dining room table, and sniffed the air, then arched his back. His tail stood at attention and grew to twice its size, and he growled deep in his throat.

"What's the matter with him?" April asked.

"He probably smells all those animals on you and thinks that you brought one or more of them home," Nessa answered.

April dropped down on her knees and called Waylon over to her. He walked all the way around her, sniffed her jeans, and then nudged her hand and started purring. She stroked his fur and said, "I wouldn't ever love those others like I do you. They're sweet and they are my job, but you're the boss."

"Amen to that," Nessa said. "He's been right under my feet most of the day. He wanted to lay on my pattern pieces, or else sleep right beside the sewing machine."

"Hey, honeys, I'm home," Flynn called out when he came through the door. "And this AC feels wonderful."

"That's 'cousins' to you, not 'honeys,'" Nessa scolded. "Go get washed up. Supper will be on the table in about ten minutes."

"Yes, Mother," Flynn teased.

Nessa shook a fist at him. "You call me that again, and you'll be eating on the porch in the heat."

Flynn laughed out loud and headed to the bathroom. He came out a few minutes later, got the salad dressings from the refrigerator, and poured three glasses of sweet tea. By then Nessa had the spaghetti on the table, and she and April were in their seats. Then he sat down at his normal place and even said a short grace when Nessa asked him to do that.

"Nanny Lucy wouldn't like it if we didn't give thanks. How was your day, Flynn?" Nessa asked.

"Amazing," Flynn answered. "I've always liked doing new things, but working with wood is more calming than anything else I've tried. How about you two?"

"Got the job, and I love it." April heaped her plate full of spaghetti and then added two thick chunks of bread to the side. "My main work is in the shelter, cleaning up the pens and playing with the animals. No one came to adopt any of them today."

"Our new normal," Nessa said.

"What does that mean?" April asked.

"You go to work at the clinic. Flynn goes to Jackson's place. I work on quilting all afternoon so that when the craft fairs start up, I'll have something to take," Nessa answered. "That's our new norm, and I think I like it, but what happens when we get the quilt finished?"

"Maybe by then Maudie will let me work more hours," April said.

"And Jackson will decide he needs me to do more." Flynn crossed his fingers up in the air like a little boy.

"Then our norm will change, and we'll have to adjust to whatever it is then." Nessa slid the salad over to Flynn.

"Yep," April and Flynn said at the same time.

After supper, Flynn shooed Nessa out of the kitchen. "You cooked. I'll take care of cleanup."

"You wash," April said. "I'll dry and put the dishes away."

"Well, thank you both," Nessa said. "I have been hunched over a sewing machine all day, so I'm going for a long walk. See you later."

She rounded the end of the house and stood at the edge of the path. Going left would take her to Jackson's place, but showing up on his porch again so soon might seem awfully forward. Still, she would love to sit and talk to him some more. With a long sigh, she turned right and headed toward the waterfall.

The sound of water tumbling over the rocks brought back memories of all those times when she and her two cousins had run all the way from the house to the falls and jumped in without even a second thought. The race had decided who was the fastest, and the last one in was the loser. Pretty often Nessa, with her short legs, was the last one to dive into the cool creek water. She had never gotten to swim at home, unless the girls' prayer group got to go on a retreat where there were only girls involved. Isaac believed that girls and boys swimming together in scanty bathing suits would cause all kinds of impure thoughts. Trouble, in a nutshell.

"Yeah, right," Nessa muttered. "My one-piece bathing suit couldn't be called scanty by any stretch of the word."

Tex came around the curve in the path and shook himself, sending water flying everywhere. Nessa laughed and dropped to her knees to pet the dog. "I wish I could just jump in the water like you can. You don't have to worry about a bathing suit or a towel." She blushed at even the thought of skinny-dipping.

"Hey, do I hear voices?" Jackson yelled.

"It's Nessa," she called out. "Are you decent?"

"Enough for company." Jackson's laughter rang out. "Come on in, the water is great."

She straightened up and started that way with Tex right beside her. "I didn't wear my bathing suit, but"—she rounded the bend and caught sight of Jackson out there in the middle of the creek—"I will put my feet in."

The dog took a running dive right into the water, paddling out to where Jackson was and then swimming in circles around him.

Lord have mercy! she thought as she plopped down on the grass, removed her shoes, and rolled up her jeans. *His smile would make ice boil.*

Chapter Twelve

*J*ackson swam over toward the bank, stood up when he could touch the bottom with his toes, and walked the rest of the way out of the water. Tex beat him to the grassy edge and gave Nessa a shower when he shook from head to toe.

"You might as well dive in, even if you do it in your clothes," Jackson said as he sat down beside her. "Tex is like a kid. He's in and out, in and out, and every time he comes out of the water, he has to do that shaking business. He'll drench you if you sit here very long."

"He's like one of those mist fans," Nessa said.

"Never thought of it that way." Jackson chuckled. "What brings you out tonight if you aren't going for a nice cool swim?"

"I just needed to get out of the house. We've been here a week now, and I'm not any closer to getting things sorted out than I was when we first got here. I quilted all day today, and I enjoyed it, but no revelations fell out of the sky like I thought they would," she said. "And I don't know why I'm telling you this. We hardly know each other."

"That's why you're telling me." Jackson picked up a smooth stone and tossed it out into the water. It made a splash, and ripples started at the site and grew bigger and bigger until the flowing water brushed them away. "Relatives and really close friends want to give you advice. A stranger just listens."

"Then thank you for just listening," Nessa said.

"When I was a kid, my folks would come see Uncle D. J. in the fall, usually between Thanksgiving and Christmas." He picked up a stick and whipped it out into the middle of the creek. Tex dived into the water and swam out to retrieve it. "Mama would bring him a box of expensive candy from one of the stores in Austin and a smoked ham. He told me later that he shared the candy with Miz Lucy and gave her the ham to fix for Christmas dinner. When I was about six, Daddy let me come stay a week with Uncle D. J. Mother told me if I got homesick to just call her and she'd come get me. At the end of the week, I cried because I had to go home."

"Yep," Nessa said. "I pouted for a week when I had to go home. I'm surprised we never met when we were kids."

"I always came the first week after school was out, sometime at the end of May or the first of June," Jackson said.

"We came for two weeks right before school started in the fall. I couldn't come before then because that way, Mama and Daddy could use my time here as a threat all summer. If I wasn't 'good'"—she put air quotes around the word—"then I couldn't come to Blossom."

"Then I take it that you liked to spend time here?" Jackson could listen to her soft Texas drawl all evening.

"It was the highlight of my year. Nanny Lucy made us go to church every time the doors opened. Flynn fussed about it, but I was used to that and more. Other than that, I thought this place was paradise. She pretty much let us run wild over the property while we were here. Until we were teenagers, she sewed shirts for Flynn and cute little dresses for me and April when we visited her. I always loved the dresses and blouses she made for me. And she had her quilting ladies on Wednesday mornings. If I behaved, was quiet, and stayed out of the way, I could watch them quilt and listen to their stories," Nessa answered.

"Did you like sharing her with the quilting club?" Jackson asked.

"Loved it." Nessa's smile lit up her eyes. "I have to admit that I kind of let my mind wander when they talked about the Bible or sang hymns, but when they got all involved with the quilt talk, it was right up my alley. I should have known then that my passion lay in that area, but then I had no idea it could be a lucrative business."

"So what are you trying to sort out?" Jackson asked. "You don't have to answer that if it's too personal."

Nessa shrugged. "It's not too personal, I guess, but the truth is I need to know myself. I need to figure out what I really want to do with my life."

"I understand," Jackson said. "It took me a while to figure out the same thing."

"What was holding you back?" Nessa asked.

"My brother and sister were teenagers when I was born. They both went into the law business, and I was expected to do the same, so I did. But I hated the job—it made me miserable. I wondered what made me so different from everyone else in my family, and it took me a while to realize I was more like Uncle D. J. than my father or my siblings."

"I hope I can figure things out like you did. It seems like whatever happened here has rolled downhill to us three kids and helped to make us who we are. If we can understand why, then maybe we can get a better insight into our own lives," she told him. "Kind of like those ripples in the water when you tossed in that rock. Nanny Lucy and Grandpa are the rock. The first ripples are their three children. The next ones are April, Flynn, and me. But there's more that go out from there, so if we ever have kids, we need to know what made us who we are."

"Why does that matter?" Jackson asked. "That's in the past."

"The past defines the present and affects the future," Nessa said.

Jackson tossed another rock out into the water. This time Tex dove in and interrupted the ripples. "Throw in an external force like the dog, and everything is in an uproar."

"Or maybe that external force will help break the pattern, so the next generation won't have to face all these problems that we're dealing with today," she suggested.

"That's an interesting thought," Jackson said. "Does that mean you want to borrow my dog to interrupt the pattern?"

"No." Nessa smiled again. "But you are right about it being easy to talk to a stranger."

"I'm here anytime you want to talk, but I'd rather be a listening friend than a stranger," Jackson said.

"Is there a girlfriend to get jealous, or a fiancée to break up with you for talking to another woman?" She turned her head and locked eyes with him.

He stared into her green eyes for a full fifteen seconds before she blinked and turned away.

"No girlfriend. No fiancée," he answered. "I won't even send you a bill for the therapy if you'll be my sounding board as well."

"It's a deal." Nessa stuck out her hand to shake with him.

He'd just taken her hand in his when Tex ran between them and shook water everywhere. When the dog stopped, their hands were still clasped over his wet back. "Does shaking hands over a wet dog mean something deep and meaningful?" He chuckled as he dropped her hand.

"Of course it does." Nessa's eyes glittered. "It means that we will both find the answers to our questions right here by this waterfall, but if you've already pretty much come to grips with finding yourself, what would you have to worry about?"

"Well"—Jackson rubbed his chin—"I do like to talk about my job, my day, and other things. But we're discussing you tonight, so what do you want to talk about?"

"Why Daddy is such a strict preacher and Uncle Matthew a womanizer. They both showed up at the house, and it was horrible. Daddy tried to bully me into leaving. He and Uncle Isaac were like two old bulls in a pasture. Neither of them would back down, and the tension seemed to be thicker than a dense fog."

"What did you tell him?" Jackson asked.

"I told him I wasn't leaving, and that I was even thinking about quitting my job. He left in a fit of anger," Nessa answered. "Seems like I can't move forward until I get my head wrapped around everything."

"I understand." Jackson had been in that same state a few years ago and knew exactly how Nessa felt. It might take a while for her to get a grip on her life—but Jackson was a patient man.

❖ ❖ ❖

Hearing those two words helped Nessa more than reading one of the dozens of self-help books that filled the bookcase in her bedroom back in Turkey. She pulled her feet up out of the water and let them air-dry. "Too bad those ancestor tests that are so popular these days can't tell us the *why* as well as the *who* we are related to."

"That could get sticky with folks who've been unfaithful to their spouses, couldn't it?" Jackson asked. "As it is, cousins can pop up and folks have no idea how they're related. If there was a record that said, 'You are kin to this person because your great-grandfather had an affair with her great-grandmother,' just think of the repercussions."

"I hadn't thought of that." Nessa shook her head slowly. Either of her grandparents ever doing anything immoral was something that, in her mind, simply wouldn't happen. "I don't think we've got a thing to worry about. Nanny Lucy was too religious to ever have an affair, and she would have killed Grandpa if he did."

Jackson swatted a mosquito on his arm, leaving a smear of blood where the little varmint had been. "That's my cue to go home. They seem to come out worse in the evening. You staying a while longer?" He extended a hand.

She put her hand in his and let him pull her up to a standing position. "Not if those bugs are coming around to suck my blood."

"I'll walk with you to the fork in the path." He dropped her hand. "You said you quilted this morning. Did you enjoy it?"

Nessa wished that he had kept her hand in his, but maybe he wasn't feeling the sparks that she was. They were so real to her that she could see them almost as clearly as she could the fireflies flitting out ahead of them.

"I don't see many of those out in the Texas Panhandle," she muttered.

"What?" Jackson asked.

"Lightning bugs," she answered. "When we were kids, I thought the only place that had them or a waterfall was Blossom, Texas. It wasn't until I was older that I figured out this place wasn't as magical as I thought when we were little."

"Today's kids are so glued to their phones and tablets that nothing much would be magical to them," Jackson said.

"When and if I ever have kids, I want to let them be kids as long as they can. Once we're grown up, we can't ever go back and recover all those simple feelings that lightning bugs and waterfalls and a new dress for the first day of school bring us," she said.

"If you bring up your kids right here on this dead-end road, you just might be able to pull that off." Jackson stopped at the fork in the road.

To her left she could see the faint yellow glow of light coming through the living room window. That was home, even if it did harbor its own fair share of secrets. Ahead was where Jackson lived, but it was far enough away that the scrub oak trees shielded it from sight.

"Thanks for the visit," she said and turned her back, and suddenly she was falling forward. She grabbed for anything to break her fall but got nothing but a fistful of air. She could see the ground coming up to meet her, and then two strong arms were around her, saving her from crashing face-first into the dirt and weeds.

Her heart thumped in her chest so hard that she could feel the loud beats in her ears. She wrapped her arms around his neck and held on to him like he was her rock in the midst of a tornado.

"Are you all right?" Jackson asked. "Did you twist your ankle? I'm going to have to fuss at Tex for not taking care of these damned gophers."

"I think I'm fine," she gasped, but she wasn't totally sure.

"I'm going to take a step back. Don't put your weight on your foot until I check it." He squatted down and, starting at her knee, ran his hand down her leg. "Tell me if something hurts."

"So far just my pride," she mumbled.

"That's easily fixed. A broken ankle is another thing," he said. "Nothing feels out of whack. Does this hurt?" He pressed on her ankle bone.

She couldn't tell him that his hands on her bare skin were sending little shocks all through her body. "No, it feels fine. I'm going to put my weight on it now."

He stood up and held her shoulders while she gingerly pressed her foot down. "See, all better," she said, and she stepped in another hole and pitched forward a second time.

Jackson caught her just like before and laughed out loud. "Darlin', we've got to stop meeting like this. If you want a hug, just ask for it. I'll be glad to oblige you."

"Then I want a hug." She hung on to him, amazed at herself for being that bold.

"Ask and you shall receive," Jackson teased as he brought her even closer. "Have you ever hugged a guy on a first date?"

"Sure, and a few times I even kissed a guy on a first date," she admitted, "but you and I haven't been on a date."

"Yet." He grinned as he took a step back. "Maybe I'd better walk you all the way to the porch, just in case you need someone to catch you if you fall again. They say the third time is the charm, and you might really break something the next time."

"But I might get another hug if I did," she flirted, even though she knew she shouldn't.

He looped her arm in his, and the instant electricity between them was like nothing she'd ever experienced before. She reasoned that it was the result of her not having gone out with anyone in almost a year, but her heart told her it was something more than that. She'd been with men, both in a fairly serious relationship and on lots of platonic dates, but none of them had affected her like Jackson did.

It didn't take long to cover the distance from the fork in the road to the porch since it was only about thirty yards. When they reached the bottom step, she pulled her arm free. "Thanks again," she said as she leaned in to give him a kiss on the cheek for saving her twice.

The next few seconds became a blur, and yet everything felt as if it moved in slow motion. Tex came from the back of the house in a dead run and reared up on Jackson's leg. Jackson turned to push him away at the same time Nessa leaned in to kiss Jackson on the cheek. Instead of landing where she intended, the kiss landed square on his lips. He wrapped her up in his arms for the third time and kissed her back— long and slow, sending tingles all the way to her toes.

When the kiss ended, she took a deep breath and said, "That's to thank you for saving me, but I really only intended it to be a sweet kiss on the cheek."

"I'm glad it was more," he said. "I guess this *was* a date since I got a goodnight kiss at the door. Maybe we'll go out again sometime."

"You've got the number here at the O'Riley house." She figured he was joking, but down deep inside she hoped he wasn't.

"Night, Nessa." He waved over his shoulder as he and Tex disappeared into the darkness.

Chapter Thirteen

April was watching a rerun of *NCIS* when Nessa came into the house. Her cousin had a glow about her that begged for answers, so April asked, "What have you been doing? You look like you just kissed a frog, and he turned into a prince."

Flynn came down the hallway and stopped at the edge of the living room. "You've been with Jackson, haven't you? He said he was going to the falls when we knocked off work today. You been out there making out with him? Don't you dare lead him on and then dump him, Nessa. I like working for him, so don't ruin it for me."

"Are you judging our cousin by your own half bushel?" April asked.

"I'm not talking to you," Flynn smarted off.

"You are now, and you didn't answer my question," April said.

"I saw him at the falls, and we talked," Nessa admitted. "You really are thinking of yourself, aren't you?"

Flynn raised a dark eyebrow. "Yes, I am. I'm a work in progress, and I really like my job. So fess up and tell us what happened."

"I believe it was you who said you didn't know us well enough to tell us all about your private life and past. Well, darlin' cousin"—she dragged out the last two words—"I'm saying the same thing right back at you. I'm going to get a piece of chocolate cake. Anyone else want one?"

April followed her into the kitchen. "You're changing the subject, so there's more to this story."

"We talked about our problems. There! Are you satisfied? You've pulled the big secret out of me." Nessa lifted the glass dome off the cake stand and cut a wedge of cake for herself. "Either of you want to join me?"

"I'll have a piece," Flynn said. "I want milk with mine. How many glasses should I pour?"

April answered both questions. "I'll have one, too. What problems did you talk about?"

She waved her arm around the kitchen. "Mine, his, ours, as in yours and mine."

"What is my problem?" Flynn poured two tall glasses of milk and set them on the table.

April wondered if Flynn even knew the depths of his problems. She sure didn't know just how far hers had gone, but she felt as if she was making progress—one baby step at a time.

Nessa pulled out her chair with her free hand and sat down, putting her cake right in front of her. "The same as mine and April's, evidently. We all want to know why we are the way we are. How our parents could have had the same parents and turned out so different. Where did the genes actually come from? It's easy to see that my daddy got Nanny Lucy's love of God and religion, but where in the world did Uncle Matthew get his penchant for womanizing, and where did Rachel get her rebellion?"

"Rachel and April weren't preachers' kids like you, but with Nanny Lucy's religious streak, they might just as well have been, and you know that preachers' kids usually have a rebellious side, either when they're young or later on in life," Flynn answered.

"And why did Nanny Lucy love you both more than she did me?" April took her seat. "It was as if she saw something in me that just flat-out pissed her off every single day. No matter what I did or how hard I tried, nothing was right."

"I don't care where the genes came from. I just want to change the ones I got from my dad and replace them with Mama's." Flynn put the first bite of cake into his mouth.

"How on earth did your folks ever get together to begin with?" Nessa asked. "They were so different."

"She got a job as a secretary at the oil company where he worked," Flynn answered. "She fell in love with him, and I believe that even after he cheated on her and asked for a divorce, she loved him until she died."

"I want to find peace, and to do that, I've got to be at peace with me. Somehow I don't see either Nanny Lucy or Grandpa doing something immoral, but maybe our great-grandparents . . ." Nessa paused to take a bite of cake.

"April, did Nanny Lucy ever talk much about Grandpa?" Flynn asked. "He was dead before any of us were born, and I never heard her mention him, except to say that the green rocking chair was his."

"He died before my mother was even born," April answered. "Nanny seldom ever said anything about him, but she did tell me more than once that raising my mother and then me was what she got for trying to punish him. She never did tell me what he did that made her so mad."

"Did she ever tell you how he died?" Nessa asked. "I've asked Daddy, but all he'll say is that his father died on the job when he was a teenager and just before Rachel was born."

"My dad says that Grandpa was away a lot and pretty much only came home on weekends. When he was home, he spent most of his time getting ready to leave again. He worked on the railroad, and Dad said that at the end of his life he was an engineer, but it wasn't on a passenger train," Flynn added.

"Freight trains?" Nessa asked. "Are there pictures of him anywhere?"

"Not that I've ever seen, but Nanny Lucy told me that he worked with freight trains, too. She said that she kept her memories in the hall closet and that I'd get in big trouble if I ever prowled around in there," April said.

"Do you think there's pictures in there?" Nessa asked.

Flynn left his cake, stood up, and started down the hall. "Let's see if there are. Could be that we'll find some answers in the pictures."

April didn't think for one second that they'd find anything helpful, but it was worth a try. Still, a shiver chased down her spine at the very idea of prying into that closet.

"Holy smoke!" Flynn yelled when he opened the door and a whole raft of items fell from the top shelf, covering him with quilt tops and crocheted afghans.

"Need some help fighting your way out of all that?" April yelled back.

"Why haven't we opened this closet before now? And with everything else in the house so neat, why did Nanny Lucy let this become such a mess?" Flynn threw the quilt tops over to the side. "I see a suitcase, but I'm not even going to try to put all this stuff back. We'll box it up for the garage. Do y'all think she might have put her memories in the suitcase? It looks ancient."

Nessa rushed down the hall and grabbed up all three quilt tops. "We've all got a messy room or drawer somewhere in our places. Mine is a drawer in the kitchen. Evidently Nanny Lucy had a messy closet. This is fantastic. I'll take care of all this after we see whatever is in the suitcase. I can get these quilted by the time I go to my first craft fair."

"I've never seen it opened, so it never registered to me that there was a closet at the end of the hall," Flynn said.

"You're welcome to all of it." April kept eating her cake.

"I can't believe we've been here a whole week and never opened that closet door." Flynn groaned when he pulled the suitcase off the shelf. "This thing weighs as much as a baby elephant."

April remembered the day she had gotten curious and opened the door. She had been about ten years old, and things had spilled out into the hallway that time, too. She had crammed it all back into the closet, but a couple of days later, Nanny Lucy had figured out that someone had been in her things.

"You look like you've seen a ghost," Nessa told April.

"I kind of have." April nodded. "I peeked in the closet once. I can still feel Nanny Lucy's glare boring holes in my soul when she figured it out. She said that this house was my Garden of Eden. She said that she provided for me, clothed me, and made sure I had a place to sleep. She reminded me that she took me to church so I would know God, but that closet and her bedroom were like the tree of good and evil, and I was never to touch either one ever again. Then she beat the hell out of me for disobeying her about never opening that door and sent me to my room for a whole day. I could only come out to go to the bathroom, and I didn't get dinner or supper, to teach me to leave her things alone."

"That was harsh," Flynn said.

"That"—April covered her face with her hands for a moment—"was minor compared to some of the other things that happened here." She removed her hands, but she didn't make an attempt to go help Nessa.

"Well, I'm going through it, piece by piece," Nessa said. "That's my job tomorrow afternoon while y'all are at work."

"Be my guest." April finished off the last bite of her cake. "But don't come whining to me when Nanny Lucy scolds all of us in our dreams."

Flynn shut the door to the closet and carried the suitcase to the living room. He set it in the middle of the floor and sat cross-legged in front of it. "Y'all going to join me?"

Nessa sat down beside him. April left the table and took a place on the other side. "I'm keeping my distance from that thing."

"She's gone, April. She can't hurt you anymore," Nessa said.

"The whole time I was in that room, I wondered if my mother had looked in the closet and that's why God struck her dead."

"You poor thing," Nessa said. "I remember being sent to my room to pray about my sins. I figured it was me God was going to punish, not my mother, who, I was sure, had a halo under all her big hair."

Flynn flipped the two fasteners holding the suitcase shut. "And all this time, I thought I wanted to live either with Uncle Isaac because you had two parents"—he glanced over at Nessa and then turned to April—"or with Nanny Lucy because we had so much fun here in the summertime, but I'm beginning to think that I might be less scarred than either of you two."

April pointed at the suitcase. "I'm not so sure I want to be close when you open that thing."

"Hey, things were tough around here, but none of it is your fault. You've got to make yourself believe that," Flynn said. "And yes, I'm speaking from experience. I blamed myself for years for not being a perfect son. If I had been, maybe Dad wouldn't have been a womanizer. Maybe he would have been content to be a single father and go to my academic meets instead of the bars to look for another lady. It took a long time, but I realized all that wasn't my fault. Nanny Lucy wasn't well, and you didn't create her problems," Flynn said.

"I always thought it was all my fault because I was like my mother." April sighed. "I'd just as soon take that thing and everything in the closet and her bedroom out in the yard and have a bonfire with it."

"But there could be answers to all our questions right here." Flynn eased the top open and let it drop back onto the hardwood floor. "Surprise! If our grandmother had evil spirits locked up somewhere, they aren't in the suitcase. Looks like old papers and packets of pictures."

"It smells like roses. Strange that through everything, I still like that scent, but that thing scares me," April said.

"It's not evil," Nessa argued. "Evil smells like hell, like something hot and on fire, maybe like what a house smells like when it's burning down. This is just an old, dusty smell mixed with the faint aroma of roses. The quilt tops had the same odor. I'll hang them out on the clothesline tomorrow and air them out."

"How do you know what hell smells like?" Flynn asked.

"Daddy describes it very well in his sermons." Nessa reached for a faded manila envelope. "Looks like this might have the important papers April told us about."

She opened it to find a marriage license for her grandmother and grandfather dated December 18, 1958, a death certificate for their grandfather, and original birth certificates for all three of their children.

"This is history," Nessa said.

"We all know that she and Grandpa got married, they had three kids, and he died." April leaned forward enough to peek into the suitcase, but she didn't stretch out her hand to touch anything.

Flynn had picked up an envelope of pictures and was studying them one by one. "Here's our answer to one of the questions. My dad is the image of Grandpa. Look at this." He passed the pictures over to Nessa.

April moved over close to Nessa so she could see, but she couldn't make herself pick up a single paper. Merely looking at the suitcase made her feel every single stinging lash of that whipping she'd gotten for opening the closet door. "He really does look like Uncle Matthew, and Uncle Isaac looks like that man right there." She pointed to the best man. So this was what Nanny Lucy had been hiding where the tree of good and evil lived. She wondered if there were pictures of her mother in the suitcase, and if April really looked as much like her as Nanny Lucy had said she did.

Nessa flipped the picture over and read, "'Me, Everett, his fraternal twin brother, Ernest, and my best friend, April, on our wedding day. Ernest and April were our witnesses.'"

"I never even knew that we had a great-uncle," Nessa said.

"She only mentioned him one time to me. She said he was a preacher, but he died a year after the wedding when a rattlesnake bit him," April told them.

Nessa giggled under her breath. "My dad got a double dose of religion. First from going to church with Nanny Lucy all the time, and then from the uncle that he looks like. And I bet you're named after her best friend, April."

"Could be, but I always figured that she just named me that because I was born in April, and she didn't want to come up with a name," April answered.

"We should all do one of those DNA tests and figure out more about our ancestors." Flynn opened another envelope of pictures.

April would rather forget all of them, not do a test to figure out things. Just looking at the stuff in the suitcase made her slightly nauseated. She grabbed a tissue from the television stand and sneezed into it. "No, thank you."

"I'd do it just to see if Daddy is a descendant of Noah or maybe Moses." Nessa laughed out loud as she pulled another piece of paper from the envelope.

"I should go to the waterfall," April said. "Lightning could shoot through the ceiling and hit you for comments like that."

"I've said far worse, and I'm still alive," Nessa said, and then she lowered her voice. "Well, well, well, no wonder Nanny Lucy didn't want you digging around in the closet. This is your birth certificate, April, and it has your father's name on it."

April's chest tightened, and her pulse raced. The room started to go dark, but she shook her head and took a deep breath. Her hands trembled when Nessa passed the paper over to her. "I've never seen this."

"And here's the adoption paper, and your original Social Security card." Nessa handed them to her.

"I never knew that Nanny Lucy adopted me, either." April laid both documents on the floor in front of her and stared at them. She had always figured that the birth certificate would have "father unknown" on it.

"Why didn't you have a copy of your birth certificate? Didn't you need it for something or other through the years?" Flynn asked.

"Nanny Lucy took it to school when she enrolled me in kindergarten. I didn't need it after that. She must've gotten my Social Security card when I was born. I've never seen the birth certificate before right now," April whispered, unable to take her eyes off the papers. "I didn't ask many questions. I learned early on that her answer to most anything like that was to tell me it wasn't any of my business." She gave the certificate to Flynn. "This is all overwhelming."

"Well, from what this says, your father was Lucas Green, and until Nanny formally adopted you, you were April Green," Flynn said as he studied the piece of paper.

April had a father somewhere out there in the world. Where had he been? Did he even know he had a daughter?

"When Nanny Lucy was mad at you, did she mention anything about your father?" Nessa peered over her shoulder.

April shook her head. "Maybe the sin she kept fretting about was that she killed him. I wonder if he loved my mother, or if I'm the result of a date rape or a one-night stand."

Flynn pulled his phone from his pocket. "You want me to see where Lucas Green is these days? I can look him up on the internet. I'll just add 'Blossom, Texas,' so we narrow it down. You might even meet him."

"I'm not sure. What if he ran out on my mother, or what if he was a married man?" April asked around the lump in her throat. Her palms got clammy, and her breath caught in her chest. "This is too much information for one night. It makes me want a double shot of whiskey to calm my nerves."

"Well, I want to know, and he's not even my father," Flynn said as his thumbs flew on the phone's keyboard. "I'm sorry, April."

"What?" April was suddenly hungry for information about this Lucas Green.

Flynn read from his phone. "I found an old obituary dated thirty-one years ago. 'Lucas Green, sixteen years old, of Paris, Texas, was killed when a drunk driver struck him as he was walking to town, two days before his junior year began. He leaves behind his foster parents, Lola and Melvin Sully, and two foster sisters, Crystal and Jamie Davidson, ages four and six.'"

"Good grief!" Nessa gasped. "Aunt Rachel was pregnant, the father of her baby was killed, and she had to live here with her super-religious mother. What a mess."

Tears flooded April's cheeks, dripped off her jaw, and left wet dots on her T-shirt. "I never knew him or even his name, so why do I feel grief for him now? Why didn't Nanny Lucy tell me these things?"

Nessa draped an arm around April's shoulders and gave her a hug. "I'm sorry, but maybe Rachel refused to tell her who your father was until you were born, or since he was already dead . . ."

April laid her head on Nessa's shoulder. "Dead, alive, married with six other kids. I deserved to know."

"Yes, you did," Flynn agreed. "Even if she didn't tell you until . . . Hey, when I scrolled down, there's a picture of Lucas. It's a newspaper print, but at least you can see what he looked like." He handed the phone over to April.

She held the phone at the right angle to get the best picture and cocked her head to the side. "He was just a kid, but then so was my mother. I wonder if Nanny Lucy even knew they were dating, or how they got to know each other, since he was from Paris."

"I'll see if I can find out for you," Flynn said. "I bet he was origi-nally from this area, and when he got put into foster care, they sent him to Paris. But I promise, I'll try to get some answers for you."

"Thank you," April sighed. "I appreciate that, Flynn."

"No problem," he said as he picked up another picture and handed it to April. "Look, here we are, all three of us. I remember when this one was taken. Nessa is still crying because we'd just buried Waylon number one."

Nessa reached into the suitcase and brought out a small pink diary with a key dangling from a faded blue ribbon tied to the clasp. "Was this yours?" She offered it to April.

"Never saw it before, and never had a diary. Do you think it was my mother's?" April handed the phone back to Flynn and took the diary.

"Only one way to find out. Open the thing." Nessa put the package of pictures she'd been looking at back in the suitcase.

April slipped the key into the lock, but it broke off when she twisted it. She was on the verge of throwing it across the room when Flynn took it from her hands, pulled out a pocketknife, and sliced through the pink leather strap.

"There you go," he said. "If it belonged to your mother, you might find something in there to bring you closure about her relationship with your father."

"Thanks." April opened the book and read out loud. "'I am Lucy Anne Anderson, and my mother gave me this diary for my sixteenth birthday. The first thing I want to say is that I'm in love with Everett O'Riley. My mother wants me to like Ernest since he's such a good boy, but my heart belongs to Everett.'"

She tossed the diary over onto Nessa's lap. "Oh, my gosh. It's Nanny Lucy's. She'll haunt me if I read any more of that thing. You read it."

Nessa flipped through it. "There's writing all the way to the last page. On that one she writes that she buried Everett that day, and that she didn't shed a tear. She'd gotten the bad boy that she wanted and had paid the price for it."

"I guess if Grandpa was a bad boy, then that's where my dad got his genes," Flynn said.

Nessa turned a few pages back, and all the color left her face. "Oh. My!"

"What?" Flynn asked.

She took a deep breath and read:

God is going to punish me for what I have done. I did it out of anger, and I deserve whatever God lays on me. I just hope I'm not punished through my boys for it. Isaac is so much like Ernest. Please God, let him be a man of God. Matthew is already showing signs of following in his father's footsteps, so I don't have much hope for him.

"What did she do?" April couldn't imagine her pious grandmother doing anything that God would deem a sin.

Nessa scanned a few more pages and then read:

I'm pregnant, and there's no way that this child belongs to Everett. It serves him right for cheating on me all these years. I knew there would be consequences for my actions, but why did it have to be this way? I have teenage boys, and I'm in my midthirties. I don't want this child, but I can't, in all good conscience, get rid of it.

"My mother didn't belong to Grandpa?" April's voice sounded like it was coming from a deep well in her own ears. The room began to spin, and she reached out to grab the leg of the coffee table.

"Evidently not," Flynn said. "That explains why Nanny Lucy was so hard on herself and on you. She viewed both you and Rachel as retribution for her committing adultery."

"Does she tell who my grandfather is? Please don't tell me it's D. J. Devereaux. I don't think I could face Jackson if it is." April covered her face with her hands.

"Why not? You don't have a crush on him, do you?" Nessa asked.

"No, but we are neighbors, and he seems like a good man," April answered. "He doesn't need to know that the uncle he adored had an affair with another man's wife."

Nessa flipped through several more pages and finally read:

Rachel was born today, and her father doesn't even know that she exists, and never will. He's my best friend April's husband, and they've moved to El Paso. April can't have children, and wants a family so badly. It's not fair. I have her husband's child and don't want it, but I'll raise the baby, even though I never wanted another child, especially a girl.

April's quick intake of breath caused both Nessa and Flynn to turn toward her. "What a mess! No wonder she got so mad at me when I looked in that closet. This is a lot to take in all at once. I know my father's name, and I have a grandfather. I wonder if he's still alive."

Flynn flipped out his phone again, then put it back in his pocket. "We don't even know the man's first or last name. All we know is that he was April's husband."

Nessa scanned through several more pages and then read:

I was the maid of honor at my best friend's wedding today. She seems happy with Joseph Wilkes, but that man has a wandering eye, just like my Everett. We'll pay the price for falling for handsome bad boys. I just know it.

Tears flowed down April's face. "I didn't have much of a chance, did I?"

Flynn grabbed his phone again and looked for obituaries in and around El Paso. "I found him. Joseph Ray Wilkes died two years ago at the age of eighty-three. He was survived by his wife, April Wilkes, and all the many children that they fostered over the years after they moved to El Paso."

"I lived in El Paso for a year or two," April whispered. "I wonder if he or his wife ever came into the café where I waitressed. I might have waited on one or both of them and not even known I was looking at my grandfather."

"Does any of this help you?" Flynn asked as he picked up more pictures and then found an old, yellowed newspaper.

"It must seem a little like a dream," Nessa said.

"More like a nightmare." April's words came out breathy, and her voice hardly sounded like her own.

"This is the paper with Grandpa's obituary in it," Flynn said. "It just says that he worked for the Missouri Pacific Railroad and gives the dates of his birth and death and tells who survived him. It mentions that he had a twin brother who preceded him in death."

"So there was the wild-boy twin who was our grandfather, and the good-boy twin who died young, and my father is the image, both naturally and spiritually, of Grandpa's twin brother," Nessa said.

"He wasn't my real grandfather." April wiped at her tears.

Nessa gave her another hug. "We're all cousins no matter who our grandparents are."

"How on earth did Nanny Lucy get to be so religious and God-fearing?" Flynn asked. "She had to have a little bit of rebellion in her to go against her parents and marry the ornery twin. Let alone have Rachel."

"It was the tornado. Think about the timing. The storm came right before she and Grandpa got married, and that turned out to be a disaster, and then there was another storm when Rachel gave birth to April," Nessa said. "She must have related the storms, both physical and mental, to bad times in her life." She flipped through the diary again, found the place, and read: "'I was so afraid when that thing went over our heads that we would die, I promised God I would go to church every time the doors were open, and I would raise whatever children that God saw fit to give me and Everett to respect Him.'"

"Whew!" Flynn wiped his forehead in a dramatic gesture. "I vote that this is enough for tonight. Let's go to bed and sleep on what we know before we go digging any deeper into that closet."

"Amen." Nessa laid the diary back in the suitcase. "I'll just straighten up the kitchen a bit before I turn in."

April placed the birth certificates back into the suitcase and closed the lid. "I'll take care of the cleanup. I won't be able to sleep for hours anyway."

"I won't argue tonight." Nessa covered a yawn with her hand.

After her two cousins had gone down the hall to their rooms, April stared at the suitcase for a few more minutes. If Nanny Lucy had known that she was going to die, would she have destroyed what was in it? Or had she left it on purpose so that they would understand why she had been the way she was?

"Who knows?" She finally stood up and headed to the kitchen to wash the dirty dishes. "I had a father, and I had a grandfather. I wonder how my life would have been different if they would have been part of it."

Chapter Fourteen

essa awoke with a start and sat up so fast that the room did a couple of spins, and then she realized that she had been dreaming. She wasn't in a king-size bed, and there wasn't a bottle of wine in a silver cooler sitting on a glass-topped table across the room. For a split second she was disappointed that Jackson wasn't there with her. After a kiss that had left her wanting to drag him off to the creek for sex under a tree, one part of her would love to have spent the night with him. The other part reminded her that doing something like that would create great big problems.

Oh, yeah, what kind of problems? the niggling voice in her head asked.

The kind that would make it awkward for us to work together or even be around each other as neighbors, she answered.

"It was just a dream, that's all, one that can't ever come true," she whispered as she threw back the covers.

She slung her legs over the side of the bed and tried to shake the dream from her head, but it didn't work so well. She knew the excitement of that first time having sex with a guy, and then the pleasure of cuddling up next to him in the warm afterglow. The trouble was, she had inherited a few of the same genes that made Flynn go from woman to woman. She liked the fun of the first date, the second one, and then sex on the third date, but then after that she always began to find something wrong with the guy, especially when he was an overbearing jerk like her last boyfriend. But it seemed like those were the kinds who came into her life. Maybe they got a kick out of trying to tame her sassiness, and when they couldn't, they moved on or cheated.

"I will own my commitment issues," she said as she got dressed for the day and headed to the kitchen. "And I've only had a few relationships that ever made it to the third date."

April was busy putting the sofa bed to rights. Her thin shoulders slumped, and she had bags under her eyes. Nessa crossed the room and wrapped her cousin up in her arms. "You didn't get much sleep, did you? Finding out that Nanny Lucy wasn't perfect is tough on me, but I can't imagine what this information overload about your father and biological grandpa is doing to you."

"Thanks for that." April bent to lay her head on Nessa's shoulder. "And no, I didn't sleep well at all. I still keep expecting to wake up in my car, or in my apartment when I could afford one, and find out this is all a dream. That some worthless man I've let con me into moving in together is going to come through the door at any time demanding I give him my last ten bucks so he can go buy cigarettes and beer."

"Flynn and I will help you get through this, April." Nessa gave her shoulders a gentle squeeze. "I smell coffee. Thanks for getting it started. Let's put all this in a box and close the lid, toss it in the back of our minds for a little while, and make breakfast."

April took a step back and finished folding the covers. "No problem. It's actually the second pot. I've been up for a couple of hours. I read through the entire diary while I drank the first pot by myself. I got to admit, I'm a little jittery."

"Then we better get some breakfast going to counteract all that caffeine." Nessa crossed the living room and dining area and opened the refrigerator. "So what else did you find out in the diary? I only read a few parts of it. Did you discover anything else that would shock us as bad as what we read last night?"

Before she could answer, Flynn arrived, poured himself a cup of coffee, and sat down at the table. "Find out what?" he asked.

"April's been up for a while, and she read all of Nanny Lucy's diary," Nessa answered as she broke eggs into a bowl.

"I started on the first page and read all the way to where she stopped writing." April's tone sounded hollow, as if she were reciting something for a school project. "The first few months of her marriage were pretty good, but then she got pregnant, and . . ." She paused. "Do I call him Grandpa even though he wasn't mine?"

"Call him whatever you want," Flynn said. "He's been your grandfather for more than thirty years, so it would be weird to me and Nessa if you started calling him Everett."

"Things started to fall apart while she was pregnant. I wonder if the pregnancy hormones triggered depression. I don't know anything about that illness or what brings it on. She did write that she had made that vow to God when the tornado hit this area, and that God wouldn't be happy with her if she divorced her husband. She was married to a man who was constantly looking at other women and even telling her how pretty they were when she felt like an ugly elephant. She had Uncle Isaac and was pregnant again when he was just a few months old, and all this before she was twenty years old. I thought I had it bad, but poor Nanny Lucy drew the short end of the stick all the way around," April said.

Nessa tossed a slice of ham into a cast-iron skillet and made toast while it cooked. "Did she ever say anything about all that to you?"

April shook her head. "But the more I think about it, the more I realize that she was lashing out at herself, not me. It sounds crazy, but it helps."

"Grandpa wasn't a very nice person," Flynn said, "but my question is, If he was such a womanizer, why did she stay with him? She was so independent and sassy that it's hard for me to imagine her putting up with that crap."

"She wrote that she'd made two vows." April set the table while she talked. "One was to God that she would go to church, and the other was to love Everett O'Riley in sickness and health and for better or worse. In order to keep her vow, I guess, she figured that she had to stay with him even if it was mostly for worse."

"Dad has vowed that same thing several times," Flynn said. "I guess saying the words means about as much to him as it did to Grandpa."

"Did her affair with Joseph Wilkes last very long?" Nessa asked. "Saying that about Nanny Lucy sounds so wrong. As if I'm already condemned just for asking."

"About a month, from what I read," April said. "She felt guilty about betraying her friend. But at the same time, Joseph told her she was beautiful and even brought her flowers when they met in secret. She just wanted someone to love her, and to *see* her. I don't think Grandpa ever really looked at her after they were married. He didn't compliment her or say nice things about her. She did write that she was glad when Joseph and April moved away so the affair would end. She didn't have the power to stop it, and yet she was cheating on her best friend as well as her own husband."

"Did she love him?" Nessa asked as she poured eggs into a skillet.

April shook her head. "I don't think she was capable of love after the way Grandpa broke her heart. But knowing all that takes a load off my shoulders. How do all y'all feel?"

"I've been just like him," Flynn whispered as he pushed back his chair and helped bring the food to the table. "But by damn, I don't have to continue to be that way. I *can* and *will* get my life turned around. I owe it to all women, like Nanny Lucy's friend, the older April, to make things right. I haven't been a decent guy, but I intend to do my best to change that. I actually came here for just that reason."

"Yes, you can, and I've got faith you will!" Nessa replied. "From what Nanny Lucy wrote, our grandfather didn't want to change. Makes me wonder why he even married her to begin with, or if things would have been different if Nanny Lucy hadn't made that vow about church."

"Who knows? The past can't be changed, but the future is another matter." April smiled.

A surge of love flowed from Nessa when she realized that April's eyes didn't look nearly as haunted as they had before. "I was worried that all this would send you over the edge for sure, but it seems to have made you stronger."

"I think it just might have." April bowed her head. "I'll say grace this morning. For the first time in my life, I truly feel like I have something to be grateful for."

❖　❖　❖

As usual, Flynn took his place between the two women and picked up his needle to start his section of the quilt. He would much rather be helping Jackson make some piece of furniture, or at the very least sanding one, but the truth was that he was getting more curious every day about what was in that hope chest. If Nanny Lucy left a diary lying about with practically her whole life story in it, then what would they find in the hope chest?

"I'm seeing more of a pattern here." He pointed to a section they were working on that day. "The quilt actually starts back here at the beginning when we were babies. I bet the first squares came from blankets that she made for us when we were born. Then there's a row or two from when we were toddlers. The first ones we actually recognized are right there"—he moved his finger back a few rows—"where we remembered the first-day-of-school things. Today I'm seeing a scrap from a shirt she made for me when I was about nine. I wanted to go to the beach so I could see the ocean, so she made me a Hawaiian shirt—at least that's what I called it. You can see the palm trees and part of the parrot in this square."

"You're right," April said. "Look ahead at some of the other squares. This whole quilt is made from remnants of the things she made for us. I didn't even know she kept them. Hey, there's a square with a stain on it! I remember when I spilled the communion wine, or I guess I should say grape juice, on that dress when I was about twelve years old."

"And there's one with a smear of mustard that I got on my blouse when she let us roast hot dogs over an open fire out in the yard. She fussed because it had dried before she got it in the washer and the stain didn't come out," Nessa said.

"That last row is the year we were all fifteen. Remember she made us matching shirts? I see part of the material over there," Nessa said. "But why would she save bits of all those things all these years? We've all just turned thirty-one. Some of this stuff has to be as old as we are."

"I think it's her way of letting us know that she loved us," April said.

Flynn couldn't believe she'd said that, not after learning so much about her relationship with Nanny Lucy the night before. "Why would she treat you like she did if she loved you?"

"All she had was her quilting. There she was, saddled with a miserable lifestyle she didn't want," April said. "Kids and grandkids that disappointed her and made her remember her sin. Her husband quit paying attention to her when she got pregnant, so that had to affect her, too. Uncle Isaac wanted to please her, so he went into the ministry, but I wonder if he truly loves what he does. Uncle Matthew is constantly looking for love. My mother probably just wanted someone to show her affection."

Complete silence filled the shed for a full minute. Flynn couldn't think of a single word to say, because April was right. His father was constantly looking for love and never finding it, just as Flynn had done.

Finally Nessa nodded. "You probably hit the nail right on the head, April, but I'm wondering what Nanny Lucy might have done with her life if she hadn't been dealt such a raw deal. Her sewing is so good, I wonder if she might have been a home economics teacher."

April held up both palms. "There are no buts here, Nessa. I can read, and a lot of what I read in self-help books is beginning to make sense now. We can't go back and redo or undo the past, but we don't have to let it define us, like it evidently has Uncle Isaac and Uncle Matthew and even my mother when she was alive, right along with all three of us."

Flynn went back to stitching. "My mother made the comment once that my father changed when she got pregnant with me. That scares the bejesus out of me. What if I break this gene thing that got passed from our grandfather to my dad and now to me, only to find out that I can have a meaningful relationship, but then I don't like my wife when she gets pregnant?"

"When does Uncle Matthew get tired of his women?" Nessa asked.

"Well, it's sure not when one of them gets pregnant. He had a vasectomy as soon as he could. Mama told me that when I asked if she thought Dad would have more children," Flynn answered.

"Think back," April said. "What's the longest he's ever stayed with a woman?"

"My mother, I guess. He was with her about six years after I was born, but he wasn't faithful." Flynn frowned. "The rest of his marriages have lasted about two years; then he's off on the chase again. You know"—he paused a moment before he went on—"I just bet that's why she treated my mama like a daughter, and the rest of her family so horrible. She kind of bonded with Mama because of her own past."

Nessa snapped the fingers on her left hand. "You're probably right about that, and it's the chase, like you said before. I bet that's what Grandpa liked, too. He liked the excitement of the chase, then the first little while of the affair or relationship, then he got bored. Nanny Lucy was just a phase that he went through. I hate to say that."

"From what I read, he had to marry her to get into bed with her. She'd never been with a man when they married," April said. "If he liked the chase, then I guess the only way he could win with Nanny Lucy was to marry her."

"Sixty years ago, that wasn't uncommon," Nessa said. "Not even around thirty years ago, because Mama says that she and Daddy were both virgins. Of course she added, 'just like God declared they should be.'"

Flynn chuckled.

"What's so funny?" Nessa turned to glare at him.

"I bet you got the talk about how it would be so much better if you abstained until you got married, right? I can just hear Uncle Isaac drilling that into your head. The idea of him trying to talk you into anything hit me as humorous," Flynn answered.

Nessa raised her eyebrows and nodded in agreement. "It was Mama who gave me the talk. Daddy would never discuss sex with me. He picked out a husband and wanted me to get married the summer after I graduated, but I refused. That came close to causing a war."

"Nanny Lucy was proud of you for doing that," April said.

"Really?" Nessa leaned forward to look past Flynn at her cousin on the other end of the quilting frame.

"Truth." April laid a hand over her heart. "I was jealous that she bragged on you for standing up for what you wanted. But then I was angry with her at the same time for not being proud of *me* when I stood up for what *I* wanted."

"We really are a screwed-up bunch, aren't we?" Maybe the happy-ever-after kind of love was just a myth perpetrated by romance books and TV shows. Even in his head that sounded like psychobabble, so he put it out of his mind.

But it didn't stay gone very long. As soon as they finished their morning quilting and went their separate ways to do other things before lunchtime, Flynn headed down the path to the waterfall. When he was sure neither of his cousins had followed him, he sat down on the grass with his back against a scrub oak tree and called his father.

"Hey," Matthew answered on the second ring, "did you change your mind about being my best man and about running from who you are?"

"No, and I'm not running *from* something, Dad, but running toward a better life. I do have a couple of questions about Nanny Lucy," Flynn told him.

"Fire away, but you've got to remember that I moved away from Blossom as soon as I graduated from high school. One of my older friends got me a job in the oil field business down around Austin, and I only went back to visit Mama for holidays," he said, "and then only if I knew Isaac wouldn't be there. I got sick and tired of his preaching at me when I was a teenager. I sure didn't want to listen to him list my sins when I was an adult."

"Did you know that your father was a womanizer?" Flynn asked.

"Oh, hell, yeah!" Matthew laughed out loud. "Everyone knew that he chased skirts, even Mama. They had some hellacious arguments about that when me and Isaac were kids. Seems like we were about twelve and thirteen when he started spending most of his nights on the sofa. I guess they tried to make it work one more time, though, because Rachel came along."

Flynn could feel the hard bark of the tree pressing into his back, but he didn't shift positions. "Did you ever feel like Nanny Lucy loved Isaac more than you?"

"That was a given, too. She always said that he was a good boy like Uncle Ernest, and I was the bad child like my father. I guess I proved her right, didn't I?" Matthew's chuckle crackled like an icicle in a child's hand. "I didn't want to end up like Daddy. I wanted Mama to love me like she did Isaac, but I got told that so much that I figured, 'What the hell. I've got the name; I'll just prove her right.'"

Sweat rolled down Flynn's face and dripped off his jaw. Was he fooling himself into believing that he could change the course of nature?

"How did that make you feel?" Flynn asked.

"After a while I didn't really give a damn," Matthew answered. "What brought all these questions out anyway? You never asked me anything like this before."

"We've just been talking a lot about her. Moving into the house has brought back memories. I wondered how you felt about the way things were done when you were here," Flynn said.

"It was life. I didn't whine or pout because I wasn't the favorite. I'm like Dad. Isaac is like Mama. Nothing could change that. It's just the way things are, and she reminded me every day of it," Matthew said. "You need to get out of there, Son. That place isn't healthy."

"I like it here, and I've got a part-time job that takes me away from the house in the afternoons. I'm hoping it turns into a full-time job later," Flynn told him. "I'm helping Jackson Devereaux build furniture."

"That's ridiculous." Matthew's voice shot up and got a lot shriller. "You're trained to manage oil rigs, not piddle around with junk like that."

Flynn hadn't expected much support, not when his father had always been affiliated with the oil business in one way or another. "I have found that working with my hands is relaxing. For the first time in ages, I whistled on the way home yesterday evening."

"And just how many women are you going to meet working out there in the sticks? You're thirty-one years old. It's time for you to settle down. Remember that you are the last living young O'Riley in our family. Having a son to carry on the family name is on your shoulders," Matthew fussed at him. "Marry a good woman, have a child or two or three until you get a boy, and then . . ."

Flynn butted in before his dad could finish: "And then leave her like you did."

"I'm sorry that you don't like the genes you got, Son. And if you want to change, then I wish you nothing but the best," Matthew said, "but you do need to remember that you really are the last O'Riley male in the family. I promise I'll quit giving you hell about turning your life around if you'll just keep that in mind."

"I appreciate that, Dad, and I never thought about being the only male heir," Flynn said. Talk about a burden! Not only was he trying to turn his life around, but now he had to think about perpetuating the family name.

Maybe it would be best if the O'Riley name died with me, he thought.

"Well, think about it, and the best of luck to you in finding a good woman and staying with her for fifty years. Your Mama was a good woman and deserved better than she got. Maybe when you figure things out, you'll be more like her than me," Matthew said. "I've got to go now. Delores needs me to look at a wedding venue. It would be nice if you'd come to the wedding, even if you are too stubborn to be my best man again."

"We'll see how things go." Flynn felt like he was becoming more like his mother, and he liked the difference it was making in his life. Just a little more work, and maybe, just maybe, he would be ready to really fall in love for good.

"Bye, then," Matthew said, and he ended the call.

Flynn put the phone back in his shirt pocket. "Well, how about that? I can't believe that my father admitted that Mama deserved better."

❖ ❖ ❖

April was fifteen minutes early to work, but she sat in the car for a while, trying to still her mind. It had done nothing but run in circles since the night before. Finally she pushed open the door and inhaled the hot air as she crossed the gravel parking lot.

Now I understand why Nanny Lucy was the way she was, but why couldn't someone love me unconditionally in my life? she asked herself as she opened the door into the clinic.

"I'm so glad you're here. I've got a chamber of commerce meeting." Maudie already had her purse thrown over her shoulder and was heading for the door. "I'll be back in an hour."

"Yes, ma'am," April said, and then she headed back to the shelter area. "Good morning, my pretties." She took a fluffy yellow kitten out of the first cage. The little thing cuddled down in her arms like a baby and began to purr.

"I love you," she whispered.

The kitten purred even louder.

"And you love me no matter how bad I messed up in the past." She almost smiled.

She sat down in the rocking chair with the kitten, and in minutes all the stress left her body. She began to hum a lullaby, and the kitten closed her eyes. This was truly the life—knowing that a little homeless kitten loved her so much it could trust her.

"Someday you'll have a wonderful home, and the people there will pet you and play with you, but until then, we need to get your cage cleaned," she whispered as she stood up and laid the sleeping kitten on the chair.

Someday you will have the same, the voice in her head said.

I'd be happy if I could just have a family of my very own. April sighed and then got busy taking care of the animals. But she hummed one tune after another the rest of the afternoon. The troubles she had brought to work with her disappeared one by one until, by the end of the day, she was happier than she'd ever been.

Chapter Fifteen

*F*or a few days, Nessa put the idea that her grandmother was not perfect out of her mind and dived into finishing one quilt top and starting another. She listened to the older country-music playlist on her phone as she worked so that she wouldn't think about what she had read in the diary. Every evening she took a walk to the waterfall and spent a couple of hours trying to make up her mind whether to go back to Turkey and teach another year or stay in Blossom. If she went back, maybe April would finally come to grips with her demons and go back to her own bedroom. Sleeping in the living room didn't give the poor girl a bit of privacy.

She must have been trying to make up her mind once and for all the night she dreamed about that messy closet for the second time. Nanny Lucy was in her dream, telling her that answers were in the closet; then she faded away in a gray fog. The next day, when Flynn and April left for their jobs, Nessa gathered up half a dozen boxes from the garage, popped them into shape, and taped the bottoms.

"Okay, Nanny Lucy, let's go find all the answers so you can rest in peace. If you've got any more secrets or anything else to keep chipping away at the pedestal that I had you on, let's get it over with." She sighed when she opened the door. Where to begin was the big question. Nanny

Lucy had always said that everything had a place, so what had happened here? Nessa stared at the messy closet and shook her head slowly.

"Might as well drag it all out and then sift through it," she muttered as she got started.

Pulling the stuff on the closet floor out into the hallway, she realized that there was an order to the chaos. She found one pink rubber flip-flop, a ziplock bag full of small items like ponytail holders and barrettes, and one Cinderella sock—all items that she'd left behind when she was a little girl. She wrote Flynn's name on one box, April's on another, and her own on a third, and then sorted the coloring books, puzzles, and all their old memories into the right places.

The stuff on the first and second shelves seemed to belong to Nanny Lucy's children, and Nessa had to guess at a few things, but most of the items didn't leave much doubt. She wrote Matthew's name on the last empty box. Matthew's toy guns with his initials on the belt went into the one labeled for him. Rachel's Barbie dolls went into hers. Isaac's first little New Testament went into his box.

When Nessa reached the top shelf, where the suitcase was stored, she had to bring a chair from the kitchen to stand on. There was very little on the shelf—an old railroad hat and a tiny box that held two gold wedding rings. What had Nanny Lucy thought when she put those rings away? Had she been relieved that she didn't have to keep up the farce of being married to a cheater, or had it made her sad? Nessa carefully opened the suitcase and added those two items to it and then carried everything, box by box, out to the garage and stacked the boxes up in one corner.

"The quilt tops were on top of the suitcase," she said as she went back into the house. "The hat was Grandpa. The quilts were you." She had picked up the chair to bring it back to the kitchen when she noticed the corner of something yellow sticking out from the bottom of the top shelf. She set the chair down, held on to the back of it, and stood on it again. Sure enough, there was an envelope stuck in the crack between the shelf and the wall. She yanked it free, got down off the chair, and then sat down.

She turned it over and over in her hands. There was no name on the front of the envelope, but it was sealed. How a corner had gotten stuck was a mystery because the thing was downright hefty. Hoping that it was a long letter from Nanny Lucy explaining more about her decisions, she ripped into the paper, and hundred-dollar bills tumbled down onto the floor.

"Why did you hide this money?" Nessa frowned. "And in that closet, of all places. Were you saving up so you could divorce Grandpa?"

Nessa counted the bills as she picked them up—twenty-four in all. Then she noticed that the date on them was the previous year. She drew her brows down in a deep frown and carried the money to the kitchen. "Are you testing me or whoever cleans out the closet? I'll share this with Flynn and April, but why did you put it up there unless . . ." Nessa clamped a hand over her mouth. "You knew you were sick, didn't you? You put this money there for us grandkids to find. This was probably the last of your quilting-business money."

She stared down the hallway at the empty closet and then looked toward the living room. "On the outside, you were prim and proper and God-fearing. But on the inside, you were like this closet—messy and locked up—and you knew your family was all in a jumble, too."

She put the chair back where it belonged, laid the money on the dining room table, and was about to leave the house when Waylon came wandering down the hallway. "I wish you could talk to me," she told him, "and tell me what was going on here those last months before she died. I guess I'll never know what she was thinking when she put that money up there on the shelf. Do you think she was really losing her mind, like my dad says?"

The cat meowed loudly, jumped up on the sofa, and curled up to take another nap.

"A lot of help you are," Nessa said. "I'm going to the falls to try to figure out why she put money away on that shelf. Did she really leave it for us cousins, or was she up there hiding things and just tucked the envelope away?"

When she was halfway there, the noise of tires crunching gravel told her that April was home. That meant Flynn would be there in a few minutes, but Nessa didn't care. There was a slow cooker of stew on the counter, and they were both adults. They could make their own supper, and she would eat when she got back.

When she reached the water, she kicked off her flip-flops and waded out into the cool water until it came up to the edge of her cut-off denim shorts. She was deep in thought about her grandmother when a big splash startled her so badly that she whipped around to see what was going on. Tex was swimming toward her, and Jackson was taking off his shoes at the edge of the creek. She took a couple of steps, and then her foot landed on a slippery rock and she lost her balance. On instinct, she sucked in a lungful of air just before the water covered her face, and then she came up sputtering. Jackson was right beside her, a big grin on his face and laughter in his blue eyes.

"I haven't seen you here in a whole week. I thought you were mad at me," he said.

She pushed her wet hair out of her face. "I've been here every evening."

"But did you get in the water or just sit on the bank?" Jackson swam over to the falls and climbed up to the top.

She followed him and sat down beside him. "I swam, but I wore a bathing suit, not my clothes."

"Well, it couldn't be any cuter than what you're wearing now," he said.

"If that's your best pickup line, it's no wonder you're still a bachelor," she told him.

"It's not a pickup line," he protested, "it's the truth. Why didn't you wear your bathing suit tonight?"

"I didn't plan on swimming. I was just coming to the falls to think for a while," she said. "I cleaned out the hall closet today. I always thought my grandmother was perfect. That's why I'm here."

"Because Miz Lucy was perfect?" Jackson asked. "I'm sorry to burst your bubble, darlin', but nobody on this earth is perfect."

"Don't I know it," she sighed. "Did you ever think that someone was?"

"Yep. I always thought Uncle D. J. was the greatest man on earth, but I found out different when I moved in with him," Jackson answered. "He had his faults, and so did Miz Lucy."

"I'm finding that out. When the court settled the issue of the will, I just knew I could find it—whatever it is—here in Blossom, because this is where I was happiest when I was a little girl. I'm beginning to think that whatever it is, it's just an elusive dream anyway."

Jackson nodded. "I feel you, but I'm five years ahead of you. I haven't found 'it'"—he put air quotes around the last word—"but I'm content, and I keep hoping that *it*, whatever it is, will find me if I sit still long enough. I read once that happiness, or *it*—whatever you want to call it—isn't a destination, it's the journey. What makes you think you won't find it here in Blossom?"

"Finding out that Nanny Lucy wasn't perfect has really, really burst my bubble. How can I find what I'm looking for when all these years I was wrong about this place?" she asked.

"Maybe fate brought you here because this is where you will begin the journey to happiness," Jackson said. "Most days I'm happy to make my furniture, go to the craft fairs, have a beer after work and a swim when it's warm weather, but there's still an ache down deep inside my heart that screams at me that there is something more than this," Jackson said. "Then I feel guilty for not being satisfied with what I have and the peace that it brings me."

"Yep," she agreed, and then she dived into the water, swam out to the edge of the creek, and sat down on the grass beside Tex.

"Are you running from me?" Jackson teased before he did a perfect swan dive into the deep water.

Nessa couldn't very well tell him that she was attracted to him and that just sitting beside him jacked her hormones into overdrive, especially when she thought about that kiss they'd shared. Or that she wondered if he had something to do with whatever she needed to be happy.

"Nope," she answered.

He got out of the water, tossed his towel toward her, and said, "Use this to dry your hair. Did you ever miss not having siblings?"

"Oh, yeah, I did." She soaked up most of the water from her thick, red hair and then handed the towel back to him. "I always wanted a sister or a brother, but Mama says God thought I was enough for her to handle."

"I have an older sister and an older brother. I was an oops baby, as Mama called it." Jackson took the towel from her, then draped it around his shoulders.

Nessa stole sideways glances at him, catching glimpses of his square jawline and his broad shoulders. But what caught her attention most was the soft black hair on his chest, still dripping with water. She would have loved to be brave enough to reach out and touch it, then run her hand down his sculptured face, look deep into his eyes, and kiss him.

"Did you get along with your siblings when you were younger?" Nessa finally asked.

"They were gone from home by the time I even started kindergarten. I really didn't know them so well until I went to work at the firm, and then"—he shrugged—"we argued a lot—and I mean a lot. My sister didn't think Dad should give me high-profile cases that she felt she deserved and could do a better job with than I could. My brother only just tolerated me even being at the firm."

"Was that the reason you left the business?" Nessa asked.

"No, I left because I was tired of the long hours, the stress, and doing a job that I didn't even like. You said you like kids, so you must like teaching. Think you'll look for a teaching job around here?" Jackson asked.

She shook her head. "I want something different. I want to give making quilts and shipping out kits like Nanny Lucy did a try. I figured out something when I cleaned out that closet. She kept all her feelings and her pain inside, and it was messy like that closet was. Now it's empty and put to rights, so I hope she can rest in peace." She sighed. "I only wish that cleaning out the closet had brought me closure. Maybe I should go to the cemetery and talk to her. That sounds crazy, doesn't it?"

"I haven't been to Uncle D. J.'s grave in a while. Want to go right now?" Jackson asked. "We've still got a couple of hours before it gets dark."

"Yes," she said without hesitation. "Give me ten minutes to change into dry clothes."

He stood up and extended a hand to help her. She wasn't a bit surprised at the sparks that danced around them or at the sudden rise in her pulse rate at the touch of his rough hand on hers. Once she was upright, he dropped her hand, but he walked close enough beside her that she could still feel the heat from his body.

"I'll drive around and pick you up in a few minutes," he said at the fork in the pathway, and then he broke into a jog toward his own place.

Nessa ran the last hundred yards to the house, dashed through the front door, and went straight to her room.

"Hey!" April looked up from the book she was reading. "What's got you in such a hurry? And what's all this money on the table for?"

"I'm going to the cemetery!" Nessa yelled as she closed her bedroom door.

She threw off her wet clothing and dressed in a pair of jeans and a dry T-shirt. There wasn't much she could do with her still-damp curly hair, so she flipped it up on top of her head in a messy bun, applied a little lipstick, and crammed her feet down into a pair of cowboy boots.

April had moved to the porch with Flynn when she made it outside again to wait for Jackson.

"I like those boots," Flynn said. "Got a hot date to go dancing at some honky-tonk?"

"Where are you really going? I know I didn't hear you right," April said.

"I'm going to the cemetery with Jackson," she answered. "I hear him driving up the road now. I'll explain everything when I get home. Take a look at the hall closet. I cleaned it out."

"Are you going to tell me about this money?" April asked.

"We're dividing it three ways. Take your third and just leave mine there," she answered.

"Where did it come from?" Flynn asked.

"The hall closet, and I'd suggest that we go back through whatever you packed up out of the coat closet. I wouldn't be surprised to find more money in pockets or old purses. There's Jackson. We'll talk later." Nessa hurried down the steps and out to the pickup truck.

"Don't do anything I wouldn't do," Flynn teased.

"That gives you a pretty wide range," April added.

Heat filled Nessa's cheeks. She hoped that Jackson thought it was just a flush from hurrying to be ready.

Chapter Sixteen

It's not a date, Nessa told herself as she fastened her seat belt. *If it were a date, he would have opened the door for me, so it's just two friends who are going to the cemetery to visit their loved ones' graves.*

Jackson waved to Flynn and April and then rolled the window up. "Flynn and April would have been welcome to come along with us."

"I didn't invite them," Nessa said. "I want a little time with Nanny Lucy by myself." *And with you,* she added silently.

"I take it that they never did think Miz Lucy was perfect?" he asked as he backed the truck around and headed down the gravel road.

"April didn't, but she lived there. Flynn might have a little bit, but he's fighting his own demons. Neither of them thought she was as perfect as I did, though," Nessa answered.

"The question is, Are you going to get over Miz Lucy falling off her pedestal?" Jackson asked.

"I think so, but it's not going to be an overnight thing. Have you ever heard that song by Miranda Lambert that talks about 'the house that built me'?"

Jackson turned south off the gravel road. "Yes, ma'am. I like Miranda's voice. It's old country. I'm not much for the new alternative stuff."

"April mentioned that song when we were talking. The house didn't really build our parents, but what happened there did, and understanding that helps," Nessa said. "I'm not making a bit of sense."

"More than you know." Jackson drove past Weezy's and made a right turn toward the cemetery. When they arrived, he parked beside Lucy's tombstone. "Did you come visit her the last five years? I keep thinking that we should have met before now."

"I'm ashamed to admit that I didn't come often enough." Nessa's eyes filled with tears, but she blinked them away. Perhaps if she'd come to see her grandmother more, she would have understood more about her trouble and could have helped her. "Were you at her funeral?"

"Yes, but I stayed close to the back. I saw you and Flynn from a distance, but I didn't know if you were April or you, or if Flynn was the grandson or your boyfriend," Jackson answered. "Why didn't you come around more often? Too far to drive?"

"It's hard to explain. I loved coming here, liked the peace I felt in the place, but the older I got . . ."—she paused and tried to think of the right words—"it seemed like I was interrupting Nanny Lucy's lifestyle. An afternoon with me around appeared to wear her out, or even annoy her. We would talk about her quilts, my job, and then she'd begin to look at the clock every five minutes."

She made a mental note to ask Flynn and April if they'd had the same feeling when they came to visit.

"She was a very private person." Jackson nodded. "We had Sunday dinner with her pretty often, and then a game of checkers or dominoes, but by midafternoon I got the feeling she was ready for us to leave."

"Maybe she was afraid she would forget and say something that would reveal her past," Nessa said. "I feel guilty that I didn't come more often than I did. Being here was strange. There was peace, but it was sprinkled with angst, if that makes a bit of sense. Nanny Lucy took that uneasy feeling to her grave with her, and that makes me feel guilty, because it's like I got the peace I wanted at her expense."

"I understand." Jackson nodded.

"Thanks for listening," Nessa said as she opened the truck door and got out. "See you in a little while?"

"Uncle D. J. is over on the other side of the cemetery. Fifteen minutes long enough for you?" Jackson asked.

"For tonight." She waited for him to drive away before she sat down in front of the stone. Most folks who were buried beside their spouses had one tombstone with both their names on it. Sometimes the stone even had their wedding date etched into the middle of the stone and their children's names on the back side. Not so with Nanny Lucy and her husband. They were buried side by side, but they had separate tombstones, and now Nessa understood why.

"I know why you didn't want to share a stone with him, Nanny Lucy. He promised to love and respect you when y'all got married, and we all know how that turned out now." She pulled a few weeds from around the stone. "I'll bring fresh flowers for the vase next time. I need to talk to you, but I don't even know where to start. I cleaned out the hall closet today. We know your secrets, Nanny Lucy. You can rest in peace." She swiped a single tear from her eye with the back of her hand.

"Thank you for letting me think everything was perfect in your life when I was growing up." She blinked back more tears. "I needed that back then, but I'm sorry you had to carry that burden alone so many years. I feel a little silly talking to a chunk of granite, but it makes me feel better. There's something else I need to tell you, Nanny Lucy. Something I'm very excited about. Something that you instilled a love in me for. I'm considering getting into the quilting business and staying in Blossom. Jackson says he'll show me the ropes when it comes to the craft fairs." A soft breeze kicked up, rustling the leaves on the oak tree that shaded Nanny Lucy's grave. If Nessa had been a superstitious person, she would have sworn it was a sign that her grandmother was giving her an endorsement of sorts.

Nessa didn't know what else to say, so she just sat there in the quiet of the cemetery and listened to the birds flitting about in the trees until Jackson drove up in front of the grave. She got to her feet at the same time that he got out of the truck, jogged around the back side of it, and opened the door for her. Maybe it was a date after all, she thought as she stepped up on the running board and got inside.

"Feel better?" Jackson asked.

"Yes, I do," she answered. "But talking to a tombstone feels kind of silly, doesn't it?"

She watched him as he walked around the front of the truck. He would probably have looked exceptionally good in a three-piece suit, but she liked him even better in those tight-fitting jeans and that chambray shirt. She couldn't take her eyes off the muscles that bulged the seams at the sleeves.

He slid in behind the wheel and put the truck in gear. "I felt like that, too, the first time I talked to my uncle. I know he's not there, but it makes me feel good to talk to him. I told him about you three cousins tonight and even let him know that you and I are on our second date."

Nessa raised an eyebrow. "This is a date?"

"I pick you up. We go somewhere. We have ice cream at Weezy's. Everyone sees us out together. I believe that's the definition of a date," he answered as he drove back toward town.

"What if I'd rather have a hamburger at Weezy's?" she asked. "I haven't had supper."

"Me either, and that makes it officially a date. And I'd also love a burger," he answered. "What do you usually do on a second date?"

"Been too long since I had a second one . . ." She stopped. "How is this a second date?"

"Last week I saved you from breaking your leg, and we had a really hot good-night kiss, and I walked you to the door. That's the first date. This is the second." He parked in the café parking lot. "Are all the men in Turkey, Texas, blind or just stupid?" He turned off the engine, unfastened his seat belt, and turned to face her.

"Why would you ask that?" she asked.

"You're a beautiful woman, Nessa O'Riley. If you haven't had a second date in a long time, then there must be something wrong with the cowboys out in that part of Texas." He got out of the truck and opened her door by the time she undid her seat belt.

He thinks you're beautiful, she singsonged in her heart. "Thank you for the compliment, but I imagine the second-date thing is more my fault than theirs. There just wasn't any chemistry, so I didn't see any reason to go any further."

He laced his fingers in hers and slowed his stride to match hers. "Well, then, we must have chemistry between us because we're on a second date."

"These are pretty unconventional dates," she said as they entered the café.

"Aren't those the best kind?" He guided her to a booth with his hand on her lower back.

When she slid into one side, she could still feel the warmth of his hand. No, that wasn't right. His handprint felt like it was permanently branded into her back, and yes, there was chemistry and lots of it. Sparks danced across the tabletop like drops of water on a hot griddle.

"It's been months since I've been in here," he said.

"Why?" She peeked over the top of her menu and tried to calm the flutters in her stomach. "The food is great."

He leaned over slightly. "The waitress, Tilly, keeps hitting on me. She seems like a nice enough person, but I don't want to start something with a woman . . ." He stopped talking when Tilly started toward them.

"What can I get y'all tonight?" she asked. "Hey, you're one of the O'Riley cousins. I remember you from a couple of weeks ago. Why hasn't Flynn called me? Did he lose my number?"

Nessa shrugged. "I really don't know, but we've been very busy." She made a mental note to tease Flynn about it when she got home.

That's not nice, her mother's voice in her head scolded.

No, but he teases me about Jackson, and turnabout is fair play, like you always say, Nessa argued.

"Well, I'll give my number to you to give to him before you leave." Tilly pulled out her pad and pen. "You"—she poked Jackson in the arm with the tip of her pen—"have lost a good chance. I've given you forever to call me, but I see you're more into red-haired ladies. Now it's Flynn's turn. Don't pout or cry. If he doesn't work out, I might still break you two up and make you the happiest man in the state of Texas."

"Do you always tease customers like this?" Nessa asked.

"Who says I'm teasing?" Tilly gave her a broad wink. "Now, what can I get y'all to drink, and are you ready to order?"

"Sweet tea for me, and I'm ready if Nessa is," Jackson said.

"The same to drink for me, and I want a double bacon cheeseburger and fries," Nessa said.

"Just double that, and afterwards we'll share one of your brownie sundaes," he said.

"Got it, and here's my number for Flynn." She tore a page from her notepad, wrote her number and a double heart at the end, and then handed it to Nessa.

"Is she always this forward? I thought it was just because she knew Flynn from way back when," Nessa whispered when the woman was out of hearing distance.

"That's why I steer clear of here." Jackson nodded. "Thanks for being my date tonight, but you do know you'll have to come in here with me anytime I want one of their big, juicy burgers, now don't you? I got to admit, though, I feel kinda sorry for Flynn. Being around that woman would be sort of like dealing with alcoholism and having someone hand him the keys to a fully stocked bar, wouldn't it?"

"Flynn isn't an alcoholic. He's . . ." Nessa slapped her hand over her mouth. "Has he talked to you?"

"A little bit, but I got a lot of his story from Miz Lucy. She said that he was like his grandfather and his father in that he liked to chase women. I got the feeling she didn't care if she saw either Matthew or Flynn very often in recent years," Jackson answered.

Tilly brought their drinks and tapped the paper that Nessa had laid on the table. "Put that in your pocket, woman. I don't want you to forget it." Then she rushed away to wait on another customer.

"He seems to be like his father, but I know *I'm* not like my dad." Nessa picked up the paper and shoved it into the pocket of her jeans. "I strive hard not to be like him, but I don't mind being like Nanny Lucy."

"Why? Don't answer if that's too personal," he said.

"I had to separate what was religion and what was Daddy. It wasn't easy, but I finally figured out that religion isn't the reason my dad is the way he is. That's just his personality. He's controlling, and if he doesn't get his way, he gets angry." Nessa was amazed at how just talking to Jackson took some of the heaviness out of her heart. "But enough about the past. Let's talk about the future. Tell me more about these craft fairs. I can't wait for the first one."

Jackson took a long drink of his tea. "Are you going to have some quilts ready?"

"I found three tops already done in the closet. I have one finished, and I'm working on a second one. As soon as we finish with the one in the shed, I'll start quilting what I've got. I might not get five finished, but is three or four enough for a start?" she asked.

"That's a pretty good start, but you'll sell as many kits as you do quilts. Miz Lucy always had a picture of a finished quilt on the top of the kit. I've often wondered how many folks really got one of those intricate ones sewn up," he said.

Tilly brought out their food, smiled at Nessa when she saw the number was gone, and set down their burger baskets. "Y'all enjoy, and tell Flynn if he doesn't call me soon, I might just bring my kids out to the waterfall to swim."

"You can't do that," Jackson said. "The waterfall is on the Devereaux property, and we've got 'No Trespassing' signs posted everywhere. If we let one person come out there to swim, then we'd be constantly overrun with partying kids."

"Party pooper!" Tilly gave him a gentle squeeze on the shoulder before she left.

"See what I'm talking about?" Jackson squirted ketchup on his fries and handed the bottle to Nessa.

"Oh, yeah." She nodded as she covered her fries with ketchup and picked up a fork. "Does she flirt like that with every guy?"

"I have no idea," Jackson answered. "But I'm sure glad Flynn is taking some of the pressure off me."

❖ ❖ ❖

Jackson had always liked tall blondes with brown eyes and delicate features. Nessa had curly red hair and steely blue eyes that looked like they could see right into his soul, and she barely came up to his shoulder. But he'd thought all week about that kiss they'd shared, and he kept sneaking peeks at her full lips as they ate their burgers. He had told himself that the sparks between them when they had kissed had only been the result of his not having dated or been with a woman in months, but now he was ready to admit that he was attracted to her.

Nessa's knee bumped against his as she slid forward in the seat to reach for the salt, and there was the same electricity between them that he'd felt every time he was in her presence. He couldn't blame the chemistry on abstinence when just the touch of her knee caused a stirring in his body and soul alike.

The lawyer in him weighed the pros and cons of having a relationship with a neighbor who might not even stay in Blossom. The pros were that she was close by, he could see her often, and she was so easy to talk to. The cons were that if things got serious and she moved back to the Panhandle, his heart might be broken, and if there was a bad breakup, things could get really awkward between them as neighbors.

"Penny for your thoughts," Nessa said.

"Do you live in the moment or think about the future?" he asked.

"That's what you were thinking about?" she asked.

He took a drink of his tea. A good lawyer never played all his cards on the first day of a trial. "In a roundabout way. I was thinking about you, but you don't have to find a penny to pay me."

"I spend way too much time thinking about the future. Living in a religious household with a father that looked forward to heaven meant that I'd better be asking for forgiveness for my past, be thankful for the present, and hope for heaven." She finished off the last bite of her burger. "How about you?"

"Living with lawyers all around me, I was trained to always look forward to the future, too," he answered. "Get an education. Become a lawyer and work for the firm. Start a retirement fund. But I've been working on trying to live a little in the moment. We only get today. Yesterday is gone and tomorrow is always a day away."

"Is that a closing statement?" Nessa asked.

"If I was defending a person, it would be." Jackson grinned. "I'd ask the jury to give my client one more chance to enjoy the day and to take time to smell the roses." He thought of all the rosebushes around Miz Lucy's house and how she had taken such good care of them.

Nessa almost giggled. "I'm sorry. You were being philosophical, and it's not funny, but something Nanny Lucy said came to my mind. She was actually talking about some girl at her church who had the attention of all kinds of good boys but settled on a bad boy who got her pregnant. She said that the girl was like a pretty butterfly that had flitted among all the pretty flowers in a pasture and then lit on a fresh cow patty."

"And why is that relevant to what I said?" Jackson frowned.

"That's what I've been doing lately. I've been focusing on the fact that Nanny Lucy fell off her pedestal instead of looking at the pretty flowers that are all around me and the freedom I had when I came here as a child. Does that make sense?" Nessa asked.

"Oh, yes, ma'am," Jackson drawled. "It surely does make a lot of sense to me."

"I've got a home that I don't have to pay rent or a mortgage for, a beautiful waterfall, a way to make a living if I don't want to teach, two cousins that aggravate me at times, but I wouldn't take anything for, and"—she paused and looked right into his eyes—"a new friend I can talk to and who understands me."

Jackson reached across the table and laid a hand on hers. "It took me about a year to realize that I'd landed in a pasture full of flowers. You're getting there a lot faster than I did."

"Maybe it's because I've had a lot more help from my new friend and my cousins than you did." Nessa didn't blink or look away until Tilly stopped at their table.

"I hate to break up a romantic moment, but are you ready to share that sundae now?"

"Yes, we are," Jackson answered without looking up.

"*Was* that a romantic moment?" Nessa whispered when Tilly had walked away.

Jackson squeezed her hand. "I hope so. I'm a whole lot rusty in that department. Did I pass?"

"Guilty as charged." Nessa grinned.

He wiped his brow in a dramatic gesture. "I'll take my punishment like a man, especially if it involves a good-night kiss."

"Well . . ." Her eyes twinkled. "Since this is a second date, and we *are* protecting you from a pushy woman, maybe it would be all right."

Tilly brought their sundae with two spoons and set it in the middle of the table, then focused on Nessa. "I sure wish I knew what you've got that I don't." She sighed.

"Red hair and blue eyes," Jackson answered.

"I could dye my hair and get contacts," Tilly said with a wink. "But I've got a feeling there's more to it than that. Oh, well, I'll just settle for Flynn. Don't forget to give him my number."

Nessa picked up a spoon and dug deep into the sundae. "I promise I will remember." She looked back at Jackson. "So you like red hair, do you?"

"I do on you," he answered as he waited for her to take the first bite.

"Well, then, I'm glad I didn't dye it black like I wanted to when I was a teenager," she said.

Jackson didn't feel like he had to fill the space with words as they finished off the sundae. Simply enjoying a meal and ice cream with Nessa—talking about the past as well as the present and future—was enough.

Tilly came by and laid the bill on the edge of the table, but this time she was in too much of a hurry to flirt. He turned over the edge, figured in a tip, and laid a twenty and a five on the table.

"Are you ready to go?" he asked Nessa.

She slid out of the booth, and he took her hand in his.

"I have to admit I've never been on a cemetery date before," he said as they left the café.

"Me either. I guess neither of us are cemetery-date virgins anymore," she said.

"Was it as good for you as it was for me?" he teased as he opened the truck door for her.

"Absolutely. I doubt another cemetery date could ever compare to it," she joked right back at him.

He drove ten miles under the speed limit and then even slower when he turned off the highway and onto the gravel road, but the trip from Weezy's to the house was still too short. She remembered that she'd wanted those last few miles to fly by when her folks took her to stay with her grandmother in the summers, but now she was wishing for a flat tire or that they would run out of gas. No such luck, though. He parked in front of the house and helped her out of the truck, draped an arm around her shoulders, and walked her to the door. "Thanks for a great evening. I really enjoyed it. Can I call you tomorrow?"

"Of course," Nessa said.

He tipped up her chin with his fist, and the second kiss was every bit as awesome as the first one had been. Heat filled his body when her arms snaked up around his neck, and she tangled her fingers in his hair. He wanted to scoop her up in his arms, carry her back to the truck, and make out with her until midnight, but when the kiss ended, he took a step back. "Good night, Nessa."

"Good night, Jackson." She was as breathless as he was when she opened the door and disappeared into the house.

Sucking on a lemon couldn't have wiped the grin off his face as he drove to his house and parked the truck in its usual spot. Tex waited for him on the porch and followed him into the house. Jackson sat down on one end of the sofa. Tex jumped up on the middle cushion and laid his head in Jackson's lap.

"I just had the most amazing, unusual date," he told the dog as he picked up the remote. "This woman makes me feel special, like I'm ten feet tall and bulletproof, as the old country song says. I don't know why. She just does."

Tex yipped once and stared at the television.

"I know. I know!" Jackson laughed out loud. "You missed watching shows with me when Waylon moved in for those months. How are you going to feel if a lady moves in with me someday?"

Tex growled.

"Not anytime soon, old boy, but for the first time, I'm thinking about it."

Chapter Seventeen

April was surprised to see Stella and Maudie having a cup of coffee together when she arrived at the vet's office that Wednesday afternoon. "Hey, it's good to see you again. Is this the day you volunteer every week?"

"Yep," Stella answered. "I volunteer a day a week, most of the time on Wednesday. Usually my sister, Vivien, and I come together, but the two of us went on a vacation last week up to Branson, Missouri, and she's plumb worn out. But I'm here to help you today. We tried our best to get Lucy to go with us on our little short trips, but she always made an excuse."

Maudie pointed toward the coffeepot. "Help yourself. I was wondering if maybe you could start coming in at eleven next week. Stella's been telling me about the quilt you kids have to finish. When you get that done, would you like to turn this into a full-time job and come in at nine every day?"

April wondered if she'd heard Maudie right. "Are you serious? I would love that."

"I'm very serious. You are a godsend, April. Bending to clean out those bottom cages has gotten to be a real chore for me. Plus, I'll be able to take a whole hour for lunch next week, and when you start coming in at nine, you can help me in the vet side of this place. Know anything about computers?" Maudie asked. "They're a cross for me to bear. I hate inputting the invoices and the animal information."

"I can do that for you. We had plenty to input at the garden center." April's heart thumped in her chest so hard that she wondered if Stella and Maudie could hear it.

"Good, then when you get here next Monday, you can work on that after you get the shelter taken care of. I'm at least three months behind," Maudie said. "Now, Stella, tell me more about Branson before you get back there with the kittens and forget the good parts."

"I'll just get to work." April poured herself a cup of coffee and felt like she was floating on air as she carried it over to the shelter side of the business. She could hear the two elderly ladies talking about the music shows Stella and Vivien had attended and the little nickel-and-dime store in town where they had tried on hats and taken each other's pictures.

"Hello, my pretty babies." She greeted the animals. "How has no one adopted a single one of you since I left yesterday? Taking care of you is so much fun, I'd do this for free," she said as she took a sip of her coffee. Then she set it down on a nearby table and opened the first cage. "Someone is going to come along and take you home one of these days. I'll miss you, but when that happens, you won't have to stay in a cage all day."

"Vivien and I talk to them, too," Stella said as she came into the shelter room. "I'll start cleaning this end of the cat cages, and we'll meet in the middle, if that's all right with you."

April must have had a quizzical look on her face, because Stella grinned and said, "You're the boss, honey."

"No, Maudie is the boss," April argued.

"Not beyond that door over there." Stella pointed. "Maudie says that you're in charge of this place."

"Oh, my!" April gasped. "This is just my second week." She felt like a little girl on Christmas morning.

"I got to tell you, girl, this is the cleanest I've ever seen this place." Stella took a small yellow kitten from a cage and set it on the floor. "You're doing an amazing job."

"Thanks," April beamed. "And I love doing it."

Stella took the water and food dishes out of the cage first, cleaned them well, and refilled them. Then she put in a clean kitty pad. "I expect when Vivien feels up to coming with me that Maudie will want you to spend those days working on the computer stuff. She really hates that. Lucy would be proud of you."

"I don't know about that." A shadow passed over her happiness when she thought of her grandmother.

"Honey, don't judge Lucy too badly. She had a rough row to hoe." Stella stopped long enough to hold and pet the little yellow kitten before she put it back in the cage.

"I know," April said. "I got in on doing some of that hoeing."

Stella clucked like an old mother hen gathering in her chicks. "Me and Vivien tried to help her, but she was bitter toward Everett by the time your mama was born, and even worse when you came along. He wasn't a good man," Stella whispered as if she was sharing something that would bar her chances of ever getting into heaven.

"We found her diary in the hall closet." April wondered if she should have shared that without asking Nessa and Flynn about it first.

"Then you know that he cheated on her all their married life. We were surprised when she got pregnant with Rachel," Stella said. "I guess it was a last-ditch effort to make things work with him. We started the quilting club earlier with hopes that it would help her depression problems, and it did. Pretty soon she was selling quilts and kits and making as much money as Everett did. We tried to talk her into divorcing him, but she said she couldn't because it would bring shame on her boys. In those days, society didn't look on divorce like it does now. Then she got pregnant and he died."

"Rachel didn't belong to Everett," April said. "Did you know that?"

Stella cocked her head to one side and then began to giggle. "Good for Lucy! She finally gave Everett a dose of his own medicine."

"But it cost her dearly. She had a daughter to raise that she didn't want, and then she had to raise me when my mother died. I've lived under that shadow my whole life, Stella." April sighed.

Stella started on her second cage. "No wonder she always said that you were a little lost soul. She wished she had been in a better frame of mind when she was raising you."

"She said that?" April was stunned.

"Yes, honey, she did. Now I know what she was talking about. I can't imagine the guilt that she must've felt. Everett died before you were even born. There she was, a widow with teenage boys and a baby on the way. She should have been grieving, but she probably only felt relief. I know I would have, and then I would have been covered up with guilt for feeling that way." Stella worked as she talked.

"Then she had to deal with my mother as a baby she didn't want, who didn't even belong to her dead husband." April felt a wave of sympathy for her grandmother. "And she couldn't even tell anyone because she thought it was a horrible sin."

"Hello, are we in the right place?" A masculine voice followed the sound of the bell when someone opened the front door to the business.

Stella was closest to the door, so she took a couple of steps and asked, "Are you looking for the vet or the animal shelter?"

"Kittens!" a little girl yelled. "It's my birthday!"

"Then come on back here," Stella said.

The little girl skipped into the shelter, sending her long blonde ponytail flipping back and forth. She stopped in the middle of the room, her big brown eyes wide, and clamped a hand over her mouth. "Look at all of them, Daddy!"

"Hello, I'm Kent Wallace," her father introduced himself, "and this ball of energy is Callie. We're here to adopt a kitten." His green eyes glittered when he looked at the child. He was over six feet tall, had thinning light-brown hair with a sprinkling of gray in the temples, and wore black-rimmed glasses.

April took a step forward and stuck out her hand. "I'm April O'Riley, and this is Stella. We'll be glad to take out whichever kitten Callie wants to play with. That might help her decide. Is it really your birthday?"

"Yes, ma'am. I am six today. Daddy said I can have a kitten for my birthday and that I can even pick it out myself. Ooh, you're pretty—blonde like me!" Callie said.

"Children have no filters on their mouths," Kent chuckled.

"Isn't it a wonderful thing that they are still innocent and honest?" April said.

"I'm naming my first kitten Belle," Callie announced as she continued from cage to cage. "When I get my second one, it will be Cindy after Cinderella."

Kent rolled his eyes and shook his head. "She's got visions of having a cat named after each of the Disney princesses. I don't share her grandiose ideas."

"What's *granny owse*?" Callie asked.

"*Grandiose* means high-and-mighty," Kent explained.

"That's a funny word." Callie went back to checking out the cages.

"One a year until she's eighteen and leaves home for college, and then you inherit the whole lot of them, right?" April asked.

"That's exactly what I'm afraid of." Kent chuckled again. "You related to Lucy O'Riley?"

"My grandmother," April answered.

"I work with Paul Jones at the law firm. I met her several times when they were working on her will. Sassy old girl." He smiled and shook his head.

"She was truly that," Stella agreed. "Callie, do you see one that you want to take out of the cage?"

Callie set her little bow mouth in a firm line. "I like this orange one right here. It told me that it likes the name Belle."

"Little problem there," April said. "That's a boy kitty."

"Show me the girl ones, then," Callie said.

April took her by the hand. "See the pink watering bowls? That says the kitten in that cage is a girl. The blue ones tell us that the ones in those cages are boys."

"Shame on you, boy kitty." Callie shot him a dirty look. "You meowed when I whispered Belle in your ear. I thought that meant you liked it." She bypassed the blue bowls and only stared intently into the cages with pink ones. Finally she poked her finger at a cage that held a longhaired yellow kitten. "Daddy, this one looks like Belle, doesn't she?"

"It's your cat, so you have to make the decision," Kent told her.

In that moment, April coveted a childhood with a father who would take her to an animal shelter and let her pick out a kitten. All she had ever known was a grandmother, who would have told her that Waylon would hate another cat in the house.

"Belle did wear a pretty yellow dress when she went to the ball, didn't she?" April said. "Would you like me to take that one out and let you play with her, or maybe rock her a little?"

Callie nodded very seriously. "Yes, please."

April opened the cage and handed the kitten to Callie, and the yellow ball of fur put a paw up on Callie's cheek. "I think she likes you."

Callie carried her over to the rocking chair and loved on her for a few minutes, then set her on the floor and picked up a long, braided piece of yarn. The kitten looked like a windup toy as it chased after the braid.

"This is the one, Daddy. She loves me." Callie's lower lip trembled.

"Why the sad face if this one likes you?" Kent asked.

Callie wiped away one little tear. "The others look so lonely. We've got a big house and lots of yard. Can't we take them all home with us?"

"No!" Kent shook his head. "Not even your well-trained tear will work today. One kitten is the limit. Now bring your new kitty cat along, and let's get out of these ladies' way." He turned to April. "Are there papers that we have to fill out?"

"Yes, but she's not a bother. We love it when folks come in and play with the kittens."

"I'll be back for y'all later," Callie whispered as she blew them a kiss and followed her father out into the vet side of the clinic to get their adoption papers filled out.

Stella giggled. "You've got your hands full, Kent."

"Don't I know it?" He laughed with her.

April knew she'd never see Callie again. But what if a daughter was part of her new future?

She could hear Callie telling Maudie what name to put on the adoption papers, and asked Stella in a low voice, "Are her folks divorced?"

"No, honey," Stella answered. "Her mama died when Callie was just a year old. Kent has raised her on his own ever since. He adores that child and is such a good daddy. The world would be a better place if there were more men like him."

April didn't know the guy, but she nodded in agreement. Any man who was that kind and sweet to his daughter had to be one of the good ones.

"I'm going to miss that kitten so much," April sighed.

"Poor little thing was half-starved when someone dropped it on the doorstep a couple of weeks ago." Maudie joined them. "It's a good thing that cats and dogs can forgive the ones that treat them shamefully. Would be good if we could be more like them."

April took what she said to heart and thought about it as she drove home that evening. Forgiveness was tough, but she needed to be more like the kitten and just be happy with the good home she had. That took her thoughts to Callie and how much love she'd showered on the kitten. Someday April really did want a child of her own. Thinking of a little blonde-haired girl put a big smile on her face.

"What's got you so happy?" Nessa asked as she motioned for April to take a seat at the table.

"I thought about kidnapping a little girl today and giving her all the kittens at the shelter," April told her cousins as she took her place at the table.

Flynn choked on a laugh. "So you're a kidnapper now? How many cats was that?" He scooped mashed potatoes onto his plate.

"Maybe twenty-five," April said.

"You do realize that none of us sitting around this table have any good role models for parenting, don't you?" Nessa asked her. "We barely know how to take care of Waylon. A little girl and twenty-five cats would be a stretch."

"Yes," April groaned. "But that didn't keep me from wanting to kidnap her and give her all the kittens she wanted. She was so cute and so serious about picking out her cat. And guess what?" She didn't give them time to guess. "Next week I go to work at eleven, and as soon as we finish the quilt, Maudie wants me to start full-time. I'll be working from nine to five thirty, five days a week. Reckon we could do our quilting a little earlier than usual each day?"

"No problem for me. I'm an early riser anyway. Are we all going to continue to live here when and if you two firm up your jobs?" Nessa asked.

"Don't see why not," April answered. "It's working out so far."

"Congratulations on getting more hours," Flynn said. "We're a little more than halfway done with the quilt, so we'll probably have it done in two weeks."

"That's what I figured." April nodded. "And Stella came to help out today. She volunteers with the shelter an afternoon a week. Her sister, Vivien, usually joins her, but she was too worn out after their vacation to come today."

"Who?" Flynn asked.

"Stella," April answered. "Remember the wiry little red-haired lady who brought us the chocolate cake the first day we were here? That's Stella. Her sister is Vivien. They were Nanny Lucy's quilting partners. Stella knew that Grandpa was a womanizer. She said that they started the quilt club to get Nanny Lucy out of a deep depression. No wonder I thought she hated me. Depression is a terrible thing."

"I never saw that in her." Nessa took a roll out of the basket and passed it over to April. "That's why I'm having such a hard time with all this information we've uncovered."

"Shocking, isn't it, that she was a different person to each of us," April said. "But now that I know some of what was on her mind, it makes her actions a little easier to understand."

"Yep," Flynn said, "and gets us closer to understanding our parents, too."

"On another note, the guy that came into the shelter with that little girl was Kent Wallace. He's part of the same law firm that Nanny Lucy used to set up her will. He works with Paul Jones." April slathered her roll with butter. "If I keep eating like this, I'm going to outgrow my jeans."

"You've got a job now. You can buy new jeans, and, honey, you need a few more pounds. I'll help you along—there were jars of blackberries in the cellar, so we're all eating cobbler for dessert," Nessa said.

Flynn groaned. "That's just my favorite pie in the whole world. It's a good thing I've got a job, or I'd be outgrowing my jeans, too."

"Might be a good idea," April chuckled.

"Why's that?" Nessa asked.

"If he didn't look like a movie star, maybe the women wouldn't flock to him," April said, dissolving into giggles.

"Oh, ha ha. But that reminds me," Nessa said. "Tilly gave me her phone number. I put it on the top of the fridge when I got home and forgot to tell you, Flynn. She said that if you don't call her, she might just show up here at the place with her kids. Jackson told her that the falls was off-limits to the public, but she could come to the house. She's the pushiest woman I've ever known, so you'd do well to steer clear of her."

"I'm doing my best." Flynn buried his head in his hands. "Burn that number. I'm not calling her, and I'm steering clear of Weezy's."

April took a long sip of her sweet tea and smiled. For the first time in her life, she was beginning to feel at home. There had never been much laughter in the house when she was growing up. Now it seemed like every time they all got tickled, a little more of the past was washed away by their happiness.

Chapter Eighteen

*H*ave you ever stained a piece of wood?" Jackson looked up from the table saw where he was working when Flynn came into the building.

"No, but I'm willing to learn," Flynn answered, glad to be trusted with another job.

"I've got so many orders that I'm getting behind. I'd sure like it if you could do the finish work for me from now on. I can get the pieces built pretty fast, but the finish takes forever and slows me down." Jackson pointed to a couple of hope chests on a worktable. "You've got those sanded. They're ready to put the dark cherry stain on them. I'll show you how to do the lid on one. It's really easy. Just brush it on until you finish one side, let it set about five minutes to soak up the color, and then use paper towels to wipe it off." He demonstrated as he talked. "Then tomorrow you can put a coat of varnish on each of them."

"That I can do." Flynn was excited to be learning something new. Sanding had taken his mind away from everything and given him time to think. Hopefully, staining would be just as satisfying. "I've done my fair share of painting, and it can't be a lot different than that."

"Not at all. Just keep the strokes even and overlapped, with no runs." Jackson handed him the brush and went back to cutting out more pieces. When he turned off the saw, he turned around and nodded. "Good job there. You've got a job here full-time if you decide to stick around once the quilt is done. And thank you."

"For what? You're paying me to do this," Flynn said.

"Nessa and I had supper at Weezy's when we went to the cemetery. You've taken heat off me and probably the entire unmarried male population of Blossom when it comes to Tilly." Jackson grinned.

"You're welcome, but I'm not getting tangled up with that woman, either. I'll just stay out of Weezy's, and if she comes up in the yard, I'll hide over here." Flynn laughed.

He could see himself in Tilly and wondered if she had ever thought about changing her lifestyle. Did she have a troubled background like he did, or maybe an ex-husband who'd made her feel worthless? "Makes a man wonder what kind of husband she had."

"I have no idea, but I'm glad that Nessa was with me, or I might be the one running and hiding." Jackson chuckled.

"What's your secret?" Flynn asked. "I'm trying to get my life straightened out, not dive into more trouble."

"Stay away from the known spots where women like Tilly will ambush you," Jackson answered. "Bars and Weezy's."

"And church?" Flynn added.

Jackson cocked his head to one side. "You've picked up women in church?"

"One of the best places," Flynn answered. "If you're going to church, they think you're a stand-up guy who would never sleep with them and then not call or send flowers the next day."

"You've been a little bit of a bastard, haven't you?" Jackson asked.

"I learned it from the best. You already know all about my dad. But now I'm doing my best to unlearn it and start over with a clean slate." Flynn looked at the hope chest he'd been working on. It had started out as raw wood, and to get to be a finished product, it had to endure screws being sunk into it, the sanding and staining processes, and then varnish. That was the way his life had been since he'd decided to come to

Blossom and get a new start. It had been a lot and would be even more, a lengthy process from start to finish. Some of it might not be pleasant, but when he was done, he hoped to be more like his mother—like his father had said. "Did you and Nessa have a good time on your cemetery date? Now that's one place I've never picked up a woman."

"Me either." Jackson's grin got bigger. "And that was the first time I ever took a date to the cemetery."

"Not even in high school on Halloween?" Flynn asked.

"We went to the cemetery once on Halloween, but it was just a group of us kids goofing off, not a date with a single girl," Jackson answered.

"Yep, same here." Flynn wiped away the stain on the end of the hope chest. "Nessa came in all aglow and happy. But as a friend, I should warn you that both of you better think about this. You're neighbors, you know."

"Big-brother cousin giving advice?" Jackson asked.

Flynn shrugged. "I'm in no place to give anyone advice on love or relationships. I've had lots of women, but I've never been in love or been in a serious relationship. Things could get weird between you two if they didn't work out. And I'd hate to lose my job here if . . ."

"Noted, and, Flynn, we're adults. I won't fire you if things don't work out. As far as crazy women go, I've got your back. If Tilly comes sniffin' around your place, just come on over here. I've got two extra bedrooms, and there's usually cold beer in the refrigerator. You've always got a hiding place." Jackson picked up a drill and started putting a hope chest together.

"Thanks, man!" Flynn began to brush stain on the front of the hope chest he was working on. He'd had drinking buddies and work acquaintances, but he'd never had a friend who would make an offer like that. He suspected most of his coworkers would have been more than happy to see him get caught.

He sure wouldn't bring in the paychecks he'd gotten used to having if he worked for Jackson, but then, he was living in a place where he had no rent and only had to buy food every third week, had a cousin who was a great cook, and even had a cat—not much was needed past that. Besides, he had a very healthy savings account, and a stock portfolio that wasn't shabby at all. And it was possible, if he was willing to put a little money into the business, that Jackson would someday make him a partner.

❖   ❖   ❖

From all accounts, Jackson was a decent guy. No red flags had popped up when Nessa was with him or when he kissed her. She had dreamed of him and awakened with a smile on her face. Every time the phone rang, her heart skipped a beat, but it had been telemarketers three times and someone who didn't know Nanny Lucy had passed away and wanted a quilt kit shipped to them another time. By evening, Nessa was thoroughly bummed out.

"Chalk up another mistake under my name," she muttered as she left the house for a walk. She'd barely made it to the edge of the yard when April pulled up in Nanny Lucy's car.

"Where are you going? And who died?"

"For a walk, and no one died. I need some time alone. Supper is in the slow cooker and on the counter," Nessa said.

"Anything I can do, other than stay out of your way?" April got out of the car.

"Nope," Nessa answered. "See you later."

"Call if you need to talk or you get lost. I know these woods like the back of my hand." April headed toward the house.

Nessa didn't want Jackson to feel like she was stalking him, so she didn't go to the falls but headed out through the path in the woods to a place she had gone to when she was a kid. Nanny Lucy had told her that the big oak tree that lay across the path had been struck by lightning when Isaac and Matthew were just toddlers, and that the two of them had played king of the mountain on it when they were little boys. Nessa had been fourteen when Nanny Lucy pointed the log out to her, and it had been hard even at that time for her to imagine that her overbearing father had ever been a child, much less a baby. Now, after the way the two men had acted when they'd both shown up at the house, it was doubly hard to imagine them ever playing together.

When she got to the old tree, she sat down on the ground and leaned against the bark. She and her cousins had been more than two-thirds of the way across the quilt when they quit that morning. Soon it would be done, and then they'd know what was in the hope chest, but it mattered less and less to her each day. If it was more money, that was fine, but none of them really needed it now. April and Flynn had jobs, and Nessa would hopefully be selling quilts come fall.

Her phone rang, and when she fished it out of her hip pocket, her father's name popped up. "Hello, Daddy, how are things in Canyon?"

"Busy," he answered. "We're finalizing our plans to go to Israel, and I'm giving you one last chance to join us. That house will be there when you get back. If y'all haven't gotten it squared away by now, then it can wait for your fall break from school. By then, Flynn and April will have given up on it anyway, and you'll have to maintain the old place."

Just like Isaac O'Riley to make judgments like that, she thought.

"April has a part-time job that is turning into a full-time one as soon as we finish with the quilt. Nanny Lucy pieced it together with scraps of clothing she made for us when we visited her, so it's been like going back in time and remembering the good times." Nessa tried to change the subject.

"If there's money in that hope chest, April will be gone the next day, and Flynn won't be far behind her. You can mark my words on that," Isaac said.

"Flynn is working with Jackson Devereaux, our next-door neighbor, in his woodworking business, so he's probably going to stick around, like April does. I've had two dates with Jackson," she said, hoping to force actual steam out of her father's ears.

"You can't seriously be considering giving up a secure teaching job to make quilts and date a Devereaux." Isaac's voice rose to the screech level. "His uncle was strange, a recluse at best. I won't have my daughter dating a man like that. It could lead to something permanent, and your children *will* be weird."

The bark began to bite into her back, so she leaned forward. "Daddy, two dates does not produce little blue-eyed Devereaux babies."

"Don't you get sassy with me, girl!" Isaac yelled into her ear. "Sometimes I wish we'd never let you go there in the summer to stay with your grandmother."

"But you did, and your choice now has consequences. I'm sending in my letter of resignation next week so that my principal will have plenty of time to replace me." She hadn't had any notion of doing that so soon until her father fussed at her, but now that she'd said it, she was content with the decision.

"You'll be sorry," Isaac said, and he ended the call.

"Maybe, but I don't think so." Nessa wiggled, but the pain in her back just got worse and worse even though she wasn't leaning against the old tree anymore.

She heard something behind her and started to stand up. Before she could, Jackson had jumped over the log, grabbed her up by her hands, and ripped her T-shirt off over her head. Then he threw it against the tree, jerked her shorts down off her hips and did the same thing with them.

As he scooped her up and ran, she shrieked. Her flip-flops flew in different directions. She held on to her cell phone with one hand, beat on his chest with the other one, and screamed. "What the hell are you doing? Are you crazy?"

"Fire ants!" he yelled as he dodged low-hanging tree limbs, took his porch steps two at a time, and rushed into the house. He came to a screeching halt in the bathroom and set her in the old claw-footed tub, jerked the shower curtain around it, took her phone from her and laid it on the edge of the vanity, and turned on the water. In seconds, he had stripped his shirt off and was standing in the tub with her.

Jackson lathered up his hands, flipped her dripping, wet hair to one side, and soaped up her back, neck, and arms, then dropped to his knees and did the same to her legs. "Have any crawled under your bra or panties?"

Speechless, she could only shake her head. She was standing in a shower with Jackson Devereaux, both of them next door to naked. His callused hands were like rawhide and silk blended together as they worked over her body a second time and then turned her around to rinse the soap away. "Crawled?" she croaked.

"Are you in shock? There's at least a hundred bites on your back alone. Do I need to take you to the emergency room?" he asked.

Nessa shook her head again. *Bites?*

"Then let's get you out of here and dried off. I've got some salve that Uncle D. J. brewed up that will help them not itch, but you're going to look like you've got chicken pox for a few days." He talked as he slung the curtain back and got out of the tub. "The important thing was to get all of the ants off you and wash the bites down with soap so they won't get infected and turn into blisters."

Nessa stepped over the edge of the tub and onto a brown rug. "Thank you."

Jackson picked up two towels from a stack on an old ladder-back chair and handed them to her. "You're more than welcome. One for your hair and one for your body. I found out a while back that the ants like to build a castle by that old log. Get dried off, and I'll put the salve on you. Are you sure you don't need to be checked by a doctor?"

"I'm sure." Nessa's heart pounded and her pulse raced, but neither had a thing to do with all the ant bites. "I should have looked before I sat down. I thought it was the tree bark biting into my back."

"You've found your voice, so you're probably not in shock." Jackson grabbed up another towel and dried most of his body, then took a jar of ointment from the medicine cabinet and rubbed a little on two bites on his arm. "I got lucky. Only two got me while I was hauling you out of there."

Nessa wrapped a towel around her head like a turban and then dried off her upper body. Today of all days, she was wearing her oldest underwear, but there wasn't anything she could do about that now. "I'm sorry you got bit, too," she said.

"No worries. It's only two. You're the one that they were really angry at. Turn around and let me get at those bites. This really does help. I should have gotten the recipe for it before Uncle D. J. passed on, but at least he left three jars for me." Jackson smeared the salve all over her back.

"That smells like the beach," she said.

"It's the coconut oil that he put in the mixture." Jackson handed the jar to her. "You can take this one with you and put some on your legs in the bedroom right across the hall. I'll hang one of my shirts on the doorknob for you. Just toss your wet underwear out in the hallway. I'll get them in the laundry."

She took the salve from him and picked up her cell phone on the way out of the bathroom. She crossed the hall and closed the bedroom door behind her. There was a twin bed on one side of the room and a dresser on the other, much as in the room where she slept at home.

Home!

The word stuck in her mind. Now that she'd told her father she was quitting her teaching job, Blossom would be home, and was, both in word and in her heart. She peeled her wet underpants down and removed her bra, held the towel up in front of her as she tossed them out into the hall, and grabbed the shirt off the doorknob. Then she applied the ointment to all the bites on her legs and slipped her arms into the red-and-black-plaid button-up shirt. The sleeves were way too long, so she rolled them up to her elbows. She was grateful that the shirt had a long tail and went down to her knees, but she still felt naked with no underwear under the garment.

She opened the door a crack and peeked out to see that her bra and panties were gone. In the distance she could hear the dryer already running. She eased the door open just a little more and stepped out into the hallway.

"Hey, want a beer?" Jackson came out of the bathroom.

"I'd love one, and thank you again for rescuing me," she said.

"No problem. I'm glad I decided to take a walk through the woods rather than going to the falls tonight." He draped an arm around her shoulders. "You must have thought I was assaulting you, but your shirt and shorts were covered in those evil little devils, so I had to get them off you in a hurry."

"Sorry that I pounded on your chest." She smiled up at him.

"I deserved it for not trying to explain, but all I could think about was getting you to a shower and getting you treated so you wouldn't be miserable for days on end. Have a seat and I'll get the beers." He pointed to the sofa in the living room.

She sat down on one end of the well-worn, outdated sofa and scanned the room. Television straight ahead, a scarred coffee table in front of the sofa, and Nanny Lucy's old hope chest over there in the corner.

Jackson returned from the kitchen with two open beers and handed one to her. She pulled the tail of the shirt down over her knees. She could wear a bikini—much to her mother's horror—and not blink an eye, but sitting there with a shirt that covered all of her body except her head and calves made her feel naked.

It's because I don't have my undergarments, she thought.

He set his beer on the coffee table and sat down on the other end of the sofa. "I see you're looking at Miz Lucy's hope chest. From what Flynn says, I may have to give it a home forever."

"You just might." Nessa turned her beer up and took a sip. Then she put the bottle on the coffee table and removed the towel from her hair.

"Just toss it on the table," Jackson said. "You don't ever plan to get married?"

"Nanny Lucy used to say to never say never." She felt the corner of her mouth quirk up—what would she think of all their *nevers* now?

"Then there's a possibility, but maybe not a probability?" He turned and locked eyes with her.

"I guess it all depends on what my heart tells me. I depend on it to steer me in the right direction in matters of love," she answered.

"Fair enough," Jackson said. "Think you'll wind up with the hope chest?"

"I wouldn't even begin to try to answer that." She crossed her legs at the ankles and noticed all the red marks. "I didn't ever have chicken pox. Do you really think this is how they look?"

"I didn't have them, either," he answered, "but my best friend in elementary school had them, and he sent me a picture of his legs and chest, so yep, that's kind of the way they looked."

"Then thank God for vaccines." She picked up her beer and clinked it with his. "Now it's my turn. Do you plan to marry, or are you going to follow in your uncle D. J.'s footsteps?"

He chuckled. "It all depends on how my heart advises me."

"I guess I had that coming," she said. "We probably should talk about whatever this is between us and decide if things will be horribly weird if . . ." She paused.

Jackson shook his head slowly. "Let's live in the moment for a few weeks and promise not to let things get awkward if we decide that we don't like each other."

"I've done passed that point. You're my knight in shining tennis shoes. You saved me from fire ants," she said.

"If I'd been a true knight, I would have saved you before you got bit." He glanced down at her legs.

"I'm not arguing at all, but you did save me from being scarred forever, so it could have been worse," she told him. "What about you, Jackson? If you were in the running to keep that hope chest, would you get married just to get it?"

"Probably not, but"—he gave her a slow, sexy wink—"since it is one of the first ones that Uncle D. J. ever made, I might think about it."

"I always thought that my grandfather loved Nanny Lucy a lot to have that made for her on their first anniversary, but now that I know more, I figure it was to make up for his guilty conscience," Nessa said.

"What would you have done if you'd found out your husband was cheating on you back in those days?" he asked. "Remember that times were different sixty years ago. Society didn't accept divorce as well as it does today."

"Yesterday, today, tomorrow," Nessa said with total conviction. "I would have either divorced him and thumbed my nose at society, or I would have shot him and buried the body under that fire-ant bed by the old tree."

"I believe you," Jackson chuckled. "If we have a fourth date, I'll be sure to remember to never cheat on you."

"Wise decision." She frowned. "Fourth date? We've only been on two."

"You don't think today counts as one? I mean, after all, you're wearing my shirt and a smile and nothing more. I saved you from near death. If that's not a third date, then I'm not sure what is," he teased.

"We have had some pretty unusual dates," she agreed.

"Have you had supper? Want to share a sandwich with me?" he asked.

"That sounds great, but only if you'll let me help make them. I'm a gourmet at spreading mayo on bread," she told him.

"I'd never turn down gourmet help." He got to his feet and held out a hand to help her up. When she was upright, he pulled her into his arms and grazed her cheek with the back of his hand. Their eyes met, and she barely had time to moisten her lips before his mouth closed on hers. By the time the make-out session ended, they were both panting.

This is *the third date,* she thought, trying to rationalize what she wanted to happen next and yet not wanting to instigate it. Could Jackson be what she was looking for? Had fate led her to Blossom so that she would meet him and be ready to commit to a long-term, maybe even forever, relationship?

He scooped her up into his arms for the second time and carried her back to a bedroom across the hall from where she'd been before. "Are you going to say no?" he whispered as he kicked the door shut with his bare foot.

"For tonight, I'm going to live for the moment, and no is not a part of the moment," she whispered.

Chapter Nineteen

April went to the refrigerator for milk on Friday evening, but there was none. "Hey, we need to make a run to the grocery store for milk, and we're down to only three or four slices of bread."

"I was supposed to buy the groceries for this whole week, so I'll go," Nessa said. "I agree with Nanny Lucy, though. We need to buy a cow."

"You going to milk it when we do?" Flynn teased.

"If I put out my money to buy it, then you should have to milk it, and April has to feed it," Nessa shot back at him. "Let's have supper, and then I'll make a run up to Paris. There are some other things I need from Walmart, so I can kill two birds with one stone."

"I'll go with you," April said. "While we're there, we might as well buy the groceries for next week. That way we don't have to go back on Tuesday evening."

"You got a hot date on that night?" Flynn pushed himself up off the sofa and took his place at the kitchen table.

"I did, but I'm standing him up next Tuesday," April said. "His name is Wally Mart, but like most of the guys I've known in the past, he's just there to take my money, and if I don't have any, he tosses me out on my butt."

Nessa set a basket of hot biscuits on the table and then sat down. "Looks to me like all three of us have had some bad luck when it comes to dating."

"Please don't marry Jackson and leave us." April picked up the bowl of mashed potatoes, scooped a big spoonful onto her plate, and then passed them across the table to Flynn.

"What . . . I don't . . . Why . . . What did you say?" Nessa sputtered.

"I still had one eye open last night when you came home," April told her. "That was not the shirt you had on when you left for a walk. You were barefoot, and you weren't wearing shorts. I don't want you to marry him and leave us. I can cook, but not as good as you, and Flynn only knows how to make soup and sandwiches. We'll starve if you leave."

"Did you and Jackson . . ." Flynn froze with a spoonful of mashed potatoes in the air. The potatoes fell off the spoon, missed his plate, and landed on the plastic place mat.

"I told you this morning that I sat down in a pile of fire ants, and that Jackson rescued me. I was wearing his shirt because my shirt and shorts as well as my flip-flops are still out there in the woods by an old log. After being nearly devoured by those miserable ants, I'm donating my shirt and shorts and flip-flops to them. I don't ever intend to take a walk down that path again. As for the rest, I'm pleading the Fifth-and-a-Half Amendment that says that a lady don't kiss and tell," Nessa said.

"Jackson is the most decent guy I've ever met." Flynn jumped up, jerked the place mat out from under his plate and tossed it in the sink, and then returned to the table. "And shame on you if you're just using him."

"Using him for what?" Nessa asked.

"For a good time. Because he's close by. Because you haven't been with a man in a while. Take your pick," Flynn said.

"Hey, that's downright mean." April accentuated each word with a stab of her fork toward him. How dare he judge Nessa when he'd done the same thing to women? To *many* women? "Are you judging Nessa by your own half bushel?"

"I'm sorry," Flynn answered. "And yes, I was."

"Apology accepted, but I'm not that kind of person." Nessa shot a dirty look across the table. "We've been here three weeks now, Flynn. Is this the longest you've gone without putting on your running shoes to chase a woman?"

April's eyes shifted from one cousin to the other and back again. She would have been willing to bet dollars to doughnuts that Nessa had slept with Jackson. There had been a glow about her as well as a smile she couldn't wipe off her face when she'd come in after midnight.

Flynn took a deep breath. "Yes, three weeks is the longest I've ever been without sex, but I don't want to be *that guy* anymore. I'm working hard to overcome the man I was, and I think I'm making progress."

"Explain, please," April said. "Did a woman do the same thing to you that you usually do to them?"

Flynn took a deep breath and let it out slowly. "That's exactly what happened, and now that I know how painful it is, I'm changing my ways. I never thought twice about having a one-night stand or a weekend fling. Last time around, I wanted more when Monday morning came, but she didn't."

"And?" April could tell by the way his eyes misted over that things had not gone well.

"She laughed in my face. Told me that she was already married and I'd just been her excitement for a weekend," Flynn answered. "I have never, ever messed around with married women. As bad as my dad is when it comes to women, he has a steadfast rule about married ladies. Maybe he didn't want to mess up *two* marriages at once. For my part, I don't know why I didn't figure things out, but I damn sure got burned."

"Uncle Matthew might not go out with a married woman, but he doesn't mind cheating on whatever woman he's married to, which is about the same thing," April said.

"I know, but I was trying to at least give him a little grace," Flynn said.

"How long ago did this happen?" April asked.

"I bet it was right before we got the court decision on this place, right?" Nessa butted in before Flynn could say a word.

"Nope, a month before," Flynn answered. "I moped around for a couple of weeks and finally decided that I needed some space to get my head on right and my life back together. If it takes a year, that's all right by me."

"Did you talk to your dad about what happened?" April asked.

"He would have just laughed at me. Two things he always told me were to stay away from married women and never go out of the house without protection." Flynn buttered a biscuit. "And for the record, I don't want you to leave, either, Nessa. Sitting down to family supper, and sometimes breakfast, has been pretty great. So thank you for doing this for us."

"No problem," Nessa said. "Your turn, April."

"My turn for what?" April wouldn't even know where to start untangling all her problems.

"Men that have let you down," Nessa said. "You told us that you'd made bad choices with bad people. Fess up."

April's hands got clammy. She had put all the past into a box, taped it shut, and then buried it in the back of her mind. She wanted to keep it tucked away and never talk about it, but evidently tonight was confession night for the three of them. "I'm on the other end of that stick that Flynn was talking about. I was the one left behind with a broken heart, and for some insane reason, I kept making the same mistakes and expecting a different outcome. Some guy would say that he loved me, and suddenly I would do anything to keep him. He could lay on my sofa and drink beer all day and take my hard-earned paycheck at the end of the week to go out with his friends and have a good time and leave me at home. But hey, he loved me, right?" She shrugged and went back to eating.

"You didn't have much of a home life here with Nanny Lucy, so you didn't know what to expect out of a relationship," Nessa said, realizing that she had pretty much been in the same kind of boat. She didn't want a relationship like her folks had and had steered toward the wrong kind of men.

"Neither did you." April shrugged again. "We were all wrong about each other. Did either of you ever go to counseling?"

"Not me," Flynn answered. "I probably should have had therapy after my mom died, but Dad was too busy with all his stuff to even think about the grief I was shouldering."

"My daddy would have told me that he could counsel me better than anyone outside the church. I heard him tell other people that. You do know that he's got a place reserved in heaven at the left hand of God. Jesus has the chair on the right hand, and Daddy respects him enough that he won't ask him to move over." Nessa laughed. "I guess y'all want a confession from me now, right?"

Flynn nodded. "We've bared our souls, so tell us why you're not married and producing a bunch of little red-haired kids."

"I want the whole enchilada when I get married." Nessa thought again of the night before and the pure contentment and happiness she'd felt when she was with Jackson. "I want the bells and whistles when he kisses me, and enough in common with him that we can almost finish each other's sentences. And then I want to trust him so much that I'm sure down deep in my heart that he won't ever cheat on me." Hopefully, that was what this relationship with Jackson would bring her.

"I guess neither one of us is going to get that quilt we're working on, Flynn," April giggled. "From the glitter in Nessa's eyes, I think she's taken the first steps toward getting it and the hope chest."

Nessa ducked her head, but that didn't prevent a blush from turning her cheeks bright red. "One can only hope," she muttered.

"As for me, I don't think there's a man out there that's wonderful enough to make me blush," April said. "I've been stung too many times, and I may never get over the pain or the feeling of stupidity when I turned around and let another man that was just like the last one into my life."

"I plan on being one of *those guys* that women can put their trust in someday, so don't say there aren't a few good men left," said Flynn.

"I'll believe that when I see it," April said.

"What's your plan?" Nessa asked Flynn.

"Just what I'm doing now. Stay away from dating until I feel like I've got something worthwhile to offer a woman. Be a gentleman and be honest. If I don't feel any chemistry on the first date, then call the lady and tell her. I'm not going to sweet-talk my way into bed with a woman on the first date, and maybe I won't even kiss her until the second date," he said, "and if it takes me a year or two, I want to be a guy like you just talked about, Nessa, not one of the jerks April just described."

"Good plan," April said. "Mine is about the same. No sleeping with a guy on a first date. No letting him move in in anything less than six months, and being up-front and honest from the beginning about what I want in a relationship. Your turn, Nessa."

"I've dated lots of guys, got to a second date with a few, and a third date with only a handful. But there were no bells and whistles, even with the few where I could say that there *was* a relationship. Daddy thought I was a rebellious daughter, but I wasn't really. I've never done drugs and actually drank very little. Been drunk maybe three times in my life. I have been sassy, and I do speak my mind, and Daddy couldn't make me get married at eighteen." She paused a moment before going on. "I wanted to experience the world, and I never want to wind up with a controlling man like my father. I guess that's what scares me most. That I would misjudge a guy, and after we got deep into a relationship, he would expect me to be a submissive little wife. Then he'd get all bossy and wind up cheating on me before we even broke up."

"So were there bells and whistles when Jackson kissed you?" Flynn asked Nessa.

"Like I said before, I don't kiss and tell." Nessa blushed again. "I'm sorry that we've all had these kinds of problems. Looks like one of us could have had a healthy relationship by this time in our lives."

"You can't build a brick house out of sticks and mud, or a relationship out of what we've had to offer." Flynn reached for the bowl of potatoes.

"You got that right." April nodded. "All we've had up until now is mud and more mud, but I'm going to do my best to have a brick house before next year."

"Amen," Flynn and Nessa said at the same time.

When they'd finished supper, Flynn offered to take care of the cleanup. "That way y'all can go on to the grocery store and get back before bedtime. I like a glass of milk before I go to sleep."

April felt as if a few more chains had fallen from her heart and soul.

❖ ❖ ❖

What Nessa liked best before going to sleep was a good round of hot sex, just like she and Jackson had had the night before. She had been expecting him to call all day and was disappointed when he didn't, but then maybe he and Flynn had been extra busy that day.

Are you making excuses for him? the voice in her head asked.

No, I am not. I'm being honest. She tipped her chin up a notch and felt liberated to be able to argue the point.

"I'll be ready in a minute." Nessa pushed back her chair. "I just have to grab my purse."

"Me too." April was on her feet and headed outside before Nessa could even push back her chair. She was already in the SUV when Nessa slid in behind the wheel.

"You must really not like washing dishes," Nessa said.

"No, I don't mind doing any kind of housework, and I can cook. Nanny Lucy made sure that I knew how to do all kinds of things before I left—like clean, cook, work with the roses, and change the oil and tires on the car." April rolled up the window when Nessa started the engine and turned on the air conditioner. "I just didn't want to talk about my failures anymore. It's depressing."

"Failure doesn't have to define us," Nessa said. "It can be the turning point in our lives that leads us to something better."

"Is that Uncle Isaac I hear?" April asked.

"No, it's straight from my school counselor. I confided a lot of stuff in her, and I remember seeing that quote hanging on her wall. I have no idea who said it. For all I know, she thought it up herself and printed it out right there in her room. But it has helped me a lot, even when I kept making the same mistakes over and over," Nessa said.

"Ever get a good outcome from one of them?" April asked.

"Not one time. Same old thing, time after time." Nessa turned onto the paved highway. "Well, that helped take care of the shake, rattle, and roll. Think they'll ever pave this road?"

"Probably not for just two houses. Every time I drive Nanny Lucy's car out onto the highway, I think the same thing." April turned on the radio, and they listened to country music all the way to Paris. Kenny Chesney and David Lee Murphy were singing "Everything's Gonna Be Alright" when Nessa found a parking spot not far from the entrance to Walmart. Nessa kept time with the beat with her thumbs on the steering wheel. April bobbed her head along with the lyrics.

"You believe that everything is really gonna be all right?" Nessa asked.

"I do, but we have to give it time. It took a lifetime for us to get in the condition that we're in, so we don't need to be over our past in three weeks. I've already got rid of one of the monkeys on my back, like they're singing about. Now I just have to not worry and for sure not hit the panic button, because . . ."—April moved her shoulders and arms to the music—"for the first time I really feel like just maybe things will be all right."

"Me too, but I'm scared that the other shoe might drop." Nessa got out of the SUV and grabbed a cart that had been left between two vehicles. "Hold up. My phone just pinged."

April slid out of her seat and slammed the door shut. "Is it Jackson?"

"No, it's Mama. She says I need to call her immediately. Hold on to this cart. I'll make it quick." Nessa sighed as she ran down the list of contacts and hit her mother's number.

"I'm so glad you called," Cora said. "Your father is making the absolute final plans for the trip to the Holy Land, and we want to give you one more chance to go with us. You'd need to be back in this area by July first."

"I haven't changed my mind. I don't want to go anywhere this summer. I'm not coming back to my old job, so I need to save my money to hold me over until I can sell some quilts this fall," Nessa explained. "I told Daddy that I didn't want to go. Does he ever talk to you, Mama, or does he just expect you to go along with everything he wants?"

"That's enough of that," Cora scolded. "A wife is to be dutiful and submissive to her husband. That's what brings peace into her heart, and for the record, I think this idea of you staying in Blossom is insane." Cora's tone turned into the same one she'd used when she threatened Nessa about going to Blossom when she was young. "I can't believe that you're giving up a good-paying, secure job to live in Blossom, Texas, and make quilts. That's a hobby, not a job. Your father tried to talk sense into you, but you've never been one to honor your father or your mother."

Nessa wondered if her mother was bossy with her to make up for the fact that she had to live with an overbearing husband. "If you're going to throw around Bible verses, you might remember the one about not provoking your children to anger."

"Don't you sass me, Vanessa." Cora's voice rose an octave.

Nothing was going to get resolved. Nessa wasn't going to budge, and her mother couldn't, so she finally sighed. "Mama, I'm standing in the Walmart parking lot with April. Y'all have a good time on the trip, and come see me when you get home."

"It might be a long time before either of us want to see you again," Cora said.

Nessa started walking toward the store, and April kept step beside her. "I can live with that." She couldn't believe those words had come out of her mouth. "Bye, Mama."

For the first time ever, silence met her ears. Her mother hadn't ended with "If I didn't love you, I wouldn't care what you do" or even "Goodbye." Nessa shoved the phone into her hip pocket. "You remember that old phone Nanny Lucy had when we were little kids? The one with a cord, and you could slam the receiver down and hang up on someone?"

"She had it when I left home." April nodded. "She didn't get a mobile phone set up until a few years ago. I saw her hang up on a few people and wondered if they would ever hear anything in that ear again."

"Mama just hung up on me, and I could swear that I felt the loud click even though I know cell phones don't work that way," Nessa said.

"Miz April," a thin voice yelled out from the exit doors.

"Hello, Callie." April waved toward the little girl who had left her father's side and was running toward her.

"Guess what? Belle loves her new house, but sometimes she gets lonely, so Daddy said I can come pick out one more kitty to keep her company," Callie said without catching her breath.

Kent pushed his cart over toward April and Nessa. "Hello, April. She's talked me into adopting another kitten, so we'll be by to see you again sometime this week."

"I'm going to name this one Cindy, after Cinderella." Callie grinned up at April. "Do you have a boyfriend?"

"No, do you?" April asked.

"Nooo. I'm just six years old. That's too young to get married, and that's what boyfriends are for, ain't it?" Callie asked.

"Calliope Wallace!" Kent finally caught up with her. "That's not a nice question to ask a lady."

"Well," Callie huffed, "I needed to know because you ain't got a girlfriend, and I bet if you got one, she would love Belle and Cindy."

Kent shot a brilliant smile toward April. "I'm so sorry," he said. "She has no filter on her mouth."

"Oh, to be young and be able to say anything on my mind." April returned the smile. "This is my cousin Nessa O'Riley. Nessa, this is Kent Wallace and his daughter, Callie."

"Pleased to meet you," Kent said, but his eyes stayed on April.

"You've got hair like Ariel in *The Little Mermaid*," Callie said to Nessa. "Daddy, can I dye my hair like that?" She looked up at him with her big blue eyes.

"Not until you are thirty years old," Kent said.

Callie crossed her arms over her chest. "That's what you always say."

"Yep, it is, and we'd better be getting on our way if we're going to the movies," Kent said.

"Bye, April. Bye, Ariel. Hey, Daddy, wait a minute. Can April go with us?" Callie asked.

"I'd love to, darlin', but I've got to do some shopping. I'll see you sometime this week when you come get another kitty cat." April thought she could see relief in Kent's eyes.

"Oh, all right," Callie said. "At least I don't have to wait until I'm thirty to see you again."

Kent pushed his cart toward the parking lot with one hand and held Callie's hand tightly with the other one. He was handsome, but it was his kind eyes that appealed to April. And then there was the fact that he was so sweet to his daughter. *That says a lot, doesn't it?* she thought as she and Nessa made their way into the store.

"Wonder what happened to Callie's mama," Nessa said as they made their way through the automatic doors into the store.

"Stella says that she died when Callie was only a year old. Callie is a lucky little girl to have a father like she has." April sighed. "He's definitely one of those good guys—the kind Flynn wants to become."

"I think he might like you," Nessa told her.

April picked up a head of lettuce and two tomatoes and put them in the cart. "Then you're thinking wrong. He's a lawyer, for crying out loud. He would never be interested in someone like me."

"Don't underestimate yourself, Cousin. Besides, you can't fool kids, and that little girl thinks you're pretty enough to be her daddy's girl-friend," Nessa said.

April flushed at Nessa's observation and then gasped. "Is that Jackson over there? And who in the hell is kissing him? I mean it's just on the cheek, but it *is* a kiss."

"I'm sure I don't know, but he's pushing the cart for her, so . . ." Nessa felt the world crumbling under her feet.

"It was just a cheek kiss. Maybe it's a cousin or a friend. We don't know all the people that he knows. It could be nothing. Just ask him about it," April said.

Nessa appreciated April's rationalization, but the way the tall bru-nette, who was wearing short shorts and high-heeled shoes, looked up at him left no doubt that she was a lot more than a friend or a cousin. "Let's go to Kroger to do our shopping. I don't want to run into him."

"You *did* sleep with him, didn't you?" April asked as she put the lettuce and tomatoes back and left the cart in the middle of an aisle.

"Third date." Nessa blinked away the tears. She'd made a wrong decision again, and now things were going to be awkward between neighbors.

Chapter Twenty

*n*essa laid her forehead on the steering wheel and let the tears flow freely. "Just another disappointment, and I'm used to those."

April patted her on the back. "The O'Riley curse strikes again. Don't beat yourself up. I thought he was a nice guy, too, but then my judgment ain't worth crap. You're just doing what all three of us have done. We've all tried the same old recipe, even though the outcome leaves a bitter taste in your mouth."

Nessa jerked her head up and slapped the steering wheel with both hands. "Don't tell Flynn. He's doing so good right now, and he has to work with Jackson. He might think he has to defend my honor or something crazy like that."

"I won't say a word to him, I promise." April leaned over the console and hugged her. "You really should talk to Jackson about this, though, in case there's an explanation."

Nessa wiped at her eyes. "She was so tall and so beautiful. If he could have her, then why would he even look at me?"

"Don't do that to yourself," April scolded. "He'll call, or you two will meet at the falls, or maybe you'll even sit in another ant bed. When that happens, just give him the chance to explain before you let that red-haired temper get ahead of you."

Nessa started the engine and put the SUV in reverse, but then sat frozen in her seat as she watched Jackson and the woman in her rearview mirror. He opened the door of his truck for her, proving that they were together. Her chin quivered, but she was determined that she wouldn't cry anymore. Evidently she was just a one-night stand to him.

Then that's what he is to me, she thought, *my first and last one-night stand. I'll never make that mistake again. Forget the third-date rule that everyone these days talks about. I'm not sleeping with another guy until we've had a dozen dates.*

"Living in the moment," she muttered.

"What does that mean?" April asked.

"Jackson and I were talking about living in the moment as opposed to always looking ahead to the future," she explained as she backed her vehicle out of the parking spot and headed toward the grocery store. "Last night I was in the moment, not thinking about what the consequences would be for the future. I wanted this to be more than just . . ." She couldn't even say the words.

"I've tried that moment thing too many times to count, and it sure didn't work for me, either. I'm going to enjoy the day, but I'm also not wasting my time on something that only lasts a day," April said. "Third date? When did you have the first two? I thought your first date was when you went to the cemetery and had supper at Weezy's."

Nessa took a deep breath. "We talked last week when we both showed up at the falls. I stumbled when I stepped in a gopher hole and wound up kissing him, so he said that was our first date. The second was the cemetery. The third was the ant bed."

"So that's what a third date is—one that involves wallowing in an ant bed." April laughed and then grew serious. "I don't think I've ever had a third date. I usually fall hard, let some sorry sucker move in with me after a week or so, and then it all falls apart because it's all built on steamy sex, but that's not the way things are going to be from now on."

"You've come a long way since we've been at Nanny Lucy's." Nessa sighed.

"So have you," April told her. "I had to make progress because I hit rock bottom. The inheritance was a godsend for me, and getting a job that I love was icing on the cake. I've found that I don't need a man to complete me. I'm good on my own, and I like myself a lot better. I'm glad I didn't have another place to go, because you've helped me work things out. I didn't have to make a tough decision about whether to quit my job and stay here, but you did. That wasn't a moment thing, Nessa. That was changing your life to fit the future that you want. As far as last night goes, you need to own your sexuality, girl. You wanted it. You got it. It didn't work out the way you thought it might, but you have a beautiful memory."

Nessa pulled her SUV into the Kroger lot, parked the car, and turned to face April. "What made you so smart?"

"I read a lot—mostly self-help books when I was trying to figure out why my own grandmother didn't seem to love me," April answered. "Thank you for even thinking that I'm not the dumb cousin, though. Hey, remember that song we heard called 'Everything's Gonna Be Alright'?"

Nessa fished around in her purse until she found her phone and searched for the song. "What's this got to do with us?" she asked as she hit the play button.

April's head bobbed with the beat of the music. "Listen to it and let your spirit float. It keeps sayin' that everything's gonna be all right, and I believe it. We'll have ups and downs, and argue and maybe cry together, or other times we'll all laugh until our sides hurt, but everything is gonna be all right."

Nessa unfastened her seat belt so she could be free to move her shoulders with the music. "You're right. As long as we all have each other, we're going to be fine. I'm so glad that we all three are staying at the house."

"Me too." April nodded. "You and Flynn have helped me understand Nanny Lucy better, and that helps me to forgive."

"I'm not there yet," Nessa admitted. "I thought she was perfect, and my bubble has been blown. I was coming back to the home where I felt peace and freedom. And you were coming back to where you felt the opposite. But in the past few years, I could kind of see this side of her when I would come visit. She was glad to see me, but then I felt like she'd just as soon that I go on and leave her alone."

"I got the same feeling," April said with a nod of understanding, "but I thought she was probably better with you. She always gave me the impression that she loved you the most. I guess we all come across to others in different ways. I was a pain and a thorn in her side. You were the kid that looked like her and was born to her favorite child. Flynn was the one she felt sorry for because he lost his mother, and yet was disappointed in because he was like his father. We can't change that," April told her.

Nessa opened the door. "Well, I'm sure glad that you are here to help me."

April pulled the keys out of the ignition and tossed them to her. "Don't forget these."

"See? Here to help me." Nessa smiled, even though she wanted to throw beer cans at the front of the store, or maybe storm over to Jackson's when she got home and use words that would fry the hair out of her father's ears.

❖ ❖ ❖

Crickets, tree frogs, and hoot owls combined their voices to serenade Flynn as he sat on the porch with a beer in his hand. A lonesome coyote lent his howling to the mix. Tex came around the end of the house and snuggled up next to him.

"Are you lonesome? Jackson had to run into town to get a gallon of varnish. He'll be back soon." Flynn rubbed the dog's ears. "A month ago, I would have been sitting in a bar, sipping on this beer and scanning the place for a woman. Know something, though?"

Tex growled down deep in his chest and focused on the road.

"I'm happier right here than I would have been in a bar. Even though we're not out hunting for women, you can be my wingman tonight." Flynn continued to rub the dog's ears.

Tex barked once as if agreeing with Flynn.

"Good boy." Flynn chuckled and then grew serious when he heard the crunch of gravel as a vehicle came down the road toward the house. "It's too soon for April and Nessa to be home. They've only been gone thirty minutes. Maybe Jackson is stopping by on his way back. You just might get a ride home, Tex."

When the vehicle came into view, Flynn stood up. It wasn't Nessa's SUV or Jackson's truck but a small compact car. "Someone has gotten lost. Nanny Lucy would give those people the big-oak-tree directions. You know what that is, Tex? It's when she would say, turn around and go back to the road, go north so many miles, or south so many blocks, then turn left at the big oak tree. I always wondered how many big oak trees there were in Texas." He laughed at the memory and waited for the car to stop so he could give directions.

His whole body stiffened when Tilly slid her long legs out of the car and waved. "Hey, just the man I wanted to see." She slammed the door and started toward the porch. "I came to kidnap you, Flynn O'Riley. We're going dancing tonight at the Lonestar Bar and Grill in Paris. Go change those shoes for some dancin' boots." She stopped on the bottom step and let her eyes roam all over him.

He had worked in the oil fields in the hot summertime. He'd spent sweaty hours in Jackson's workshop. But the way Tilly let her eyes linger on the zipper of his jeans made him feel like he needed a shower more than any other time.

"Thanks for the invitation, but . . ."

She butted in and held up a palm. "There are no buts. Either we go dancing tonight, or else we spend time together right here on this porch."

"But I have other plans. I was just going out to my truck to go to Paris when Tex showed up and I stopped to pet him." Flynn hoped that God realized his little white lie was better than the much bigger sin that Tilly had in mind. Besides, he could go to Paris, get one of those waffle cones of soft yogurt, and call that his plans.

She squinted her overly made-up eyes at him. "That's too bad, darlin'. I got the feeling we could be good together, both in vertical dancing and horizontal. Is it another woman you've got plans with?"

"Yes, ma'am," Flynn lied again, and then his conscience pricked his very soul. "But come on up here on the porch and sit a spell. I've got a few minutes."

With a big smile on her face, she swaggered over to the porch and sat down on the steps beside him. "What do you want to talk about, darlin'?"

"I've been the male version of you, and I woke up one morning and didn't like myself so much. I'm taking baby steps toward a change, and I like myself better each day. I just want you to know that I'm not interested in dating right now—not just you, but anyone. A woman deserves respect and honesty, and . . ." He paused.

"What do you want in the end of this big change?" she asked.

"I want a solid relationship built on love and, like I said, respect, not just sex," he answered. "What do you want from life?" He could tell Tilly that she would never find anything stable by chasing after men the way she was doing, but she needed to come to that conclusion on her own for it to do a bit of good.

Face your fears. Be a good person. Do what's right. Words of wisdom from Nessa's father came back to him.

"Are you serious?" Tilly whispered.

"Yep, and it may take a year or even two before I feel like I've got something good and decent to offer a woman," he said, "but I want to be honest with you." God, it felt good to feel like he was helping someone, but it felt even better to realize that it didn't mean he had to be there *for* someone. He was talking to himself as much as or more than he was to Tilly, and it was downright liberating.

"I appreciate that." She cocked her head to one side. "You asked me what I want from life. I want the man you are working to become."

"Then I'd say that you have to become the woman that would appeal to that man. Maybe it won't be me, or even someone else, but you have to want that bad enough to work on yourself," he said.

"Why wouldn't it be you?" She winked.

"Because when and if I ever settle down, I don't think I want a ready-made family, and please don't take that wrong. I'm not being hateful, just honest," he said again.

"Thanks, Flynn." She stood up and started down the steps. "I appreciate you talking to me, but I'm not willing to work on that much change. I want my second husband to be someone like what you're talking about, but I don't want to give up my good times just yet to get him. I like to flirt. I like the thrill of the chase."

"Who's taking care of your kids while you live like that?" Flynn asked.

"That's really none of your business, but the girls and I live with my mother. She's not well, so they do a lot to help her. She's more than willing to let me have my weekends to cut loose and let my hair down." Tilly took a couple of steps toward her car and then turned around. "If things go in the crapper, honey, and you change your mind about all this changing stuff, I'm right here for you. Did your red-haired cousin give you my number?"

"She did." Flynn couldn't make himself head to his truck.

"Well, okay then." Tilly sighed louder than the crickets. She blew him a kiss just before she slid in behind the steering wheel, and then she rolled down the window. "Thanks again for being up-front with me. At least I know you don't think I'm ugly or too brassy. It's one of those 'It's me, not you' things, and I can live with that." .

"You are so welcome, and if you decide that you want something else out of life and need to talk, just holler at me." Flynn waved. "And Tilly, you are a very attractive woman. You have such a lovely smile. You should kick any man who makes you feel ugly out the door."

"Thank you for that." Tilly laid a hand over her heart, and then blew more kisses toward him. She drove away, leaving a puff of dust in her wake. Flynn made sure he had his wallet in his hip pocket, crossed the yard with Tex right behind him, and got into his truck. "Want to go with me and be my wingman at the drive-in window of the ice-cream shop?"

Tex didn't need a second invitation. He bounded up into the truck and sat down in the passenger seat. When Flynn drove past the fork in the road, Tilly fell right in behind him. Evidently she had been waiting to see if he was telling the truth.

"That was downright liberating, Tex. Maybe she'll think about what I said. Maybe not. But it sure helped me to say it," he said as he watched her pull her car in behind his truck.

He drove five miles below the speed limit, hoping that she would go on past him, but she hung back. Then he drove five miles over the speed limit and hoped that she might lose him, but she didn't. When he finally pulled in at the ice-cream shop, she honked.

He hoped that she would think about what he'd said and wished her the best in her quest to find happiness. He rolled his windows down slightly so Tex could get some air. Then he got out of his truck and jogged across the parking lot. When he went inside, the first people he saw were April and Nessa at a booth on the far side of the place. He crossed the room in a few strides and said, "I thought y'all were going for groceries."

"We did, and now we're treating ourselves to brownie sundaes." April scooted over. "You can help me eat mine. It's pretty good, but Weezy's beats it all to pieces."

"I would, but Tex is in the truck. The windows are down a little, but it will get hot in there pretty quick. Tilly showed up at the house and tried to drag me to a dance with her. I'm just getting my ice-cream cone to go," he explained.

"You can't drop that on us and then leave. At least give us the short version of what happened," April teased.

Flynn told them what he'd said, but that Tilly wasn't ready to change. "She's a lot like my dad. She likes her life just the way it is."

"I admire you for trying," Nessa said.

"I feel sorry for Tilly." April finished off her ice cream. "If she'd admit it, she just wants someone to love her. I've been where she is, to some degree."

"Maybe so, but she knows now that she and I want two different things out of life," Flynn said. "I can't leave Tex alone in the truck much longer. See you at home."

He got his ice cream and then got in behind the steering wheel. Even with the windows up and the AC going, he had to eat fast. When the cone was half-done, he offered what was left to Tex. The dog gobbled it up in one bite, his tail thumping against the seat the whole time.

"That didn't last long, did it?" Flynn smiled. "Ready to go home? As a thank-you for keeping me company, I'll even drive you to your house this evening."

A vehicle turned off the paved road right behind Flynn, and for a minute he thought Tilly was back. Maybe she'd taken time to think about things and had decided that she *did* want to talk some more. He was actually looking forward to visiting with someone who had the same problems he was trying to overcome. Then he realized that the vehicle was a truck and not a car. Jackson must have gotten his business taken care of and was on his way home, too. Flynn took the fork leading up to

Jackson's house and parked in the front yard. He opened his door, and Tex bounded out between him and the steering wheel.

Jackson got out of his truck and waved. "You didn't have to bring him home. He knows the way."

"No problem. He and I went to Paris and had an ice-cream cone." Flynn took a few steps toward the porch. "Tilly came to seduce me, and I needed some time to think about what I told her."

"And that was?" Jackson smiled.

Flynn told the story again, and Jackson stopped to pet Tex when he reached him and then leaned on the fender of the truck. "I've only been gone a couple of hours, and you went visiting." Then he focused on Flynn again. "Come on inside and we'll have a cold beer. Sounds to me like you were trying to help Tilly, and that's a good thing."

"Thanks for the offer, but April and Nessa will be home soon with groceries. I should get on back and help unload. I guess Tilly has to realize she has a problem before she admits that she needs help. I sure did," Flynn said. "See you tomorrow."

"Sure thing." Jackson picked up a gallon of varnish and headed toward the shop with Tex right at his feet.

❖ ❖ ❖

April had never been good at keeping secrets, but she was determined not to say a word to Flynn. But—and there always seemed to be a *but* where her life was concerned—when they got home, Flynn noticed that Nessa's eyes were red.

"Have you been crying?" Flynn asked.

"Allergies." Nessa brushed away his question with a flip of her hand.

April had to bite her tongue to keep from telling him that Jackson had broken Nessa's heart. She felt a kinship with both her cousins these days, and she wouldn't do anything to hurt either of them, even if some of their friends weren't working out. "We want to hear the long version of the story about Tilly," she said as she helped Nessa put the groceries away. "Sit down at the end of the table there and start talking."

"April saw the lawyer tonight, the one who has a little girl and who came to adopt a cat, so you both need to talk," Nessa said.

"What lawyer?" Flynn asked. "Why do you need to talk to a lawyer? Are you in trouble?"

"The lawyer and his daughter adopted a kitten, remember," Nessa explained. "I think he has a crush on April, and I know his daughter does."

"Oh, hush." April blushed.

"You know the story. Tilly came. She offered. I refused and tried to talk to her about her lifestyle, like I did with my dad. I felt like a fifth wheel too many times when Dad would bring home a woman that had kids, and he showed them more attention than he did me," Flynn said as he poured himself a tall glass of milk. "Your turn, April."

"That's just like a man," Nessa fussed. "Just the bare bones, and no feeling. We want to know how you felt when she was standing out there."

"Guys don't talk about things like that," Flynn protested.

April got a wine cooler from the fridge and sat down in her regular place at the table. "Yes, they do, but they just do it with other guys. Pretend we are guys and tell us how you felt."

"This feels like one of those therapy sessions I've seen on television," Flynn said, "and honey, in my wildest imagination, I can't see either of you two as guys. But I'll give it my best try just for y'all."

Nessa brought a glass of sweet tea to the table and sat down on the other side. "Do your best, and then we'll hear from April."

"If this is group, then we should hear from you, too," Flynn argued.

"I'm the therapist in this scenario," Nessa said. "I might have something to say when you two get done, or I might not."

"I felt panic when she drove up," Flynn admitted, "and I felt like I'd done the right thing when she left."

April could sure relate to that moment of panic, because she'd felt the same way when Kent and Callie greeted them in front of Walmart.

"My chest got tight, and I wanted to shake my fist at God. Why would He blast me with a test like that after less than a month? Then I felt sorry for her and tried to make her realize there was no future in that lifestyle." Flynn looked miserable just talking about the whole ordeal.

Nessa patted him on the shoulder. "You can't save the world, Flynn."

"You'll do good to save yourself." April wondered what would happen if Callie ever did convince her dad to ask her out for ice cream or coffee. The little girl seemed to want her father to have a girlfriend, but Kent Wallace was a lawyer, for goodness' sake. He had a graduate degree, and April had barely made it through high school. They were just too different to even go on a first date.

"I don't think Tilly is close enough to God for Him to use her for a test," Nessa giggled. "I reckon, if she was bringing the test to you, it was straight from the devil himself."

Flynn nodded in agreement and stood up.

"We're not done," Nessa said. "Group sessions last an hour."

"I'm not going anywhere except to the pantry. I saw y'all unload a package of oatmeal cookies. They won't be as good as what you make, Nessa, but I need something to go with my milk. And besides, talking about this makes me hungry," Flynn said.

"Does talking about it make you nervous, too? Surely you've sweet-talked lots of women," April asked.

"That's just spreading on the bull crap," Flynn said. "Talking about feelings is tough for guys. Flirting comes easy."

"Yes, it does, and then . . ." Nessa clamped her mouth shut.

April raised her eyebrows. Was Nessa going to fess up about sleeping with Jackson? Flynn could probably offer Nessa some good advice on the matter, but she could see that Nessa wanted to keep quiet.

Poor Flynn would have to work with the man tomorrow, knowing that Jackson was seeing another woman. Flynn wouldn't be able to judge his boss, because most likely he had done the same thing in his past. But Nessa was his cousin, and they'd all gotten pretty close this past month, so he might feel that he should defend her.

Be quiet, Nessa! April tried to convey the message through telepathy.

"But I'm the leader of this group therapy. I'm supposed to be listening to y'all. Did you have any other feelings about Tilly?" Nessa asked.

Good job. April heaved a short sigh of relief.

"She'd probably hate me for saying it, but I pitied her. I feel like I've made progress, and it's like when you're in school and algebra finally works for you. Suddenly, you want to help your friend get a handle on it, too," Flynn answered. "Then I felt kind of deflated because she didn't want my help."

"Darlin' cousin, you're just like me in some ways. We've both been living in the moment so long that we can't believe we're ready for something with a future." April took a cookie from the package Flynn had brought from the pantry and bit into it.

I like the future I'm seeing, she thought.

"That's a good way to put it, but what if, after a year or two, when I settle down, I'm not happy? My dad tried to start a new life when he married my mother, and within two years he was cheating on her. I saw how it affected Mama. I don't ever want to be *that guy*." Flynn dipped a cookie in his milk.

"Then don't be," Nessa told him.

"That's easier said than done," April argued.

"Why do you say that? If Flynn gets a wandering eye, then he should . . ." Nessa paused to take a cookie. "I was about to sound like my father and say he should pray about it, but that's not right. We three cousins need to set aside some time each month for one of our sessions. What's wrong with us was thirty years in the making. We won't solve everything in one week, but we understand each other. This is the house that will *re*build us, kind of like we hear about in Miranda's song. We've helped each other come this far. April and I were listening to another song—Kenny Chesney's 'Everything's Gonna Be Alright.' We decided that was our new theme song. The lyrics might not all match our situation, but the title sure does."

Flynn laughed, shaking his head. "I guess you're right."

"And you deserve as many cookies as you want for not falling into bed with Tilly." April grinned.

"Well, thank you." Flynn smiled back at her. "Now it's your turn, April."

"Hello, my name is April O'Riley." She held up a hand like a grade-school child. "I'm a messed-up woman, but I'm trying to get my life back together. I've always lived in the moment and never worried about the future." She lowered her hand and kept talking. "If people can smell fear in others, then I wonder if they can also get a whiff of something from folks like me who would do anything just to get someone to love them. That's all I've ever wanted—and that's what kept getting me into trouble. Some old boy would say those three magic words, and I'd fall into bed with him. I've decided to trust no one for a long time, not until I figure out how to tell the difference between love and lust."

"Have you been to an addiction thing before, like drugs or AA?" Flynn asked.

"I went to an AA meeting," April admitted. "Even though I'm not addicted to alcohol, I thought they might help me understand why I was addicted to the wrong type of man. They didn't. I took one of the guys that was there that night home with me and let him move in the next week. He stole all my money, and the café I had been working in closed its doors. Times have been tough these past couple of years, so I was living in my car when I got the call about this place."

"How did that make you feel?" Nessa asked.

April fidgeted with a cookie, turning it around and around in her hands. "Angry, sad, and relieved, all at the same time." All the emotions she had felt following that phone call came rushing back. According to everything she'd read in the self-help books, talking about it got them out of her heart. Tears rolled down her cheeks. "Of all the places I didn't want to go, this was right up there at the top of the list. I hated the idea of having to come back here and hoped that there would be money involved so I could leave and find a place to live. But the closer I got, the more I realized that if I didn't face my demons, I was never going to do anything but keep making the same old mistakes. Right now, I feel like I don't deserve this chance to get my life together. Nanny Lucy would come to me at night in my dreams and say over and over, 'I told you so,' and I'd wake up so angry that I hadn't proved her wrong."

"It's amazing how we all saw her in a different light, isn't it?" Nessa said. "I'll take a turn now. My name is Nessa O'Riley"—she raised her hand like April had—"and I have trust and commitment issues. I had a fairly decent childhood, even if my folks were ultra-religious and overbearing. The only time I was ever happy was right here, which is strange since this is where April was the unhappiest. I thought I could find that childhood happiness when I got back, but all I got was disappointment. That makes me wonder if my past relationships failed because I wanted the same sense of contentment and happiness that I felt when I came here."

April's head bobbed up and down with every word. Her problems hadn't been the same as Nessa's, but she could relate to wanting something permanent and not just a flash in the pan. "Looks like coming back to Blossom is helping us all."

"Good session." Nessa yawned. "I'm going to get a quick shower and read until I fall asleep."

"Me too," Flynn said, "and thanks to both of you. I guess it does help to talk about our feelings."

"Yep." April grinned. "And what is said in the kitchen over milk and cookies stays in the kitchen, right? We're trying to tear up the roots that made us who we are and plant better seeds for the future."

"Yes, ma'am," Nessa and Flynn said at the same time.

Flynn went straight to his room and shut the door. April leaned over the table toward Nessa and whispered, "Are you all right?"

"No, but one thing Mama used to say feels pretty good right now. She said that all your problems look better at sunrise than they do at sunset. I'm going to believe that tonight," Nessa answered.

"If you can't sleep tonight, just wake me up. We can talk more if you need to," April offered.

Nessa stood up and gave April a quick hug. "I like having you for a cousin, but I like having you for a friend even more."

April beamed. "Thanks. Right back at you."

Chapter Twenty-One

The third's the charm," Nessa said when she finally got thread through the eye of the needle. "I can't believe we're finishing this in three weeks." A part of her was glad to have the quilt done so she could get busy on her own quilts for the craft shows, but on the other hand, she would miss the time the three of them had spent together every morning. Now the others would go off to work every morning, and she would be alone.

"Seems like we've been here months instead of weeks." Flynn put the last of his stitches in the quilt. "We've finished this job a full week ahead of time. I'm glad to have it done, but I'm going to miss the times we've had together. That does not mean I want to make another one, but . . ."

"But we need to be careful that we don't wind up going our own ways and forget to set aside time to talk to each other," April suggested.

"Be home in time for supper," Nessa said. "I read that in a book. That was the writer's secret to a happy family life. Her kids could have their friends over or play outside, or whatever, but when it was supper-time, they had to be home. They all sat around the table, just the family, not a bunch of friends, and talked about their day. They vented if they had problems, told funny stories or jokes. That's what we need to do."

"Yes!" Flynn and April said at the same time.

Then April shook her finger at Flynn. "Don't get out your bragging britches just yet. We still have to roll the backing up over the edges and do the hemming."

"Can we do it tonight after supper?" Flynn asked. "I'd like to be able to go to work full-time tomorrow morning."

"I'm willing if y'all are," Nessa agreed. "I want to get this out of the frame so I can begin one for the craft shows this fall."

"What are you doing first?" April asked.

"The double wedding ring one that fell out of the closet on Flynn's head. While I'm quilting it, I want to think about the good times I had when we were kids," Nessa answered.

"We did have fun, didn't we? You two coming to stay a few weeks was the highlight of my summer. I waited on the porch for your folks to bring you, and the day you left I spent a lot of time at the falls crying." April smiled. "I'm glad we all came back home."

"I'll tell Jackson that I can start work full-time tomorrow. Shall we take it out of the frame?" Flynn asked. "I'm not willing to work on another one, but I will admit that doing this has helped me. April, coming here was the highlight of my summers, too."

"I don't have to tell y'all how much I loved my time here. Seems like it took coming back as an adult to realize that although I loved Nanny Lucy, it was spending time with y'all that was the real prize." Nessa undid a few clamps. "I'll get it all pinned while y'all are at work today, and we'll get the hemming done after supper."

Flynn got to his feet and rolled the kinks from his neck. "Sounds like a good plan to me. I'll miss our time together out here, though."

April pushed back her chair and stood up to help fold. "Let's get this folded and . . . Oh, my goodness!"

"What?" Nessa undid the last clamp.

"Look at the back side." Tears flowed down April's cheeks.

Flynn flipped the quilt over, and all three of them went speechless. There was a photograph, maybe an eight-by-ten, right in the middle of the backing. Nanny Lucy was sitting on a quilt with all three of them gathered around her, and underneath she had written: *Good memories.*

"How did we not see or feel this?" Nessa wiped tears from her eyes with the back of her hand.

"Dammit!" Flynn's voice cracked as he moved from his spot and hugged both of his cousins at once. "Grown men don't get all weepy."

"They do at times like this." Nessa soaked his shoulder with tears.

"I hope Nanny Lucy meant it when she said the quilt brought good memories for her," April said between sobs. "She deserved to have something good in her life."

Flynn took a step back, pulled a white hanky from his hip pocket, and dried his two cousins' eyes before he wiped his own cheeks. "She wouldn't want us to carry on like this. Let's get this folded and taken in the house."

"Putting a quilt in the frame needs more than one person. I bet Stella and Vivien helped her, but how did she know that she wouldn't be quilting anymore? Did she ever tell y'all that she was sick?" Nessa blinked away more tears. Flynn was right. Nanny Lucy had been strong, and she'd expect the same from them.

"Not me," April answered. "She didn't open up to me about anything—ever."

"Me either." Flynn frowned. "Looking back, I don't think she said much about herself to anyone."

April moved from one side of the frame to another. "The only thing she ever told me was the story about the tornado."

"I'm familiar with that one, but my dad told me, not Nanny Lucy. Sometimes when he was between women, he would share things that happened when he was a kid. That wasn't often, and he had to be in a bit of a melancholy mood, but I liked it when he talked to me about this place," Flynn answered.

Together they worked until the quilt was folded neatly. Nessa carried it into the house like what it was—a priceless piece of their history.

"That's exactly what it is," she muttered.

"What was that?" Flynn asked.

"This thing is worth more than whatever is in that hope chest," she said.

"Yes!" Flynn and April said in unison again.

When they were inside the house, April stood back and stared at the quilt on the wall. "And Nanny Lucy got even more strict and twice as mean after we were all sixteen. I wonder if that's because that was when my mother got pregnant, but that picture she had put on the quilt back says that she did have good memories of us up until then. I think it might make her happy if we hung the quilt we just finished on the wall behind the sofa. We could put the one that's up there in the hope chest, and we could still abide by the rule that the first one married gets the chest and this quilt."

Nessa nodded, but had misgivings. "But that wasn't in the will. That wouldn't be what she wanted, so we shouldn't do it."

Flynn kept walking straight to the kitchen. "Maybe she would be proud that we wanted to hang all those memories up to enjoy. Besides, according to her diary, she never got what she wanted in life anyway, so why start now?"

Nessa plopped down on the other end of the sofa. "That sounds a little harsh."

"Not to me," April said. "And truthfully, I think she'd be honored if we hung it up. It wouldn't be disrespecting her wishes but showing her that we've accepted our past and are moving on to the future. We could even make a pact right now that it would always hang there instead of going to the one who gets married first."

A wide smile covered Nessa's face. "Maybe she wouldn't mind if we did it with a good heart, and not out of vengeance. I'll sew loops in the top of it so we can hang it up, and then I'll get that one"—she pointed to the quilt on the wall—"washed and ready to put in the hope chest for the one of us that marries first."

"I vote yes," Flynn said.

"My vote is yes, too." April went to the kitchen, and in a few minutes brought out a small lunch pail.

"What's that?" Nessa asked.

April flipped its latch open to show that it was filled with stuff for her lunch. "I found this in the garage last night. I carried it to school every day until I was in the seventh grade, when Nanny Lucy decided that I could start buying my lunch. It was one of the few things that I had like the other girls, and it brings back good memories. So I'm going to use it. See you later, and Nessa, don't worry yourself crazy about whether we're doing the right thing with the quilt."

Nessa opened her mouth to say something, but April and Flynn had already left. She went to her bedroom and pulled out the trundle bed, where she had stored the quilt tops that had fallen out of the closet. "I'm going to start with the double wedding ring one," she muttered as she studied each of them.

The house phone startled her when it rang. She hurried to the kitchen and grabbed the receiver. "Hello," she said with caution. After what she'd just said, she wasn't sure where the answer might come from.

"Are you mad at me?" Jackson asked bluntly.

"Should I be mad at you?" she fired back.

"I hope not. I really like you," Jackson said. "I waited for you by the waterfall the last few nights."

"When you figure out why I'm mad, then you can call back." Nessa returned the receiver to its base.

That was kind of mean, Nanny Lucy's voice scolded her.

"I was expecting an answer to my question," Nessa grumbled. "And besides, I'm not ready to talk to Jackson."

She couldn't get a clear thought pattern going. April had said she should give him a chance to explain, but the woman had kissed him right there in public. There wasn't much to explain there. And yet the Jackson she thought she knew wasn't that kind of man.

"It's like trying to see the sunshine through mud," she said as she took a step away from the kitchen.

In seconds the phone rang again. She picked it up on the second ring. "That was fast, and I'm not through being mad, so call back tomorrow." She wasn't ready to hear his excuses.

"What was fast?" Stella asked in her unmistakable gravelly voice.

"I thought you were someone else, ma'am." A red-hot blush heated up Nessa's cheeks.

"I'd be nosy and ask who you're mad at, but I don't have time. April told me yesterday that the quilt was about done. Vivien and I are planning a little two- or three-day road trip to Jefferson to do some antique shopping, so we were wondering when we might inspect it," Stella said.

"Anytime tomorrow." Nessa touched her face to see if it was as hot as it seemed. "We're hemming the border tonight."

"Great, we'll be by about nine o'clock, and we'll leave on our trip from there," Stella said. "I've got about five minutes before I go to the shelter to volunteer today. Want to tell me who you are mad at and why?"

Nessa almost smiled. "Miz Stella, it would take all day to make you understand, so I suppose the answer is no, ma'am."

"In that case, goodbye, but if you ever need someone to talk to, I'm here," Stella said.

"Thanks for that. Bye now," Nessa said, and she hung up the receiver a second time.

She went back to the bedroom and picked up the double wedding ring quilt top and carried it out to the shed. She planned to have all of them finished by September, plus at least one of the tops she had sewn up. She hung it over the edge of the wooden frame and went into the garage to forage for batting and backing. There was plenty of both, so she carried the bundle of batting and the precut muslin backing out to the shed. She would rather have gotten things into the frame, but it would be quite a job for one person, so she would wait until later when April and Flynn were home to help.

She went back inside the house and started rolling and pinning the border of the quilt they'd just finished. The whole time she thought about the picture on the back of the quilt.

"You had it tough, Nanny Lucy, but thank you for helping us to understand your reasons for what you did. I wish that none of us three would have inherited that O'Riley curse, though," she said as she worked. "I want to be happy, not miserable the rest of my life, and you've helped me take steps toward that, but I'm still hurting from what happened with Jackson." *Listen to your heart.* Nanny Lucy's voice was so clear that she looked over her shoulder to see if her grandmother had truly risen from the grave.

❖   ❖   ❖

April was in the middle of doing the daily cleaning when Stella and Vivien came inside. She looked up from a kitten's cage and waved. "Hey, it's good to see you out and about, Miz Vivien. Been a long time since I've seen you, and you haven't changed a bit."

"Bless your heart, darlin'." Vivien beamed. "It's good to feel better, but this sister of mine is dragging me off tomorrow on another mini vacation." Vivien went straight to the dogs' side of the room and took a half-grown Chihuahua out of a cage. She carried him over to the rocking chair and held him up on her chest like a baby. "This is kind of like a hospital nursery with a bunch of unclaimed babies that need love. And speaking of babies"—Vivien rubbed the little dog's fur as she talked—"April, you look so much like your mother that it's uncanny."

"Thank you." April grinned. "I just wish she would have lived, so I could have known her. When I was a little girl, I used to pretend that she and I were sitting beside each other at the waterfall. I would talk to her as if she was really there. Then when I was having really rough times as an adult, I'd do the same. It kind of brought me comfort."

Stella patted her on the shoulder. "I believe that the spirits of those who have passed can come back and help us when we need them. There's a reason for everything, and most usually it all falls right into place when we look back on it. I was there right after your mama gave birth to you. She loved you so much. I could see it in her eyes." Stella took a step back. "And now we've got to talk about something else or I'm going to start bawlin' like a baby. I hear that we're inspecting the quilt tomorrow. What did you kids learn while you were working on it?"

"To talk to each other, and that it's made from scraps of material that Nanny Lucy used to make clothes for us when Nessa and Flynn came to visit in the summer," April answered. "Did y'all know about the picture she had on the back of the quilt?"

Stella smiled and nodded as she got a puppy out of a cage and kissed him on the nose. "We did. We saw a place that could take a picture and fix it like that, and when we told her about it, she wanted that one of her and you kids the last time you were all home together put on the back. When did you find it?"

"When we were taking it out of the frame." April still got misty eyed just thinking about how much the picture meant to all of them.

"Stella told me you girls even made Flynn sew on the quilt." Vivien giggled.

April finished cleaning another cage, put the kitten back into it, and then moved on down to the next one. "Of course we did. Nanny Lucy taught us all three the goose and gander law."

Stella nodded as she recited the saying. "What's good for the goose is good for the gander."

"Yep, that's exactly what she said." April felt a weight lift off her shoulders at that good memory of her grandmother.

So you applied that law when you had an affair, didn't you, Nanny Lucy? April asked, but she got no answer.

"Hey, anyone here?" Kent called out from the vet side of the building.

"Come on back," April yelled.

Callie beat him through the door and ran across the room to wrap her arms around April. "Daddy finally brought me! Do you remember what I'm going to name my kitten?" She stopped long enough to suck in a lungful of air and went on. "Cindy, for Cinderella, because she has long blonde hair like you, and I like you." She ran out of air again.

"She's been bugging me ever since we saw y'all at Walmart to come back for the second kitten." Kent's smile lit up the whole room. "But two cats in the house is my limit."

"But our house is so big," Callie argued. "We could take all these poor little kitties home with us, Daddy."

"Two!" Kent held up two fingers.

"But how will I ever see April again?" Callie's chin began to quiver.

April stooped and gave the child a hug. "Darlin', you can come see me anytime you want to. You don't have to adopt a cat every time you come visit. And if your dad ever needs a babysitter so he can go on a date, maybe I could keep you for a few hours."

"And maybe you can come to my house to keep me and see the kitties?" Callie's expression changed from one of sadness to one of pure joy.

"We'll see when the time comes." April patted her on the back.

"Daddy needs a girlfriend, but he never, ever goes out." Callie pouted. "Maybe you could just come for a playdate sometime."

"Maybe, but right now, we've got to see which one of these kitty cats looks like a Cindy." April guided Callie gently over to the cages.

"Thank you," Kent mouthed.

"There's a yellow one with a pink bowl, so she's a girl." Callie pointed to a fluffy kitten with blue eyes. "She looks like a twin to my Belle. I think they will like each other a lot."

April took the kitten out of the cage and handed her to Callie. "Why don't you take her over to the rug and see if she likes to play?"

Callie nodded seriously, carried the animal to the area rug in the middle of the floor, and sat down. The minute she turned the kitten loose, it swatted a toy mouse halfway across the rug, then grabbed it up in its mouth and laid it in Callie's lap.

"This is the one, Daddy." Callie looked up at her father. "She loves me so much she brought me a present."

"Then I guess we better go talk to Miz Maudie about the adoption paperwork," Kent said. "But you have to promise me to not beg for another one."

Callie didn't budge from her spot on the rug. "I won't if you'll make a playdate with April. She likes cats just like me. I want her to come see my room and play with the kittens with me. Promise me?"

"Heaven help me," Kent groaned, but he promised.

"Miz Maudie isn't here. She left for lunch," Stella said, "but I can fill out those papers for you. April, you might come on with me, and I'll show you where they are and how to get them done."

"I'll be right here playing with the puppies," Vivien said.

Callie carried the kitten into the office right behind Stella. Kent had stepped to one side, but when April passed him, her arm brushed against his. Sparks danced all around the whole room, but she took a deep breath and gave herself a lecture.

This isn't the first time you've been attracted to a man, so ignore the electricity between the two of you. Besides, this is not, absolutely not, something you should even think about. He's a lawyer, and you work in an animal shelter. He's only humoring his daughter, so if and when he ever calls to set up a playdate, tell him you have plans.

"Okay, the adoption papers are always in this drawer," Stella said.

The squeaking noise the drawer made brought April back to the present. "Here, April." Stella handed three sheets stapled together at the corner to her. "I'll tell you what to write down. Once you do one, you will know how the next time."

When April finished, she had Kent's address and landline and cell numbers, as well as Callie's full name, her birthday, and what she planned to name the kitten. She gripped the pen so hard that her fingers ached when she finished. But dammit, Kent was leaning over her shoulder while she wrote, and his warm breath on her neck sent shivers up and down her spine. And that wasn't all—remnants of his aftershave lingered in the air, filling her nostrils with something woodsy with hints of cedar and ginger all mixed up together.

"Now, Kent, you and Callie sign your names on these lines." Stella whipped the paper around to face them. "Then we'll make a copy for you and put these in our files."

"When are you going to call April?" Callie asked her father as she carefully printed her name.

Kent's cheeks turned a little pink. "Well." He drew the word out to four syllables.

"I'll check my calendar for a day when I'm not working," April assured Callie. "You're going to be busy for a few weeks getting Cindy used to your big house and used to Belle."

"Thanks again," Kent mouthed over the top of Callie's head.

April smiled and nodded. She didn't expect him to ever ask her to babysit. And she wasn't sure what she would say if Kent called her and asked her to come spend time with his daughter. She really didn't have to worry about any of that, or the attraction she felt for the man, because she would probably never see him again.

Chapter Twenty-Two

Flynn found that sewing through two layers of fabric and the batting in between them was nothing compared to hemming a big quilt by hand. He was all thumbs when it came to doing something that Nessa called blind stitching. If the women from the quilting club didn't like the part of the quilt that he had hemmed and didn't pass them on their job, he would never know what was in the hope chest. More importantly, Nessa and April would never forgive him.

"Y'all need to stop hemming about three inches from the corners," Nessa said from her side of the quilt, which was draped over the kitchen table. "Mama taught me how to make perfect angles, so I'll do that part. Looks like we just might get finished by bedtime. Stella said she and Vivien are coming by tomorrow morning to look at it."

Flynn looked up at the clock above the stove and muttered, "Yeah, if we work until midnight."

April used a tape measure to figure out where the three inches fell and marked it with an extra pin. "Nanny Lucy always told the quilting club that she would do the corners, too. She was a perfectionist when it came to her sewing. And it's only eight o'clock, Flynn. I remember Nanny Lucy saying it took about an hour to do each side, so with three of us working, that's maybe an hour and a half."

"We need music." Nessa reached for her phone and brought up a playlist. "That will make the time go by faster. When I was a little girl, I figured out that each hymn Daddy played as we traveled was three to four minutes. That meant that about seventeen songs took up about an hour, and it was five hours from Canyon to Blossom, so I kept count with the gospel songs. Now I do it with what I have on my playlist."

"Don't tell me it's church songs," April groaned. "That's all Granny wanted to listen to when I was home, and I felt like religion was being shoved down my throat."

"Not a single hymn on the list," Nessa said as she hit the icon to start the music. "I think you'll like this first one."

The first notes of a guitar were joined by fiddle music, and then Travis Tritt started singing "I'm Gonna Be Somebody."

Flynn sang with Travis that someday he was going to break the chains and be somebody. "You're right," he said when the song ended, "music helps, and I believe that song was written just for me."

"This next one is for April," Nessa said.

April smiled when Travis started singing "Where Corn Don't Grow." The song talked about leaving home and going somewhere where corn doesn't grow. "I did feel I could find the answer where corn didn't grow, or in my case, anywhere but Blossom, Texas."

"And this one is for all of us." Nessa stopped sewing and wiped a tear from her eye when Chris Stapleton began singing "Broken Halos." The words talked about not going to look for answers because they belonged to the by-and-by.

By the time the song ended, all three of them had laid their needles to the side as tears welled, and then soft piano music began and those tears began to flow as Vince Gill sang "Go Rest High on That Mountain."

"We should have played this at her funeral," Flynn said. "It's Nanny Lucy from beginning to end. Like the words say, she wasn't afraid to face the devil, and she was no stranger to a lot of pain."

"I listened to this on the day she was buried," April said. "Her life on earth was troubled. I hope she's found the peace in eternity that we've found while we've been working on this quilt."

"Me too." Nessa nodded.

"Yes." Flynn's voice had become hoarse.

They listened to several more songs while they kept sewing, and then Flynn finished his last stitch, tied it off, stuck the needle he had been using in a spool of thread, and held up both hands.

"This one is for all of us, and it's not as sad as some of the others," Nessa said. "It's 'Storms Never Last.' We need to remember that as we go on with life."

April put the last stitch in her part of the quilt. "All done, and I never want to quilt again. How you can enjoy this is beyond me, Nessa."

"Everything is peaceful when I quilt." Nessa neatly folded the fabric to make a perfect ninety-degree angle, pinned it, and blind-stitched the last few inches of each side and then the corners. "It seems like my troubles and worries just fade away."

"My job at the shelter does that for me," April said. "Those animals love me. They don't care about my past. The puppies wag their tails and the kittens start to meow when I walk in the door. They're happy to see me, and that brings me peace." She left her chair, turned a rocking chair around in the living area to face the table, and sat down. "Oh, I forgot to tell y'all that Kent Wallace brought his little girl, Callie, in today for another kitten. She was determined that he would invite me to his house for a playdate with her."

"How did that make you feel?" Nessa asked.

"Scared," April answered with a single word.

"That's weird. What would you be scared of?" Flynn asked. "You've practically lived on the streets, or at least in your car, and you dealt with men who were pretty low down."

April covered a yawn with the back of her hand. "I don't know why I felt fear. Kent is a lawyer. He seems like a great guy, and Callie is a precious child. Maybe I'm still afraid to trust myself around people—we're pretty isolated out here. But I don't have to worry about any of that. He told Callie that two kittens was the limit, and we don't get many repeat customers at the shelter. She'll start school in the fall and forget all about me."

"We've all proven that sometimes the unexpected happens," Flynn said. "As far as my work, we need the repeat business over at Jackson's. Which reminds me, April and I probably won't be here tomorrow when they come to look at the quilt, Nessa. Will you text me when they leave?" Flynn asked.

"Yes," Nessa answered. "I'm a little nervous about the whole deal, but I wouldn't be any less if y'all were here. So I will let y'all know when it's over." Nessa didn't look up from her work.

"Thanks. When are we going to take that one down?" April pointed to the quilt behind the sofa.

"Tomorrow after y'all get home from work," Nessa said. "Maybe we should have champagne or at least a beer when we hang the new one up."

"I'll stop by the store on my way home and pick up a six-pack." April pulled the sofa cushions off, stacked them by the door, and popped out her bed. "I'll be in town every day, so if we need anything, I can pick it up."

"All done!" Nessa said. "Three weeks and we've got it done. I can't expect to finish one on my own in that time, but it gives me an idea of how long it will take. I'd thought I could do four this summer. Boy, was I dreaming big!"

April stopped straightening the sheets on her bed and yawned again. "Awww, come on now. If you quilt all day while we're at work, I bet you can get more done than you think."

"You're right. I should treat this like you treat your jobs," Nessa said. "Thanks for the encouragement."

"You are so welcome, but I'm not just whistling Dixie. I believe what I said. You are good at what you do, girl. I'm going to bed. Y'all can stay up and talk all night if you want to, but I'm tired and sleepy."

"Just one thing before we all turn in," Flynn said. "I'm glad that we did this quilt project together. This has been an emotional night to end a lot of days of work that has brought us all together. I'm going to bed before I get all weepy again. Jackson has agreed to let me work full-time, so I'll be getting up and around earlier than usual."

"Good night," April and Nessa chorused.

"Night to you both," Flynn said with a wave as he walked away.

❖ ❖ ❖

"Are you going to be all right going over to Jackson's tomorrow when we open the hope chest?" April whispered.

"I'm a grown woman. I've made man mistakes before. This isn't the first and it won't be the last. I'm sure it will be awkward, but I'll live through it. Besides, tomorrow evening we'll find out what's in that hope chest. I won't let Jackson take the fun out of that." Nessa folded the finished quilt neatly and carried it to her room.

The truth of the matter was that she absolutely dreaded going over to Jackson's place. She shoved the quilt onto the trundle part of the bed and stripped out of her pajama pants and oversize T-shirt. She opened the bottom dresser drawer, took out Jackson's button-down shirt, and put it on. Tomorrow she would wash the garment and take it back to him, but tonight she wanted to feel his arms around her again—even if it was just a shirt.

The next morning Nessa had taken a pan of chocolate chip cookies from the oven when someone knocked on the door. Expecting it to be Stella and Vivien, she raced across the room and opened the door to find Jackson barely two feet from her. She forgot to breathe, and her chest tightened. Her pulse raced, and her hands got all sweaty. Then she remembered that she was still wearing his shirt. She really had intended to put it in the wash that morning. A blush rushed from her neck to her cheeks, coming close to setting them on fire.

"May I come in?" Jackson asked.

She stepped to the side and motioned him inside. "Of course. Is Flynn all right? What are you doing here in the middle of the morning?"

Jackson stood just inside the door. "Flynn has gone to town to get more sandpaper. I thought I had enough to last until the first of the month, when a new shipment comes in, but with two of us working, we're down to the last piece. But that's not why I'm here. I've gone over the night that we slept together a dozen times in my mind, and I can't figure out why you're so angry." He took a step to the side and eyed her from head to toe. "You're wearing my shirt. If you are so mad at me over something I did or didn't do, then why would you be wearing my shirt?"

Her cheeks turned so red that they burned. "I was on my way to the garage to throw it in the washing machine. See?" she stammered. "Can we please talk about that night later, even this afternoon or evening when we come over to open the hope chest? Stella and Vivien are coming over to inspect the quilt. They'll be here in five minutes."

"I can't leave. Miz Lucy's lawyer says that I have to be here when the ladies check out the quilt. That will keep everything aboveboard and legal. If they say y'all did it right, then you can open the hope chest. If you didn't, I guess I'm stuck with the thing forever, and no one will ever know what's in it." Jackson's tone was downright icy. "I would appreciate it greatly if you would bring my shirt home tonight when you come over to my house."

"I can do that." Nessa felt like someone had sucker punched her in the stomach. "Have a seat. I'll change into a different shirt and put yours in the washing machine." She whipped around and went to the garage.

"Sweet Lord, why didn't I think about him being here for the judging?" she muttered as she removed his shirt and put hers on. She tossed his into the machine and added detergent. Then she turned her back and slid down the front of the washing machine with her back to it. She drew her knees up, wrapped her arms around them, and closed her eyes. She hadn't really prayed in a year, but that morning she did.

Lord, please let Stella and Vivien give us a pass on the quilt, and help me to not look at Jackson's eyes when I tell him what I think about the way he's treated me, she said silently.

When she opened her eyes, Stella was standing right in front of her. "Are you all right, child?"

"I'm fine. Just a little headache." Nessa couldn't say that the headache was over six feet tall and had gorgeous blue eyes.

"Should we wait to look at the quilt?" Stella extended a hand to help her up.

Nessa took it and forced a smile. "Thank you, but no, let's go take a look at it. We're all anxious to see what's in the hope chest. If I put off letting you see it for a week, Flynn and April would disown me."

"Then let's get it over with, but"—Stella lowered her voice—"what is Jackson doing in the living room?"

"The will says he has to hear you, or some member of the club, say that the quilt passes muster," Nessa said.

Stella's laughter echoed off the walls and drowned out the noise of the washing machine. "Lucy really took care of things, didn't she? We were just told to make sure the quilt was finished. We didn't come here to rake you over the coals about your stitching. We just want to have a look at the final product."

Nessa bit back the tears that were dammed up behind her eyelids. She wasn't sure if they were tears of relief that the quilt wasn't going to keep them from opening the hope chest or if they were tears of anger.

Or jealousy? the aggravating voice in her head asked.

Nessa shook that idea from her mind and led the way into the house. "I'll bring it out, then, and you can see that it's all done."

"Great, then me and Vivien can be on our way." Stella followed close behind her.

"Well, look at you. If you're not the image of Lucy when she was about your age," Vivien said from Lucy's rocking chair. The woman was pretty much a mirror image of her sister, Stella, except that she'd dyed her hair jet black and wore bright-red lipstick.

"Thank you." Nessa managed a weak smile.

"You are quite welcome. Lucy had her bad moments, but when she wasn't suffering, she was the best friend we ever had," Vivien said.

Talk about bad moments. It took all of Nessa's willpower not to shoot a knowing look right at Jackson.

Vivien went on, "She was a good Christian woman, and I always thought she was a beauty."

"Well, then, thank you a whole bunch more times." Nessa went to her room and brought out the quilt. She flipped it out on the back of the sofa. "What do you think?"

"It's the ugliest thing that Lucy ever made," Stella answered.

"And we both told her so." Vivien nodded. "But it's finished, and you kids did a great job, so our part of this—whatever this is—has been done. You can open the hope chest and put this in it."

"Then my work is done. I'll be seeing all y'all around, I'm sure." Jackson pushed himself up out of Grandpa's rocking chair and waved over his shoulder as he left the house.

Dozens of thoughts vied for first place in Nessa's head. She was relieved and yet sad at the same time that the quilt was done. What had started out as a chore had turned into something she looked forward to doing each morning with her cousins. She wanted to clear the air with Jackson, but she didn't. What if it turned into a big fight that put a virtual fence between them even just as neighbors?

"Looks to me like Jackson done found a cockroach in his morning bowl of cereal," Vivien giggled. "He's never been that curt with us before."

"Could be that he doesn't want the O'Riley kids to open that hope chest," Stella added. "We should be . . . Whoa!" She paused for a good fifteen seconds. "What are those loops on the side of the quilt?"

Nessa had hoped that they wouldn't even notice, but it's near impossible to put a cat back in the bag when it's already out. She figured she might as well just tell the truth, and she did. When she was through explaining what she and the other two had decided, both Stella and Vivien had tears streaming down their faces.

"Are you crying because you think we're doing the wrong thing by not following Nanny Lucy's wishes?" Nessa wiped a tear from her own cheek.

"Oh, no, honey." Vivien pulled a tissue from the box on the end table and dabbed at her eyes. "I just think that's the sweetest thing ever."

"Me too." Stella wiped her eyes on a handkerchief that she took from her purse. "Hanging it up there on the wall means that you are remembering the good times and not the ugly ones. Lucy wanted you three cousins to be close."

"Did she say that?" Nessa asked.

"More than once," Stella answered. "She hoped that making y'all work on that quilt would help."

"She got her wish. We've talked about the good, the bad, and the crazy while we worked on the quilt. We do plan to take down the one up there"—Nessa nodded toward the one hanging on the wall—"and put it in the hope chest. That way whoever gets married first will have a quilt that she made."

Nessa didn't miss the look that Vivien shot Stella or the nod that Stella gave her.

"We've got something to tell you. We knew that Lucy was dying, but it wasn't the first time we intervened and made her go to the doctor. That quilt up there on the wall was the last one that we all worked on together. After that, she had trouble concentrating on sewing anymore. We helped her get the ugly one that she made with remnants of all you kids' clothes in the frame just weeks before she passed. She had a bubble in her brain, and the doctor said that when it burst, that would be the end," Stella said.

"We begged her to tell Matthew and Isaac, or even you kids, but she refused." Vivien's chin quivered, but she didn't break down. "We think it was because she didn't want to have the surgery, and the boys would have tried to force the issue. With it she would have had a fifty-fifty chance to survive, but she wouldn't do it."

"What kind of surgery?" Nessa asked.

"She had an aneurism in her brain," Stella answered. "The doctor said there would be risks if she had surgery. Like she might lose her motor skills and have to go to a nursing home or live with her sons."

"Did it hurt?" Nessa pulled two tissues from the box and blew her nose.

Vivien and Stella both shook their heads.

"No pain, but there at the end, she kept telling us that she wanted to go before Christmas Day. You kids usually found a way to come home sometime during the holidays, and she was afraid you might suspect something was wrong," Stella answered.

"She just got absentminded. We didn't know if that thing on her brain was pushing on something that made her forget things, or if maybe it was worry, or if the depression she'd fought for years was the cause," Vivien chimed in.

"I'm so sorry, honey." Stella sighed and headed for the door with Vivien right behind her. "We hate to leave you after telling you all that, but I'm glad you know. We'd best get on our way."

"Thank you," Nessa said, and then she remembered that she'd made cookies and had planned on offering them to the ladies while they examined the quilt. "Let me give you some coffee in a to-go cup and some cookies to snack on as you travel."

"That would be great," Vivien said.

Nessa hurriedly filled two disposable cups with coffee and put a dozen cookies in a paper sack for the ladies. They each gave her a hug and told her again what a great idea it was to hang the quilt the three of them had finished. She followed them out to the porch and waved until they were out of sight.

"Nanny Lucy used to do this when Mama would come and get me," she remembered, and she wondered if her grandmother had been truly sorry to see them leave—or relieved. *So many secrets.*

Chapter Twenty-Three

*N*essa thought back over the past three weeks as she ran a brush through her hair that evening. In her mind, Nanny Lucy's place had always been the house of freedom. To April, it had been a prison. To Flynn, a place of sorrow because his mother had died while he was in Blossom. She still thought it was strange that one house could be so different for each of them. But then, Nanny Lucy hadn't treated April the same as she had Flynn and Nessa.

"You about ready in there?" Flynn rapped on the door. "I told Jackson we'd probably be over there at six thirty."

"Give me one more minute," she called out. *I don't know if I'm anxious because we're going to open the hope chest or if I'm nervous because I have to face Jackson again. I can't avoid it, no matter what, so I might as well suck it up and get it over with.*

"Ten, nine, eight," Flynn counted down. When he got to five, she opened the door.

He used both hands in a flourishing gesture to point at the quilt hanging above the sofa. "What do you think?"

"It's still ugly as sin"—Nessa forced a smile—"but I love it. It's the good, the bad, and the ugly of our lives hanging up there to remind us of the summers we got to spend together. It's kind of like a whole array of family pictures."

Flynn and April both nodded, and then April held up the folded quilt they were taking to Jackson's house. "Are we driving or walking?"

"We should drive this time," Flynn answered. "We don't know what's in the hope chest. It could be nothing, but then it could be too much to try to carry back here."

"We can take my vehicle," Nessa offered. "Do either of you even want to take a guess about what's in the hope chest?" She wanted them to talk so that it would take her mind off seeing Jackson again.

Flynn opened the door for April since she had her hands full. "Not me," he answered. "If we hadn't already found the stuff in the closet, I would have said pictures and important papers."

"I just hope one of you gets married first," April said. "I don't want anything that's in that old chest. I got sent to my room for a whole afternoon for just sitting on the thing one time. Nanny Lucy put high value on *things*, more so than people's feelings. I'm never going to put something like a wooden box above the feelings of a person."

Nessa was right behind April, and she hurried a little and gave her cousin a gentle sideways hug. "I'm so sorry that you had to live with the angry side of Nanny Lucy."

Flynn closed the door and brought up the rear. "I loved our grandmother, but I'm just now coming to grips with the fact that she didn't offer to let me stay here when Mama died. She knew what kind of man my dad was, and yet she sent me to him instead of raising me here, but I understand now that she was hoping that if I lived with my dad, he would shape up."

Nessa slid in behind the steering wheel, waited until Flynn and April were settled into the SUV, and then started the engine. "Seems like y'all didn't put her up on a pedestal like I did, but we've sure come a long way in just three weeks."

"Yes, we have, and I'm glad for it," April said from the back seat. "She must have felt real time pressure there at the end. I believe that she wanted us to make amends with the past, and maybe even with her, and that's the reason we had to make that quilt."

"Yep," Flynn agreed. "I figured I would spend this month helping you two clean out the house and then go back to South Texas."

"And I never thought that I'd be doing a job that I love," April said. "Today Maudie and I set up a plan for me to take over the computer work for her. I'll work half a day in the shelter and the other half in the vet office."

"What can I say?" Nessa pulled to a stop beside Jackson's pickup. "I came here with the idea that I would probably stay. I just hope this quilting business makes enough money that I can survive."

Flynn stared at the white frame house. "This is it, girls. This is the day we've been waiting for. Do you feel a little like it's Christmas?"

"Not me," April answered. "It's more like Halloween. I'm going to stand way back when Jackson opens that thing."

"Thinking something scary might pop out of it?" Nessa's chuckle caught in her throat.

"With Nanny Lucy, you never know. It could be filled with switches or dollar bills, but I'm not taking any chances." April's voice quivered.

Nessa shut off the engine and slung open the door. She had two things to worry about that evening, and the hope chest was the second in line.

Jackson stepped out on the porch and waved at them. "Y'all come on in. I've got cold beers or coffee waiting."

"Thanks. A beer sounds good," Flynn yelled across the yard.

Nessa noticed that April took a little longer than necessary to open the rear door, pick up the quilt, and get out of the vehicle. Could it be that she was serious when she talked about what could be in the hope chest? Nessa rounded the back of the SUV and waited for her cousin. "It's going to be all right," she reassured her. "Whatever is in there can't hurt you now."

"Probably not, but I still don't want that hope chest. If I get married first and have to take it, I'll give it to you or Flynn or make a bonfire out of it," April declared as she hugged the quilt to her chest. "Guess I've still got a long way to go before I'm completely healed."

"We can't expect to be over the past in only three weeks, but we can close the door to it and choose to be happy one day at a time." Nessa gave her another sideways hug.

"I can do that." April nodded in agreement.

Jackson held the door for the two women and took the quilt from April. "Flynn told me this morning what you're doing with the quilt you just finished. I think Miz Lucy would like that. So are we ready to open this thing, or should we have a beer and some kind of ceremony?"

Nessa glanced his way and saw as much confusion in his eyes as was in her heart. *Good Lord,* she thought, *what if I judged him wrong? What if not simply asking him about the woman has ruined any chance of a relationship we might have had? I could just have asked.*

"Let's have a beer," April answered.

"I'll bring them out." Jackson smiled and headed to the kitchen. "Take a seat anywhere you like. I'll drag the hope chest out into the middle of the floor to open it so you can all see what's inside. Once we're done, I can scoot it back in the corner again." He brought a six-pack of cold beers out and set them on the scarred coffee table.

April had taken the rocking chair, and Flynn sat on one end of the sofa. Since there were only two places left, and they were both on the sofa, that meant Nessa and Jackson would be side by side until someone opened the hope chest. She chose the other end so that at least she wouldn't be between the two guys.

Jackson twisted the cap off a bottle and handed it to Nessa, and then did the same for Flynn and April. When he sat down in the middle of the sofa, his whole right side was pressed against Nessa. She was surprised that the sparks didn't light up the whole room.

"Does anyone want to guess what might be in the chest?" he asked.

Nessa took a long drink of her beer, but it didn't touch the fire raging in her hormones. Right then she didn't care if there was a million dollars for each of them, or if the hope chest turned out to be empty. She just wanted to talk to Jackson alone and figure out where she stood with him. She was through being mad and was ready to get things settled.

April was the first one to speak up. "I think there's keepsakes in there that were valuable to her but not worth much. But I wouldn't be surprised if a bomb went off when the lock is turned. She was so disappointed in us that she might be ready to end the O'Riley line right here and now."

Nessa's blood ran cold. Poor Nanny Lucy had had so many disappointments in her life, beginning with Grandpa, that she just might have put his head in the hope chest, too.

Flynn turned up his beer, took a long drink, and then set it on the coffee table. "Let's just get it over with. Anyone want to send up a prayer or make a confession just in case April is right?"

"There's not a bomb in there," Jackson chuckled. "She might blow y'all into eternity, but she wouldn't harm a hair on my head. She liked me."

"You willing to bet on that?" Nessa asked.

"Yep, I am." Jackson turned and gazed into her eyes a second time.

"If you're that confident, then drag it out here," April told him. "But let's make a pact right now between us three. If there's something in there that will tear apart the friendship we've built, then let's burn it tonight and pretend it was never there."

"I agree," Flynn said.

Nessa took one more swallow of her beer and set it beside Flynn's bottle. "Me too."

Jackson pulled the chest away from the wall and removed the key that was taped to the back. He didn't make a big fanfare but simply slipped the key into the lock and turned it. "Does one of you want to have the honor of lifting the lid?"

April shook her head.

Flynn just stared at the thing.

Nessa got to her feet, took a couple of steps, and eased the lid up. It bumped onto the floor. "There now. It's done, and it did not blow up in our faces."

"What's in it?" Flynn asked.

Nessa bent down and picked up an envelope from the bottom of the hope chest. "Just this. Looks like a letter. Either of you want to read it, or should I?"

"You do it," April said. "If she had a favorite among the three of us, it was you."

Nessa sat down on the floor and tore open the envelope, fully expecting to find some legal paper, but it was a handwritten letter from her grandmother. She recognized the perfect penmanship from the birthday cards she had received from Nanny Lucy through the years. "It's a letter," she whispered. "Are you sure you want me to read it out loud?"

"Maybe you'd rather do that with just you three . . . ," Jackson said.

Nessa held up a palm in protest. Jackson was a part of this whether the two of them got things straightened out or not, and her heart told her that he should stay for the reading. "She trusted you to keep this thing, which is more than she trusted one of us, so you can hear what she has to say. Here goes."

To my grandchildren,

If you have opened the hope chest, I'm dead and the quilt that I left for you is finished. Knowing Nessa and her neatness, I'm pretty sure she cleaned out the hall closet, and you've found my diary in the suitcase by now. I've been in the ground for a while, so I don't care if you kids know about the O'Riley dirty laundry. Do with it what you will, but I do hope you are more honest with your children than I have been with you. It must have come as a shock to hear that your grandfather was a womanizer, that I had an affair with my best friend's husband, and that Rachel didn't belong to your grandfather. But you know all that by now, so there's no need rehashing it in this letter.

Nessa laid the first page in her lap. "What if we hadn't found her diary and all those papers?" Even after just one page, she felt even more numb than she had at Nanny Lucy's funeral.

"Then you can bet your sweet soul we would be rushing over to the house to find it," April said.

"We have all had our share of secrets," Flynn said, "and no one is perfect."

Nessa began to read the second page:

I thought about leaving all my money to you kids, but then that didn't seem fair to my boys. Matthew would go through the inheritance like he does his women. Isaac might do something good with it, but I've been mad at him for a long time now. He tried to make Nessa marry a man of his choosing. When she didn't bow to his wishes, he cut her off, and that didn't set well with me. That went against the Christian values I thought he had. He might be a preacher, but he's got a controlling streak like his father had, and I don't want to give him a single dime.

When the doctors told me that the ugly mass in my head could explode at any time, I stayed up all night, trying to figure out what to do with my money and my things. I had a million dollars in the bank, plus what I had in my checking account. The quilting business has been very good to me. Finally, I made the decision about the house and land. You know that, of course. Then right after Thanksgiving I donated my money to a research lab that is studying bipolar disorder. Maybe my mood swings are what made your grandfather start cheating on me, or maybe his cheating happened and then my system went out of balance. At this point it doesn't really matter.

I hope you weren't expecting to find money in the hope chest. I want you to make your own way and find your own happiness. Don't depend on someone else like I did to make you happy. Be content and complete within yourselves. Then, when and if one of you finds someone to love, you can give them your whole heart. I gave you each a little seed money and a place to live. If you decide to live in Blossom, you've got that much. If not, then you've got a vacation place. I do hope that you spend some time there each summer and rekindle that closeness that you kids had back when you were young.

That said, I'll move on to the quilt. I hope you recognized the fabric I used in the quilt top and remembered the good times you all had in the summer when you got to be together for a couple of weeks. I tried to make those times happy for all of you.

Now, to each of you individually.

Flynn, I'm sorry I didn't offer to take you in and raise you when your mama died. Sometimes I felt as high as the clouds in the sky. Other times I was so low that I couldn't lift my head off the bed. I couldn't bring you into that world. It was tough enough on April to have to live in it. It wasn't until April left home that Stella and Vivien made me go to the doctor, and I got medicine for my problem. I still got bouts of sadness when I *thought about the wrong choices I'd made in life, but I did get better than I was.*

Nessa stopped reading and focused on Flynn. He was blinking back tears, and his voice cracked when he spoke. "Maybe I did have it better with my dad than I would have if I'd stayed here."

"You did," April said. "At least you knew exactly where you stood with him. I never knew from one minute to the next what to expect out of Nanny Lucy. Go on, Nessa."

Nessa found her place and read:

April, I apologize for everything. I tried to love you, but it just wasn't in me. I could blame it on my bipolar disorder, but that would be a lie. I didn't want a third child, and I sure didn't want to raise another one when you came along. Your mother was such a disappointment, and then you came along right behind her. You deserved better than you got. I sincerely hope that I didn't completely ruin your life. I won't try to justify the way I treated you, because that's not possible. You would have been much better off if I had given you out for adoption after Rachel died, but I felt so guilty about the way I treated Rachel that I felt like I owed it to her to keep you in the family.

Nessa looked up to see tears streaming down April's face. "If she had given me up for adoption, I would have never known y'all or this moment. I forgive you, Nanny Lucy, and I hope you have found peace in eternity. Lord knows you sure didn't have much here on this earth. I just wish you'd have talked more about my mother so I could have known her through what you could tell me. And I wish Mama and I hadn't been such a huge disappointment to you."

Flynn sucked in a lungful of air and let it out in a whoosh. "That's a hell of a lot to forgive, April."

"You don't forgive someone just for them," April told him. "You forgive to take away the hard spots in your own heart. You forgive for your own peace of mind." She remembered what Maudie had said about the first little kitten that Callie adopted and about how forgiving animals were.

"Okay, I've only got one page left," Nessa said.

Last, this is to Nessa. I've seen that you struggle with what is true service to God and what is your father's version of what it should be. I was so proud of him for going into the ministry, so proud that he wasn't like his father. But I've come to realize that he just hides his controlling nature behind a pulpit. Don't let him taint your idea of religion. I'm probably confusing you, but what I want you to know is that I'm proud of you for standing up to him.

Now that I've tried to make amends for my misdeeds, I pray that none of you will make the same mistakes I did. I wish you all a happy, fruitful life.

Nessa expected to see it signed "Love, Nanny Lucy," but it ended right there.

"And that's all." She could hear disappointment in her own voice and looked up to see the same thing in Flynn and April's expressions.

"Well, now we know." April tipped up her beer and took a sip. "I can't help but wonder if she would have been a different person if she'd gotten help sooner. She must have held so much in when you and Flynn visited so that we could have a good time together."

"What makes you say that?" Nessa folded the letter into the envelope and dropped it back in the hope chest.

"Because she was a nightmare for a few days after you left. I thought it was because she loved you and Flynn so much more than me. I figured out that she was going to be in a horrible mood when you were gone, and I'd stay away from her as much as possible." April brought the quilt from across the room and laid it in the hope chest on top of the letter.

"Should I push it back in the corner? Or has one of you gotten married? In that case, you can take it home," Jackson asked.

"Well, that lightened the mood, but hell, no!" Flynn chuckled. "We're just now making progress in getting our lives in order. I'll take care of putting it back."

"I can understand that. As they say, been there, done that," Jackson said, but his eyes were on Nessa. "This has been kind of anticlimactic, hasn't it?"

"Little bit," Flynn said.

"I'm just glad to still be breathing," April joked.

Jackson laid the key on top of the quilt. "There's no reason to lock it up, is there?"

"None that I can think of," Nessa answered, feeling mixed emotions about the way Jackson was looking at her.

He returned the chest to the corner and sat down on the other end of the sofa from Flynn. Nessa didn't budge from her place on the floor. She finished off her beer and set the bottle on the coffee table. She wondered if it would be rude to say that they needed to leave. No one was saying anything, and a gloom hung over the room like smoke in an old Western bar.

Flynn frowned. "Do you think what Nanny Lucy suffered with is hereditary? Do we have to worry about it?"

"I have no idea, but if I start showing symptoms, I'm going to go straight to the psychiatrist and get medicine for it," Nessa answered. "There are a number of kids each year in my school who meet with our counselors. It makes a big difference."

"I'm with Nessa and would treat it, but maybe it's not something we have to worry about," April said. "Talking about it is hard, though."

"She wouldn't want this to be a sad night," Jackson said. "Y'all want to play a board game to get our minds off that letter? I've got Pictionary or Monopoly."

"Yes!" April's smile reached her eyes. "I choose Flynn for a partner. Nessa, you can have Jackson."

"What if I wanted to play guys against gals?" Flynn asked.

"I remember us playing Pictionary when we were kids, and you were the best, so either it's me and you against those two"—April swung her forefinger around to include both Nessa and Jackson—"or I'm going home to watch reruns of *Criminal Minds* on television."

"She's been hanging around you too much, Nessa," Flynn said. "She's almost as bossy as you are."

"That's a good thing," Nessa said. "Don't knock it. I'll play Pictionary, but if you'd decided on Monopoly, I was going home." She still wished that she had piped up and said that they should be going as soon as the hope chest was pushed back into the corner.

"I guess it's me and you, doll, against the pros," Jackson drawled like an old-time gangster. "Think we can whip them?"

Nessa shrugged. "Of course we can, but . . ." She gave him a long sideways look.

"But first we need to talk, right?" he asked.

She nodded.

"Our conversation might take a while," he said. "Could we put it off until tomorrow morning when all the tension of opening the hope chest has passed?"

Nessa nodded again. She would have liked to have gotten it over with, but then, on the other hand, she might feel better if she slept one more night on the matter. Nanny Lucy always said that things looked better after a good night's sleep and in the daylight, instead of darkness.

Chapter Twenty-Four

As they had left his house the night before, Jackson had asked Nessa to come over the next evening after work so they could have their talk. The day dragged by like a crippled snail, and something akin to crackling electricity had hung in the air ever since she'd woken up that morning. She busied herself by cutting the pieces for a quilt kit. Jackson had said that Nanny Lucy's kits sold even better than her finished products, so Nessa intended to have several ready for the fall craft fairs. "And four quilts, too," she told Waylon, who was watching every move she made from a kitchen chair.

"I'm home!" April dropped her purse on the rocking chair nearest the door.

Nessa heaved a huge sigh of relief. She was so ready to get this visit with Jackson over with.

"Did you hear that we're under a tornado watch?" April asked.

"I usually get that kind of notice on my phone, but I guess I wasn't paying attention." Nessa cut the last piece of cloth and put it into a ziplock baggie. "And I haven't had the television or radio on all day. How did your day go?"

"Great!" April crossed the living room and dining area and went straight to the kitchen. "What do I smell?" She removed the lid from the slow cooker and sniffed.

"Kidney bean soup," Nessa said. "Yeast rolls are on the stove to go with it."

"I'm not waiting on Flynn." April filled a bowl with the thick soup and put two rolls on a plate. "I'm starving. Nanny Lucy never made this. Where did you get the recipe?" She set the food down on the end of the table and took a bite. "Sometimes I had to do some basic cooking when Nanny Lucy had bad days. I wonder now how on earth she cared for me during those times."

"One of the church ladies used to bring it to soup-and-sandwich nights at my dad's church. When I asked her for the recipe, she gave it to me," Nessa said.

April buttered a hot roll and took another bite of the soup. "Is it hard to make? I could eat this stuff every week."

"Might be the easiest soup in the world to make," Nessa answered. "You crumble up a pound of hamburger in a pot with a small diced onion, cover it with water, and boil until the meat is done and the onions are tender. Pour in two cans of kidney beans and a can of tomato sauce. Then add about a cup of ketchup and a fourth cup of Worcestershire sauce and simmer. I make it and pour it into a slow cooker and let it simmer on low for a few hours. Daddy liked to add a little more Worcestershire sauce to it. Mama always served it with hot rolls and an assortment of sliced cheese."

"Well, it's really good," April said.

"Glad you like it." Nessa put away the sewing machine and cleared the table of quilting scraps. "I've kind of felt something in the air all day, so I'm not surprised there's a tornado watch."

"Maudie says every time a little breeze kicks up around these parts, the weather folks issue a tornado watch. She says we shouldn't start to worry until they call it a warning. Then we shouldn't get our under-britches in a twist until we feel it in the air," April said between bites.

"She must be a hoot to work for." Nessa thought of her previous principal, who had never seemed to smile. Then she thought of the electricity she'd felt in the air all day. Could it have been the approaching storm and not her anxiety over talking to Jackson?

"Yes, she's more like a friend than a boss, and honey, the electricity in the air around here isn't a tornado." April giggled. "It's just sparks jumping back and forth from our house to Jackson's. I could almost see them when we played Pictionary last night. You ever think that you might have been wrong about the woman with him in Walmart? Maybe she was just a good friend. When are you going to have it out with him?"

"I'm going over there right now," Nessa answered. "I'll either feel like a fool because I was jealous, or like an idiot because I didn't give him a chance to tell me what was going on. At least it will be out in the open."

Flynn came in the door, kicked off his shoes, stopped to pet Waylon, and headed to the kitchen. "I'm starving, and I smell yeast rolls."

"Supper is on the stove and in the slow cooker," Nessa told him. "Help yourself. There's a lemon chess pie in the refrigerator."

"I'm sure glad that I'm working every day. If I was just sittin' on the porch watching the clouds roll in, I'd gain fifty pounds before Christmas," Flynn said as he dipped up a bowl of soup. "Aren't you going to eat with us, Nessa?"

"I've been too antsy to eat. I'll see y'all later," she said.

April gave her a brief nod and went back for a second bowl of soup.

Nessa kept her eyes on the ground to avoid stepping in a hole or stumbling over a rock. She went through a dozen scenarios about how to even ask Jackson about the woman, and none of them worked. When the wind picked up and blew her hair back away from her face, she looked up at the sky and saw the dark clouds in the southwest.

"I guess that's what caused the warning," she muttered as she rounded the corner of Jackson's house.

He was standing on the porch, his hands on the railing, with Tex right beside him. His eyes were on the clouds, and he didn't even notice her until Tex barked. He whipped around and yelled, "What are you doing out in this weather? We've been issued . . ." His voice was blown away in a sudden burst of wind, and his finger shot up to point at a funnel swirling down from the dark clouds that looked like it couldn't be more than half a mile away. He jumped from the porch to the ground in one leap and grabbed her hand.

"That thing is coming right at us. Run, Nessa!" he screamed.

She glanced over her shoulder to see the whirling vortex devour a tree, roots and all, and almost froze in her tracks, but he yanked on her hand and she started running. The noise above them sounded like a freight train as Jackson guided her into the storm cellar right behind Tex. He pulled the heavy door shut and barred it with a long length of wood. Then the sound got louder and louder.

Nessa dug her cell phone out of her pocket and used it for a flashlight. "Do you have electricity down here?" Her heart was beating so fast that her words came out between breaths.

Jackson struck a match and lit the wick of an oil lamp. "No electricity. Wouldn't do us much good—every time the wind blows, we lose power for an hour or two. I've got a generator for the shop, but this is as good as it gets down here. Have a seat. We might be here . . ."

His voice was cut off again when it sounded like a full-grown elephant landed on the cellar door. Nessa's hands went to cover her ears. Tex whimpered and crawled under the twin bed against the wall. Nessa took her hands down at the same time that something else landed on top of the cellar.

Jackson motioned toward the bed, then took her by the hand. "We're safe. That was a close call, but we're alive. You're shivering. Are you cold?"

"No, just the aftereffects of the bejesus getting scared out of me."

He draped an arm around her shoulders and led her to the bed, then pulled her down beside him. She was reminded of the song on her playlist about storms never lasting. "Is it over? Can we go outside?" she asked.

"I think it's just rain and hail right now, but if that was the big pecan tree in the backyard that fell on the cellar door, we'll be here until someone comes to see about us," he answered.

"Or maybe the tornado threw that other tree it grabbed up down the road back down on us." Nessa's heart pounded in her chest even harder, and her hands felt clammy. Her eyes darted around the small space. Shelves stocked with canned goods at the end of the oblong room and a small table where the oil lamp sat were all that was down there, except for the twin bed. She wasn't sure what was storm fear at that point and what was fear of finally being in a place where she and Jackson could talk.

Face your fears. Her father had preached that so many times. *Don't be afraid to put your trust in God. Give Him your life and your heart.*

But Jackson isn't God. He's just a man, she argued.

"I'll try to open the door, but I can tell you right now that we're here until someone rescues us." Jackson got to his feet and put his shoulder and both hands against the door, but it didn't budge. "I just hope the house and shop are still standing when we get out of here. That still sounds pretty fierce out there. Uncle D. J. and I had to come down here a few times, but we never saw anything like that funnel."

The idea of the tornado and wind blowing Nanny Lucy's house away hit Nessa harder than the idea of being stuck in a cellar until someone came to rescue them. A lump formed in her throat when she thought of Flynn and April being covered up with the debris from the house with no way to get out of the cellar under the garage floor. She pulled her phone from her hip pocket and groaned when a message popped up saying she had a low battery. She sent a quick text asking Flynn if they were all right, and got one back saying they were safe and about to survey the damage at Nanny Lucy's.

> We're stuck in Jackson's cellar. Send hell..p

She started to correct the spelling but hit send instead.

"Did you bring your phone?" she asked Jackson.

"It's in the house, if it's still standing," he groaned. "Did you get a message out?"

She nodded. "But it's misspelled. I hope they know I meant for them to send help and not hell."

Jackson's chuckle relieved some of Nessa's tension. "I'd take a little hell if it could remove whatever is laying on the door. I sure hope it's a tree and not my table saw. But the important thing is that we're safe." He draped an arm around her shoulders. "Another minute and you would have been caught right in the middle of the thing."

Nessa shivered from her neck to her toes.

"Cold?" Jackson asked again as he pulled her closer to his side.

She shook her head. "I saw that funnel tear a tree out of the ground like it was a toothpick and swallow it whole just before we got into the cellar. I thought we would both be sucked up into that thing and never get to have our talk."

"We're a couple of lucky people," Jackson said, "but what were you doing out in this weather, anyway? Not that I'm complaining. It would be lonely down here with just Tex to talk to. I'd thought maybe I'd call you and ask if we could meet at the waterfall."

Nessa drew in a long breath and let it out slowly. "I don't know how to approach this without sounding like a jealous fishwife. The day after our third date, when we . . ." She paused.

"When we made love," he finished the sentence for her.

"Yes." She was going to say "had sex," but she liked his phrase better. "That next day you were with a tall brunette woman at Walmart, and she kissed you on the cheek. Then you drove off with her in your truck."

Jackson drew his dark brows down and cocked his head to the side. After a minute, his face relaxed and he smiled. "Oh, that was Brenda. She's the wife of a lawyer friend of mine in Paris. She was practicing for a new play over at the Paris Community Theatre. She got a flat tire between the theater and Walmart, so I gave her a ride to the store. Her husband was at work, and her dad and brother were going to be a little while getting a tire and taking care of her car, so I took her home."

"Did you ever do theater work?" Nessa asked.

"No, musicals aren't my thing." He grinned. "So, jealous fishwife, huh?"

"Are you just a knight in shining armor, coming to a stranded damsel's rescue like that?" She avoided the question.

Jackson's grin got bigger. "Yep, I guess I am, but I know the family. Her husband tried to recruit me into his firm when I first came here. His name is Grady. He and Brenda bought a hope chest from me for their daughter's sixteenth birthday, and every now and then, Grady still calls to see if I'm ready to go back to the law business."

"That woman has a sixteen-year-old daughter?" Nessa gasped.

"Yes, and four kids younger than that one. The sixteen-year-old helps out in her dance studio over in Paris, but they live on a ranch out north of Sun Valley," he answered. "Is that why you were so distant the past few days?"

Nessa nodded. "I judged you by another man's half bushel."

"Uncle D. J. used that expression pretty often. I'd never heard it before I moved to Blossom. He told me it meant judging one person's actions by someone else that you know. So who did you judge me by?" Jackson asked.

"Uncle Matthew and my father all rolled into one. My uncle because he's a womanizer, and my dad because he preaches love and Jesus, but he's got a lot of anger in him," she answered honestly.

"I'm not either of those guys," Jackson said. "If I'm in a relationship, then I'm faithful. And honey, after I have sex with a woman, I don't dump her and never call. I'm thirty-two years old, and my mama would still come after me with a switch if I ever showed that kind of disrespect to a lady. So tell me, are we in a relationship or not?"

Nessa nodded. "I'd like that, but we've only known each other a month."

Jackson tipped her chin up with his rough knuckles and leaned in to kiss her. When the kiss ended, he whispered, "I fell in love with you the first time I laid eyes on you."

"It was dark then," she said with half a giggle. "You couldn't even see me clearly."

"I could see enough," he said.

"When we get out of here, and if it's still the light of day, are you still going to be able to say that?" She laid her head on his shoulder.

"Of course." He toyed with a strand of her hair. "I'll even shout it from the rooftop if you want me to. That is, if I've got a roof left."

"Hey, if the tornado took your shop and house, you can have the quilting shed to work in, and I'll suspend my quilt rack from the living room ceiling. You can stay with us. All I've got is a twin bed with a trundle underneath it, but I'll make Flynn trade rooms with me," she said.

"Well, whether your quilting shed is gone or not, my house has three bedrooms. You can have the bigger one to set up your sewing machine and do your quilting. You'll have air-conditioning in the summer and heat in the winter," he said.

"That almost makes me hope the shed is gone," she laughed, but then she grew serious. "No, erase that. I wouldn't want Nanny Lucy's shed and all the memories, good or bad, to be gone."

"Whether it's there or not, that offer still stands." He kissed her on the forehead. "I'd ask you to move in with me tomorrow, but that might be moving too fast."

"Probably so," she yawned.

"Looks like it's going to be a while before we get out of this place." His eyes were twinkling.

"Not in front of Tex," she whispered.

At the sound of his name, the dog came crawling out from under the bed and jumped up on the foot of it.

"I don't think he'll mind if we just cuddle and talk," Jackson said as he stretched out on the side of the bed nearest the wall.

Nessa kicked off her shoes and snuggled up next to him, her cheek on his chest. His arms around her made her feel safe and warm, no matter what was going on outside because of a tornado.

Chapter Twenty-Five

Flynn was frantic to get over to Jackson's place after the storm to see if Nessa, Jackson, and Tex were all right. That text he'd gotten from Nessa had him wondering if she'd lost service or had been swept up by the tornado.

"Do you think they're all right?" April's voice was totally breathless.

"I hope so," Flynn said as he and April emerged from the cellar at their house. Hard rain had continued to fall for more than an hour, and hail the size of marbles had turned the yard white. Then, as suddenly as it had blown up, the rain had stopped, and now the stars danced around a lover's moon.

April gasped and pointed. "The quilting shed is gone. All I can see that's left are the file cabinets. We've got to get to Jackson's and see about Nessa."

Flynn started for his truck. "God, I hope they're all right."

April beat him to his truck and was fastening her seat belt when he slid in behind the wheel. "Her message did say they were stuck in his cellar, right?"

"Yep, and then she asked for help before something kept her from finishing the text." Flynn gripped the steering wheel so hard that his hands started to hurt.

They made it to the fork in the road, only to find an uprooted tree blocking their way. Flynn stopped the vehicle and got out, with April right behind him. "Guess we'll be walking from here."

She nodded and started jogging toward Jackson's place.

Flynn was in good shape, but his stride wasn't any longer than hers, so they ran side by side until Jackson's house came into view. He stopped and put his hands on his knees. "The shop and house are still there. We might have to replace the shingles, but they're still standing, thank God. Now we just have to find them and hope to hell they're all right."

"Amen." April huffed right beside him. "Now let's go see what's going on that they need either hell or help." She circled around the house and gasped. "Flynn, there's no way we can get that tree off the cellar door. The roots are taller than I am."

"I'm going to the shop for the chain saw," Flynn said. "We don't have to get the whole thing off. We just need to saw a section off big enough to . . . No, wait a minute."

"What?" April asked impatiently.

Flynn pushed aside some tree branches and took a better look. "Forget taking part of the tree away. There's enough room below the tree trunk for them to crawl out if I can saw through the boards that make the door. Jackson and I can make a new door later."

April followed him to the shop. "What can I do to help?"

"When I cut the branches off the tree, you can pull them out of the way." Flynn searched until he found a chain saw, revved it up to be sure it would work, and then carried it to the cellar door. He had used chain saws before, but that night he was helping free Jackson and Nessa, and that made him feel like he was making giant steps toward his goal. He could almost feel the virtual shackles that had been holding him to a negative standard just floating away.

"Hello!" Jackson called out when they returned.

"Sit tight and stay away from the door," Flynn yelled.

"Are y'all okay?" April hollered.

"We're fine, and so is Tex," Nessa yelled back.

"Hold him back away from the door, too." Flynn started up the saw and cut away the branches.

April dragged them off to the side as he worked, and in a few minutes, they could see the door. "Now what?" she asked.

"Now I cut away the door and hope I don't hit concrete and ruin Jackson's saw." Flynn put the nose of the saw down to make the first cut and carefully made a hole big enough that he thought Jackson and Nessa could crawl through. He dropped to his knees and poked his head inside. "Turn Tex loose and then y'all come on out. It's muddy out here, so watch your step."

"Are y'all all right? Is the shop still standing?" Jackson asked as he let go of Tex's collar.

"We're fine, and your house and the shop are still standing, but this big-ass tree is going to be tough to get hauled out of here," Flynn said.

Tex came like a shot through the opening Flynn had made and ran straight to the porch. Nessa came up the stairs on her hands and knees. Flynn reached for her, but Jackson said, "I've got her."

When she had a foot planted on the ground, she slipped and fell flat on her face. Flynn laughed in spite of himself—their cousin was not going to be happy about that.

"Thanks a bunch," Jackson said when he came out of the hole behind Nessa. "Holy smoke! That's not the pecan tree. It's a big scrub oak, but right now, we've got to get Nessa cleaned up and make sure she's not hurt." He ripped off his T-shirt and gave it to her to wipe her face, then took her elbow to guide her to the house. "Y'all come on in. Help yourselves to a beer or anything you can find." He led Nessa to the bathroom and turned on the water for her to take a shower.

289

"I closed my eyes when I fell," she muttered. "I can see just fine."

"Good. Then I'll go change out of these dirty shoes and jeans and meet you in the kitchen when you're cleaned up," Jackson said.

"Thank you. I guess you *are* a knight in shining . . ."—she stopped and giggled—"armor who comes to a damsel's rescue. Look at us. We're both a muddy mess."

"Kind of romantic, isn't it?" Jackson chuckled.

"When you consider that we've had a date at a cemetery, it is." She rose on her toes and kissed him on the cheek.

"Never forget that or that I told you I fell in love with you at first sight," he whispered.

"I don't know if it was love or lust, but it's turned into love," she said just loud enough for him to hear.

He leaned in and kissed her again. "Mud never tasted so good."

"I agree, but I'm going to need to borrow your shirt again," she said.

"This time you can even keep it." He washed up at the sink while she stripped out of her muddy clothing, then went to his bedroom and put on clean clothes. He still had her undergarments that they had washed when she had gotten into the ant pile, so he put them on the vanity in the bathroom, along with the shirt she'd asked for.

April and Flynn looked like they'd just lost their best friend when he made it to the living room. "I can't thank you enough for what you've done tonight," said Jackson.

"No thanks necessary," April sighed. "But if you could help Nessa through the next couple of days, that would be great. We thought we were all fine over at our place, but then we looked at the quilting shed. The roof is completely gone, and everything that was in it is gone except for the three filing cabinets."

"She's going to be devastated," Flynn said. "I'm just glad we got that quilt done before the tornado hit us."

Jackson grinned. "I've already offered her the use of one of my bedrooms as a quilting room if she needed it, and she offered me the quilting shed if my shop had gotten blown away."

"Thank you," Flynn said. "She wants so badly to make this quilting business work out. You can't imagine how much that helps."

"We can get a quilting frame ready and hung before the week is out. Did any of the stuff in the garage get water damaged?" Jackson asked.

"No, the tornado left that alone." April heaved a sigh of relief. "Flynn and I have found jobs, but Nessa . . ."

"Don't worry." Jackson sat down in the rocking chair. "We'll have a nice quilting room put together for her real soon."

"Did I hear something about a room?" Nessa came down the hall wearing jeans and his shirt, which hung to her thighs. "How bad is it really over at our place? Are y'all keeping something from me?"

"No, but . . . ," Flynn started.

"The quilting shed is practically gone," April spit out.

Nessa stopped in her tracks. "Nanny Lucy's frame. Is it still there?"

"It's gone," April answered. "The file cabinets are still standing, but we didn't check to see about water damage to the stuff inside them. I'm so sorry, Nessa."

"But I've already told you that you can have a room here," Jackson assured her. "Two rooms, if you want to live with me and let April have her own room instead of sleeping on the sofa. One for the quilting business, one for you to sleep in. Tex and I wouldn't mind the company."

"Are you asking Nessa to move in with you?" April asked.

"I'll take you up on that quilting room, and maybe later, when April is ready to reclaim her trundle bed, we'll talk about the other room," Nessa said before Jackson could answer.

"Yes," Jackson said as he locked eyes with Nessa. "I'm asking Nessa to move in with me."

Chapter Twenty-Six

*n*essa woke up at five o'clock, eased out of bed, got dressed, and walked home before the sun was even a tiny orange thread on the eastern horizon. This had been her regular routine for the past several weeks—ever since the night of the tornado. She was surprised to see the yellow glow of light flowing through the living room window and even more shocked to smell coffee brewing when she opened the door. But neither of those shocks compared to the adrenaline rush she got when she saw Flynn and April sitting at the table having pancakes and bacon. Bad news was the only thing that would make them get up that early and cook. Was it about one of her parents?

"Good mornin'." April smiled.

How could she be happy when something was so terribly wrong? Nessa glanced around the room to see four boxes sitting in the middle of the floor. The sofa had been put to rights, but the coat-closet door was open, and there was nothing in it.

"What's going on?" Nessa whispered.

Flynn motioned to the chair where she always sat. "This is an intervention. Come on in here, sit down, and have some breakfast."

"I'm not addicted to anything." She walked around the boxes and eased down into her chair.

"We beg to differ," Flynn chuckled. "You are addicted to Jackson."

"And he's addicted to you," April told her. "I packed your things last night. That's what's in the boxes over there, and I put all my stuff in my old bedroom. The ghosts are gone. I slept like a tired toddler last night. No nightmares, and the bad memories are fading. I think my mother and Nanny Lucy are finally resting in peace. And so am I, because the past is finally fading away, and the future is looking brighter every day."

"What has all that got to do with me and Jackson?" Nessa asked.

Flynn forked two pancakes over onto Nessa's plate and then slipped four pieces of bacon beside them. "You have been going over there every day to work on your quilts for the past few weeks. Then you rush home early in the morning to make breakfast for us, then come back again in the evening to cook supper for all of us, and most of the time, Jackson comes with you. We are cutting the apron strings."

"You are what?" Nessa picked up a piece of bacon and bit off the end. "What about our pact to be home for supper and have a visit over the meal?"

"You said the night the tornado demolished the quilting shed that you would think about moving over there into Jackson's spare bedroom when I was able to sleep in my own room," April reminded her.

"It's time you have your own life and quit worrying about taking care of us," Flynn told her. "As you can see, we can make our own breakfast, and we aren't going to starve when suppertime rolls around. We're both working, and we've already worked up a plan for groceries and the electric bill to be divided in half rather than three ways. We're going to be all right, and we'll have our little visits most every day anyway. I, for one, need them still."

April laid a hand on Nessa's arm. "We're kicking you out, but not permanently. This is still your place as much as ours, and you will always have a key."

"But your place right now is with Jackson. He's ready for you to move in with him," Flynn added. "But only if you are ready, Nessa. We can see things from our viewpoint, but what does your heart say?"

"To trust it, and I'm ready, even if it has only been a couple of months since the tornado." Nessa smiled. "And it says to tell you both thank you and to admit that I'm in love with Jackson."

❖ ❖ ❖

Jackson was awake when Nessa slipped out of bed that morning. He gave her enough time to get out of the house before he kicked off the covers and slung his legs over the side of his king-size bed. He dressed for work in a pair of faded jeans and a T-shirt, pulled on his steel-toed boots, and laced them up.

He hoped he'd given Flynn and April enough time for their intervention when he got in his pickup truck and drove over to the O'Riley place. The guys who worked for the county had finally cleared the tree that had blocked the road. He parked in front of the house and took a deep breath as he walked up the steps. If he'd learned anything the past couple of months, it was that Nessa did not take to having decisions made for her.

"Here goes," he muttered as he raised his hand to knock.

Nessa opened the door before he could make contact and stepped out onto the porch. "I hope you were really serious all those times you asked me to move in with you."

"I was." He wrapped his arms around her.

"They're kicking me out, and they already have my stuff packed. April slept in her room last night." She rose up on her toes and kissed him. "And something tells me that you already knew."

"I did," he said as he gave her another kiss. "Let's load your things up and go home, darlin'."

"*Home*," she repeated.

"Has a nice ring to it, doesn't it?" Jackson said.

"Are y'all going to stand out there all morning?" Flynn yelled from the kitchen. "Come on in and have some breakfast, Jackson."

"I guess I'm getting a family, along with you." Jackson chuckled.

"*Family* is another wonderful word." Nessa took his hand and pulled him into the house.

"I love you, Nessa," he whispered.

"I love you right back, Jackson." She stopped in the middle of the living room and kissed him one more time.

Epilogue

One year later

Flynn noticed the T-shirt hanging on the wall when he walked into Weezy's that cool September evening. It read: "Where the heck is Blossom, Texas?"

"It's the best-kept secret in all the world, and is right next door to heaven," he muttered as he headed toward the booth where he and his two cousins had their group therapy once a month. He had just slid into the booth when Nessa and April arrived. Nessa hadn't changed much since the first time they'd met there, but April had put on a few pounds and looked amazing. They crossed the café and sat across from him.

"Thanks for coming here, even though we do see each other almost every day. Nanny Lucy would be so glad to see us keeping up the tradition of meeting like this. I want us to remember her, so I decided to make a donation in her memory to a bipolar research facility each year on the anniversary of when we came back to Blossom," he said.

"Great minds." April smiled. "Kent and I were just talking about doing something like this for his firm to support a few days ago."

"Tell me more," Nessa said.

Flynn spoke up before April could and told her the name of the organization he'd chosen and then said, "It's a nonprofit organization supporting research on the causes of, and treatments for, schizophrenia and bipolar disorder. It's been around since 1989, and from everything I could read, it's legit."

"That's the one Kent chose, too," April said. "He did a lot of research on several charities that support Nanny Lucy's illness, and this is the one that looked best to him."

"I'm in," Nessa said. "Jackson and I were just talking about what charity we should support this year. This may be our choice forever."

"Mine, too," Flynn said. "And thanks for agreeing with me. We just need to do something to help folks who have the same difficulties she had. Now let's talk about the honeymoon, April."

"It was absolutely wonderful, but it wasn't a honeymoon as much as it was a vacation, because we took Callie with us," April said. "I just couldn't leave her with either of you guys, as much as she'd love to stay."

"She's so full of life that she brings sunshine when she just walks into a room," Nessa said. "Someday I hope Jackson and I have one just like her."

"Your biological clock is ticking," April teased. "And you do have a hope chest to keep all the baby things in until your daughter gets here."

"Hey, if my clock is ticking, so are both of yours," Nessa shot back at her. "We're all three pretty much the same age."

"Guys don't have biological clocks, and I need a little more time to get my ducks in a row before I get into a relationship," Flynn said.

"Who would have thought that a year would make this much difference in our lives?" April said. "Or that Nessa and I would be married at the end of the year? I really thought you would bring a plus-one to my wedding, Flynn."

"I was my own plus-one." Flynn grinned. "I've learned to be a patient man. My time will come, and I don't intend to rush things. When I do tie the knot, I hope the woman of my dreams wants to go to the courthouse, like Nessa and Jackson did."

"I didn't want to have to deal with my dad insisting on doing the ceremony," Nessa said.

"And I don't want to deal with my dad even being there," Flynn chuckled. "He's in mourning now because Delores left him. And when he's sad, the only thing that cheers him up is chasing another woman. He'd spend the whole time at my wedding looking out over the congregation for his next victim. I don't want him to choose one from Blossom. I think we'd all have to save Tilly."

Tilly came over to the table, almost as if she'd heard them, and sighed. "You still tryin' to shape up?"

"Yes, ma'am, and makin' progress. What about you?" Flynn asked.

"Still happy with my life." She grinned. "What are y'all havin' today?"

"I'll have a large sweet tea and a chicken-fried steak." He figured that when he was close to a finished product, he might be able to eat a hot dog again, but that wasn't today.

"I want a sweet tea, chicken-fried steak, and a peach fried pie," April said.

"And I'll have a sweet tea and a burger basket," Nessa added.

"Same thing every time y'all come in here," Tilly said.

"If it ain't broke, don't fix it." April smiled up at her.

"Well, my pitiful little heart is broken." Tilly sighed again. "I've missed out on two good men in one year. Jackson and now Flynn."

"Maybe your luck will change next year," Nessa said. "But just a word of advice you can take or leave. If you want a change, you have to work for it."

"I've always been a little bit lazy." Tilly grinned and then hurried back to the kitchen.

"A year can change luck for sure," Flynn said. "A year ago, I was the one who wasn't going to be in Blossom but a month or six weeks at the most, and now I'm the one living in the house. If and when I ever get married, y'all realize the wife will make changes to the place, right? Is that going to bother either of you?"

"Of course not." Nessa shook her head. "I made lots of changes to Jackson's place when I moved in. Y'all ever think that fate had a hand in bringing us all back to Blossom?"

"Oh, yes, I do," April answered. "Call it fate or the will of God or good luck—whatever you want to name it—but it's a miracle that we're all sitting here together tonight."

"And we *have* found the happiness we were looking for, right?" Nessa asked.

"Yes!" Flynn and April said at the same time.

Dear Reader,

There really is a Blossom, Texas, and a Weezy's Restaurant. Mr. B., our son Lemar, and I enjoyed a little research trip to that area before I started writing this story. We had planned to stop at Weezy's, but it was closed when we were there. Hope Creek and the waterfall are just places that I felt should be near Blossom, so I took the liberty of putting them there.

I've approached the delicate subject of bipolar disorder in this story and the effect that it has on a family if it goes undiagnosed and untreated. I hope I've done justice to it.

As always, I have many people to thank for their help in taking this from a rough idea to the book you hold in your hands today. My thanks to all of the following awesome people: My agent, Erin Niumata, and my agency, Folio Management. My editor, Alison Dasho, at Montlake, and my team there. My developmental editor, Krista Stroever (I hope you never retire). My family, for all their support. My husband,

Mr. B., who has my undying love still, even after fifty-five years. My readers, who continue to support me, write notes to me, and tell their friends and family about my books. Y'all deserve so much more than just a simple thank-you!

Happy reading to all y'all.

Carolyn Brown

About the Author

Photo © 2015 Charles Brown

Carolyn Brown is a *New York Times*, *USA Today*, *Publishers Weekly*, *Washington Post*, and *Wall Street Journal* bestselling author, as well as a RITA finalist with more than one hundred published works to her name. Her books include romantic women's fiction, historical, contemporary, and cowboys and country music mass-market paperbacks. She and her husband live in the small town of Davis, Oklahoma, where everyone knows everyone else, knows what they are doing and when—and they read the local newspaper on Wednesdays to see who got caught. They have three grown children and enough grandchildren and great-grandchildren to keep them young. For more information, visit www.carolynbrownbooks.com.